HE WALKED INTO THE DOORWAY
AND HALTED

Ten years compressed in the nerve-racking space of a few seconds.

This tall, broad-shouldered stranger was her husband. Every memory she had of his appearance was there, stamped with a brutal decade of maturity, but there. Except for the look in his eyes. Nothing had ever been bleak and hard about him, before. He stared at her with an intensity that could have burned her shadow on the floor.

Words were hopeless, but all that they had. "Welcome back," she said. Then, brokenly, "*Jake.*"

He took a deep breath, as if a shiver had run through him. He closed the doors without ever taking his eyes off her. Then he was at her in two long steps, grasping her by the shoulders, lifting her to her toes. "I trained myself not to think about you," he said, his voice a raw whisper. "Because if I had, I would have lost my mind."

"I never deserted you. I wanted to be a part of your life, but you wouldn't let me. Will you please try, now?"

"Do you still have it?" he asked.

Anger. Defeat. The hoarse sound she made contained both. "*Yes.*"

He released her. "Good. That's all that matters."

Sam turned away, tears coming helplessly. After all these years, there was still only one thing he wanted from her, and it was the one thing she hated, a symbol of pride and obsession she would never understand, a bloodred stone that had controlled the lives of too many people already, including theirs.

The Pandora ruby.

Silk

and

Stone

Deborah Smith

BANTAM BOOKS
NEW YORK · TORONTO · LONDON · SYDNEY · AUCKLAND

SILK AND STONE
A Bantam Book / March 1994

Grateful acknowledgment is made for permissions to reprint from
the following:

Reprinted with permission of Charles Scribner's Sons, an imprint of
Macmillan Publishing Company from LOOK HOMEWARD, ANGEL
by Thomas Wolfe. Copyright 1929 Charles Scribner's Sons; copyright
renewed © 1957 Edward C. Aswell, as Administrator, C.T.A. of the
Estate of Thomas Wolfe and/or Fred W. Wolfe.

TALES FROM THE CHEROKEE HILLS by Jean Starr. Reprinted
with permission of John F. Blair, Publisher, Winston-Salem, NC.

ISBN 0-553-29689-2

Published simultaneously in the United States and Canada

Bantam Books are published by Bantam Books, a division of
Bantam Doubleday Dell Publishing Group, Inc. Its trademark,
consisting of the words "Bantam Books" and the portrayal of
a rooster, is Registered in U.S. Patent and Trademark Office
and in other countries. Marca Registrada. Bantam Books, 1540
Broadway, New York, New York 10036.

PRINTED IN THE UNITED STATES OF AMERICA

RAD   0 9 8 7 6 5 4 3 2 1

For Nita and Andrea

Whisper the words.
Say that name as little as you can,
Don't draw their attention.
Raven Mockers.
They can look old or young, man or woman,
Beautiful, ugly, kind, mean . . .

The Mockers take the shape of others,
Seeming to be old Grandfather, Grandson,
Wife, harmless friend,
Sweetly speaking, coming closer,
Placing a gentle hand on the forehead,
Looking at the helpless one
With pitiless two-hundred-year-old eyes,
Waiting, waiting, until heads turn,
Until others leave the room,
Then, in a flash, ripping out the heart . . .

These who love life so much
That they would steal it
Are not evil strangers, but kinsmen,
And every Raven Mocker
Is one of us,
One of us.

JEAN STARR
Cherokee storyteller

Prologue

She had everything ready for him, everything but herself. What could she say to a husband she hadn't seen or spoken to in ten years: *Hi, honey, how'd your decade go?*

The humor was nervous, and morbid. She knew that. Samantha Raincrow hurt for him, hurt in ways she couldn't put into words. Ten years of waiting, of thinking about what he was going through, of *why* he'd been subjected to it, had worn her down to bare steel.

What he'd endured would always be her fault.

She moved restlessly around the finest hotel suite in the city, obsessed with straightening fresh flowers that were already perfectly arranged in their vases. He wouldn't have seen many flowers. She wanted him to remember the scent of youth and freedom. Of love.

1

Broad windows looked out over Raleigh. A nice city for a reunion. The North Carolina summer had just begun; the trees still wore the dark shades of new spring leaves.

She wanted everything to be new for him, but realized it could never be, that they were both haunted by the past—betrayals that couldn't be undone. She was Alexandra Lomax's niece; she couldn't scrub that stain out of her blood.

Her gifts were arranged around the suite's sitting room; Sam went to them and ran her hands over each one. A silk tapestry, six feet square and woven in geometrics from an old Cherokee design, was draped over a chair. She wanted him to see one of the ways she'd spent all the hours alone. Lined up in a precise row along one wall were five large boxes filled with letters she'd written to him and never sent, because he wouldn't have read them. A journal of every day. On a desk in front of the windows were stacks of bulging photo albums. One was filled with snapshots of her small apartment in California, the car she'd bought second-hand, years ago, and still drove, more of her tapestries, and her loom. And the Cove. Pictures of the wild Cove, and the big log house he'd built for them. She wanted him to see how lovingly she'd cared for it over the years.

The other albums were filled with her modeling portfolio. A strange one, by most standards. Just hands. Her hands, the only beautiful thing about her, holding soaps and perfumes and jewelry, caressing lingerie and detergent and denture cleaner, and a thousand other products. Because she wanted him to understand everything about her work, she'd brought the DeMeda book too—page after oversize, sensual page of black and white art photos. Photos of her fingertips touching a man's glistening, naked back, or molded to the crest of a muscular bare thigh.

If he cared, she would explain about the ludicrous amount of money she'd gotten for that work, and that the book had been created by a famous photographer, and was considered an art form. If he cared, she'd assure him that there was nothing provocative about standing under hot studio lights with her hands cramping, while beautiful, half-clothed male models yawned and told her about their latest boyfriends.

If he cared.

The phone rang. She ran to answer. "Dreyfus delivery service," a smooth, elegantly drawling voice said somberly. "I have one slightly used husband for you, ma'am."

Their lawyer's black sense of humor didn't help matters. Her heart pounded, and she felt dizzy. "Ben, you're downstairs?"

"Yes, in the lobby. Actually, I'm in the lobby. He's in the men's room, changing clothes."

"Changing clothes?"

"He asked me to stop on the way here. I perform many functions, Sam, but helping my clients pick a new outfit is a first."

"Why in the world—"

"He didn't want you to see him in what they gave him to wear. In a matter of speaking, he wanted to look like a civilian again."

Sam inhaled raggedly and bowed her head, pressing her fingertips under her eyes, pushing hard. She wouldn't cry, wouldn't let him see her for the first time in ten years with her face swollen and her nose running. Small dignities were all she had left. "Has he said anything?" she asked when she could trust herself to speak calmly.

"Hmmm, lawyer-client confidentiality, Sam. I represent both of you. What kind of lawyer do you think I am? Never mind, I don't want to hear the brutal truth."

"One who's become a good friend."

Ben hesitated. "Idle flattery." Then, slowly, he added, "He said he would walk away without seeing you again if he could."

She gripped the phone numbly. *That's no worse than you expected*, she told herself. But she felt dead inside. "Tell him the doors to the suite will be open."

"All right. I'm sure he needs all the open doors he can get."

"I can't leave them all open. If I did, I'd lose him."

"Parole is not freedom," Ben said. "He understands that."

"And I'm sure he's thrilled that he's being forced to live with a wife he doesn't want."

"I suspect he doesn't know what he wants at the moment."

"He's always known, Ben. That's the problem."

She said good-bye, put the phone down, and walked with leaden resolve to the suite's double doors. She opened them and stepped back. For a moment she considered checking herself in a mirror one last time, turned halfway, then realized she was operating on the assumption that what she looked like mattered to him. So she faced the doors and waited.

Each faint whir and rumble of the elevators down the hall made her nerves dance. She could barely breathe, listening for the sound of those doors opening. She smoothed her upswept hair, then anxiously fingered a blond strand that had escaped. Jerking at each hair, she pulled them out. A dozen or more, each unwilling to go. If it hurt, she didn't notice.

She clasped her hands in front of her pale yellow suit-dress, then unclasped them, fiddled with the gold braid along the neck, twisted the plain gold wedding band on her left hand. She never completely removed it from her body, even when she worked. It had either remained on her finger or on a sturdy gold chain around her neck, all these years.

That chain, lying coldly between her breasts, also held his wedding ring.

She heard the hydraulic purr of an elevator settling into place, then the softer rush of metal doors sliding apart. Ten years compressed in the nerve-racking space of a few seconds. If he weren't the one walking up the long hall right now, if some unsuspecting stranger strolled by instead, she thought her shaking legs would collapse.

Damn the thick carpeting. She couldn't gauge his steps. She wasn't ready. No, she would always be ready. Her life stopped, and she was waiting, waiting. . . .

He walked into the doorway and halted. This tall, broad-shouldered stranger was her husband. Every memory she had of his appearance was there, stamped with a brutal decade of maturity, but there. Except for the look in his eyes. Nothing had ever been bleak and hard about him before. He stared at her with an intensity that could have burned her shadow on the floor.

Words were hopeless, but all that they had. "Welcome back," she said. Then, brokenly, "*Jake.*"

He took a deep breath, as if a shiver had run through him. He closed the doors without ever taking his eyes off her. Then he was at her in two long steps, grasping her by the shoulders, lifting her to her toes. They were close enough to share a breath, a heartbeat. "I trained myself not to think about you," he said, his voice a raw whisper. "Because if I had, I would have lost my mind."

"I never deserted you. I wanted to be part of your life, but you wouldn't let me. Will you please try now?"

"Do you still have it?" he asked.

Anger. Defeat. The hoarse sound she made contained both. "*Yes.*"

He released her. "Good. That's all that matters."

Sam turned away, tears coming helplessly. After all these years, there was still only one thing he wanted from her, and it was the one thing she hated, a symbol of pride and obsession she would never understand, a bloodred stone that had controlled the lives of too many people already, including theirs.

The Pandora ruby.

Part

One

Chapter
One

The living room of the old Vanderveer family home, Highview, had been transformed into a glorious wedding chapel of white satin bows, enormous white urns filled with flowers, and, at the end of the aisle between rows of white wooden chairs, a white wooden trellis strung with garlands of white orchids. Judge Vanderveer's wedding was the biggest social event the town had seen in decades. Life moved slowly in Pandora; the mountain gentry rarely ventured into the lowlands to find brides.

Mountain people were clannish. Indian or white, they looked down on the rest of North Carolina in more ways than one.

The bride, swaddled under a white veil and miles of

pearl-encrusted white satin, floated up the aisle, as perfect as Doris Day. Standing beside the trellis with a bouquet of orchids trembling in her fists, Sarah Vanderveer Raincrow stared in horrified disbelief. This couldn't be happening.

Held by a delicate gold setting, shimmering in the light, the Pandora star ruby gleamed at the end of a long necklace on the bodice of Alexandra Duke's wedding gown.

Sarah felt smothered by disbelief, as if the pink tulle and satin of her matron-of-honor's dress had become a hot blanket.

My ruby. My heirloom. A gift from my husband's ancestors. William gave it to her. No, no, no—how could he, like this, without even an explanation or warning? There must be some terrible mistake. Her head swam. Her brother would not ignore generations of tradition. *But he has.*

There were gasps from the Vanderveers and Raincrows. The Dukes reacted with awkward, stony silence. Rachel Raincrow gaped at Alexandra as if she'd grown horns and a tail. Sarah had never seen anything rattle her mother-in-law's serenity before.

Sarah turned toward Hugh desperately.

He stood under the trellis beside her big redheaded, red-faced, stern brother, and next to William he looked lean and exotic and achingly handsome in a black tuxedo. His dark gaze was already on Sarah. Her husband seemed as stunned and betrayed as she.

In the electric silence the minister cleared his throat. People waited, fidgeting. Sarah gave her future sister-in-law a venomous stare. Alexandra returned it.

Five minutes later Alexandra Duke took a giant step up the social ladder, and became Alexandra Vanderveer.

The parlor doors were shut, a hundred guests milling outside, confused and curious. William looked uncomfortable but firm, his eyes shifting away from Sarah's wounded, condemning questions. His new wife kept one hand in his and the other delicately posed over her ruby in elegant horror. "I didn't realize Alexandra would wear the necklace today," William said gruffly.

"Oh, William, I'm sorry," Alexandra answered. "You said Sarah would understand. I thought you were going to discuss it with her after the rehearsal dinner."

"I decided to wait until after we returned from our honeymoon." William looked away, scowling. "This is a damned mess. My fault."

Sarah cried out harshly and pointed at Alexandra. "You let *her* talk you into this. You'd never hurt me this way otherwise."

William had tears in his eyes. "I believe"—he cleared his throat and his troubled gaze went to Sarah—"I believe, because our parents are dead and there are only the two of us to carry on, Sarah, that an invaluable heirloom should remain with the one of us who bears the family name. You've never expressed much interest in the ruby. All these years it's been locked away in my office safe, and you don't care for jewelry—"

"This isn't about a piece of jewelry, it's about *trust*. And our family's traditions." She turned toward Hugh, who stood beside her, somber and alert, one broad hand pressed against the small of her back in silent support. "And about Hugh's family traditions too," Sarah added urgently.

"Will, you're as fair a man as I've ever known," Hugh told him grimly. "This isn't right. Not to Sarah, and not to me. My people gave that ruby to yours. The Vanderveers have always passed it down from mother to daughter. It belongs to Sarah."

"William, I don't want your sister to be jealous of me," Alexandra interjected. She slid her fingers up the necklace, fingering the clasp. "I'm certainly not trying to *steal* a family heirloom. It's just that I'm so *proud* to be your wife, to be a Vanderveer, and when you showed me the ruby, I admired it for what it *means* to you, William." Her mouth trembled. "To me, it symbolizes a very dear, fine old family—one I want to be part of." She undid the necklace. "Here. Sarah, please—take it."

William, who looked protective and upset at her

speech, grasped her hand. "*No.*" He glared at Sarah. "Sister, I've raised you and looked after you, and to do it the best I could, I gave up dreams I had of traveling— seeing the world, being footloose and fancy-free. Now I ask this one thing of you—not to throw family traditions in my face when I've upheld the *best* traditions a family can hope for. I've done my duty. You will always be my sister, and I love you, and there's no call for you to feel threatened because I've brought Alexandra into this house."

Sarah gasped. "You think I don't want you to have a wife? Good Lord—no. But not a wife who'd deliberately make trouble between you and everyone who respects you."

"You're the one who's making trouble, sister. You're ruining my wedding day, and that is the legacy people in this town will remember—that you destroyed the happiest day of my life with your bickering."

Sarah's hand rose to her throat. Stricken with betrayal, she gazed at Alexandra. "Why did you marry my brother? You had dozens of boys at college."

"I have to explain why I cherish your brother? He's so much more of a man—a gentleman—than anyone else I've ever met. How can you imply that I have ulterior motives. I love him."

"Liar. William is crazy about you—blind in love with you. But you don't love my brother—you love his name, and his title, and his money. And having our family's heirloom is a way you can show everyone that you've moved up in the world—you've got more respectability than any Duke could earn with a thousand mills. You aren't a Duke anymore—not a money-grubbing, slave-driving Duke. *That's* what my brother and my ruby mean to you."

"Those are damned lies," William shouted. "Sarah, you apologize!"

Sarah stared at him in heartbroken defeat. "I was born and raised in this house. My mother sat in this very room and told me the story about the Pandora ruby, and how it would belong to me someday. If you don't honor that, I'll never set foot in this house again." Her brother's mouth moved silently. His agony was obvious. Alexandra touched his arm, and he looked away from Sarah. "I've done what I think is best. Please try to honor that."

"No. I can't." She walked toward the door. "Hugh, stop her," William said, starting forward, then halting, looking from his sister to his wife, who gave him a beseeching stare.

"She's right," Hugh said. He followed Sarah out of the parlor.

Hugh's mother commanded a place of honor in the middle of the crowded hallway. Small, wide, and calm, she balanced an enormous paisley handbag on the lap of her print dress. An outlandish blue hat decorated with a single spring daffodil sat jauntily on her head, above a coiled braid of graying black hair. Around her neck hung a half dozen strings of garnets and rose quartz stones, all of which she'd collected herself over the years.

Rachel Raincrow's bright-black eyes nearly disappeared under folds of honey-colored wrinkles when she squinted at Sarah and Hugh. "Is that woman keeping the stone?"

Hugh nodded.

"She's a thief, then. And William is a fool." Rachel Raincrow, daughter of a white road-construction engineer who'd passed through on a Roosevelt WPA project during the Depression without leaving her his name, was a first-class rockhound. No one understood quite how she did it, but she had an uncanny knack for finding anything that glittered. She'd supplied Pandora's jewelers with local stones for years. A few of her more illustrious finds had paid Hugh's way through medical school.

And no one took her pronouncements lightly. Alexandra's reputation was doomed among the oldtimers.

Sarah caught Alexandra's kid sister, Frannie, looking at them miserably. Frannie Duke was a little blond beatnik, a truly odd, gentle character among the Dukes, which was why she was the only one of the clan Sarah would have welcomed as a sister-in-law. Too bad Frannie was only seventeen and didn't have Alexandra's Barbie-doll beauty. Too bad that quiet, sweet, aging-bachelor William had fallen in love with the wrong Duke sister.

"I'm sorry, Sarah," Frannie said tearfully.

Sarah bit her lip and refused to answer. Hugh pressed his fingertips against her spine and smoothly guided her up a hallway to the front door. She looked up at him, tears in her eyes. "I'm not greedy or jealous. This isn't about the ruby—it's about broken promises."

"I love you," Hugh answered. "Let's go home."

Frannie crept into an upstairs bedroom as Alexandra was changing into her traveling suit. Her sister was alone, standing like some slim, perfect mannequin before a full-length gilded mirror in nothing but her ruby necklace, white silk panties and a white bra with cups as pointed as nose cones on rockets. Alexandra could kill somebody with those big, pointed bosoms. Frannie felt, as always, as if there were only so much space in the world for egos, and Alexandra had taken both their shares long ago. Frannie had always been in awe of her willpower. Alexandra had alternately defended her and ignored her, all their lives.

Frannie was the black sheep—a mousy little daydreamer, not good potential for upgrading the family's position by snaring an important husband—a mission for which both she and Alexandra had been instructed all their lives.

Alexandra was crying silently, tears sliding down her face in streaks of pink rouge. Frannie couldn't remember the last time she'd seen her sister in tears. When Alexandra heard her close the door, she pivoted, wiping her face quickly, frowning. "What do you want?"

Frannie took a deep breath. "What you did was *wrong*." There. It was said. For the first time in her life she'd overcome cowardly inertia and confronted her sister. Like a boulder pushed over the crest of a hill, her courage rolled out of control. "I know how you operate," Frannie continued breathlessly, straightening her back, hands knotted by her sides, defiant. "You act so innocent, but you're always thinking of yourself first. You . . . you persuaded Judge Vanderveer to give you his family heirloom, even though you knew it shouldn't be yours. You don't care at all that you came between him and Sarah."

"You're right—I don't." Alexandra sank wearily into a chair. "Nobody cares about *my* happiness. Why should I have any pangs of conscience about making other people miserable?"

Frannie knelt beside her and awkwardly touched one of her hands. "I care about your happiness. I thought marrying Judge Vanderveer is exactly what you want."

Alexandra laughed bitterly but clasped Frannie's hand. "You live inside your books and your daydreams. You think you're safe from reality that way. You don't have the foggiest idea what's going on, do you?"

"I know that you didn't have to marry him if you didn't want to."

"Don't you understand? I want to be somebody. I was *raised* to want that—it's all I know. Either a girl marries well, or she's nothing."

"You sound just like Mom and Dad." Frannie tugged at her hand. "But there's so much *more*. Women don't have to be measured by their husbands' importance."

"Oh, hell, Frannie, what else can we be measured by? I wanted to go to law school. You know what I was told—it wouldn't do me any good, it was a waste of time, forget it. End of discussion. Men have all the choices. Women have only one—pick your targets, get what you can, use it before you get fat and wrinkled and nobody gives you a second look. Well, that's what I intend to do—and everybody better get out of my way."

Frannie rocked back on her heels, staring at her older sister with open-mouthed distress. "You *did* talk Judge Vanderveer into giving you that ruby."

"Hell, yes, I did. Just to prove that I could. And I'm *never* letting it out of my cold-blooded little fists either. Sarah Raincrow has more than she deserves already. Nobody keeps her from doing what she wants. Good God, she got to marry the man she loves, and he's an *Indian*."

"Do you *want* to make your own husband take sides against his sister?"

"I want him to do *exactly* what I tell him to do. That's the only power a woman has, and I intend to use it."

"You don't love him. Alexandra, you took vows, but you lied."

"It makes no difference to him. He wanted a prize, and he got one."

"No, he loves you. He really does."

"He's forty years old and about as exciting as stale bread. He doesn't love me—he loves the idea that he can *have* me."

Frannie's shock turned to righteous anger. Dropping Alexandra's hand, she stood. "I know about you and that law student. I know you sneaked out to see Orrin Lomax even after you got engaged." She shivered with frustration. Her shoulders slumped, and she turned numbly toward the door. "You could have married Orrin."

Alexandra was silent. Her eyes shimmered with new tears. "Orrin has a lot of ambition but no money, and no clout. If I married him, I'd have to give up my horses. We couldn't afford them."

Her horses? Alexandra was an avid rider, and her two Arabians were champion stock, and she doted on them, but to marry money just to keep them. . . . Frannie shook her head in dull amazement. "You love Orrin, but you can marry somebody else so you can keep your horses."

Alexandra stiffened. "Do you think your future is going to be better than mine? You think you can just traipse off and do as you please?"

"I can try."

"Frannie, Carl Ryder was the first in a series of long, hard lessons you're going to learn about reality."

Frannie stared at her. Even the mention of Carl's name brought an ache to her chest. In a small, shattered voice she asked, "What do you mean?"

"I mean that Mom and Dad arranged to have your soldier transferred out of state. Did you really think they'd let you meddle around with the son of mill workers? You can mumble about social equality all you want—you can turn up your nose at the family's money and call us all a bunch of snobs, you can talk about brotherhood and freedom until you're blue in the face, but you not only can't do anything about it, you don't even suspect what you're up against. They'll have your soft little hide nailed to a respectable altar by the time you turn my age. I made the best of my choices, and so will you."

Frannie stumbled to the door and held its cold, crystal knob for support. "They got rid of Carl?"

"Of course they did. And the same thing will happen with anyone else who isn't good enough for a Duke. They threatened to disown me if I even talked about marrying Orrin. If I can't get around them, why in the world would you assume you can?"

"But . . . but why do you have to *care* about being disowned?"

"Because I won't be a *nothing*, you idiot. I won't struggle along in a cheap apartment with a law student and be treated like a fool!"

Cold sweat trickled down Frannie's back. She jerked at the door, opened it, and looked back at her sister miserably. "I'm not going to lose Carl. And I'm not going to be like the rest of this family—patronizing and narrow-minded. You're just taking the easy way out," Frannie whispered. "You know it, and you hate it, and it'll make you sorry."

Alexandra rubbed her arm across her swollen eyes, a bitter, girlish gesture that made her look vulnerable for just an instant. But when she lowered her arm, her gaze was hard, set. "Just keep my secrets for me, Frannie. I'll worry about the rest."

Frannie nodded. "You're my sister."

She left Alexandra alone with that small vow, and fled.

Frannie huddled miserably in the azalea garden beyond the backyard lights at Highview. The house blazed with lights and music as Dukes danced with

Vanderveers and all were impeccably polite to one another. Alexandra and Judge Vanderveer had left hours ago in the judge's shiny Edsel, showered in rice and confetti. Frannie's last image of her sister was burned deeply in her mind: smiling, as sleek as a model in her beautiful white suit, looking like a blond Jackie Kennedy, with the ruby dangling prominently down the front of her jacket.

Frannie had been reduced to hiding from their parents and thinking about Carl Ryder. They'd met last year at a dance hosted by the Raleigh Young Ladies' Progressive Club. The club performed its civic duties by busing fresh-faced second lieutenants up from Fort Bragg.

Carl was no second lieutenant; he was a sergeant who'd been assigned to drive the bus. The club matrons let him into the dance but were in high lather over the situation: He was not elite pickings for progressive young ladies.

He was, in fact, the orphaned son of mill workers, and he'd been on his own since he was sixteen, had joined the army at eighteen—four years ago—and loved it dearly. His one ambition in life was to be a soldier. But when he saw Frannie across the dance floor, and she saw him from her corner behind the punch table, where she was trying furtively to read Jack Kerouac without anyone noticing, it was love at first sight. She could almost hear "Some Enchanted Evening."

He'd walked up to her, spit-and-polished, very formal and polite, and then he'd bowed and said, "You're a sight for sore eyes, miss."

It was love at first sight on both sides, and they found ways to meet in secret, until her parents discovered them and put a stop to the romance. Dukes didn't carry on with mill workers, they'd said, as if Carl were destined to be a mill hand simply because of his bloodlines.

She'd vowed not to forget him when he was transferred to Fort Benning, down in Georgia. His letters came every week, squirreled away for her by her parents' sympathetic housekeeper, and Frannie feasted longingly on his earnest, simple, carefully spelled words for months.

She doubted she'd ever see him again. Knowing now what her parents had done to get him out of her life, she hated them.

"Frannie." Her name came out of the darkness beyond a row of juniper shrubs. Her name, spoken in Carl's deep drawl. She ran to him, astonished, frightened, and ecstatic. They held each other and kissed with frantic welcome. "What are you doing here?" she whispered. He was dressed in trousers and a plaid shirt. "Carl, you didn't desert, did you?"

"Of course not. What kind of man do you think I am? I'm on leave, Frannie. I got a week. I borrowed a car and drove the whole way from Georgia without a stop. I had to come find you. I'm getting shipped over to Germany."

"Oh, no."

He got down on one knee and took her hands. "We don't have much time. I know this sounds crazy, but . . . come with me. I love you. Marry me. Please."

Her mind whirled. What did she have to look forward to here? College, next year, but she wanted to study philosophy and her parents had already said no because they thought it was ungodly and maybe even Communist. No one thought her worthwhile; she wasn't a go-getter like Alexandra, and didn't want to be.

But more than any of that, she adored Carl Ryder. "I—I—I—of course. Certainly. *Yes.*" She dropped to her knees and kissed him. He threw back his head, on the verge of whooping, and she clamped a hand over his mouth. "How?" she asked.

Carl kissed her hand and murmured thickly, "I'll go in and just *tell* your folks that's what we're going to do, Frannie. That's how. They can wail and carry on all they want about my pedigree, but this is the U-nited States of America, which I signed up to protect and serve along with all its freedoms, and, well, hell, Frannie, you and me having the freedom to get married is what this country's all about."

His passionate and simple ideas about constitutional rights wouldn't hold a drop of water in a debate, but she loved Carl's way of looking at things, loved him right to the bottom of his honest, red-white-and-blue soul. "No, no, no. You don't understand." She clasped her throat. "They'll lock me in a room and have you carted away. By the time they let me out again, you'll be speaking German like a native."

"I'm no coward. I'm not about to carry you away like a thief—"

"You're no thief. Believe me, I *know* what a thief is like." She cupped her hands to his face. "I love you. If you really want to marry me, then let's go. Let's just go. It's the only way. My clothes are at a motel in town. I'm staying in a room with two of my cousins and an aunt. I have a key."

He scowled. "Frannie, if I take you away from your family like this, they'll say I didn't have the guts to do right by you. They already think I'm after the Duke money."

"I don't need them. I don't care if I ever see any of them again. I'll write to them when it's safe. After we're married. They can't do anything about it then." She looked at him firmly. "I love you too much to risk losing you again. If you love me that much, then don't you take the chance either."

He pondered this in grim silence, then sighed and said, "Frannie, are you sure?"

"Yes. Are you?"

"I was sure the second I laid eyes on you. Still am. I'll be good to you. I don't have a bad temper, and I don't drink, and I work hard, and—"

"I know."

"But I don't think we'll ever be rich on a sergeant's pay, Frannie."

"I don't like *rich*. In fact, I hate *rich*."

"Don't go crazy, now."

"Crazy about you."

"That's good, then." He stood and helped her up. They looked at each other in solemn consideration. "I wish we could have a wedding like this," he said, nodding toward the house. "You deserve what your sister has."

Frannie shuddered. "I hope not," she answered. She grabbed his hand. They disappeared into the darkness, and she never looked back.

Sarah lay deeply entwined in Hugh's arms, but even his warmth and the peaceful darkness of their bedroom couldn't comfort her. She tried to concentrate on the sounds of the old comfortable log house—the soft creak of an oak limb against the second-story roof, the murmur of spring crickets outside the open window, the faint, tinny drone of Rachel Raincrow's radio coming from the bedroom across the hall.

Hugh stroked her shoulder. Dr. Hugh Raincrow. What a lovely piece of work he was. There had been plenty of gossip when they married, lots of "He's a credit to his race, *but* . . ." talk, and she hadn't ever listened. He loved her as much as she loved him, and the world was opening up for couples such as them. Camelot had arrived with the Kennedys.

Sarah curled closer to him, his bare thighs warm and hard under her leg, his chest rising and falling slowly under her palm. He stroked her hair, each soft caress absorbing her misery. She was thinking that there was one story in the history of Pandora that deserved special reverence: The friendship between the Vanderveers and the Raincrows, and the Pandora ruby. Two families, two cultures, one symbol of loyalty, stretching back more than 120 years. There might be no Raincrows left in Pandora if the Vanderveers hadn't helped them hide when the army rounded up the Cherokees for removal.

The ruby had been a gift from the Raincrows for that friendship. Generations of Vanderveers had cherished the heirloom, and each passed it down to the next generation through the eldest daughter. Where there was no daughter, it had passed to a Vanderveer niece.

Next year, when she turned twenty-one, it should have come to her.

But not now.

Her thoughts turned to the woman who had appropriated her brother—and her ruby. Alexandra Duke had more kin than a dog had fleas. The Dukes were a respectable-looking bunch: Sarah gave them that. They had money all right, a potful of it, but they were social outcasts, and they knew it. They liked to hint that they were distantly related to the tobacco-dynasty Dukes who'd endowed Duke University, but everyone knew that was just wishful thinking: This Duke clan had scratched its way upward in the textile mills, paying their workers slave wages for long hours at the looms, holding their people hostage during the hard years of the twenties and thirties. Some of the ugliest strikebusting in the history of the state had occurred at Duke mills.

Society didn't forget stories about mill workers being beaten and threatened. To Sarah, like most self-sufficient people born and bred in the mountains, the idea of controlling other people's lives, or being controlled, bespoke a sinister loss of grace.

Plus the Dukes were lowlanders, and that conveyed a lack of proven durability in the eyes of mountain people. Life in the rolling, accessible regions of the piedmont, with its big cities and industries, was easy and safe compared to the existences people carved out among mountain peaks and steep gorges. In every sense of the word, the Dukes were on their way up now. But she didn't want her brother, Judge William Vanderveer, to be one of their ladders.

William was nearly twenty years older than she—shy around women, scholarly, infinitely strict but honorable. Their parents had died when she was a child; William had raised her like a father. William had put that responsibility ahead of his own social life, she realized sadly, and now, with her grown and married, he was desperate to make up for lost time. Too desperate.

Hugh's deep, sympathetic voice distracted her. "Is the stone worth alienating yourself from your brother?"

Sarah sighed. "How can I face our children if I won't fight for what's theirs?"

"Sarah, when we have children, they'll know what's important, just like you ought to, and I know—"

"You ought to listen to your mother. She says it's a medicine stone."

"I know, I know." Hugh kissed her, his breath feathering her face softly. He recited dryly, as if his mother were speaking, "And if I used real medicine instead of white medicine, I'd appreciate its power. But I can't work both sides of the road. If I start chanting and tossing tobacco to the four winds whenever a patient walks into my office, I suspect I'll lose my practice. And my medical licence. The old ways are useless, sweetheart. They won't get the people anywhere."

Because she was tired and depressed, she blurted out, "Is that why you married *me*? To get ahead?"

He raised himself on one elbow and looked down at her. A trace of moonlight glittered harshly in his eyes. He was the most gentle, loving man in the world, slow to anger, quick to forgive. At the moment he was angry. "I lost a dozen white patients in town when I married you. And when I made my rounds at Cawatie after our wedding, one of the Keehotee boys slashed my tires. *Slashed my tires*, even though my brother died in the same platoon with their uncle in Korea. My own aunt Clara trotted out of her house and threw a bean dumpling at me."

"You never told me," Sarah whispered.

"Because I didn't want to hurt you. When you hurt, I hurt. That's why I don't want you to brood over the damned ruby. I want you to forgive your brother and tolerate Alexandra, even if she's a first-class—"

"Witch. She's a witch." Sarah hissed the words. "Your mother says witches are real, and I believe her."

"She's a horned toad, for all I care."

"William's the one who hurt me." She swallowed hard, her throat on fire. "He was always so much older— after our parents died, he was . . . he's more like a father than a brother." Her voice rose. "She's going to make him miserable, Hugh. He loves her and he can't see that. And if I let her run over me too, I'll be helping her ruin him. No. I won't pretend it doesn't matter."

"I understand, but—"

"No, you don't. I'm *pregnant*."

After a startled moment, Hugh pulled her closer and kissed her. They murmured questions and answers to each other softly, joy mingled with the day's poignant disappointment. For a while he thought she'd forgotten about her brother's blind betrayal. Touches, kisses, small smiles, segued between them, and she seemed content. He drew her head into the crook of his neck and sighed happily.

But she breathed against his ear, "Your mother told my fortune. She says we're having twins. That ruby is theirs too."

Exasperation strained his serenity. "It's just a rock when you get down to the facts. An expensive rock."

Hugh moved over her, stroking her belly with one hand, then settling between her thighs when she shifted under his teasing fingers. Sarah shoved lightly at him. "What are you doing?"

"Paying a visit to our babies. Distracting their mama so they can get some sleep." He brushed a kiss over her mouth. "Do you want their first words to be 'Where's my ruby?' "

"No." Sarah put her arms around him and buried her face in the crook of his neck. *Yes,* she admitted silently.

Depending on which story a person liked best, their beloved North Carolina town had been named for a Greek myth or a local whore, or both.

Today she was inclined toward the Pandora whore story. It seemed appropriate, considering the woman her brother had just married.

Chapter Two

_P_andora's town limits encompassed most of a small plateau at almost precisely 5,280 feet above sea level—one mile high, in the tops of the Cawatie Mountains. The town had more than twice as much altitude as residents—maybe 2,000 people, and most of them scattered on tiny, secluded farms along the ridges and deep in the coves below town.

The earliest Scotch, Irish, and Dutch immigrants had been drawn to the misty, ancient mountains of western North Carolina by rumors of rubies and other precious gems mined by the Cherokees. The rumors were more than true. The newcomers plucked fine stones from the riverbanks, from the hillsides, from the ruts in deeply churned wagon roads. They riddled the mountains with mine shafts, looking for more. But the easiest pickings were taken within a generation, after bloody feuds over the mines.

25

When the mines played out, the hardiest survivors stayed on, independent and passionately devoted to a land of breathtaking beauty and isolation, of freedom.

The Indians were reduced to hiding, for some years, from federal troops. Those fugitives were all that remained, after thousands had been marched to the Indian Territory out west. The whites opened shop, built churches, farmed the creek valleys, and ran lumber mills supplied by an endless vista of virgin forest. The Cherokees— those who survived despite starvation and threats—did the same after the government granted them amnesty. Some intermarried with the newcomers, some withdrew bitterly to reservations, and others simply kept to themselves, clinging to pieces of land so rugged, no one would challenge them for it.

Clara Big Stick clung to traditions just as tenaciously.

The Raincrow babies were a matter of professional concern to Clara. As a medicine woman, it was her duty to give them the proper protection against evil after they entered the world, even if she disapproved of their parents' mixed marriage. She was, after all, honor-bound to treat members of her own clan, which the Raincrow twins were, but only on a technicality.

Clara brooded over the ethical quandary as she followed Rachel Raincrow's spry path up the brick steps of Pandora's small hospital. Certainly she had an obligation to Rachel Raincrow—a respected elder, and her distant cousin—who had requested her services. She figured the matter of the babies' clan would have to be accepted, problems and all. By rights they belonged to their mother's clan, but because Hugh Raincrow had seen fit to marry a white woman, and whites had no clans, traditions would have to be juggled.

The spirits might not be entirely fooled, but some protection was better than none at all.

Short, sturdy, and strong—at forty, she was in the prime of her career—Clara easily shouldered a heavy woven bag filled with her materials. She cast dour looks at the squat little hospital's lobby as Rachel Raincrow led her through, ignoring the curious stares of the nurses.

Sacred ceremonies could not be confined to impersonal places. White people were so ignorant.

"My son is not here right now," Rachel whispered in Cherokee as they made their way through a maze of short hallways and then double doors marked MATERNITY WARD. "He went home to sleep. Sarah said we should come now. She knows this is important, and he doesn't believe."

Clara frowned thoughtfully. "She's a wise woman, even if she's not one of the people." This fact reassured Clara. Surely the mother's good heart would account for something.

They entered a small private room filled with flowers—that was a good sign—but smelling unpleasantly of useless things like antiseptic. Clara saw immediately she had her work cut out for her: Rachel's freckled, red-haired daughter-in-law was lying in the bed, and looked none too well. This show of weakness might encourage bad spirits to waltz right in. "Sit up," Clara told her, dropping her medicine bag into a chair and going to Sarah.

Sarah groaned. "Mrs. Big Stick, I had a cesarean twelve hours ago."

"I can't help that. *Sit up.*"

She nodded wanly. Clara and Rachel helped her scoot back and lean against the pillows. They smoothed her frilly cotton nightgown, and Clara made a satisfied mental note of the stains on the front. "You're feeding them yourself?" she asked.

Sarah chuckled. "Oh, yes. They eat like horses. The nurses think I'm being peculiar, but I don't want bottles."

"Nurses are crazy." The poor, abused girl had the courage to smile at her. "See my beautiful babies?" She pointed to a pair of bassinets beside the bed. Clara nodded brusquely and went to them, shaking her head in disgust when she saw how many clothes they wore. Goodness, the spirits would think these two couldn't survive at all.

She removed their tiny shirts, their caps, their diapers, then sighed with relief. One boy, one girl. A good balance. "What do you think?" Rachel asked, peering over her shoulder worriedly. She spoke only in Cherokee, as Clara had instructed. Best that the spirits think these babies belonged entirely to the people. "Big, with clear eyes," Clara noted approvingly. "Strong genitals." She peered into their eyes and stroked their fine black hair. Their skin would be awfully pale, she feared, and their light eyes would undoubtedly be green, like their mother's.

"They have it," Rachel said proudly, laying one gnarled hand on each of their heads. "Like me. They have the gift. I can feel it."

"Are you certain?" Clara looked at her, impressed but worried. This complicated things. Extra precautions would be necessary.

Rachel nodded. "They'll know how to find things."

"You must teach them how to go along carefully, then."

"I will."

Clara quickly moved vases of flowers off a little table, and rolled it near the bassinets. She set out a black pottery bowl that had been made by her great-grandmother in Oklahoma, then broke dried tobacco and herbs into it. "What are their names?" she asked Sarah in English.

Sarah smiled wider. "Jacob, for Hugh's brother, and Eleanore, for my grandmother."

"Strong names. You did well."

Sarah's smile faltered. "No, I almost died during labor. But I love them so much. Please do your best for them. I don't think I'll be able to have any more children."

"I had only two," Rachel Raincrow said. "Two are plenty if they're the right two."

Sarah's face brightened. "I agree. And Hugh said the same thing."

Clara struck a match and dropped it in the bowl. Seconds later, fragrant smoke wafted up. Clara stroked it with both hands, urging it to spread and purify the room. She concentrated on the bowl, chanting sacred prayer formulas. When the time was right, she would hold each newborn baby over the smoke, enveloping the new souls in a cocoon of goodwill from the spirits.

"My God, what's going on here?"

Clara jerked her head up, appalled at the damage this intrusion might do, and its rudeness. Two people stood in the doorway—a young blond woman with disrespect in her eyes, and an older man whose red hair signified some relation to Sarah. The woman was dressed in high heels, a straight skirt, and a flowing maternity blouse with a soft white bow at the throat. Her belly made a distinct mound under the expensive-looking material.

Sarah's brother frowned. He was the one who had spoken.

"William, what are you doing here?" Sarah asked, leaning forward with painful urgency. "Don't interrupt. It's a ceremony."

"Sarah's brother," Rachel whispered darkly. "And his wife. The one who stole the ruby."

Clara drew back in alarm. Oh, this was a terrible sign. "I'm working," she said as calmly as she could. "Please, stay out."

The man fumbled with a large, wrapped present he held in both hands. "I don't intend to interfere, sister. I merely wondered what this is all about. I brought"—his face flushed, he held out the package—"*we* brought the babies a gift."

Sarah cupped a hand over her mouth. Tears flowed down her cheeks. "I can't accept it."

"Please." His tone had a sad urgency. He set the package on a chair by the door. "Please take it. I'd like your children to know their uncle cares about them. No matter your disagreement with me, please don't shut me out of their lives. They'll be welcome at Highview."

Sarah looked away and swallowed hard. "They'll make up their own minds about you. Hugh and I won't raise them to hate their own uncle."

"Thank you," he said, his voice ragged. He went over to the babies and looked down at them tenderly. "They're perfect, sister. Absolutely perfect."

Smoke billowed from Clara's pot. William stared at it curiously but said nothing. Clara fanned the fragrant cloud and kept one eye on his wife, whose pretty face had grown darker. A shiver crept down Clara's backbone. A shiver—and the intuition that made her such a good medicine woman. There was danger here. Her eyes widened, and her hands froze in the blue-white smoke. She scrutinized the wife with unrelenting concern. "What about me, Sarah?" the wife asked coolly. "Will you raise your children to hate *me*?"

"I'll tell them the truth," Sarah shot back. One of the babies sneezed. Sarah's brother scowled at Clara, but took his wife's arm. "Let's leave them to their ceremony," he said firmly.

His wife covered his hand with hers and looked from him to the babies with a meaningful nod. "They're probably catching a cold. And this smoke can't be healthy for them—my eyes are beginning to water. Think what it's doing to them."

"Well, I don't think—"

"William, is this the kind of, well, *bizarre* ritual you want performed for *our* baby? It makes me nervous."

"No need to be alarmed," he answered quickly, patting her arm. "It's a Cherokee custom. No harm in that."

"Sarah's lying here looking exhausted, and the babies are having trouble breathing."

"They're *fine*," Sarah interjected. "And so am I."

The wife gazed at her sympathetically. "You're trying to honor Hugh's family customs, I'm sure. But, Sarah, this is primitive and, well, unnecessary."

"There is something unnecessary in this room," Clara announced loudly. "But it's *you*, not my smoke."

Sarah's sister-in-law drew back with a wounded expression. Her eyes shifted to her husband. "I'm concerned only for your nephew and niece. Don't let me be insulted for feeling that way."

Her husband shifted uneasily to Sarah. "Perhaps she's right, sister. This kind of ceremony, no matter how well-intentioned, doesn't belong in a hospital room. You'll set off the sprinklers."

Sarah was sitting upright now, rigid, her eyes glittering. "Leave. Just leave, before you ruin it."

"Your sister's glassy-eyed from pain medication," the wife whispered. "*Do* something, William. She's not thinking straight."

His mouth moved in silent distress. He was plainly caught between two hard walls, Clara thought. Rachel Raincrow waved her hands. "Judge, you let us finish. We know what we're doing."

"*William*," Sarah added, her voice slurred but full of warning. She scrubbed a hand loosely across her perspiring face. "Don't meddle. Don't let your mealy-mouthed wife cause more trouble."

Sarah's brother stiffened. Clara sighed heavily. Sarah had said the wrong thing. Never provoke a man to take sides against his wife. "Alexandra's right," he told his sister. He looked at his wife. "Call one of the nurses."

Sarah yelped. "No, Alexandra, wait—" But she had already pivoted on her high heels and hurried out. Clara stood in furious silence. Rachel wrung her hands together. "Judge, you fool. You blind fool."

"I'm doing what I think is best," he said, a muscle popping in his jaw. "Sarah, you have to believe that."

Sarah sank back on the pillows, gaping at him. "That's what you said when you gave our family's heirloom to her."

"There. Look at what these two characters are up to." His wife appeared in the doorway again with a starched nurse glowering beside her. The nurse said swiftly, "Mrs. Vanderveer, I swear I didn't know what they were doing." The nurse barged in, grabbed a cup of water from the bedside stand, and dumped it in Clara's bowl.

Rachel Raincrow gasped. "Clara, fix it."

"It's too late," Clara announced in Cherokee. She stared in horror at her bowl. "The spirits have been insulted."

"No, oh, no—"

Sarah pounded her fists on the bed. "Get your meddling tramp out of my room."

Her brother turned anxiously, his hands out. "Don't talk that way. Please—" His jaw worked spasmodically. "Alexandra, apologize."

His wife raised her chin and looked at him. "I'm sorry for trying to take care of your sister and her children."

"Dear, I didn't mean anything like *that*. I meant—"

"Enough," Clara said. She knew this was a lost cause. She emptied her bowl in a sink in one corner, then packed her things in her bag. Rachel Raincrow huddled over the babies as if she had the power to undo the harm. Sarah Raincrow said other things to her brother and his wife, bad things, not what family should talk of.

Clara shivered. Still speaking Cherokee, she said, "Rachel Raincrow, we must go. I'm getting dirty. Come on, please. We need to discuss this alone."

"Rachel, I'm sorry," Sarah cried. "Tell Mrs. Big Stick I want her to come back later. Or she can come to the Cove next week—"

"No." Clara faced the poor girl and shook her head sadly. "This is not like giving a shot of penicillin. There is a time for it, and when that time is past, well—you'll have to do the best you can. I'll pray for you and your children."

Clara hoisted her bag and marched out of the room. She waited in the lobby, grim-faced, until Rachel Raincrow joined her. Rachel's hooded eyes were terrified. "Tell me the truth," Rachel said.

Clara stared at the floor. Giving bad news to people was the only unpleasant part of her work. She stalled. Maybe Rachel wouldn't pressure her. "Tell me," Rachel repeated, grasping her arm. "I have to know."

Clara lifted her head. Her eyes met Rachel's. "I'll try to help you with the children. I don't know how much good it will do. For now, I need to know all you can tell me about that woman."

"Oh, Clara, why? I'm already worried about her being a witch."

"It's worse than that." She could barely say the word, it was such a horrible threat. She whispered it furtively. "*Ravenmocker*."

Rachel Raincrow moaned. Bowing her head, she shielded it with both arms.

Ginger Monroe Flemming had done even better in marriage than Alexandra, a fact Alexandra secretly loathed. Her old schoolmate had married into the South Carolina Flemmings of Flemmings Pharmaceuticals. *Very* old money, very big money, very much the epitome of Charleston society. It galled Alexandra when Ginger arrived for a weekend visit driving a Rolls Royce sedan and accompanied by her own maid.

William and she had only a grumbling housekeeper who served double-duty as a cook. William was devoted to the furtive black creature and her equally recalcitrant husband, who kept the gardens up as well as caring for the two Arabian mares Alexandra had brought to Highview after their marriage.

Alexandra couldn't convince him to fire them and let her staff the house with people of her own choosing. Since the birth of his sister's children, and that bizarre incident at the hospital, William had been moody with her. She was treading lightly, coddling him these days, as she waited out the last two months of her pregnancy.

Ginger's visit only made the frustration worse.

"It's absolutely lovely here," Ginger said, leaning back in a white wooden chair on the lake dock to catch the spring sunshine. Behind them, crickets droned sleepily in the grass of the back lawn; before them a secluded inlet of Pandora Lake stretched to steep hills covered in giant firs and rhododendron.

Sipping iced tea, Alexandra lay on a cushioned lounge beside her, feeling bloated and encumbered by a belly that was growing more enormous every day. "You live in paradise," Ginger continued heedlessly, stroking wavy brunette hair back from her forehead with one hand and rubbing suntan lotion on her face with the other. "No humidity, no gnats. I can work on my tan without sweating and swatting at things. The air is so clean. My sinuses haven't bothered me since I got here. And the scenery—oh, Alex, I can't believe the views you've shown me outside town. And *town* is the *cutest* place, right out of a Norman Rockwell painting. I envy you."

Alexandra scowled behind black sunglasses. "We have five churches and no movie theater. The owner of our only restaurant thinks yeast rolls and overdone sirloin are haute cuisine, and the best clothing shop we have stocks dungarees next to the dress rack. Once you drive off the main roads, nothing is paved, and the electricity went out for an entire week last winter. Deer eat the shrubbery, and last month the postman totaled his new pickup truck when he ran into a bear. It made the headlines for two weeks in our newspaper."

Ginger laughed. "Don't you see? That's why this place is so fascinating to lowlanders. It's quiet and unspoiled, tucked up here in the top of the mountains."

"It's lonely. William's relatives are gentrified hicks. They look down on anyone who can't trace the family tree to some grubby mountaineer settler." She paused. "Or to some shabby Indian."

Ginger looked intrigued. "How funny. Are there many Indians around here?"

"A lot. But most are so shy and backward, they keep to themselves. There's a nothing little community across the mountains called Cawatie Township. About five miles from here. William dragged me over there once to some sort of cermonial dance. Indians stomping and chanting. Half of them either can't or won't speak English. William thinks they're wonderful. His sister even married one."

"My God, you're kidding."

Alexandra smiled wearily. "Of course, *my* sister ran off in the middle of the night with an army sergeant."

"Where's Frannie now?"

"On an army base in Germany, with her dearly beloved. My parents won't even write to her. I sent her some money and told her to get a divorce and come home. I'm sure she married the man just to spite us all. It won't last. I told her she could live with William and me. I even had William write to her—invite her to come here."

"What did she say?"

"She sent the money back and told me she was happy."

"Maybe she is."

"My sister," Alexandra said grimly, "thinks I'm the unhappy one."

Ginger laughed. "You've got everything a girl could want. Including a baby on the way."

Alexandra was silent. William was thrilled with her pregnancy; he doted on the idea of having a child. That was the main reason she wanted to give him one. Extra insurance. "I'm so bored I could scream," she said suddenly. "I wish I had a job. I wish I could do something, *anything* to put this godforsaken place on the map."

Ginger sat forward eagerly. "*Alex*. Help me find a piece of property to buy. Something irresistible. John would love it up here. We have a summer cottage in Maine, but it's so far away. We should build one here. I *know* he'd go crazy for the place."

Alexandra pushed herself upright. A thready coil of excitement erased her lethargy. "Really? And you'd bring friends to visit?"

"Dozens of them. Think about it—a whole crew of people with money to burn, drooling over the fresh air and the mountains, buying land, building homes, tennis courts—God, a country club even. A golf course. Something private, of course. But everything would hinge on finding the perfect setting."

"I've already got it. William owns a thousand acres of the most gorgeous property you've ever seen. Only a few miles from here."

Ginger yelped with glee. "Empty land? What does he do with it?"

Alexandra waved a hand in disgust. "It's as good as empty. He rents it to a handful of tenant farmers."

"Would he tell them to move?"

"Not even if his life depended on it. They can barely scratch together rent payments, and half the time they show up on our doorstep with truckloads of vegetables instead of money. But he lets them get away with it because they treat him like some kind of adored land baron. I've pointed out that they're cheating him blind, but he just mutters about traditions and loyalty, as if they're his personal responsibility."

"Well, then, why do you think he'd change his mind?"

Alexandra lay back happily. "Don't worry about it. I'll think of something."

Not much work was getting done around the Cove these days because Sarah and Rachel couldn't keep from playing with the babies. At four months, the two put on an endless show of smiles and gurgles and wide-eyed charisma. Every wave of a tiny arm, every kick of a fat leg, was cause for admiration. And Hugh wasn't much better, rushing home in the evenings to spend every spare moment with them in his arms.

Deep in the narrow secluded valley below Pandora, with the Saukee River whispering just out of sight beyond a grove of poplars and the steep granite face of Razorback Bald rising in the background like a protective wall, Sarah was never lonely. She had the big two-story log house to manage, chickens to feed, a cow to milk, a garden and fruit orchard to tend. She had three frisky mutt dogs and five fat cats to keep out of trouble. She had her paintings—bright, gentle watercolors of landscapes and flowers, with an occasional portrait of any willing souls who would sit long enough to be copied. She had her children, Rachel's friendship, and Hugh's love.

Most days, it was almost enough to keep her from brooding about her ruby and her brother, and his wife.

She and Rachel were picking tomatoes in the garden beyond the log barn, with little Jake and Eleanore asleep on a blanket in the shade of a yarrow hedge, when Rachel raised her head toward the road. "Somebody's coming," she said, and frowned.

Rachel's hearing was an extraordinary thing, like her talent for finding gemstones. The dirt road that ran through the Cove intersected a turn in the Saukee so far in the distance that the drive to the house took a full five minutes. To get into the valley a person had to drive through the river at a shallow ford, then traverse the road down the mountainside in steep and winding curves. Hugh's father had built a wooden bridge off a narrow side road to cross the river when the water ran high, but even when visitors rumbled across the bridge, their approach couldn't be heard at the house.

Even the dogs hadn't barked yet. But Rachel was rarely mistaken about these things. "A big truck," she added, pushing herself up from the herb bed and brushing dirt off her faded work skirt. Her long braid of brindled hair swung along her back as she nodded to Sarah. "You'll see."

Sarah got up, tucking thick garden gloves into a back pocket of her overalls, then trying in vain to puff up her damp helmet of teased hair. Mountain hospitality called for the lady of the house to be presentable—and in warm weather armed with iced tea. She thought quickly. She had a fresh gallon in the refrigerator.

A few minutes later, the dogs began barking. Sarah walked into the front yard between towering clumps of nandinas and the wide shade of huge oaks, peering through dogwoods that lined the narrow dirt driveway off the road. A lurching, ancient flatbed truck with tall, slatted-wood side panels pulled into the driveway. A half-grown boy drove the old truck, and the cab was crowded with small children, all standing up. She immediately recognized the dozen women who stood in the bed of the truck, clinging to the side panels. Weathered, tough, young, old, two of them black women. She knew their shy faces and simple Sunday-go-to-church dresses as if they were family.

The wives of William's tenant farmers.

"Well, hello," she said when the truck came to a stop and the growling engine went silent. "What are y'all doing out and about in the middle of a workday?"

They climbed out silently, their faces grim. She was startled to see evidence of tears. Rachel came up beside her, a baby cuddled in each brown arm, and whispered, "Look at 'em. There's bad trouble."

Sarah waited politely. One of the older ones edged forward, her knotty hands wound together in front of her. "We come to you for help, ma'am. You bein' the judge's sister. We don't know what else to do."

"Help for what, Lucy? What's wrong?"

"Revenuers. Government men. The law carried our husbands off. Busted up their stills and caught 'em."

Sarah gaped at them. Making liquor was a revered hobby in the mountains, not a booming industry anymore. Swapped and sold by people who were proud of their homemade brands, it amounted to a local craft, not a crime. Government agents hadn't seriously hunted for moonshiners since Sarah was a child.

"What happened?" she asked.

"We don't know exactly. But they're sayin' our men's going to jail for six months."

"Yes, we *do* know what happened." A crying young woman, hardly more than Sarah's age, came forward. "We ain't never spoke ill of the judge before, ma'am. He's been so good to us. But now he's turned on us."

"No," Sarah said quickly. "My brother wouldn't do that. He'd never—"

"It was his wife," another woman added.

Sarah felt the blood draining out of her face. "What did she do?"

"She come to visit, like she just wanted to be polite. Bringing little gifts—cakes and things. Everybody got together at Lucy's house to see her. Everybody brought her presents—just like we do when the judge comes to say hello. We give her a basket of liquor, 'cause we always give a basket to the judge. She asked all about it, real sweet, about how it was made, and where the stills is at. We figured—ain't nothing to worry about, people around here know what's right, and how to behave."

Lucy said slowly, "But that was a week ago, and last night the gov'ment men come. Ma'am, we hate to think your sister-in-law put the revenuers on us, but we don't know what else to say."

Sarah dimly heard Rachel's hiss of anger. Shame and

fury strangled her. "Y'all go on back to your homes,"
Sarah said evenly. "I'll take care of this. I promise."

She left the babies in Rachel's care and drove to the
next town—the county seat—as fast as she could push her
old Jeep. She remembered her brother's court schedule—
it was Wednesday afternoon, and everything in the county shut down after twelve on Wednesdays. William would
be finishing up paperwork in his office.

Sarah barged into the big, paneled room lined with
bookcases. William sat at his desk with his head in his
hands. "You *know*," Sarah said, horrified. "You know
Alexandra called the law on your tenants."

He jerked his head up. His expression was anguished.
"I don't know anything of the kind."

"Who else would?"

"There's no reason on God's green earth for her to
do something like that. I asked her. She swore to me it
wasn't her. You forget how it used to be. People make
enemies. They get some little feud going and turn each
other in out of spite. It could have been anyone in the
county."

"You don't believe that. I can tell by the look on your
face. She hurt those people. What are you going to do
about it?"

"Sarah, I love her. I love her, and she's *not* cruel at
heart. She's got this . . . this need to be important, and
it's because she's defensive about her family's reputation.
People still gossip about the way they treated their workers at the mills." He thumped the desk. "It was thirty
years ago, by God."

"The Dukes haven't changed that much. Life isn't
that much better for their employees, even now. Besides,
Alexandra's creating her own reputation, and it's damned
bad, and she's dragging you down with her."

He slammed his fist on the desk. "She's my *wife*, and
we have a child on the way. My first duty is to stand up
for her and that child."

"What about honor? What about self-respect? And

loyalty to the other people who've come to depend on
you? All right, putting Alexandra aside, what are you
going to do to help your tenants? Those families can't
keep their farms going with the husbands locked up for
six months."

"I'll take care of them."

"They're proud. They want fair treatment, not charity." She paused, her jaw working. "That's all I want too.
Fair treatment."

"Sarah, I'd cut off my right arm if it would take away
your disappointment."

"You know what you owe me. It's not an arm. Don't
you understand? You're my brother, and I love you. I
don't want to be at odds with you."

"Then try to forgive and forget. I'm being torn apart
here, sister."

"Judge? Excuse me for interrupting, but it's an emergency." His secretary stood in the doorway, wringing her
hands. "They called from the hospital. Mrs. Vanderveer
has gone into labor."

William leapt up and grabbed his hat from an ivory
peg on the wall. He shook his head at Sarah. "I've got to
get over there. Trust me, sister. I'll make things right."
He rushed out past her, running.

Alexandra knew the moment William took his newborn son into his arms that her power and influence
were forever secure. Tears in his eyes, William cooed to
the red, wrinkled baby, then kissed the top of his head.
"He has my red hair," William said in a husky, rever-
ent voice. "He's the most perfect . . . thank you, darling,
thank you."

"It was my pleasure." She relaxed on the hospital pillows with peaceful exhaustion. Once was enough. William
wanted more children, but she would simply find a doctor
out of town who'd prescribe birth control pills for her—
thank God for that new resource—and she'd take them
without telling William. "Would you mind if I hire a
nanny for him?"

"Well, I suppose not, but why?"

"Because he deserves it. Because it's the responsible thing for parents of our status to do."

"If it makes you happy." William cuddled the baby and stroked his curled fingers. "I'd like to name him Timothy, after my . . . after my and Sarah's father."

"Certainly. I'd love to think that gesture would make your sister feel more generous toward me. Maybe she'll see that I want to be friends with her—and that our children should grow up playing together, like cousins ought to."

William sank into a chair beside the bed and looked at her tenderly. "No one will ever say you don't have this family's best interests at heart."

"I don't want to be an outsider. I don't want people to be suspicious of me. Oh, William, I *hate* that your tenant farmers think I caused the trouble for them. There's no way I can prove my visit was innocent. I was such a fool for encouraging them to tell me all about their homemade liquor. Of *course* they think I was prying into their secrets, when it was just my clumsy way of showing polite interest."

"Shhh, I know that." He rocked the baby in his arms with absurd delicacy for such a big, bearish man. Alexandra took a deep breath and added, "You're going to think I'm cruel for what I say next. But I'm thinking of *you*. Of us. Of what we have to do to protect our good name—Timothy's good name."

William shifted uneasily. "I do believe you want what's best. That's not cruel or selfish. Tell me."

"No matter how sad it is about your tenants, or how harmless their intentions were—they broke the law, William. You're a judge. You have to set an example. We can't have your career ruined by people saying you condone criminal activity whenever it suits you. And you *know* that as soon as those men come home, they'll be back at their stills." She reached out and entwined her fingers in his. "You have to put those families off your property."

He protested. He cajoled. She insisted. She cried, and begged him to consider how he'd explain to their son why he'd let personal sentiment override the sanctity of the law. In the end, she won. He sat with his head bowed to Timothy's, beaten. She controlled him with the very qualities that had drawn him to her; her unbending pride and beauty, and the steely grace that had seemed so charming when they first met. It shamed him to love her more than his own conscience, but he could not stop. After so many years of self-denial and loneliness as he played the role of both father and mother to Sarah, as he toiled in his law practice single-mindedly and rose to a judge's bench by the dull forces of intellect and unending attention to others' problems and needs, she was the one gift he had given himself.

It shamed him to need her pampering so much, to slavishly pursue her gratitude and her willing sensuality. He was humiliated but unable to deny her anything she wanted for fear he'd lose her. There was no looking back now.

That night, for the first time in his sober and dignified life, he drank heavily and sat in the dark of his office, in the home that had been his family's for generations, the Pandora ruby lying in the palm of his hand. He had given her everything dear to him. His name, his home, his protection, and his self-respect.

Chapter Three

"*Atmen Sie aus*, Frau Ryder. *Atmen Sie aus*."

Breathe out? Frannie thought desperately. The pain was so bad, she couldn't remember *how* to breathe, much less which way. "*Ja*," she answered in the middle of a groan, her head arching back on the sweat-soaked pillow, her gaze fixed blankly on the ceiling of the bedroom in her and Carl's tiny apartment. And then, as her updrawn legs convulsed and she thought the baby was going to rip her apart, she called, "*Nein, nein!* Oh, shit!"

"What is *shit*?" the German midwife asked, huffing. "Push, Frau Ryder."

"She's dying," Jane Gibson said darkly. Jane, the wife of a staff sergeant and a cheerful friend ordinarily, was kneeling on the bed with her hands wound around one of Frannie's fists. "She's been in labor for a day and a half. This is crazy! We've got to take her to the base hospital."

"Too late for the *Krankenhaus, ja,*" the midwife muttered. "The baby, it comes out."

And it did, like a piano squeezing through a keyhole, while Frannie screamed. If she were dying, she didn't see her whole life flash before her eyes, but only the last four years—four miscarriages in four years, and a platoon of army doctors patting her head while they told her and Carl to keep trying. Four years of hope, failure, and heartache had driven Frannie to this point. She didn't believe in doctors anymore.

Carl did though. Thank God he was away on maneuvers for two weeks and didn't know she'd been studying natural childbirth. He was unhappy enough, already, about her interest in bizarre ideas.

"Oh, Lord, she's not breathing!" Jane yelled. Frannie heard the words dimly as the agonizing pressure inside her slipped away. *I am too breathing, I think*, she decided. *No, the baby. She means the baby.* Frannie lurched upright, staring in horror at the limp blue baby girl lying between her legs on the bloody sheets.

The midwife enclosed the baby's head in her beefy hands, bent over her, and closed her mouth over the baby's entire face, it seemed. "What the hell are you doing?" Jane screamed.

Frannie pushed at Jane's hands, which were grabbing the midwife's curly gray wig. "She's giving her air," Frannie explained. She leaned forward, shaking, praying. "Please let her be all right. Please don't let my stupidity kill her."

The baby shuddered. Its frail chest puffed out vigorously, and the incredibly delicate-looking arms and legs began to move. The midwife sat back, hoisted her across Frannie's abdomen, and lightly slapped her rump. A faint, angry wail filled the room.

Frannie huddled over her daughter, crying, stroking slick wisps of blond hair on the baby's head. "Do you think she's hurt?"

"She's *mad,*" Jane said, collapsing beside them. "And Carl is going to be mad as hell too, if you tell him how this went. You could have delivered this baby hours ago, in the hospital, with a nice spinal block and a pair of friendly forceps to help you, instead of only me and this . . . this Aryan soothsayer."

"Hush. Everything's all right. I'm sure."

But she wasn't sure, she was terrified, and later, when the baby had been cleaned and dried and put in her arms, she looked down into her eyes and swore she saw rebuke. "Don't be upset with me, Samantha." she whispered. "I love you. I really, really do."

"Samantha?" Jane sipped a cola and sat, cross-legged, on the end of the bed. The midwife ambled in from the kitchen, belching and taking deep swallows from a mug of dark beer.

"Carl and I talked about it. Sam for a boy, Samantha for a girl."

"Family name?"

"No." Frannie brooded over that, thinking about Alexandra and the rest of her family. She didn't write to anyone but Alexandra, and even her letters to Alex were dutiful. Alexandra sent pictures of her son, who was almost four now, and brief, polite notes occasionally. Frannie thought her sister had not forgiven her for having the courage to run away. "She's named for Elizabeth Montgomery." Frannie told Jane finally.

"Huh?"

"Samantha. On *Bewitched*."

"You're naming your daughter after a TV witch? You *want* your kid to grow up being named after a witch?"

"A *good* witch," Frannie corrected her. "Like the good witch in *The Wizard of Oz*."

"Huh? That witch was named Samantha too?"

"*No*. She was named Glenda. The point is, there are good karmas and bad karmas, and Samantha represents the good."

"Karmas?"

"Never mind." Frannie rubbed a fingertip across one of the baby's tiny hands. "Look at these beautiful little hands. Frau Mitteldorf, would you read her palm for me?"

"Oh, jeez," Jane said, and left the room.

The midwife shuffled over and sat down heavily beside them. Balancing her beer on one broad knee, she pressed the baby's right hand open and peered at it. "*Gut* hands," she proclaimed.

"Good? Really?"

"*Ja*, good luck in her hands." The woman squinted and frowned. "She will need it."

Frannie was too guilt-stricken to ask why.

Almost two years passed in agonizing denial before Frannie admitted that something was wrong with Samantha. "Say 'Daddy,'" Carl coached every morning, hunched beside Samantha's high chair while his breakfast turned cold. And every morning Samantha solemnly smeared baby cereal on her mouth and said nothing. "Say 'Mama,'" Frannie would croon. "Look, Carl, she almost did it." Frannie was sick with fear.

But every morning Samantha merrily whacked her baby bowl with her spoon and simply stared at them.

One evening, sitting in the living room watching Samantha, Carl threw his newspaper on the floor, scrubbed his hands over his eyes, and muttered hoarsely, "She can't talk or won't talk. This is killing me."

"There's nothing wrong with her." Frannie huddled next to him and struggled—as she did every day—not to cry. Samantha sat on the living room floor, appearing cute and normal in a pink jumper, as she solemnly stuffed bits of twine into a shoebox, then pulled them back out, arranged them in neat rows on the carpet, then put them back in the box. Her chubby little hands were extraordinarily graceful and precise. "She has a real love for order," Frannie noted hopefully. "Just like her adoring daddy."

Carl grunted. "She's training to be a pack rat." He sat on the floor, and Samantha toddled over to him, grinning, as he held out his arms. "You'll make a damned fine pack rat too," he said. "But I'm taking you to another doctor."

That specialist did the same tests as the ones before him, and told them the same thing: He could not diagnose the mystery that kept words locked inside their little girl.

On her second, silent birthday, Carl paced the living room with his hands knotted in his trouser pockets, watching her methodically examine a stuffed bear, her eyes bright, her hands quick. "She's not an idiot," he announced loudly. "Goddammit, I don't understand her. There's nothing wrong with her. She's not feebleminded."

Two years of guilt flooded Frannie with confession. She made a garbled sound and blurted out, "Something's wrong with her, and it's my fault."

Carl halted, rammed his hands through his short-cropped hair, and stared at her. "What?"

Frannie shivered. "I lied to you. She wasn't born at home unexpectedly. I was so afraid something would go wrong if I went to the hospital—everything had gone wrong with our other babies. I'd heard about a German woman—a midwife who specialized in natural childbirth—no drugs, no doctors. When I went into labor, and you were away on maneuvers, I called her." Frannie sank to their small, rump-sprung couch and put her head in her hands. "I was in labor for over thirty-six hours. When Sammy came, she wasn't breathing. The midwife had to help her. Oh, Carl, I'm *sorry*. I hurt our daughter somehow, and I'll never forgive myself."

"You put our baby in danger to test out some damned fool idea about what's 'natural'?" Carl's voice shook with anger. "I've tried my best not to make fun of your queer ideas, but this is the limit." Frannie looked at him miserably as he flung a hand toward Samantha, who had stopped playing to stare at them with huge, worried blue eyes. "What's *natural* about a two-year-old who can't even say 'Mama' and 'Daddy'?"

Frannie straightened, crying silently, but determined. "She will talk. I know she will. And when we have another baby, I won't take any chances. No more midwives. No more 'natural' anything. Nothing but good, modern, dyed-in-the-wool methods. I swear."

"I don't think we ought to have another baby until we get this mess straightened out."

"Carl!"

Frannie rose and reached out to him, but he shrugged her hands away and left the room. Samantha, her eyes filled with tears, chirped sadly.

At the wise old age of six, Jake already knew what he was: a tuning fork. A tuning fork like the one on Mother's straight-backed piano in the living room, and that was why, Granny explained, he could hear a kind of music no one else could hear, the music of hidden things, lost things. Eleanore was the same way. Ellie didn't ponder their uniqueness the way he did. It worried him—being different. At a county fair he had seen bottles filled with baby animals so strange they'd died before they were even born. Tiny, two-headed calves, and three puppies joined at a single pair of hind legs. He'd asked Father if there were children, somewhere, like that—dead little babies floating in bottles, with extra parts. Father had looked at him oddly and answered—Yes, son, at medical school I saw babies like that.

Did someone kill them because they had extra parts? Jake had asked, horrified. And Father—who didn't beat around the bush (that was what Mother was always telling him)—said most times they just died on their own, and it was nature's way of making sure they didn't suffer.

But what about the ones that don't die on their own? Jake persisted. What if Ellie and I had been born with extra parts?

Father had had to think about that a minute. Well, I'm a good doctor. I'd just have cut them off, he said. Then he turned Jake around, felt his arms and legs, his back and stomach, looked into his mouth, and said, Nope, nothing there that isn't supposed to be there.

Jake had wanted to confess that he and Ellie *did* have an extra part—like Granny—only no one could see it. But the fear that Father might look at him as if he ought to be in a bottle was too awful to risk. He explained this problem to Ellie, and she agreed that they'd better keep quiet.

So they didn't tell anyone, not even their parents, that they were tuning forks; Granny was the only one who knew, because she was a tuning fork too. She was their teacher—a whole lot more interesting than any teachers at the elementary school, in town. They happily toted Granny's spade and pick for her on long walks into the mountains to hunt for rocks, and she showed them how to tell what was what: garnets and topazes, aquamarines and sapphires, and when the music was very, very sweet, rubies.

Most were just rocks, Granny said, but some were so special, she took them to a jeweler in town and sold them.

Being able to find things was a sacred gift, Granny said, a secret gift that bad people might try to steal or use if they knew about it. And the mountains were full of watchful spirits—big, coiled *Uktenas* who hid in the deep pools of the rivers, trouble-making elves and tricky witches who would pounce if they learned how powerful Jake and Eleanore were.

The world of the people was turning upside down, Granny explained. There were strangers on the high ridges outside town now, strangers who put gates on the roads to their fine new houses, strangers who cut down the forest and planted more grass than a million cows could eat, strangers who played games like golf and tennis, which they didn't want to share with anyone else, strangers who bought the old buildings in town and filled them with beautiful, useless things they could sell only among themselves.

The scariest thing was, the world outside the mountains was in just as much of a mess, Granny said. Hard as it was for her to believe, shows about sex, dope, and naked people were going on up in New York, right on the same street where Grandpa Raincrow had taken her to see *Annie Get Your Gun*. More than 30,000 soldiers were dead over in Vietnam for no good reason Granny could figure. The space people were getting ready to send men to the moon—who could know what horrible evil might come from meddling with the moon?

And a bunch of fools had added division playoffs to baseball.

Over smoky campfires Granny told them all her stories and gave them all her secret warnings, and they listened, hypnotized. Everybody loved Granny, and she'd lived a long, long time without anyone noticing her extra part. As long as Granny was okay, they would be okay too.

Jake decided odd people had to stick together, and look out for each other.

Another year passed, and Carl's grim silences began to match Samantha's innocent ones. Desperation made Frannie forget her vow about not seeking unorthodox help.

Madame Maria was a transplanted Italian, the wife of a German bureaucrat who worked in the mayor's office, and she gave psychic readings every Wednesday afternoon in her small, cluttered house on a back street where the windows were so close to the sidewalk that the cats who lounged in the flower boxes flicked their paws at the hair of unsuspecting visitors.

One of the cats had pulled a clump of hair loose from Frannie's long braid, and Frannie toyed with the hair nervously with one hand while the small, sparrowlike Madame Maria gripped her other hand. Madame's little living room was as pretty as a dollhouse; Madame looked like a faded porcelain figurine, with rigidly permed blue-gray hair even her cats couldn't destroy.

"You have a problem," Madame said in a guttural, soothing accent—English overlaid with Italian and German. "You have come to see Madame Maria because you need help."

"It's my daughter," Frannie said, forgetting her hair and letting her hand drop wearily to the table between them. "She's almost three years old, but she's never spoken a word. We've taken her to doctors. They can't find anything wrong with her."

"Ah, your daughter. I suspected. I feel your . . . fear. And your guilt. You wonder if you caused her silence, some way."

Frannie leaned forward eagerly. "Yes. God, yes. She was born at home. I should have gone to the hospital, but I believe in natural childbirth. My husband was away, and I didn't tell him what I intended to do. I hired a midwife, and I almost died. I didn't tell my husband the truth for a long time—I prayed our daughter was all right, but when she didn't start talking . . ." Frannie swallowed hard and looked away.

Madame stroked her hand. "You have a strong interest in the spiritual."

"Yes, I do! I had four miscarriages before Samantha—that's my daughter—"

"I saw a name beginning in *S*."

"That's her—yes. Before Samantha, I lost four babies. No conventional doctors could do a thing to help me. I was so afraid. I was ready to try anything. But I'm afraid I hurt my little girl."

"Perhaps the fact that she was born at all is because you chose a different path during that pregnancy."

"I've wondered about that." Frannie hesitated, a knot of emotion still hurting her throat. "But my husband has never forgiven me for what happened. Oh, Madame, every month that goes by without Samantha saying a word is . . . my husband doesn't say so out loud, but I know he blames me more and more. I've got to find out what's wrong with her."

"Is she a nervous child?"

"Oh, no, she's just the opposite. She's so calm and, well, sort of *dignified*. She's an old woman! Sometimes I think she blames me too, for putting her through a hard labor."

"The child is under pressure. She senses all the anger and fear around her." Madame cupped Frannie's hand in both of hers and shut her eyes. "You are blocking her spirit. You are unhappy. How long have you lived in Germany?"

"Seven years."

"Homesickness," Madame proclaimed.

Frannie chewed her lower lip. "I haven't seen any of my family in all that time. I have a sister—"

"I see her. Blond, yes?" Madame opened one eye and peeped at Frannie. "Like you."

"Yes! We write to each other, but we don't have much in common. She's rich, Madame. Money and prestige mean everything to her. I'm just the opposite. There were bad feelings between us when I left home."

"Ah! You must go home and resolve this. You envy your sister, but you don't know it."

"Envy Alexandra? I don't think so."

"Alexandra. Hmmm. I knew her name began with an A. She is . . ." Madame squinted at her. "Older."

"Yes. Four years older."

"Pride is your mistake. Go to your sister. Take your daughter. Clear away the bad feelings. Ask your sister to pay for specialists to perform medical tests on Samantha."

"No, no, I could never do that. I don't want my sister's money. My husband and I agreed a long time ago not to accept any help from my family. I—"

"Pride," Madame repeated, waving a thin finger. "Pride keeps your daughter from speaking."

"What?" Frannie said, frowning at her.

"Pride. Like yours. Go home. Set a good example." Madame placed Frannie's hand on the table, then leaned back. "That will be five dollars, please."

Frannie's thoughts whirled. She hadn't had time to mull over everything Madame Maria had said, but the woman seemed so confident. Madame had, after all, divined Samantha and Alexandra's names, the color of Alexandra's hair, and the fact that Alexandra was an older sister. No one could convince Frannie that psychics weren't legitimate. She was so desperate for guidance, for ways to protect the daughter she'd birthed after so

many disappointments, and to salvage Carl's respect
for her.

She paid Madame Maria and nodded vigorously.
"You're amazing. Thank you. I'll do exactly what you
suggested."

She was going home to visit Alexandra. She would
humble herself.

Alexandra walked quickly out of the house. William
was pitching a softball to Tim on the back lawn, where
the grass was just beginning to turn green for spring.
Her thoughts distracted, she noted wearily that Tim, at
six, was chubby and awkward and had no discernible
potential for sports. That galled her—she, who had been
riding a pony over jumps by the time she was his age,
she, who played tennis and golf with expert skill. She had
birthed this clumsy little dumpling who started crying as
William's slow, underhanded pitch bounced off the tips of
his splayed fingers.

"It's all right," William said quickly, striding over
to him with the thick, ponderous movements Tim had
inherited, and lifting the boy into his arms. Tim sniffled
loudly. William patted his back and coddled him, which
set Alexandra's teeth on edge.

She announced loudly, "Frannie called. She's coming home. I invited her to stay with us."

William turned and stared at her. It had been sev-
en years since Frannie ran away with Carl Ryder, with
never any hint that she'd ever come back. "Is anything
wrong?"

"Samantha still isn't talking. Frannie asked me to
loan her the money for more tests. I'm arranging them
with the medical center at the university. The best specialists I can find. Those army doctors are cheap quacks.
There are no retarded children in my family. Samantha
isn't going to be the first." Alexandra hesitated, frowning.
"Who knows what the child had bred into her from Carl
Ryder's people?"

"Don't talk about her as if she ought to be dropped from the breeding registry, dear. She's not a horse."

"People are no different from horses. If you breed carelessly, you get weak traits." Alexandra glanced at their son, then looked away quickly. "Put him down, William. He's not a baby. He's six years old, and you're encouraging him to whine at the drop of a hat."

William set their son down slowly, ruffled his pale red hair, and told him to go wash up for dinner. When the boy was safely out of earshot, William straightened and looked at her with the hangdog resignation she'd come to despise. "He needs brothers and sisters to look after. If I pamper him, it's because he's an only child."

"If you wanted a whole brood of chicks, you should have had my uterus checked for cysts before you married me." She clapped her hands. "Now let's talk about Frannie. She'll arrive here in two weeks. We'll have a dinner to introduce her to Ginger and the gang, and I want to do some redecorating in the two upstairs bedrooms with the shared bath. I'll move the double bed out of the small room and replace it with a child-size one. Something gorgeous—with a canopy. I'll buy a pretty little toy chest and fill it with dolls and picture books."

He advanced toward her, fists clenched. "You changed the subject. You won't discuss our own shortage of children, but you gleefully make plans for your sister's child."

"There's nothing to discuss. We've said it all before. You want more children in the house? Fine. We'll have Frannie's little girl."

"You talk as if you expect to keep her."

"I do." Alexandra took a wary step back from him as he halted close to her. She smelled the bourbon that was on his breath constantly. "Her, *and* Frannie," Alexandra explained. "I'm going to do my level best to persuade my sister not to go back to Carl. I've always suspected that Frannie regrets marrying him but is too proud to say so. If I give her some tactful encouragement, she'll probably jump at a chance to put the marriage behind her."

William snatched her by one arm. "I won't have you conniving to break up Frannie's marriage and meddle in the upbringing of her little girl. See to the problems in your own household, woman, and if you want a daughter, produce one of your own!"

"I can't have another child! Stop trying to humiliate me!"

He jerked her arm. "Can't, or won't?"

"Let go of me! Tim might be watching from a window!"

"Then let's get some of your precious privacy." Alexandra gasped at this sudden and unexpected violence. He nearly dragged her across the lawn to a hidden spot behind tall boxwood hedges, then swung her to face him. "Stop lying to me." he said. He shook her so hard her head snapped back. "By God, I've kept quiet because I didn't want to hurt your feelings—I didn't want to make you think I'm blaming you for your inability to become pregnant again. But I know the truth. I talked to your doctor. You don't have any goddamned cyst."

"You went behind my back!"

"You're my wife. I deserve to hear the truth."

"I can't give you more children, and all you can do is humiliate me about that fact by investigating my medical records!"

He shook her again. "Why can't we have more children? That's all I want to know. I had tests too. I know there's nothing wrong with me." His voice rose. "I'm a . . . middle-aged drunk, but I've got the wherewithal to get my own wife pregnant if she'd give me half a chance!"

"Prove it!" she yelled, shoving at him. "Prove you're good for something besides boring my friends and drinking yourself into a stupor every night!"

His face flushed crimson. He shoved her to the carefully manicured apron of pine bark behind the hedge and fell on her, jerking at his trouser button. The breath knocked out of her, dizzy with a fear she had never felt before, she fought him. She was dressed in a blue pullover and long, sheer blue skirt to play bridge at a banker's cottage at the club; William pushed the skirt to her waist and tore at the panty hose she wore over silk panties. Shoving the material aside, he took her, ignoring her groans of fury and pinning her arms over her head.

It was over almost as soon as it began. One halfhearted thrust and he seemed awash in the shame done to his own honor, if not hers. He lay heavily on her, very still, with his head buried on her shoulder. Limp with relief, she stared at the hedges overhead, and tried to breathe.

"I'm sorry, I'm so sorry," he whispered raggedly. "Forgive me. I was insane for a few seconds. Please, please, forgive me."

Alexandra shuddered. Years of helplessness and rage had been summed up in those seconds. But now her head cleared and she forced herself to remember who she was, and how she had always managed her rigidly goal-oriented life, and him. "Let's forget it happened," she said. "I'm not going to give you any more children. Accept that. I can't help it."

He moved away from her and sat with his shoulders slumped. Alexandra pushed herself upright, straightening her clothes and staring at his hunched back with mixed emotions. She neither loved nor hated him; she felt sorry for him at times, and occasionally even wished she could make him happy. But she was rarely happy or content herself, and she wasn't about to give him happiness at her own expense.

He was inferior. His son was inferior. Alexandra could not tolerate weak results in her horses *or* her children. She deserved to raise the best. She had seen pictures of Frannie's daughter. Despite what she'd said about the Ryder bloodlines, Alexandra thought Samantha was the most perfect child imaginable. A carbon copy of herself. She could be proud of Samantha.

"We do need more children around this place," she said with a hint of tragedy in her voice. "Please, will you support me in trying to keep Frannie here with Samantha, where we can help them both?"

William lifted his head and gazed at her with dull acceptance. "Do you forgive me?"

"Yes. Yes, of course."

"Then if you have your sister and your niece's best interests at heart, I won't say another word."

"I do. Thank you." She stroked his sweaty, thinning red hair. He sighed heavily, either relieved or resigned. It didn't matter. She had what she wanted. As always.

Chapter
four

~~~

$f$rannie stood in an ice cream shop, staring at a chalkboard behind the tall marble counter, where the gourmet flavor of the week was listed. Chocolate mocha mint. She knew it was absurd, but this meant something. Pandora, which Frannie remembered as a simple and unpretentious town, was now a place that catered to people with a taste for fancy flavors.

Alexandra had written to her over the years about bringing new people with big money into Pandora—had mentioned how eager entrepreneurs had begun "improving" the town to serve the interests of the new-comers. Frannie felt awe mingled with a distinct sense of unease. Her sister had transformed the whole town. Her sister was far more powerful than she'd expected.

You're here to make peace, she reminded herself. And to be precise, since she was trying very hard to take things one day at a time, without dwelling on Carl's unhappiness and Samantha's problem, she was here to buy a pint of vanilla ice cream. Sammie was at Highview with Alexandra, who had captivated her with a truckload of gifts, and the situation made Frannie feel competitive. She could buy her daughter vanilla ice cream, if nothing else.

The cool breeze from the opening of the shop's door distracted her, and she glanced over her shoulder. Frannie's mouth dropped open. "Sarah?"

"*Frannie?*" Sarah Raincrow stood there, frowning mildly at her, head up and green eyes troubled. Seven years had filled out Sarah's skinny frame, and changing styles had softened her. The severely tamed helmet of red hair Frannie remembered had become a long, dramatic tangle of curls, held back by a twisted blue bandanna. Dressed in tennis shoes, a long print peasant skirt with a white T-shirt tucked into it, Sarah looked about as glamorous as an Earth shoe.

Frannie recognized a kindred spirit, and wished desperately that she and Sarah could be friends. She took a deep breath and went to Sarah with her hands out. "It's good to see you again."

For a moment Sarah didn't budge, and Frannie felt a hot blush creeping from the roots of her straight blond hair down to her leather choker with the cameo at the center. Alexandra never mentioned Sarah or their feud, but Frannie doubted Sarah had ever forgiven her for marrying William and maneuvering the Vanderveer ruby into her possession.

Sarah wavered, appearing torn, then exhaled loudly and took Frannie's hands. "It's good to see you too. I thought you'd flown the coop and might never come back. I was sorry your family gave you no choice." Sarah smiled thinly. "You caused quite a commotion, from what I've heard. Running off like that."

"My parents haven't spoken to me in all these years. Not a word. Not a letter."

Sarah's expression became sympathetic. "But Alexandra has obviously welcomed you home."

"She's not as cold-blooded as you think. I'm here for a visit."

"Well, the fact that she's smart enough to recognize a good sister when she's got one is a small vote in her favor, I guess."

Every word seemed sincere, but grudging. Frannie looked at her wistfully. "You were always so nice to me, despite how you felt about Alexandra. I'm so glad that hasn't changed."

"No sense blaming you for your sister's faults." When Frannie sighed in dismay, Sarah looked apolgetic. "Sorry. We don't have to discuss her."

"Oh, it's all right," Frannie answered quickly. "She's my sister, and I love her, but I know how she can be."

Sarah drew her to one of the small, delicate tables by a curtained window. They sat facing each other in a pool of bright sunshine. Sarah held her gaze with straightforward honesty. "I haven't set foot in Highview since the day William married her and gave her our family's ruby. My brother and I don't speak anymore. I have twins—seven years old, a boy and a girl. Hugh and I let them visit Highview to play with Tim, because cousins shouldn't grow up hating each other. But that's the only concession I'll make."

"Oh, *Sarah.*"

"Alexandra peddles the land around town to her rich friends. They're changing everything, which I'm sure you've noticed. A lot of our stores have been bought by outsiders. The hardware store is an antique store now. So are the old Farmer's Seed and Feed, and Miller's Dress Shop. We can't buy a cheap meal in town. The diner's a wine and cheese shop. We can't buy fabric and thread, or shoes, or work clothes, because all of those shops have become boutiques that sell designer outfits. A retired bank president from New Orleans bought my great-aunt's old Victorian house and turned it into a bed and breakfast. Local people have very little access to the lake anymore, because most of the shoreline belongs to outsiders who've built huge vacation cottages there."

"But . . . but with all the growth, there must be a lot of jobs for the locals."

"Jobs working for the new people," Sarah said with contempt. "Jobs as maids and salesclerks, or golfing caddies. Folks around here used to be pretty self-sufficient. Besides, the jobs don't pay well enough for them to afford the new taxes. Last year's property assessments tripled taxes overnight. Families that have owned land here for generations are being forced to sell out. Hugh and I are saving every penny just to pay this year's taxes on the Cove."

"But Hugh's medical practice must be booming—"

"My husband has a major attitude problem." Sarah's face softened despite her grim tone of voice, and her eyes shimmered. "He thinks a doctor is supposed to treat any person who needs help, regardless of their ability to pay for it. If it weren't for Hugh, half the old-timers around town and over at Cawatie couldn't afford medical care." Sarah bit her lip. Her face became strained again. "There's another problem too. The people who have been here all their lives sure have their prejudices, and they gossiped up a storm when I married Hugh, but most of them have a little Cherokee blood somewhere in their family trees, and they respect the Indians. They respect Hugh." She shook her head disgustedly. "Most of the newcomers can't seem to get past the idea that a man who's part Indian couldn't possibly be as good a physician as their lily-white selves deserve. They go to the two white doctors Hugh works with at the hospital."

She paused, gazing out the window blindly, contempt drawing her mouth into a grimace. "All these so-called sophisticated people, coming up here from big cities all over the South. You'd think they'd be smarter." Her harsh eyes met Frannie's agonized ones again. "I never knew how much ignorance there was in the world until Alexandra invited it to this town."

Frannie knuckled her hands under her chin and bowed her head. "I'm sure Alexandra doesn't realize that she's ruining a lot of what made this place so special. She's so proud of the town. She's told me so."

Sarah leaned toward her and said evenly, "She's alienated my brother from all his old friends. He's miserable, and he drinks too much. From what I'm able to find out, the only time he's not stewed is when he's in court. He's so withdrawn and defensive that I can't get through to him to help him. I tried to talk to him a couple of years ago. I told him my bitterness about the ruby was a symbol of the real problem: I wanted him to take control of his life again." Sarah swallowed roughly. "He said, 'Alexandra is my life.' "

Sarah sank back in her chair, her face so pale and exhausted that Frannie, on the verge of tears, grasped one of her hands. "I'm so sorry . . . so sorry. I can't change my sister any more than you can change William. I can only try to live my life by my own morals, my own ideas of what's right, but—" Frannie choked up and struggled to continue speaking. Her shoulders drooped. "—But right now I can't even do *that*."

Frannie told her about Samantha, and the expensive specialists Alexandra had arranged for Samantha to see soon at the university medical center at Durham, and how generous Alexandra was being to loan Frannie the money. Sarah listened so gently, squeezing Frannie's hand in sympathy, that Frannie broke down and also told her that Carl blamed her for causing Samantha's problem. "I can't go back to my husband without some kind of success," Frannie finished, her voice trembling. "I *have* to solve our daughter's problem, no matter what it takes. All my ideals are just hypocritical bullshit, because I'll accept every bit of my sister's help and generosity even though I despise the way she lives her life."

"Listen to me, Frannie. Don't let pride keep you from doing what's best for Samantha. Just don't assume Alexandra's help is unselfish." Sarah pushed her chair back and stood. "I have to go. I promised my kids a gallon of French vanilla." Sarah looked away again, her eyes shadowed and distracted. "They need something to cheer them up, and that's the best I can do."

Frannie rose anxiously. "What's wrong?"

"Their grandmother died a couple of weeks ago." Sarah

hesitated, frowning. "I think, in some ways, they needed her more than they need Hugh and me. She always seemed to know what they were thinking." Sarah and Frannie traded a somber look. "Do you ever look at Samantha and wonder if she sees the world in a way you can't quite understand?"

Frannie's shoulders slumped. "All the time. All the time."

Chapter Five

The western drive across the state from Durham to the mountains took several hours. Alexandra kept the big gray sedan to the back roads, to stretch the drive out as long as possible. Time for her to talk Frannie into an agreement.

The car moved smoothly through the rolling piedmont, past broad pastures dotted with cattle and through small heartland towns with aged brick courthouses. The trees were budding; everything had the delicate patinas of new greens, and the dogwoods scattered in sunny spots along the road were at the full peak of their white blooms. Alexandra glanced occasionally at Frannie, who stared straight ahead, oblivious to the pretty scenery, her hands clasping a sweating paper cup of melted ice and cola, her blue sweater hanging ajar around her rumpled pantsuit. Frannie was inconsolable.

Samantha lay asleep, curled on the car's deep leather rear seat, one arm around the new doll Alexandra had given her. The week of medical tests in Durham had not been wasted, Alexandra thought. The expensive pediatric specialists had confirmed the brilliant conclusions made by army medical hacks.

Samantha did not talk. She was extremely bright and alert, had extraordinary motor skills for a three-year-old, and was unhampered by any discernible physical or emotional problems. She was potty-trained, fearless, and ate like a horse. She made a variety of noises and imitated animal sounds, which had led one doctor to joke that perhaps she'd invented her own language and simply expected everyone else to learn it.

Alexandra liked that whimsical idea—the notion of her niece molding others' expectations to fit her own. She liked the child's amazing, self-possessed grace, the clear spirit in her blue eyes—in short, the qualities that Tim lacked, qualities that reminded Alexandra of herself.

She was now convinced that Samantha was the child she deserved to raise.

Her hands tightened on the steering wheel, and her heart pounded. *Careful, now*, she told herself. *Don't be obvious*. "I wish I could cheer you up," she said to Frannie.

Her sister dropped the drink cup into a small vinyl trash bag hanging from the car's ashtray, then pressed her fingertips to her temples. "Those specialists were my last resort." Her voice was hollow. "I don't know how I'm going to tell Carl they couldn't help us. What it might do to his feelings for me."

Alexandra cleared her throat. "I have a suggestion. It's not a perfect plan, but if you're willing to consider it—"

"What?" Frannie swiveled toward her. "I'll consider anything at this point."

"It would mean a hard decision on your part."

"Tell me. Please."

"If you don't go back to Germany—if you'll stay here, where there's access to the best care money can buy, I'll pay for Samantha to have speech therapy. You know, the doctors said that was an option. Regular one-on-one sessions with a therapist." Alexandra hesitated tactfully. "It might take weeks. It might take months. But surely, in time, it would work."

Frannie sank back and hugged herself. Alexandra cast a furtive look at her. She appeared to be lost in agonized thought. Alexandra added, "If Carl wants what's best for Samantha, I know he'll agree—even though he'll miss the two of you."

"I'm not sure he'd miss me," Frannie said wearily.

"Sweetie, of *course* he will. And think how wonderful it will be when you eventually take Samantha back to him, and she calls him 'Daddy.' That will make the separation worth it. You'll have Carl's respect again, and you'll both be happy. Then you can work at having that second baby you want so badly."

"Alex, you're being so wonderful to me. But I'll just have to think about this." Her voice shook. "Not seeing Carl," she said slowly. "For months, maybe. I miss him *now*, and it's been only two weeks."

"Can you honestly say you want to go back right away, as a failure?" There was silence. Alexandra let those skillfully painful words sink in.

Frannie gave a soft moan. "No, I don't want that."

"You think it over, but I'm going to make plans." Alexandra reached over gently and squeezed her sister's cold, clammy hand. "I adore Samantha. There's so much I can give her. Don't deny me the chance to pamper your little girl. I promise I'm not trying to run her life, or yours. But I can't have—you know—William and I don't have a little girl of our own. I'm not a cold-blooded creature, even if I act that way sometimes."

Slowly, Frannie's hand closed around Alexandra's. "I believe you."

Alexandra smiled.

Granny was gone, her room empty, her bed always made up, her big flowery work dresses hanging lonesomely inside the closed closet, the smell of liniment and old-lady things getting thinner every day.

Jake and Ellie sat on her bed a lot, talking to her. Granny had explained more than once that someday she'd mosey away to be with Grandpa Raincrow and Father's older brother, Graham, who'd died in Korea. She'd promised that when that happened, she'd still listen to them and that if they paid close attention, they'd know it.

So far they had watched and listened intently, with no luck.

"Somebody's coming," Ellie said, pushing her long black hair back from her face and turning toward Granny's window.

Jake eyed her hopefully. "Granny told you?"

"No, I heard the dogs bark."

"Oh." Disappointed, he shoved himself off Granny's bed. "Let's go see."

"You go." Ellie flopped back on the old quilt. "If Granny says anything, I'll let you know."

Jake bristled, and his eyes burned with tears. "She's not going to talk to you without talking to me too."

Ellie peered at him with one eye shut. "Well, I always know where you are, so I just guess Granny will figure that out, won't she?"

Ellie had an easy way with words that left Jake behind. There was no arguing with her. His mouth set, he stalked out of the room.

He heard the car now, crunching along the narrow gravel path that snaked through the woods back toward the river. Father said the mountains were like a fat lady lying on her back with the Cove hidden in a crease; town was on top of one of her tea jugs.

Jake pictured the lady with concrete roads around her pink teat like spokes on a bicycle wheel. Visitors turned off onto the shadowy dirt road to the Cove, driving down the lady's jug. In this way Jake had formed a satisfying mental map of the world as he knew it: Asheville, a big city, was way up on the lady's head, and Cawatie Township, where their Indian relatives lived, was just above her belly button. Durham, an even bigger city than

Asheville, was at her right elbow when she had her arm stretched out, and the ocean started at her fingertips. Her left arm lay across Tennessee, her feet were Florida, and her left knee was Atlanta, Georgia.

Mother and Father had taken them to Atlanta for a weekend once, and Atlanta was so big, it deserved a whole knee.

He hadn't decided what belonged in the spot at the top of her legs yet, but having studied Mother and Ellie in the bathtub, he didn't see how anyone could live there anyway.

Lost in this and other distracted, tired thoughts, he went down the cool central hallway, dragging a hand along one of the log walls. Mother came out of the kitchen door, wiping flour on a dishrag tucked in the waist of her blue jeans. She hurried ahead of him to the screen door, peered through it at the yard beyond the porch rafters, and called Father. "It's Frannie Ryder," she added. "Good Lord."

Jake leaned against the broad opening to the living room and watched with somber curiosity as Father got up from a desk full of books and papers in one corner and walked over, rubbing his eyes. Father moved slowly. Jake had seen him cry twice—once when he wrapped Granny's body in an Indian blanket to carry her to the station wagon, and when the preacher finished talking over her casket, at the cemetery in town.

Jake had an abiding determination to watch over Father and make certain he felt better.

Father and Mother went out on the porch. Jake slipped up to the screen door and leaned against the smooth-worn facing. Granny had taught him and Ellie to stay back and take in a situation carefully.

A lady with straight gold hair got out of a big car. Squinting, Jake noticed the back of another blond head— a little one with a ponytail, above a ruffled white collar— craned out the open window on the car's far side. White dog paws were planted on either side of the small head. Rastus was too short to reach car windows, but he liked to rear up and offer air kisses with his tongue.

The lady came up on the porch. "I'm sorry to show up on your doorstep without calling," she said. "But what I want to ask you would sound even stranger over the phone."

Mother said, "Frannie, you're the only Duke I'd have at my house."

Duke. Jake knew what that name meant. It meant his aunt Alexandra's family, and for reasons he and Ellie hadn't figured out yet, they were no good.

But Mother and Father asked the lady to sit with them on the porch, so she must be different. Jake couldn't quite see around the doorjamb. He listened to the rocking chairs creak.

"The doctors in Durham didn't tell me anything about Samantha that I didn't already know," the woman said. "She can't talk. She's not deaf, she's not retarded, she's just . . . *slow*." The lady's voice cracked on that word. "I hate that term. She's not slow, she's . . . I don't know what she is, but *slow* isn't it. You should see her when she gets her hands on something that interests her. She ties knots like a sailor. She braids my hair. Once she took a woven hemp place mat apart a string at a time. By the time I caught her, she had all the strings laid out in crisscrossing rows. I swear she looked as if she were scrutinizing them to figure out the design. Even the doctors admit she's remarkable for a three-year-old—in some ways."

She's got an extra part, Jake thought suddenly. Maybe not like his and Ellie's, but something just as strange.

"Give her time," Father said. "It sounds like the talking will come soon enough. I had a cousin who grunted like a pig for years."

"What happened to him?"

"Runs a barbecue joint over in Wasoga."

"*Hugh,*" Mother said. "Frannie, go on."

"Alexandra has offered to hire a private speech therapist for her. But it means we'd have to stay in Pandora, maybe for months."

Jake heard nothing but silence for what seemed like a long time. Finally Mother said, so softly he had to cup a hand behind his ear to catch it, "You take your little girl and go back to your husband, Frannie. Your sister is closing doors faster than you can even *find* them."

"No, I swear, it's not like that. I can't turn down a chance to give my child all the help she needs."

"Don't you get it, Frannie? Alexandra doesn't want her sister married to an army sergeant whose parents worked in the mills. Dukes don't marry into a class of people they *own*. And I'd bet money that Carl figured that out a long time ago. He's got to hate the fact that you came back here to ask for your family's help."

"He does," the lady answered, her voice so sad it sent shivers down Jake's back. "But everything will be all right if Samantha learns to talk."

"Carl agreed to let you stay here awhile?"

"He said"—the lady made a snuffling sound—"he said I'm looking for excuses to give up on our marriage. But I'm *not*. What kind of marriage do we have as long as he blames me for Samantha's problem? I blame myself too."

"Let's get down to brass tacks." That was Father's voice, deep and calm. Jake felt proud. Granny had always told him and Ellie that Father had a gift for looking at only one tree at a time. *He can't see the forest for the trees*. That was how Granny put it. "There's no love lost between your sister and the Raincrow family. From the day she married Sarah's brother, she's caused nothing but hard feelings. I suppose as long as she holds on to William and the old ruby, that won't change. I've watched Sarah mourn the situation for years, and I'm not going to put up with anything that makes her grief worse. So, Frannie, have you come to ask us to meddle in your affairs? I can't see how that will cause anything but more trouble."

Jake's heart fell. Father wasn't going to fix the lady's little girl? He wouldn't even try?

Mother said quickly, "I'm sure Hugh will take a look at Samantha if you want him to. He doesn't mean he'd turn his back on an innocent child."

"Never have, never will," Father answered, sounding exasperated. "But I'm no magician. I just meant—"

"I appreciate your feelings, I really do, Dr. Raincrow,"

the lady said. "But I didn't expect you could accomplish some miracle. I . . . I came here to ask about, well, *different* help. I heard you have a relative over at Cawatie who's a medicine woman. I was hoping you'd ask her to look at Samantha."

Jake slapped both hands to his mouth to cover a gasp of surprise. This lady wanted Mrs. Big Stick instead of Father? Boy, she had just stuck her head in a hornet's nest.

"Frannie," Father said slowly, as if the breath had been knocked out of him, "it would make more sense for you to sit on a hill and bay at the moon."

"Clara and Hugh don't see eye to eye," Mother added. "She wants to consult on all his patients at Cawatie, and most of them won't let him touch them without her peeping over his shoulder."

"I didn't become a doctor to work in the shadow of ignorance and superstition," Father said. "I grew up watching Indians die because nobody gave a damn whether they survived the twentieth century or not. My own father died of the measles when he was fifty years old. The *measles*. And it's well-intentioned old-timers like Clara Big Stick who keep pulling the people back into the dark ages."

"But . . . but," the lady said, "Dr. Raincrow, I've read a lot about alternative medicines, and I think, well, I think there's something *unnatural* about just poking people with needles and dosing them with drugs. I mean, there's a *lot* of research into herbs, and vitamins, and, uh, spiritual healing, and—"

"Clara talked my mother into throwing away her blood pressure pills," Father announced, his voice getting louder. "I'll tell you what's unnatural—letting your 'patient' die of a stroke."

Jake was stunned. Surely Father was wrong. Mrs. Big Stick hadn't hurt Granny. Granny would have known better than to trust Mrs. Big Stick's medicine if it wasn't good.

"I'm sorry," the lady whispered. Then she cleared her throat and added, "But *please*. Clara Big Stick can't do any harm to Samantha. She might help her. *Please*. I'm desperate."

"I won't have any part of hocus-pocus," Father said. His chair creaked. His heavy footsteps clumped across the porch's wide wooden planks. Jake slid behind the heavy wooden door and flattened himself to the rough wall. "*Hugh*," Mother called in her don't-rock-the-boat voice. The footsteps halted. "I want to do this for Frannie."

"Not inside this house," Father answered. Jake held his breath. Father and Mother never argued. Jake touched them sometimes when he saw them frowning at each other, and he always felt a warm, shared space between the frowns. "In the yard," Father said finally. "Just keep her in the yard, where I won't have to watch."

Father stalked into the house and disappeared into the living room. Jake scooted out from behind the door, eased the screen door open, and ambled out as if he just happened to be passing through. He wanted to get an up-close look at the little girl who'd caused all this trouble.

Mother gave him a squint-eyed look with one eyebrow cocked, as if she knew he'd been listening. "This is Jake," she said. "Master of the oh-so-casual arrival. Honey, this is your aunt Alexandra's sister, Mrs. Ryder." Jake offered his most solemn Hello, ma'am. The lady was crying, but she smiled at him. Reassured, he asked, "Can I . . . *may* I take your little girl to see our cow?" He was amazed at the amount of words he managed in one sentence. He was a watcher, not a talker, everyone said. What a strange day this was turning out to be.

The lady looked at Mother. Mother nodded. "Jake won't let her out of his sight. And if he did, he'd find her."

Taking that as permission, Jake ran to the big car, slowed to a dignified walk, and circled it carefully, his eyes riveted to the passenger window.

So this was Samantha "No-Talking" Ryder. She was pretty small, and very still, with her little hands clutching the window's edge and her big blue eyes staring right back at him without blinking.

"My name's Jake," he offered. Her mouth crooked up at one corner. "Want to see a cow?" he added.

She didn't say a word. He tugged the door open with both hands and gave her a good look-see. Her ruffled white collar was part of a white shirt, and she wore pink shorts with white sandals. Sunshine slid back and forth across her pulled-up hair, but even her ponytail didn't move.

He'd never seen a kid so gold and pink and, of course, quiet. "Well?" he said.

She hopped out and stood with both feet planted apart, then watched him like a hawk while he shut the door. He held out a hand, tanned and big compared to hers. She looked up at him as if he were some kind of jigsaw puzzle she hadn't quite put together yet. "Cat got your tongue?" he asked slyly.

Her eyes crinkled, and she smiled. She closed her hand slowly around his, each small finger curling tight. Jake knew what to expect when he touched people— a tingle of feelings that weren't his but *were* his, like smoke creeping into his thoughts, so that he suddenly knew things he hadn't planned to know, but most of the time the smoke faded before he could decide what it meant.

But not this time. He judged her for a thinker—she made up her mind, then she wouldn't let go. Strangely enough, that made him not want to let go either. *We've been together as long as I can remember, and for as far as I can see.*

Now, that didn't make sense, and it startled him so much he pushed the thought and the smoke away.

He tied Blossom to an iron ring in the milking stall, proud to demonstrate his fearless command over a huge animal who could have stomped anyone to pieces if she weren't too fat to move that fast. Samantha watched from a few feet away, and he hoped she was impressed. "C'mere," he said, crooking his finger. She sidled closer to Blossom's orange and white side. Jake bent down and wrapped a hand around one of Blossom's dangling pink teats. "Want to see where milk comes from?"

Samantha squatted and stared at the teat. Jake squeezed expertly, and a stream of milk shot out. It hit her in the mouth. She bolted up. Her eyes widened. She wiped her chin and made a face. Jake bent his head to Blossom's side and chortled loudly. The next thing he knew, Samantha was behind Blossom, reaching for the long switch of white hair at the end of her tail. Her mouth set in a firm line, she wound her small fingers into the thick hair and began braiding-it.

Jake watched in awed silence. When she finished, she held the end of the braid and looked up at him with a satisfied nod. He nodded back. "All she needs is a ribbon, and she can go to a party." He found a piece of baling twine among the matted straw of the stall's dirt floor, and handed it to her gallantly.

She tied a bow around the end of Blossom's tail, then stood back, eyeing her work. Jake sat down in the straw and studied her quietly. "You're not putting any bows on me," he announced.

She cocked her head back and studied him the way she'd been studying Blossom's tail. Like she would fix him up, too, one of these days.

If anything could make a person talk, being dunked in the cold water of the Saukee would do it. Jake watched anxiously from a knoll under a sassafras tree, his knees drawn up and arms wrapped tightly around them. Samantha looked over Mrs. Big Stick's shoulder at him, her mouth clamped shut. She didn't look scared, she looked mad, as if he should have warned her about this.

Her mother stood on the bank beside his mother, holding all of Samantha's clothes and her sandals. Mrs. Big Stick, her jeans rolled up to her fat brown knees, stood in a dark pool, where the river barely moved. She had her head thrown back, and she'd been talking to the wind for a long time. Jake knew enough Cherokee to pick out a sentence here and there. She was telling the spirits to fix Samantha's voice, ordering them around as if she might come looking for them with a baseball bat if they didn't do it.

Suddenly she stopped, nodded so hard that her long braid of gray-black hair bounced over her shoulder, then bent down and shoved Samantha underwater.

Jake grimaced. He knew what *going to water* was about. It cleaned you outside and inside, Granny had said. It made you think, and feel new all over, and remember how to breathe. All the old folks at Cawatie did it every morning, even if they could only get to a little pee-trickle of branch water outside their cabins and house trailers. He and Ellie had gone with Granny to a spring in the hollow every day, and boy, you could breathe like nobody's business after sitting in that spring in the wintertime.

When Samantha came up, she took a big gulp of air and latched on to Mrs. Big Stick's braid with both hands. Jake covered his mouth to hide a laugh. She wasn't going under again without taking Mrs. Big Stick with her.

Mrs. Big Stick grunted and carried her back to the bank. "She's done." Jake looked away politely as the medicine woman handed poor Samantha, who still looked mad, to her mother. Naked girls of all sizes were interesting to study, and he didn't get that many chances, but Samantha was special. He wouldn't forget the strange idea that had come to him when she took his hand; maybe there'd be chances to see her *nekkid* in the future.

He glanced over after her mother scrubbed her dry with a towel and put on her clothes. While her mother combed her wet hair back, Samantha stared straight at him, eyes narrowed, her hands knotted in little fists by her shorts.

"She'll talk," Mrs. Big Stick announced. "Sooner or later."

"Sooner, I hope," Mrs. Ryder said. "Thank you for coming."

"Faith is a powerful tool," Mrs. Big Stick told her. "If you believe in something strong enough, it will happen." She looked at Mother solemnly. "I believe I'll have that drink now."

"One bourbon on ice, coming up," Mother said. "We'll sit on the porch."

"Hugh doesn't want me in the house. I know it."

Mother's face turned red. She didn't answer, and walked up the path to the house with her head bent. Jake had to know the truth. He walked over and halted in front of Mrs. Big Stick as she rolled her jeans legs down. Her eyes were squinty and brown as chocolate, and when she met his gaze, they nearly disappeared between her cheekbones and eyebrows. "Are you keeping the faith for your granny, Mr. Jake?"

"Yes, ma'am. But I haven't heard from her yet. She said she'd let Ellie and me know she's still listening."

"She might not talk in a regular voice. It's up to you to know what she means."

"But how will I figure that out?"

Mrs. Big Stick bent close to him and whispered in his ear, "When you use the gift God gave you, just like he gave it to Granny, and it does something good for other people, that'll be your granny talking to you."

She knew. Mrs. Big Stick knew about their extra parts. Jake laid a trembling hand on one of the big brown forearms beneath her rolled-up shirtsleeves. Sad. Mrs. Big Stick felt so sad when she talked about Granny. She missed her as much as he and Ellie did. "You didn't make Granny stop taking her pills, I bet."

Mrs. Big Stick blinked. He could see her eyes again. "No, but I didn't fuss at her when she threw them away."

"Why?" he asked, breathless.

"Because she said they made her head feel too thick. She couldn't find things anymore. And that made her unhappy. How would you like it if you took a pill that made that part of you go to sleep?"

He shot a gaze at Samantha, who was still having her hair combed, and still glaring at him. To never be able to find someone like her again? He didn't sense that she could find things the way he and Ellie could. He couldn't decide what was *extra* about her, but someday he'd figure that out, and it would be important. "I'd feel pretty empty."

"Then that's how your granny felt. Understand?"

"Yes, ma'am."

"Good. There's a lot of evil around here, and now that your granny's busy with other things, you and Ellie come to me if you've got worries about it."

"Okay."

Mrs. Big Stick straightened up. "Now, why don't you take your little chick down to the spring and tell her how Granny used to dunk you and Ellie when you were her size? Even if she's too young to know her fanny from a hole in the ground, you might coax that thundercloud off her face." Mrs. Big Stick eyed the two of them, then turned to Mrs. Ryder. "Your baby girl looks like she's had a bone to pick with the world since the day she was born."

Mrs. Ryder got a funny look on her face. Jake said, "I won't let her fall in, ma'am. It's only a foot deep, anyhow."

"All right."

He felt a punch on his arm. Samantha stood beside him, mouth flat, as if daring him to explain what in the world the grown-ups had done to her. Jake snagged her fist and pulled her along behind him. *Born mad and still fighting*, he thought. *That's why she won't talk*.

Stunned by this sudden knowledge, and wondering if it was just a lucky guess, he practically dragged her in his hurry to reach the spring, which was down another path through a tall stand of poplars. She wound her hand in his and ran to keep up with him.

When they entered the shady hollow, where water bubbled in a clear hole as wide as he was tall, he sat down among half-curled ferns and tugged at her hand. She wouldn't budge. Jake stared at her firmly. "I know why you won't talk. Once you make up your mind, you don't let go. You're just like an old bottle with a stopper in it. Just need to have your plug pulled."

When she didn't make even a squeak in return, he dropped her hand and folded his arms on his crossed legs. He leaned over the spring's smooth surface, studying their reflections—a frowning boy with short black hair and a wobbly front tooth that was being pushed out of line by the new one growing in behind it, and a red-faced little girl with yellow hair sprouting fuzzy, dry tufts around her face. She was less than half his age and size; he was no baby-sitter.

"I got more important things to do than try to talk sense to a baby," he told her. "*You* don't even know what *taxes* are. Taxes are the money people have to pay to keep the sheriff from taking their homes away." He waved an arm. "And this place costs a lot of taxes. My granny could find garnets and topazes and sapphires—Granny could even find little-bitty *rubies* sometimes, and those things are worth a lot of taxes. She *died*—she went away, okay? So now me and Ellie have to find those rocks to pay taxes. Ellie's not nearly as good at it as I am, but I don't know if I can find things without Granny's help. She said she'd still talk to us, but I can't hear a peep."

All the misery of the past few weeks welled up inside him, and his eyes burned. He tried to squeeze the tears back, but one slithered down his cheek. "Granny won't talk, and neither will you. *Damn.*"

Ashamed of crying in front of her—bejeezus, it was bad enough to cry in front of a girl at all, much less this tough little critter—Jake turned his head away and scrubbed the back of his hand across his eyes.

Suddenly he felt her small, soft hands on his head. She patted his hair. He shot a stern, embarrassed look at her, but she huddled against his side, then put her arms around his neck. Tears puddled in her eyes. She took a huge breath, then let it rattle out.

"Jake, don't cry," she whispered. "*I'll* talk to you."

Her words were clear as a bell, not like baby talk. It took several seconds for him to believe he'd really heard her. But then he realized what had happened. He had brought Samantha to Granny's spring, and Granny had worked a miracle. Granny was listening, and just like Mrs. Big Stick said, she had found a special way to let him know it.

～

Frannie ran across the back lawn at Highview, leaving the car door open, carrying Samantha in her arms and laughing. Alexandra had bought a pony for Tim, and she was leading it around, Tim clinging to the pommel of its miniature English saddle for dear life, and crying. William stood on the edge of a stone patio nearby, his hands shoved in his trouser pockets and his expression dark.

Alexandra grabbed the pony's bridle and brought it to a stop. Tim clutched its mane and whimpered. "Where have you been?" Alexandra called.

"She *talked*." Frannie kissed Samantha's cheek and gazed down at her happily. Samantha sighed and patted Frannie's shoulder. "I took her to see the Raincrows, and they called a medicine woman from Cawatie, and not more than ten minutes after she performed a healing ceremony on Samantha, Samantha started talking to Sarah's son. Dear Lord, Alex, you should have been there! They came walking up from the spring, and she was jabbering to him as if it were the most ordinary thing in the world. I nearly fell down getting to her, and when I hugged her, she said, "Jake pulled my plug, Mommy. *Mommy*. She called me Mommy."

Alexandra's face turned white. "You took my niece to visit people who've treated me like dirt. You relied on *them*?"

"It's good for us all," Frannie answered, too overjoyed to care about her sister's feuds. William sprang off the patio with clumsy enthusiasm and, giving Alexandra a thin smile, put his arm around Frannie's shoulders. "That's fantastic," he said. His face was wistful. "I wish it were so easy for me to visit my sister and her family."

"It can be, William. Anything's possible. I *do* believe in miracles!"

"No, I—" His eyes were shadowed, but he smiled sadly at Samantha. "So Jake 'pulled your plug,' did he? I've always thought that boy had a special way about him. Can you say something for your Uncle Will, Sammie?"

Her brow furrowed. "Tim tried to push me down the stairs."

William's smile faded. Frannie jostled Samantha and said quickly, "I'm sure he was just playing, sweetie."

"I want to go home. Let's take Jake with us."

"We *are* going home, sweetie. We're going home right away. What will you say to your daddy when you see him?"

"Hi, Sarge, I missed you. Can Jake live with us?"

Frannie laughed and looked at Alexandra in dazed delight. "From silence to full-blown sentences in one fell swoop. She's a genius. Alex, I *know* you're happy for me."

"Of course I'm thrilled that Sammie's talking. But I'm disappointed by the way you went behind my back."

"I had to try everything I could think of. I knew you'd think I was silly to take Sammie to see an Indian medicine woman."

"God bless Sarah Raincrow and her pack of Indians." Alexandra's voice was flat. She stared at William. "Sarah wouldn't spit in our direction if we were on fire, but she'll meddle in my sister's life out of pure spite."

"Alex, *I* went to *her*," Frannie said. "What difference does it make? She helped me. *Sammie is talking*. Aren't you happy for me at all?"

"I . . . yes. Of course." Alexandra held out her hands. "But I was so hoping for some more time with you and Sammie. I love having a little girl around here. Can't you stay? What if Sammie still needs therapy?"

"Therapy? She's ready to deliver the State of the Union address."

Alexandra stroked a trembling hand over Samantha's hair and smiled at her with painful appreciation. "Wouldn't you like to stay at Aunt Alex's house a while longer? I'd teach you to ride Tim's pony, and I'd teach you to swim in the pool at the country club, and take you to meet a lot of nice little girls who don't speak German."

"We don't need a little girl around here," Tim said, sniffling. "Mom, you've got me. You don't need *her*."

"Be quiet, son. You know better than to interrupt me. Sammie, don't you like it here? Wouldn't you like to visit with me?"

Samantha watched her without blinking. "Jake says you're a witch."

Frannie gasped. "Oh, sweetie. Oh, Alex, don't pay any attention to—"

"Sarah has even coaxed her children to hate me." Alexandra turned away, her face strained and eyes gleaming with tears. "You see, William? See what's happened? My own niece is afraid of me because of something Sarah's son planted in her mind."

"I'm not afraid of you," Samantha added, speaking in her astonishingly mature way. "I been dunked in the river. I got my plug pulled. I got *Jake*. He won't let a witch eat me."

"Oh, God." Alexandra pressed her hands to her temple and walked into the house. Moving leadenly, William went to the pony and lifted Tim off. "I'm happy for you," he told Frannie, but his voice was hollow. "I'll call for your plane tickets. You need to go on home with Sammie. Go back to your husband. Alexandra will be all right."

Frannie bowed her head against Samantha's and exhaled wearily. "You can talk," she whispered. "That's all that matters."

Samantha stared at Tim, who wavered beside the pony, his face screwed into a knot of fury as he looked back at her. "I hate you," he said loudly.

And before William could catch him, he turned and ran to the house.

After he collected them at the airport, Carl sat in the driver's seat of their VW with Samantha standing on his lap. Tears ran down his face. She patted his cheek gently. "Don't cry, Daddy."

Carl sighed heavily. "Why wouldn't you talk to us before, honey?"

"I don't know."

"Why'd you talk to Mrs. Raincrow's little boy?"

"*Jake*," Frannie whispered.

"Why'd you talk to Jake, honey?"

"He missed his grandma. She wouldn't talk to him,

so I did." Carl gave Frannie a puzzled look, but she shook her head. "Don't try to figure it out. I can't. She's crazy about Jake. I had a real problem calming her down after I explained that Jake couldn't come to Germany with us. I was afraid she'd clam up again. But I took her to see him right before we left, and he promised her they'd see each other again. It was sweet, but sort of eerie. Like they had some sort of secret bond. At any rate, it satisfied her."

They were quiet as Samantha stroked her fingertips over Carl's damp face, her eyes wide with distress. "Don't be sad, Daddy."

He laughed. "I'm not sad. I'm damned happy to see my girls." He leaned across to Frannie, who was crying too, and kissed her. They bowed their heads together. "I was afraid you might not ever come back," he said gruffly. "Even if Sam never spoke a word, I didn't mean to drive you away."

Frannie nuzzled his face and smiled. "We're together again, and everything's finally all right."

Samantha watched them kiss some more. "Jake promised," she said, and sighed.

A year later they brought the new baby home from the base hospital, sat on the living room couch, and introduced her to her older sister. "Samantha," Frannie said softly, holding the pink bundle with squinty eyes and blond hair on her lap so Samantha could stand close to her. "This is your baby sister. This is Charlotte."

"Named after my hometown, not a witch," Carl interjected.

Samantha stood for a moment, gazing at Charlotte with giant, somber blue eyes. Then she nodded, patted the baby's head carefully, and said in a calm, strong voice, "I'll take care of you, Miss Charlotte. Stick with me. I have lots to tell you." She looked at her parents evenly. "And when you're old enough to talk, we'll go to visit Jake."

Chapter

Six

E llie and I turned ten last week, Jake wrote in the
dog-eared notebook he kept stuffed under his mattress. The old people at Cawatie said it was important to keep track of where you were going, so you'd have
trail markers if you got lost. Like Father, who said he'd
never forget being sent to Indian boarding school on the
reservation, where the teachers washed his mouth out
with soap whenever he spoke Cherokee. Like Mother,
who remembered every bit of the day Uncle William
married Aunt Alexandra and gave her Mother's ruby.

*Ellie and me found five aquamarines along the creek
at Eagles Gap last week,* he added. *Father sold the two
biggest ones for $100 each. He put it in the bank with the
rest of our stone money. Mother says it's for college. But
I don't want to go to college. I want to stay in the Cove
forever and pay taxes.*

Mother and Father promised the taxes were getting paid without their stone money. As long as the sheriff didn't come to make them move, Jake felt reassured. Ellie actually *wanted* to go to college and be a doctor, like Father, so he guessed their stone money wasn't being wasted in the bank.

I wonder about Samantha, he wrote next. *Mrs. Ryder sent a picture in a Christmas card. Samantha is six, and she has a baby sister. She still talks. Me, Jacob Lee Raincrow—I taught her to talk. When I get old enough, I'll take my college money and go to Germany, and visit her. I hope she doesn't just talk German by then. If she does, I guess I can learn it. It couldn't be harder than Cherokee, and I learned Cherokee when I was only a kid.*

He closed his notebook. There. Birthdays, stone money, the Cove, and Samantha. He had recorded all the important markers.

Moe Pettycorn was one of Father's patients, and he'd just come back from Vietnam a month ago with his right foot missing and a rainbow of pink scars along the right side of his neck. He'd played quarterback on the state all-star team, and everyone said he could have gotten into college on a football scholarship if he hadn't flunked out of high school on the third go-round of his senior year. But the army got him after he flunked the last time, and he went off to war, where he drove a jeep over a mine and got blown up.

His parents bought him a brand-new TransAm as a welcome-home present, and sometimes when Jake was hanging out at Father's office on Main Street he saw Moe creep by, sitting up straight and rigid, clutching the steering wheel with both hands, his face pale as a ghost's. People joked that squirrels could outrun Moe, the way he drove.

Moe limped into Father's waiting room one Saturday morning when the receptionist had gone to buy light bulbs. Jake and Ellie were manning her desk. "You got no appointment," Ellie told him.

Ellie was like Father. She took medicine seriously, and didn't beat around any bushes.

Moe stared at them in his tight, skittery way, his scars turning redder where they showed above his shirt collar. "I need a refill on my prescription," he said. "I got the shakes."

Jake felt sorry for him. "I'll get Father," he said. But Ellie made a huffing sound. "Father's cuttin' off Mrs. Simpson's corn. If he stops, she'll keel over like she did the other time." She nodded at Moe. "You gotta wait."

"I can't wait!" Moe fumbled with his car keys, and they flew over the desk and landed on the floor by Jake's feet. Jake picked them up, thinking sadly that Moe probably couldn't throw touchdown passes anymore. The keys felt warm in his hand, and he got one of his certain feelings. He held them out to Moe, and when Moe grasped them in one big, shaky hand, Jake said softly, "There aren't any mines around here. You just think there are right now."

Moe gaped at him. "You're just a kid. How'd you know that?"

Jake and Ellie traded a cautious look, then gazed at Moe innocently. "I reckon I'm old enough," Jake said, "to know you're not likely to get blown up driving to the grocery store."

Moe swallowed hard. "You two are strange little dudes. You give everybody the willies."

He stomped out. The next time he saw Jake and Ellie on Main Street, he drove faster. Before long he was up to the speed limit.

There was power in using what they knew about people. Jake began to feel cocky about it.

He and Eleanore draped their arms over a low board in the white wooden fence of the ring and watched their cousin ride a tall Welsh pony around in circles. It seemed to Jake that Tim rode the way Moe Pettycorn used to drive a car—as if he were scared to relax, as if he were always waiting for something to explode.

They wore dungarees and T-shirts. Their tennis shoes lay somewhere along the dark green lawn between the brick stable and the riding ring. They were sweaty and dusty from prowling around the barn's loft. Tim liked to go up there and play General Custer at the Little Bighorn, which didn't bother them because their part in the drama was a lot more entertaining than his.

They got to run around the stacks of hay and yell like warriors. Tim only got to stand on top, waving his arms at some invisible army, waiting to be scalped.

Tim wore a neat white pullover with his name sewn in tiny gold letters on the collar, and hilarious brown pants that bulged out between his butt and his knees before the legs disappeared into shiny black boots. He also wore a hard little black hat with a chin strap.

The pony's name was Sir Lancelot, and he wore a flat brown saddle and a bridle with a gold name plate on the jaw piece. Tim showed the pony in jumping classes, and his mother had paid a lot of money for it, he bragged.

They had a pony too, at home in the Cove, but it was a present from old Keet Jones, who lived in a trailer somewhere in a hollow at Cawatie. Mr. Keet had given it to them after Father fixed Mr. Keet's gallbladder. Old Keet had taught it to do tricks, like bowing and counting with one front hoof. If you put a saddle on it, the pony lay down and rolled until the saddle fell off. A bit only made it clench its teeth, so they rode the pony bareback with a halter and two lead ropes.

Father said it was so ugly it would never win anything but the label on a can of dog food. The first time she saw it, Mother laughed and called it grade A glue. *Grade A* became *Grady*, so that was its name. Watching Sir Lancelot plod around the ring without making any attempt to throw Tim off, Jake decided that Grady was a good deal more exciting.

"Wanna ride him?" Tim asked, pulling Sir Lancelot to a stop by a pair of braided leather reins. "I bet you never thought I'd let you."

Eleanore grinned and cut her eyes at Jake. "Sure." His twin sister oozed trouble like a new scab. So he smiled as they crawled through the fence.

"I'll show you how to do it *right*," Tim said firmly, climbing off Sir Lancelot as they walked over. " 'Cause you're my cousins, and I don't want you to act like dumb Injuns."

Jake just shrugged. Eleanore bristled like a cat. "Injuns aren't dumb," she retorted. "My father's not *dumb*. He's a doctor. Would everybody in town let him fix 'em up if he was dumb?"

"He's not dumb 'cause your granny and grandpa Raincrow were half breeds," Tim told them. "I know all about this stuff. My mother told me." Tim looked at them smuggly. "Your mother's all white, so you know what you are? You're *quadroons*."

Eleanore squinted. "What's that?"

Jake was tired of the whole discussion. He didn't care what they were. "A cookie," he explained. "Like a *macaroon*." He elbowed Eleanore and gave her a be-quiet look. Mother and Father always reminded them that Tim and Uncle William were blood kin of theirs, and that they had to be polite for that reason. Even if Mother never visited Highview, she let them come. They didn't have to like their aunt Alexandra or her ideas about Indians, but they weren't supposed to say so.

"I'll show you how to ride," Jake told Tim. Ignoring his cousin's exasperated protests, he undid Sir Lancelot's saddle and pushed it off. Jake swung himself onto the pony's back and slapped him on the rump. Sir Lancelot jumped and went around the ring at a gallop.

Tim bawled at him to stop, but Eleanore bounded forward and caught Jake's arm, then swung up behind him, just like they did with Grady.

But Sir Lancelot was no Grady. He stumbled sideways, and they fell off in a heap, laughing uproariously as soon as they caught their breath. The ground was soft sand, after all. Eleanore had landed in a pile of dried horse poop. Jake held his stomach and guffawed, and she threw one of the hard round turds at his head. He threw one back. It knocked her plastic bando off and crumbled in her long black hair.

When Tim ran over, his eyes wide, they both threw turds at him. He shrieked, then started giggling. It was soon all-out manure war in the ring, with dried green missles flying everywhere. Sir Lancelot trotted to the gate and kept out of the way. Grady would have chased somebody.

Jake thought it was a wonderful time, even when Tim hit him in the jaw with a dung ball that was still ripe enough to make a sticky *splat*. He chunked one of the fresh turds back at his cousin, and it smacked Tim's chest with a glorious wet *plop*.

Tim froze. As he stared down at the big green smear on his white shirt, his mouth screwed up and his face flushed bright red. When he looked at Jake and Eleanore from under the narrow brim of his black hard hat, tears streamed down his face. "My mom"—he choked up, and his mouth quivered—"my mom is going to be *mad* at me."

Jake traded a worried look with Eleanore. They liked their cousin despite his stuck-up attitude, and hadn't meant to get him in trouble. "He's scared of her," Eleanore whispered. "He's really scared. We gotta do something."

Jake nodded. "We'll tell her it was all our fault." They pulled Tim into the barn and scrubbed his chest with water from a spigot there, but succeeded only in making the stain spread like one of their mother's watercolors. Tim howled.

The three of them walked across a pasture to the big stone house in silence, except for Tim's ragged sniffling. Highview sat on a hill overlooking town, with Pandora Lake behind it and a handsome lawn around it, and a wrought iron gate at the end of a rock drive. It had belonged to the Vanderveers as long as anyone could remember, and if Uncle William hadn't married Aunt Alexandra, it would still be a place where everyone felt welcome, Mother said.

Aunt Alexandra's black housekeeper, Miss Mattie, came out a back door under a grape arbor and made nervous sounds when she saw Tim's shirt. She wrinkled her nose at the way they smelled, then hurried them into a kitchen. "Hush up," she told Tim, who couldn't stop making noises. "Your mama hear you, she'll come lookin'." Miss Mattie jerked his shirt over his head, then ran to a deep metal sink set in marble counters along one wall and turned the faucet on.

Tim dried up. Jake, ashamed for him, tried not to look at his bare pink chest and swollen eyes. Eleanore went over and unfastened his silly hat. "There," she said, removing the thing and placing it politely on a worktable filled with silver waiting to be polished. Jake scrubbed a friendly hand over his cousin's short red hair. "Hey," he said. "Hey, now."

That was man talk for sympathy.

They jumped to attention at the sound of sharp heels clicking on a marble floor somewhere in the house. Miss Mattie hummed under her breath, but her hands worked faster, rinsing Tim's shirt.

Aunt Alexandra came into the kitchen through a swinging door. She had long, smooth blond hair, and she always wore a dress, except when she was out riding her Arabians.

She smelled of perfume, and she painted tiny dark lines along the tops of her eyes, so they turned up at the corners. She was fastening an earring to one ear, and she had a wad of jewelry in her hand. Dropping it in a silver dish perched on the corner of the kitchen table, she stared at Tim and put her hands on her hips.

Jake looked at the dish. The ruby gleamed like a frozen drop of blood among all the silver and gold. It wasn't really hers, he thought grimly. It was Mother's.

"What have you done?" she asked Tim in a voice as smooth as glass. Mother said she'd learned to talk that way at a place called the school for social climbers.

"Just had a little accident, Mrs. Vanderveer," Miss Mattie said, nodding and scrubbing at the sink. "Just got a spot on his shirt."

"Alexandra?" Uncle William's soft voice came over a speaker on the wall. "You there, dear? I need my briefcase. I'm late for court."

Aunt Alexandra went to the speaker and pushed a button. "Look for it yourself. I'm getting dressed for lunch at the club."

She spoke to Uncle William in a sharp, ugly way Jake never heard his own parents use with each other. Uncle William was as friendly as a big, redheaded Santa Claus, but Jake couldn't remember ever hearing him laugh.

Mother said Uncle William had laughed a lot before he married Aunt Alexandra. Uncle William smelled funny—like mouthwash—all the time, and whenever he hugged him, Jake felt sad and lonely. Ellie said Uncle William made her feel that way too.

Aunt Alexandra glided over to the sink, pulled the shirt out, and made a face. It smelled. Boy, did it smell like horse turds, Jake thought. The whole kitchen did.

"What sort of accident did you have?" she asked Tim. Tim hugged himself and shook his head.

Jake squared his shoulders. "I threw a horse tur—a piece of manure at him."

"Me too," Eleanore added. Jake looked at her. She was no sissy. They could count on each other.

Aunt Alexandra made another face. "Oh? And how did you two come to be covered in horse droppings?"

Jake said solemnly, "Bad aim."

"Someone in this group's telling fibs—or not telling the whole story. Miss Mattie, call my sister-in-law and tell her to come get her children. This visit's over." Aunt Alexandra and Mother didn't speak. They hadn't for years.

She put a hand on Tim's shoulder. His shoulders drew up like he had a string down his backbone. "Son?" she said in her soft, smooth tone, "What have I said, over and over, about taking care of your belongings? Hmmm. What?"

"God helps those who help themselves," Tim said hopefully.

"Besides that. *Think*."

"We get as good as we give."

"That's right. Do you deserve to be punished?"

"No," Jake interjected.

"No, ma'am," Eleanore added.

Aunt Alexandra stared at them. She wadded the stained part of Tim's wet shirt and cupped his jaw in one hand, as though he were a horse who was getting his mouth pried open to take a bit. Tim's eyes filled with tears, and he made a little gagging sound.

Slow horror crawled through Jake's stomach. She stuffed that shit-dirty shirt in Tim's mouth. Jake could taste manure as if it were on his own tongue. Eleanore coughed and put a hand over her mouth.

"Go to your room," their aunt told Tim. "Mattie, go with him and get him cleaned up."

Tim stumbled out behind the housekeeper, bumping into the kitchen table, his hands clutching the shirt and tears sliding down his cheeks again.

Fury rose up in Jake like a dark cloud. He couldn't let their aunt get away with this awful thing. The ruby drew him; without understanding why he wanted to touch it, he couldn't help himself.

Jake sidled over to the table, dug his hand into the silver bowl, and closed his fingers around the stone. His hand jerked, but he couldn't let go. Once he'd touched a frayed spot on the cord of Mother's iron. The *zap* of electricity was like this; it had nearly knocked him down.

He swayed, his eyes half shut. A scene flashed in his mind, clear as a picture, then gone. "What are you doing?" Aunt Alexandra said loudly. Dropping the ruby, his head cleared. She was staring down at him. He couldn't breathe. *Never let pride get the best of you,* Granny had told them. *Keep what you learn to yourself. Don't let the spirits know what you know.* "Nothing," he answered.

"Nothing? I think you were about to take my necklace."

He was horrified. "I wouldn't steal anything!"

"Jake doesn't even sneak grapes out of the bin at the grocery store!" Ellie added, her voice cracking. She looked flabbergasted. "And everybody does *that*."

Aunt Alexandra kept her hard eyes pinned on him. "Then why did you pick up something that doesn't belong to you?"

"I was only looking at it."

"You keep your itchy fingers off the things in this house, you understand? I've gone out of my way to put up with you and your sister because you're Tim's cousins, but I'm fed up. You're lucky I let you come here at all, after the ugly thing you did to my niece when she was just a baby."

His breath pulled short. "Samantha? What'd I do to her?"

"You scared her. You told her I was a witch. She has nightmares because of you."

"That's not true." He knew he wasn't supposed to argue with grown-ups, but he couldn't help himself. "You wanted to keep her. You would have kept hold of her and Mrs. Ryder, and now you'd be doing terrible things to her, just like you do to Tim." He was unhinged; his mouth was working without his permission. "But you can't hurt her, because she's *mine*, and I'll take care of her."

Aunt Alexandra stared at him as if he'd lost his mind. "My God," she said under her breath. "Sarah's behind this nonsense." She cleared her throat. "Well, let me tell you something, little man, and you be sure to tell your mother. I *am* a witch, and if any of you meddle with my family again, I'll turn you into lizards."

That was too much. His mind whirled with what he'd glimpsed when he touched the ruby; he had power; he'd show her. Jake blurted out, "You kissed that lawyer from Asheville. You were in a room with books on the wall, and you kissed Mr. Lomax, and he put his hand up your dress. *And you let him.*"

Her face turned so white, her eye makeup stood out like a raccoon's mask. She clutched the corner of the table and leaned down slowly, and for one terrible second he imagined her opening her mouth, and that it would be filled with fanged teeth. "If you ever"—she bit each word off between those fangs—"*ever* tell a lie like that, again, I'll—"

Tear your heart out and eat it.

She didn't say that, she said something about paddling him until he couldn't sit down, but his mind insisted that *Tear your heart out and eat it* was what she really meant.

"I don't see Jake as a liar," Uncle William said. Jake spun around. Aunt Alexandra's hands went to her throat. Ellie's arm jerked and knocked a silver cup on the floor.

Uncle William stood in the doorway. His face made Jake think of a skinned rabbit—the hide peeled down to bare white meat with red splashes like bloodstains on his cheeks. Uncle William's eyes were awful dead spots in that skinned face. "Tell me exactly what you saw, Jake," Uncle William said. "And where you were when you saw it."

Aunt Alexandra leaned on the table. She gasped for air. "William, he's just a *child*. He's mad at me, and he made up that lurid story."

"Tell me, Jake. Don't be afraid. Just tell me the truth."

Jake was paralyzed, only his thoughts working at super speed. *What have I done? I did what Granny told us to never, ever do. I let pride get hold of me. I let our secret out.* His knees were weak. He'd hurt Uncle William. He couldn't tell how he knew about Aunt Alexandra and Mr. Lomax. Ellie had a grip on his arm, he realized finally. Her fear poured into him. She knew what a crazy, stupid thing he'd done.

"I lied," he said, choking. "I did make it up. I'm sorry."

"You see?" Aunt Alexandra said. Her voice shook.

But Uncle William walked to him slowly, almost shuffling, as if his feet couldn't quite find the floor. He bent down and took Jake by the shoulders. "I don't think a boy your age knows enough about the ugly things adults do to make up a story like that."

Ellie tried to rescue him. "Moe Pettycorn left a magazine in Father's waiting room," she said. "It had pictures of naked women in it. I think that's where Jake got the idea."

"That's right," Jake added quickly. "That's it."

Uncle William still had those dead-looking eyes fixed on Jake's. "No, that's not it." His jaw worked. "Did you hear your mother and father talking about Aunt Alexandra? Did they say she's been doing something bad?"

"No!" Jake shook his head numbly. "I swear on a stack of Bibles. I made it up."

Uncle William sighed so hard that the air rattled in his throat like a moan. His fingers were digging into Jake's arms, sending sensations like wasp stings into his muscles. Pain. A clamp squeezing down until not even a butterfly's wing would fit inside. Jake was feeling his uncle's pain, and his head reeled with it. *He knows I saw something. He's sure.*

"You and Ellie better go on home," Uncle William said. "Go on now." His hands fell by his sides.

Jake turned, grabbed Eleanore's hand, and pulled her out the back door. They ran down the driveway and through the gate, and didn't slow until they were on the sidewalk into town, walking toward Father's office. Then Jake looked at his sister sickly. "I'll never do it again. Granny was right. We can't tell *anyone*. Not even Mother and Father."

Ellie bobbed her head like a jerky puppy. "Maybe Uncle William will forget about it. Sure. Sure he will." She tucked her chin and studied him worriedly. "Was it really awful when you touched that ruby?"

"*Worse than anything.*" Jake's mouth was bone dry. He wanted to gag. "Don't ever touch it. It's not like a game. It's full of *her*. She really is evil."

Evil. They'd heard that word in stories Granny told them. There were *evil* things in the world, and, most terrifying of all, *ravenmockers* who ate people's hearts.

"I bet nothing will happen," Ellie said loudly, as if saying that would make it so.

Jake wanted to believe that. Despite all Granny's warnings, he had let a ravenmocker know that he recognized it.

Now he understood how Moe Pettycorn must have felt, always worrying about bombs no one else could see.

He began to think, by that night, that everything must be all right, like Ellie had said. Nothing strange happened; Aunt Alexandra didn't show up to make good on her lizard threat; Uncle William didn't come to accuse Mother and Father of telling stories about his wife.

Mother finished one of her watercolor paintings of the mountains while the Saturday-night chicken and dumplings bubbled lazily on the stove. Father pulled the summer's first ears of corn in Mother's garden, then sat on the front porch, cranking a churn of peach ice cream and listening to a baseball game on the portable radio.

Jake and Ellie sat in the middle of the cow pasture as the sun set, discussing the day endlessly, while tiny bats zipped across the purple sky above the granite chin of Razorback Bald, and deer edged out of the forest to steal grass beside the wire fence.

The Cove was as peaceful as ever. They dragged themselves to supper and ate enough to keep Mother from noticing their mood. By then it was ten o'clock, and they escaped to get ready for bed. "See?" Ellie whispered when she met Jake coming out of the hall bath. "Nothing happened."

He didn't think he could sleep, and for a while he lay in his bed with the sheet thrown back, his skin damp and sticky inside one of Father's old T-shirts, and he watched fireflies make yellow pinpoints of light against the screen of his open window. They were eyes, winking at his secret. Exhausted, he drifted into dreamless sleep.

"Son, wake up." Father bent over him. Jake rubbed his eyes and tried to focus. The hall lamp made a box of light across his bed; the air had the cool, settled feel of deep night. Jake looked at him groggily. Father's inky-black hair made a ragged outline against the light; he was dressed in a fresh shirt and pants. "Get up and pull some clothes on," Father said. "We have to go to town. Ellie's already up. Hurry."

That cleared away the cobwebs in Jake's drowsy mind. He heard Mother's quick footsteps moving around hers and Father's bedroom, next door. He got a terrible sinking feeling around his heart. "What's the matter?"

"Uncle William had an accident."

Chapter

Seven

The little tree in a corner of the hospital sitting room had dropped most of its leaves on the floor, and the dirt in its pot was sprouting cigarette butts like some kind of seed pods. Jake kept staring at it from his and Ellie's seats on the cold plastic chairs along one wall. His throat dry as old glue, he whispered to Ellie, "How can Uncle William get well in here if they can't even keep that tree going?"

"I don't know," she answered, glancing around worriedly. "But when I'm a doctor, I'll take care of my trees."

A lady in a candy-striped dress pushed through big double doors and jerked when she saw them. "What are y'all doing in here?" she asked. Her voice echoed in the empty room. "Dr. Raincrow sent me to check on you. You're supposed to be waiting in the car."

Jake slid off his chair and faced her. He couldn't sit

still. He couldn't wait in the dark, in the car. "How's our uncle? What happened to him?"

"He fell down and bumped his head. Now, you two ruffled chicks come with me, and I'll buy you some hot chocolate from the snack machines, and—"

"I'm scared," Ellie announced, running over to the lady and sticking her hands up. "Will you give me a hug?"

The lady's mouth made an *oh* of sadness, and she put her arms around Ellie. Jake gazed at his sister in wary surprise, and Ellie peeped back at him with green-eyed slyness from under one of the lady's pink-striped bosoms. "I'll tell you what," the lady said. "Y'all wait right here, and I'll bring you some cookies from the nurses' lounge. Okay?"

"Okay," Ellie said, still staring at Jake evenly.

The lady disappeared up a narrow hallway off the sitting area, and the second they were alone, Ellie turned toward Jake. "He's hurt real, *real* bad, and he's behind two big doors with signs that say EMERGENCY ROOM STAFF ONLY."

They nodded at each other. Then they hurried through the doors into the belly of the hospital, and began searching.

She was free, finally free, and she had the dead husband to prove it. Alexandra huddled on a metal stool with a blanket around her shoulders, her bare feet tucked under the torn hem of her pale silk nightgown. She felt stiff and swollen; her left shoulder ached where she'd fallen against the sharp edge of the bedroom dresser, and there were rug burns on her elbows.

The pitiless overhead lights hurt her eyes; the room was all glaring light and stainless steel and shades of white. Nurses moved around her, and ambulance drivers, and the sheriff stood in one corner, making notes on a small pad. Someone pressed a cold cloth to her forehead, but she didn't acknowledge it. "Your friends called," a nurse whispered. "They gave Tim half a Valium, and he's sound asleep in their guest room."

Alexandra nodded woodenly.

Her eyes stayed on the gurney where William lay, a long, large mound under a white sheet. One of his pale, beefy arms was draped on the gurney atop the sheet. Sarah sat on a chair next to him, crying, her head bent to his arm and her hands clutching it. Hugh stood beside her, rubbing her shoulders as he talked with the emergency room doctor, too softly for Alexandra to hear through the buzz of shock in her ears.

She wanted to scream that she did love William in a way, and she'd played by society's rules as best she could through ten years of a completely mismatched partnership, and why hadn't anyone ever cared when she was a fresh-faced girl being squeezed into a narrow future by her family's ambitions?

Her stomach churned, and she hugged herself hard. *I could have backed out. I could have run away with Orrin, the way Frannie—*

No. The brief stab of guilt fluttered uselessly against the brutal truth. She was not suited to noble sacrifice; she'd been raised to equate self-esteem with a husband's money and social clout. No matter how much the women's libbers talked about new horizons, mo matter how many women put on pantsuits and carried briefcases, or how many college girls slept around to prove their sexual independence, nothing had changed.

Except that now she had all of William's money and prestige, and a son she would mold into an asset, and she was free to make her own choices. She had, in effect, more than Frannie or any other woman would ever get by pointless rebellion.

She was sorry William had paid the price, but relieved that he was gone.

The sheriff came over and squatted in front of her. He was an accommodating man from shabby mountain beginnings, and he preened over the new jail, the new patrol cars, the crisp, tailored uniforms—all paid for by rich new residents who laughed at him behind his back. "I'm sorry, Mrs. Vanderveer," he whispered. "Just let me go over this here terrible night one more time. Then I'll leave you alone, ma'am."

"I understand. Go ahead."

He looked at his notepad. "The judge got in a bad way from drinkin', and he come upstairs from his office a little after midnight."

"Yes."

"He come into the bedroom, where you was reading a book, and you tried to get him to sleep."

"Yes."

"But he was in an ill mood, and said he meant to go out for a drive. Seeing that he could hardly walk, you begged him not to."

"Yes."

"You tried to stop him, but him, uh, bein' not in his right mind, wrestled over the car keys with you, and you got knocked—you, uh, you fell down."

"Yes."

"He run out to the upstairs hall, and before you could get to him, he tripped at the top of the stairs. He hit his head on the top post and fell on down to the bottom."

"Yes."

"Little Timmy got woke up by the noise, and come out to see, and you took some time gettin' him calmed down."

"Yes."

"And then you called the ambulance."

She shivered. "Yes."

The sheriff nodded and flipped his notepad shut. "A terrible thing. I'm real sorry, ma'am."

She had no trouble crying. She was overwhelmed by the idea of how well she'd survived, and a sense of being invincible, and reliving every sacrifice that had brought her to this point in her life.

"Now, now," the sheriff said, patting her shoulder. "There won't be much talk. Poor Judge Vanderveer just tripped and fell down the stairs. That's all I'm gonna say in the report."

"Thank you. I don't want his good name hurt by gossip."

The sheriff solemnly tore scribbled pages from his notepad, crumpled them, then tucked the wad in his shirt pocket. "Done," he said.

"Uncle William's *dead*?"

The boyish voice rang with horror, bringing everyone in the room to shocked attention. Hugh Raincrow whipped around, and Sarah swiveled on her chair, her swollen eyes filling with ragged alarm. Alexandra inhaled sharply. Goose bumps scattered down her spine.

Jake and Ellie stood just inside the room's doors, staring at the gruesome scene, as dry-eyed as bandits. The sight of her nephew frightened Alexandra more than anything she'd expected, bringing a dizzy sense of the unexplainable, the threatening. *But he's just a child. Just a child. Just a child who's listened to Sarah's vicious gossip about me.*

Just a child who, somehow, had guessed her most damning secret.

"Hugh, take them out of here," Sarah cried. "Sweeties, go outside. Go. I'll be right there. I promise."

"But he's dead," Jake said, clenching his hands by his sides.

Hugh looked at them sadly. "That's right. Come here." Alexandra recoiled in amazement and dread as he brought them to William's side, an arm around each of their slender shoulders. With a detachment that belied the strain in his face, he calmly explained to them about skull fractures, and edema of the soft tissues surrounding the brain—on and on, in his most professional tone, until Alexandra realized the wetness in her palms came from her fingernails digging convulsively into the flesh. *Goddamned doctor*, she thought hysterically. *Goddamned eccentric Indian, showing off his tough little mongrel children.*

"He fell," Ellie said, crying, and looked at her brother. "He had an accident, and his brain swelled shut."

Jake broke away and stumbled toward Alexandra, his chalky face and brilliant green eyes a weird contrast to the Indian-black of his hair; his eyes searing her with an intensity so startling, she leaned back on her stool. When he stuck out his hands, fingers splayed, she used all her willpower not to shield her face.

The sheriff rose from his crouch and waved Jake forward. "That's right, boy," the fool said somberly. "Your aunt could use a hug."

Her breath rattled in her throat. Her hand darted in front of her eyes. "*No!*" she yelled, not caring what anyone thought of her strange reaction.

But it was too late. Jake latched on to her wrist and gripped like a vise. Some stunning emotion flooded his face; his mouth opened in a silent gasp. Alexandra jerked her arm away. "Get them out of here! They shouldn't be here! I can't take this!"

Nurses surrounded her. She was dimly aware of Hugh guiding the children out, but before the doors closed behind them, she caught one last glimpse of Jake's face.

It was filled with pure contempt. He couldn't know anything, but he did. She collapsed into a nurse's consoling arms.

Just when her future belonged solely to her for the first time, a new and unimaginable threat had taken seed.

He lay in his bed with the covers pulled up to his shoulders. He felt feverish; Father had given him two aspirin and apologized for upsetting him in the emergency room.

Father and Mother had no idea what upset him.

"Jake, Jake, don't feel bad," Ellie begged. The house was filling with dawn sunlight and unfamiliar sounds. There were a dozen people in the kitchen, some of their kin from Cawatie, friends from town, all come to keep Mother company and cook mounds of food for the next few days of respectful visiting. Ellie had crept out of her room to keep Jake company. She sat next to him, her legs curled against his hunched back. "*You* didn't hurt Uncle William," she told him. "It was an accident."

"What I said made them have a fight," Jake answered raggedly. "And now there's nothing I can do about it. Nobody I can even tell, except you. And you can't do anything either." He shivered. "I hate her. *Hate* her. What about Samantha? Just what am I going to do about Samantha?"

"Aunt Alex's niece? What about her? Huh?" Ellie sounded completely bewildered.

Jake sighed. Even Ellie wouldn't understand if he tried to explain about a little girl he'd met only once. "I have to protect her from Aunt Alexandra."

"Why?" Ellie asked, leaning over him. When he didn't answer, she shook him without much sympathy until he rolled over in self-defense and stared at her. "What did Aunt Alexandra do, God durn it?" she demanded.

He could barely whisper the words. "Uncle William hit her, and she *pushed* him down the stairs."

Mom heard a different drum in her head. And she danced to it. That explained a lot, Sam thought. At six years, she had figured out one of the great mysteries of life.

Mom was not a hippie as some of the other American kids in school teased; that would have been the opposite of what Daddy believed in, so it just couldn't be true.

But she knew she was right about Mother. One of her earliest memories was of losing Mother in the base PX. Not that Sam had wandered away—Mother had, in absentminded pursuit of a lady she'd recognized as one of her palm-reading people. So Sam had suddenly been left in the confusing wilderness of the grocery aisles, holding baby Charlotte by one hand. Even then she'd recognized that she had to be in charge, and it wasn't quite the way things were supposed to be for a kid. Humiliated but stoic, she'd led Charlotte to a riser with big cans of nuts stacked on it, and they'd sat on the edge, gazing up solemnly at the shiny cans, waiting.

Before Mother came hurrying back, a half dozen grown-ups asked them if they were lost. To which Sam replied each time, "No, we just like to hang around with nuts."

She was not, and never would be, like Mother, no matter how sweet and good Mother was. Daddy would not give up if he were in this predicament. Neither would Sam.

"When will I get to see Jake?"

Sam had asked that question when Mom told her they were going to visit Aunt Alexandra, and when they were packing to leave Germany, and again on the plane, and on the second plane after they switched planes in Atlanta, and in the big car Aunt Alexandra had sent to get them in Asheville, and now, in the quiet of their bedroom in Aunt Alexandra's gigantic house.

They had come back to the town where she'd said her first words, the place where she vividly remembered wanting to talk, for the first time—all because of a dark-haired boy who'd made her feel needed.

Many things weren't clear to Sam, but that was. She understood that Uncle William was dead, and that dead, for a person, was the same as dead for Frau Miller's schnauzer, Schnapps, who had lived next door to them until he'd been run over by a bus. She understood that dead people were buried with more hoopla than dead dogs. Frau Miller had wrapped Schnapps in newspapers and put him in a garbage can.

Obviously, since Mom had gone to the trouble to leave Daddy and Charlotte for a week, and had taken Sam with her to fly in planes all the way back to America to see Uncle William get buried, he was not just going to be put in a garbage can. There wouldn't have been much use in coming here just to see *that*.

"Sweetie," Mom said now, sitting cross-legged on the white carpet with her long skirt in a heap between her knees as Sam faced her resolutely, "You were such a little girl when you met Jake. That was three years ago. I thought you'd forget all about him."

"I don't forget. Because I talked to him, and you said it was magic. I don't think there are many people in the world who can do real magic, so Jake must be special."

"There's something I need to explain to you about Jake." Mom smoothed a wrinkle in Sam's shirt. "Jake's

mother and your uncle William were sister and brother,
okay? And because Uncle William married *my* sister—
your aunt Alexandra—that makes Aunt Alexandra Jake's
aunt too."

"That's nice."

"Well, when Aunt Alexandra married Uncle William,
he gave her a very special present." Mom held up her
left hand, where her ring, with its tiny glass wedding
rock, caught the light from sunshine pouring through
the bedroom window. "When two people get married,
the man gives the woman a present to show everyone
that they love each other. Uncle William gave your aunt
a present like my diamond. He gave her a big red rock
called a *ruby*."

"He must have loved her a lot."

Mom looked sad. "Yes, I'm sure he did. But the ruby
he gave your aunt was one that had belonged to his family
for a long, long time, and, well, some people thought he
should have given it to Jake's mother—Uncle William's
sister—instead."

"But that would mean he'd be married to his sister.
I don't think that's the way things are done."

Mom looked up at the ceiling for a while, as though
she were trying to figure out what held it up. "The ruby
wasn't the kind of present a man gives to his wife. It
was supposed to belong to Jake's mother." Mom exhaled
the way she did whenever Sam asked several questions
in a row. "The point is, Jake's mother doesn't like Aunt
Alexandra because Aunt Alexandra owns her ruby. And
now that your uncle William is . . . gone, Jake's mother
and Aunt Alexandra don't have to be nice to each other
for any reason."

"Aunt Alexandra should give the ruby to her."

"Well, your aunt won't do that. Which is why Jake's
mother and nobody else in her family likes her." Mom
paused, and looked at Sam with her head tilted. "You
know what honor is. Daddy talks about it all the time."

Sam nodded. "It's the Ten Commandments and the
Pledge of Allegiance rolled into one. It's the rules good
people have to use."

"That's right. And so the rule is: Because your aunt won't give the ruby back, Jake's family can't be friends with her. And because you and I are part of Aunt Alexandra's family, they can't be friends with us either."

Sam stared at her. "Jake won't be my friend?"

"Not the way you think he is, sweetie."

"But he was my friend before."

"He didn't know the rules then. And neither did you. Now you're both old enough to understand them."

"No! Then I don't want any honor!"

"Sammie, I'm sorry. You can say hello to Jake at Uncle William's funeral, but I don't know if he'll talk to you. He's a big boy now. He's going to be so sad about Uncle William. He may not feel like talking to—"

"He talked to me before I could even talk back." She clenched her hands, squinted, and fought a tide of tears that burned behind her eyes. Crying was not honorable either, Daddy said. She did not want to have any honor, but she didn't want to break Daddy's rules. Still, none of this made sense. "He talked to me," she repeated. "And I'm going to talk to him some more. Whether he wants me to or not."

She ran to the window, where the sunshine was so bright it made her eyes cry all by themselves, so no rules were broken.

"This is all about a dumb *rock*," she whispered angrily. "A dumb red rock."

Jake stood stiffly in the crowded church vestibule. At his eye level, the whole world was made up of men's ties and women's bosoms, a suffocating wall of adults who brushed him as they jostled their way into the sanctuary, leaving behind a cloud of cologne, perfume, and perceptions. Judges and lawyers, bankers and mayors— and they felt more sad for themselves than for Uncle William, because the weather was nice, and there were other places they'd rather be. He was wounded by their boredom; why had they come for the funeral then? He stared into their middles and hated them; he wanted to be alone, away from their false kindness.

Ellie had already gone inside, with Mother and Father. He was supposed to go right now. But he thought he'd punch someone if he bumped into many more lies. He edged along the wall, got to a staircase, and bolted up it two steps at a time. The narrow loft at the top was empty and cool. He leaned on the railing, looking down on the sanctuary already packed with people, and took deep breaths of air untainted by fake flower scents and fake leather scents, by fake sorrow and selfish curiosity.

Mother, Father, and Ellie sat on the front pew on the left side with some of Mother's relatives. There was a small space for him beside Ellie, but he thought he'd strangle if he had to sit there. He'd be within spitting distance of Uncle William's bronze casket covered in white roses.

I killed him. Maybe Samantha would hate me if she knew what I did, even if it was an accident. Maybe she's already decided to hate us Raincrows, just like her aunt.

The front pew on the right, across from his family, was empty. But as he watched, a door opened on the side near the organist's box. Aunt Alexandra walked in, thin as a whistle and wearing a black dress, holding Tim's hand. Tim wore a black suit and tie as spiffy as any adult's, a high contrast to Jake's brown jacket, rumpled tan trousers, and skewed brown tie. Behind Tim was a lady with long straight blond hair, a black skirt that swung jauntily above the tops of black platform shoes, and a short black jacket with puffed shoulders.

Mrs. Ryder. Jake craned his neck and clutched the balcony's railing. She turned and held out a hand to some person who hadn't appeared yet.

Samantha walked into the sanctuary, and his heart did a slow flipflop. She was twice as tall as he remembered, which meant her head now reached her mother's elbow, and she was dressed in an identical black suit, even down to the platform shoes, with long golden hair streaming down her back.

He, who had little interest in girls for girls' sakes, felt heat zoom up his cheeks and knew, without doubt, for right or wrong, that she was as fine a girl as he had ever seen.

He had promised himself to Aunt Alexandra's blood niece. But Aunt Alexandra had murdered Uncle William. His uncle. What could he do? Father said, If you don't stand for something, you'll fall for anything.

If he didn't warn Samantha, knowing what he knew about her aunt, he would be a coward. But he *couldn't* tell her what he knew—he couldn't tell anyone.

Shivering with the dilemma, he watched her sit with her mother and aunt. People were still rambling around, finding their seats. The minister hadn't come out of the back yet. But there wasn't much time. Unless Jake took bold action, he might never get to talk to Samantha. Aunt Alexandra certainly meant to keep her away from him. Samantha would go back to Germany, and who knew when he'd see her again?

Hardly thinking, he reached into a back pocket of his slacks. Hidden under the tail of his jacket was a foot-long piece of hollow river cane—a miniature of the long cane blowguns the old people sold in the tourist shops up at Cherokee, the main town on the reservation. Keet Jones could kill a rabbit at fifty yards with a sharp wooden dart; he'd taught Jake and Ellie how to shoot.

Jake glanced around the loft for a safe missile. He grabbed a hymnal from a wooden rack attached to one of the pew backs, and opened it. Could you go to hell for tearing a page out of a church song book? What if he took only the very first page? It was blank.

He compromised by tearing off one corner of that page, easing the scrap along, convinced each tiny ripping sound could be heard in every corner of the church. He put the hymnal back and fixed a hard pebble of paper and spit, then loaded his piece of cane and took aim at the back of Samantha's head.

His heart pounded like an engine. It was a long way from the loft to the front pew. If he hit the wrong head, or

Samantha squealed on him for hitting *her*, he'd find out exactly what hell was like, right here, today.

He gave it his best shot. The spitball hit home squarely in the middle of Samantha's hair. She slapped a small hand at the back of her head, pulled the gummy wad out, stared at it, then twisted around and searched the crowd with glaring eyes.

Up, up, up. She saw him. Her mouth popped open. He leaned on the railing as casually as he could, holding the blowgun in the air like a peace offering. He couldn't think what else to do.

She whipped around and leaned close to her mother. He could see that Samantha was saying something to her.

Telling what the awful Raincrow boy had done to her, in *church*, at their uncle's *funeral*, no less? Jake sighed heavily, and waited.

"I need to go the bathroom," Sam whispered.

Mom, who sat between her and Aunt Alexandra, and was holding Aunt Alex's hand, leaned down and whispered back, "Can't you wait?"

"I know where it is. I can go by myself. *Please?*"

"Well, *hurry*. And don't talk to any strangers."

Sam looked at her solemnly. *It's him. It's Jake.* "Oh, I won't," she promised.

Chapter Eight

$\mathcal{B}$ ack through the cool hallways inside the church. Through a door into the hot, bright sunshine. Around the hedges and along the edge of the lawn. She ran, breathless and uncertain, but determined. She darted among the grown-ups on the front steps, into the little room at the back of the sanctuary, and halted.

He was waiting on the stairs. Gosh, he was so tall, and his hair was black as night, with little bits of red in it. And he was a *boy*, one of those creatures she disdained. But not like the boys in her first-grade class at the school for kids of servicemen, a big boy, at least a fifth-grader, she guessed.

It was heady stuff. It was the same feeling she got when she hugged her favorite stuffed animal, only a thousand times larger.

She approached him slowly. His eyes stayed right on

her, as if she might be from outer space. Then he held
out one hand. A distant memory returned, of being much
smaller, of looking up at him the way she was doing now,
and of taking his hand. It had been all right then; it would
be all right now.

She grabbed his hand and followed him up the stairs.

"Go find your brother," Father whispered to Ellie.
Father had one arm around Mother, who was staring
straight at Uncle William's coffin, her hands clenched in
the lap of her black suit. "And tell him to get his fanny
back in here right now. The service is about to start."

Ellie's skin itched with the feeling that Jake wasn't
too far away, in fact, that he was at the back of the sanctuary. She eased around furtively, looked up, and inhaled
with a long, low sound of alarm when she saw him sitting
with Aunt Alex's niece in the tiny loft. She whipped
around and gazed steadfastly into space. She didn't want
to get her brother in trouble. He was going to be in
enough of that. "Go on now," Father said. "Go get Jake."

"I—I—hmmm, he, well—"

The minister came out of a side door, and the organist
started playing. Mother jumped as if she'd been asleep,
and glanced at them. Her eyes were red and tired.
"Where's Jake?"

Ellie gazed at her parents, mouth open in silent
torture. Father squinted at her. "*Ellie*," he said, drawing
her name out.

She motioned numbly toward the back of the church.
They looked. "My God," Mother said under her breath.
"They did manage to find each other. I won't have it. I
won't have him sitting with Alexandra's niece. I'm sorry.
I just won't."

"Let's allow William one day of peace," Father said
grimly. "Let it be for right now."

Mother faced forward, looking ashamed, Ellie
thought, and said nothing else.

"I know about the rock," Sam said carefully. They sat
in the middle of a pew in the empty little hiding place

upstairs. His long legs reached the floor. Hers didn't. "The rock that makes you hate my aunt Alexandra."

"It's not just a rock, it's a star ruby. It belonged to my family way back when there was nobody else except Indians around here. Aunt—your aunt, she won't give it back to us."

"Do you hate me too?"

"No."

"Then why do you look mad?"

"Because you're a Duke, and it's not right for me to like a Duke."

"My name's *Ryder*. My daddy's an M.P. for the army, and he's *Sergeant Ryder*, okay? I'm not a Duke."

"Yes, you are." He looked at her sadly. "Because your mother is one."

"There's nothing wrong with my mom!"

"I didn't say there was. Just that she's your aunt's sister. And your aunt is a Duke."

"Aunt Alexandra is your aunt too."

"Not anymore. Not since Uncle William . . ." His voice trailed off, and he stared away, frowning. "Not anymore," he repeated, and sighed. "Listen to me. Your aunt wants you to belong to her. She'd be real happy if you could live with her like you're her daughter, because you're special, and she knows it."

"I'm not gonna live with Aunt Alexandra. Why would I do that? Mother and Daddy wouldn't let me, and I wouldn't go anyhow." She peered at him to see if he was joking. What a crazy idea.

"I'm just saying—don't ever think she's your friend. She's a mean person. She's . . . she's like a spider, and if you get stuck in her web, she'll run over and wrap you up before you can bat an eyelash."

"Oh, no, she won't. I'm a spider too. I know how to make webs." She pulled something from a deep pocket in her odd black skirt. Her eyes became even more serious. "Here," she said softly, pressing something into one of his hands. "I made this for you."

He studied the odd little knitted blue square, no wider than his palm, with a perfect gold *R* stitched in one corner. He couldn't remember him or Ellie being able to make anything so delicate when they were her age. "You made this all by yourself?"

"Sure." Her mouth flattened and she scrutinized him as if insulted.

"I told you you're special." He carefully tucked the gift in his jacket pocket. His skin tingled. *California.* The name came to him out of nowhere. His heart sank. Her family was moving to California. "I like it. What is it?"

"I don't know. But I worked on it a long time. My daddy says it could be a blanket for a bug's bed."

Jake fished in another jacket pocket, sorting through odds and ends he carried with him all the time. Bits of quartz and other rocks. His touchstones. He could feel the mountains in them. He produced his favorite, a lumpy, purple-brown rock with a silvery glimmer. Holding it on his palm, he told her, "This is a kind of ruby."

She bent over it. "It's not red. Looks like a rock to me."

"A lot of them aren't red. I didn't say it was a very good ruby, but it's my favorite." He popped the stone in his mouth, plucked it out, and polished the uneven surface on his jacket sleeve. "Look." He tilted his hand, and light shimmered across the surface. "It's got silk."

"Silk's a kind of cloth, silly. My mom has a silk shirt, and my baby sister threw up on it."

"Well, when a ruby has light inside it, the light's called silk too. And sometimes the silk makes a little star."

"I don't see any star."

"You have to cut and polish the stone first. Besides, maybe this one has caught the middle of a star. A star so big you can't see the ends of it. That's what I think. And the light won't ever go away." *That's how I feel about us,* he thought, but the feeling was too hard to say. He turned one of her hands palm-up and placed the stone in it. "So I'll give it to you, so you'll always have, hmmm, part of a star."

She uttered a low sigh of pleasure and closed her

fingers around the stone. Sam suddenly thought about Mom's diamond rock, the one Daddy gave her when they got married, and what Mom had said about Uncle William giving Aunt Alexandra the bad ruby when they got married. "You sure I'm supposed to get it?" she asked plaintively. "It's not like Aunt Alexandra's ruby, is it? You aren't supposed to give it to somebody else?"

"No." He ducked his head and looked away, red spots climbing up his cheeks. "Just to you. It'll always belong to you. Even if you live so far away it's like another planet. Even in California."

She could barely breathe. "How'd you know the army's sending us to live in California?"

"I . . . heard about it somewhere." He added gruffly, "California is in America at least."

"But it's on the other side!"

"Doesn't matter. I'll always know where you are."

She opened her hand and touched a fingertip to the ruby. "Does this mean we're *married*?"

His attention shot back to her. For a minute he didn't say a word. Then he nodded. "Yes, I reckon that's what we are."

"Why hasn't Samantha come back?" Alexandra asked Frannie the question in a hushed, strained tone, as if Frannie had failed at motherhood. "You shouldn't have let her go alone."

"She's very mature for her age." But Frannie twisted in her seat and scanned the packed church anxiously. She reminded herself that her sister was distraught. She didn't want to argue with Alex at William's funeral.

"You treat her like a friend, not a child," Alexandra continued. "You've let her become too independent."

"Alex, she only went to the bathroom, not to hitch-hike around the world."

Frannie caught a glimpse of movement in the tiny balcony. Sam, feet dangling from the seat of a pew behind the white balustrade, peered down at her stoically. Sitting beside her with his feet planted firmly on the loft's floor was a somber-faced boy whose vaguely exotic hair and features Frannie instantly recalled.

Sammie, already, at the tender age of six, as strong-willed as a brick wall, had found and claimed her long-awaited prize. Frannie studied her daughter with pride, awe, and dread.

"*Mom.*" Tim's petulant, anguished whisper made Frannie look around quickly. Tim was watching the balcony too, and tugging on Alexandra's sleeve. "Mom," he repeated while the organist's morbid rendition of "Amazing Grace" throbbed louder in the hot, still air. "Samantha's upstairs with *Jake.*"

Alexandra's chalky face became a mask of fury. She swiveled gracefully in the pew, flashing Frannie a scalding stare, then riveting her gaze on the rebellious pair in the balcony. Inspired by the widow's bizarre behavior, other people followed suit, until Frannie noted with rising alarm that most of the eyes in the church were fixed on Samantha and Jake. She glanced furtively across the aisle and met Sarah's bleak gaze.

The objects of the disruption seemed frozen in place, like deer caught in the headlights of an oncoming tractor-trailer. Frannie grabbed Alexandra's clenched fist. It was cold and clammy. Frannie stared at her sister, who shivered violently. The minister had stepped to the altar behind William's casket. He began speaking, but his words were a blank jumble to Frannie's distracted senses, frightened by the electric rage and strange, unfathomable fear she saw in Alexandra's face. "They're not hurting anything," Frannie whispered, pulling at her sister as delicately as she could. "*Leave them alone. The service has started. Alex, calm down.*"

But Alexandra bolted to her feet and jerked her hand away from Frannie's fervent grip. Her voice rang out. "*Samantha,* come down here, where you belong."

The astounding spectacle of Judge Vanderveer's grieving widow shouting in the midst of his funeral service had the power to stop the minister's voice, "Amazing Grace," and every heartbeat in the sanctuary. Frannie felt cold sweat trickling down her back.

Slowly, Samantha shook her head. Jake stared down at his aunt in black defiance. It was as if the two of them had merged into one force, an unspoken vow of alliance so poignant that a surge of maternal command faded in Frannie's thoughts, and she wanted to cheer for them.

But the spell snapped when Alexandra left the pew and strode up the central aisle. Frannie bolted after her. Sarah and Hugh were on their feet too, hurriedly following.

They caught up with Alexandra as she reached the open doors to the vestibule. Frannie pushed in front of her, blocking her way. "My daughter," Frannie said with garbled passion. "*Mine*. I say she stays where she is." She broke down and added desperately, under her breath, "Alex, *please* go back to the front. Have you lost your mind?"

"I'll strangle him. I'll strangle the little bastard for flaunting my own niece as if he owns her."

That remark brought audible gasps from the people in the back pews. A drama worthy of legend was unfolding before their eyes, an event that would weave its way into Pandora's oral history for years to come.

Sarah caught Alexandra's arm. "You ruined my brother. You killed him just as surely as if you'd pushed him down those stairs with your own two hands. If you ever so much as lay a finger on my children, I'll—"

"Keep your quirky brats out of my life, you hear? Keep your son away from my niece." They swayed together, Alexandra grabbing Sarah's shoulders. Hugh pried an arm between them, and Frannie latched on to her sister's waist with both hands.

"We're done," Jake said.

Everyone froze. Sarah jerked away from Alexandra and gazed at them with churning emotions. He and Samantha stood in the vestibule, at the bottom of the stairs. *Two old souls, watching us as if we're fools*, Frannie thought, stunned. He turned to Samantha, looked down at her wearily, and said, "It may be a long time before we see each other again, but don't worry. I'll find you."

Samantha had tears in her eyes, but she smiled at him. "Okay. I'll wait."

Samantha was gone—gone back to Germany with her mother—and Jake had to deal with his infamous reputation for disrupting Uncle William's funeral alone. Rumor got around that he'd *lured* Samantha upstairs, that he'd hidden her there and bullied her into staying, so her mother and her aunt would be worried and have to go looking for her.

Before long that gossip octopus had a hundred tentacles. He was practically a kidnapper, a bad influence. The principal even called him into the office for a lecture. He had, the principal said, the kind of attitude that could lead to dope smoking, flag burning, and draft dodging.

Father's patients gave him sour looks in the waiting room when he carried lunch to Father on Saturdays. The Presbyterian minister gave a sermon about the failing morals of youth, and the Baptists sent a lady to the Cove to ask Mother if she wanted to send him to their summer Bible camp. Mrs. Steinberg, the only Jewish person they knew, who ran one of the new dress boutiques in town, called to tell Mother and Father that Jake wasn't nearly as embarrassing as her sister's son in Atlanta, who had set off a stink bomb at his own cousin's bar mitzvah.

For their parts, Mother and Father were more puzzled than angry over what he'd done. Mother had her own part in the sorry drama to live down; everybody suspected she'd been one second away from punching her own brother's widow in the face. She was nearly sick with guilt over everything she wished she'd said and done while Uncle William was still alive. Jake and Ellie listened late at night to the muffled voices from the living room, and Mother's sobs.

Jake stared at his aunt across the polished conference table in the offices of Uncle William's attorney. Beside him, Ellie waited with her hands wound in the skirt of her cotton dress. She fixed her gaze on Aunt Alexandra too.

Mother, her face stony and her eyes glittering with disgust, sat next to Ellie. Father, big and calm and watchful, held one of her hands, rubbing the ball of his thumb over the back of it, trying to keep peace at the reading of the will.

Jake's grim attention moved to his cousin. Tim sat on a bench along the wall, his light red hair shagging over his forehead, his eyes droopy and despondent. He was nine, a year younger than Jake and Ellie, skinny and freckled, with a nervous habit of chewing his fingernails to the quick. Jake felt old by comparison. In his black suit, Tim looked like a kid dressed up to play a banker.

Jake's stomach twisted into knots of frustration. *We can't tell him what really happened to his father. We can't tell him about his own mother. She's all he's got left.*

Uncle William's attorney read a list of bequests—little impersonal things first—his law books for the town library, donations to two churches, a piece of land for a playground. Then, family matters: a silver pocket watch to Father, a prized antique rifle to Jake, a set of crystal vases to Ellie.

Jake felt the tension climbing, as if the darkly paneled room were losing its air. Mother sat on the edge of her chair, staring into space, her expression tight with dignity. She'd told them she didn't expect anything from her brother, that they would come here today regardless of the humiliation, because it was the only honor she could give him.

There was no mention of Mother in the list the attorney recited. Finally, clearing his throat and smoothing the paperwork he held on a leather-bound ledger, he read a wordy passage that, at its core, left everything else he owned to Aunt Alexandra and Tim. Aunt Alexandra sighed, closed her eyes, and pressed her fingertips to her lips as if saying a silent prayer of thanks to Uncle William.

Jake sank back in his chair, angry for his mother's sake, wondering why in hell Uncle William had wanted her to listen to this.

"With one exception," the lawyer added, then hesitated. Clocks could have stopped on that second of waiting. The lawyer looked at Mother. "I ask my beloved sister for her forgiveness, and to her I leave what has always been hers. The Pandora ruby."

"Oh, William," Mother said softly, and covered her face. Aunt Alexandra's blue eyes flew open. Her fingers convulsed into a fist, and the fist hovered at her mouth. Father put his hand on Mother's shoulder, as if holding her still. Ellie, mouth open, turned to Jake. They traded an astonished look.

Aunt Alexandra gazed furiously at Mother, who lifted her head. The look Mother gave back was a silent shout of hatred and victory. "You took my brother away from everyone who loved and respected him," Mother said in a low, icy voice. "You thought you owned him. But you *didn't*. Dear God, you made it so hard for him to do what he knew was right that he had to die before he could admit it."

Aunt Alexandra lowered her fist to the table. Slowly she uncurled her fingers.

"*You're* the greedy one, Sarah. You're the one who made William miserable. You shunned your own brother over a piece of *jewelry*."

"If I could throw it into a bottomless pit—if that would bring William back, I'd do it. I doubt you can say the same. Not honestly." Mother's distraught eyes flickered to Tim, who looked miserable. She inhaled sharply and looked at Aunt Alexandra again. "I've let you bring me down to your level. That's my fault. But I'm done with you. Done. You've got the home I grew up in, and everything else. Fine. Tim deserves his father's possessions. But for my children, and their children, and their *grandchildren*, I want my ruby. And I want it today."

Jake and Ellie were on the edges of their seats. Father said softly, "I'll come by Highview this afternoon and pick it up. If my ancestors had known what damned misery it would bring, they'd have hidden it from human hands."

Aunt Alexandra stared at them without blinking, without giving an inch. "It was mine—a gift from William. You made me feel like an outsider. Like rich white trash not fit to be a Vanderveer. William gave me the ruby to make a statement. *I belong here.* And no one, not even his own jealous sister, can take that away from me."

"You don't belong here," Mother answered. "And the only jealousy I've felt is for my brother's good sense and honor, both of which you corrupted."

Aunt Alexandra shuddered. "I buried it with him."

Mother gasped. Father, a muscle working in his cheek, leaned back slowly in his chair. Jake stared at his aunt with such intensity, he felt his eyes would burst. Beside him, Ellie gave a soft squeak.

Mother was clutching the table. Father said something filthy under his breath and held her shoulders. His dark eyes could have burned holes in Aunt Alexandra. Jake's head swam. He looked at Ellie numbly.

Jake's eyes shot to Tim. His cousin looked like a forgotten Howdy Doody puppet, his red hair ruffled around his chalk-white face, his eyes glazed. "They're not gonna dig my dad up, are they?" he asked loudly. He jumped up and stumbled to his mother, and, crying, crumpled down beside her legs with his arms around her waist. "Aunt Sarah can't dig Dad up, can she?"

"I hope not." Aunt Alexandra bent over him, holding him, stroking his hair. "No, I won't let her do that."

Mother made a gagging sound. "You . . . you . . ." Her voice trailed off into words Jake could barely hear. *You sick monster*, was what Mother whispered.

"No one will wear the ruby again," Aunt Alexandra said, oozing sadness. "It's where it belongs. Live with that, Sarah."

They eased through the cemetery with fearful resolve, glancing back through the big hickories and firs that surrounded the Vanderveer plots, sidestepping shadows cast by looming granite angels and tall tombstones. Jake shivered with a horror that bound his chest like an iron fist. Ellie skittered along with small strides, holding the end of her long black braid in one hand, as if she were ready to pull herself back to the safe road to town, beyond the trees.

"Hurry," she told Jake.

They had detoured to the cemetery on their way from Father's office to the grocery store on the other end of town, where Mother would be waiting after her shopping was done.

"If I could fly, I sure would," Jake answered. They broke into a trot up a low knoll, circled a cluster of tombstones, then plowed to a stop under a gnarled oak tree. Uncle William's grave was marked with a mound of funeral flowers, a terribly colorful hump of wilting flowers and limp ribbons.

They stood, paralyzed, staring down at it. "We have to touch it," Jake said, his own voice sounding eerie to him. "For Mother's sake. We gotta know."

Ellie exhaled. "I will, if you will—at the same time."

They squatted beside the flowers and, stealing looks at each other to make sure neither of them backed out, each slid a splayed hand under the flowers, into the soft, cold red dirt.

Jake grimaced and shut his eyes. In his most terrible imaginings he dreaded feeling the ghosts of a hundred curious Vanderveers. Maybe they would seep underneath his hand like ground water, as if he were dowsing for a spot to dig a well, as he'd seen an old man do at Cawatie, once, with a pronged stick to guide the way. Maybe he'd strike a well full of spirits—the Vanderveer grandparents who'd died in a car wreck when Mother was not much older than him and Ellie, leaving her with Uncle William, who had given up his internship with a state supreme court judge in Raleigh to come home and take care of her.

Or maybe he'd see Great-Aunt Melanie Vanderveer, who'd strangled on a peach pit one Fourth of July, while they were still babies. Or maybe Mack Lee Vanderveer, the second cousin who'd gotten burned to a crisp in a tank battle during World War II.

Jake didn't want to encounter the toasted Mack Lee, most of all.

But he felt nothing. Nothing. His eyes jerked open. He looked at Ellie. Her eyes were round green dots in her face. Her mouth was open, and she was staring into empty air.

"Our ruby's not down there," she said like a sleepwalker. She blinked, pulled her hand away, and fell back on the mowed grass, pushing herself away from the grave fanny-first. Jake jammed his hand deeper into the soft dirt. "I can't tell anything," he said frantically. "Why can't I know what you know? What's wrong with me?"

He hunched on his knees and pressed both hands into the grave. The blankness inside him was more frightening than any roaming Vanderveer ghosts might have been.

"Maybe you're thinking too hard," Ellie said. "When I think too hard, I only get a headache."

"You're sure it's not down there?" He looked over his shoulder at her as he clawed at the dirt. She nodded firmly. Her eyes glittered. "She lied to Mother. She's still got our ruby. *My* ruby." The angry way Ellie said that made Jake twist toward her, frowning, his dirt-stained hands thrust out. "Your ruby?"

"It's supposed to be Mother's, and then mine. I know the rules." Her voice rose into a wail. "But I'll die after I get it." With that amazing statement she turned over and flung herself down with her face burrowed in the crook of one arm. "I'm going to die. I just know it."

Jake's mouth had the bad taste that came from not quite throwing up. "That's the craziest thing I've ever heard," he said finally. But his heart was thudding in his ears, and he felt dizzy. "Where'd you get that feeling?"

"I don't know." She clenched her hands into fists. "I thought it. I don't know why."

"Well, don't *think* it. It's not true."

"Aunt Alexandra's got the ruby. *That's* true. Can't you tell?"

Jake pawed the grass with his hands, scrubbing the grave dirt off as fast as he could. "No." He shook his head urgently. "No, I can't. It's not right. Something's not right, but I don't know what it is."

"Dirt daubers," a low female voice thundered behind them. Jake whirled around as Ellie shoved herself upright. Mrs. Big Stick stood a few feet away, a straw hat drooping around her brown face, garden gloves and a trowel hanging from one blunt brown hand. Dressed in a long print skirt with a man-size blue shirt hanging out over it, and her mud-stained tennis shoes bulging with toe humps at the tips, she made a comfortable but commanding sight. "What are you doing here?" she asked in Cherokee.

"Visiting Uncle William," Jake said quickly. He remembered that Mrs. Big Stick came to the cemetery regularly to tend the holly shrubs near her relatives' graves. There was a section of Big Sticks. Father said they'd been lured away from the Cherokee churches at Cawatie by a visiting evangelist in a Model T. They'd come to Pandora to see the Model T, but got caught up in the excitement of a church membership drive.

Mrs. Big Stick dropped her gloves and trowel, then hunkered down with her skirt wadded between her broad knees, and studied them through squinted eyes. "Some things are best left alone," she said, nodding. "Some fights are best buried and forgotten."

Jake bit his tongue and feigned a neutral look. Everyone had heard about Aunt Alexandra burying the ruby with Uncle William. A thread of dismay curled through him. But Mrs. Big Stick understood more about him and Ellie than other people did. "If," he said carefully, "*if* a person came here to look around, and if that person didn't *find* anything, that'd be pretty interesting, wouldn't it?"

She shook her head. "That'd be a blessing. Because a person ought to stay out a ravenmocker's business. Only a foolish person goes stirring up a ravenmocker."

Ellie crossed her arms. "What if the ravenmocker is a *thief*?"

"All ravenmockers are thieves," Mrs. Big Stick answered. "That's what they do—they steal the innards right out of people. And once they do, nobody can change it." She wagged a finger at them. "The trick is to keep the ravenmocker from stealing your soul in the first place."

Jake tilted his head. "You mean a person can't get back what a ravenmocker has stolen?"

"No. And who'd want it back anyhow? Once a ravenmocker gets its claws on something, the thing will always be nasty. Soiled. It will only bring unhappiness to people."

Ellie sighed. "Then we . . . a person should just keep quiet and steer clear of the ravenmocker?"

"*Yes.*"

Jake frowned. "What if one person figured out that the ravenmocker had stolen something but another one couldn't be sure about it. And they'd always been alike before."

Mrs. Big Stick's dark, hooded eyes settled on his with alarming wisdom. "Now, that is a mystery. But your granny used to tell me that her . . . *music* would shut off sometimes. Sometimes when she wanted to hear it the most."

"Did she know why?" Jake asked breathlessly.

"She reckoned her music was protecting her from secrets she didn't really want to hear. Some mysteries are better left alone." Mrs. Big Stick thought for a moment. "What you don't know can't hurt you."

That awful glimpse of Aunt Alexandra and Mr. Lomax came back to Jake's mind, and he could almost feel the ruby burning his hand when he held it, and the horror of causing Uncle William's death returned with strangling swiftness. He nodded at Mrs. Big Stick. "A person would have to be careful of who he cares about."

"That's right. And not expect the music to come when it's called. It's got a mind of its own."

Ellie got to her feet. She looked shaky. "Well, I'm staying away from ravenmockers, and *my* music will do exactly what I ask it to do."

Mrs. Big Stick pursed her lips. "You'll be fine if you don't forget that. Now, scat."

Ellie looked happy to do that, and headed back toward the road. Jake rose slowly, his eyes never leaving Mrs. Big Stick's. His misery over Uncle William was a dark pain inside his chest. And when he thought with hatred and fear of Aunt Alexandra, he also thought of Samantha, and a knot of confusion crowded his already-jumbled emotions, until finally, one startlingly clear thought came free. He faced Mrs. Big Stick. "A person can't fight a ravenmocker without hurting other people," he offered cautiously, watching to see if she understood. She nodded. Jake sighed. "And if a person loves those people, it's downright impossible. A person has to listen close. And be patient."

One corner of Mrs. Big Stick's mouth curled upward, but she seemed more sad than anything else. "Just listen to your music. It will tell you the right thing to do."

He loped after Ellie, who was nearly at the road. Her strange talk about death zoomed back into his thoughts, and he walked close to her on purpose. "You're not going to die," he announced grimly. "Because we're going to let the ravenmocker keep her damned secrets. That way, no one else will get hurt because of her."

Ellie looked at him gratefully under her wispy black eyebrows. "It's a deal."

"I've missed you," Alexandra whispered, the words muffled against Orrin's stomach. They lay in a damask-draped canopy bed before an open window that let in the winter light and the soft, cold roar of the ocean. "It's been hell these past few months. You don't know how much I've looked forward to this trip. Hmmm, I love the Outer Banks in the wintertime. I put a photo of this island on the mirror of my vanity. I've looked at it every morning—thinking about us."

Orrin stroked her bare back. "Decorum, sweetie. I couldn't just move into Highview the day after—"

"Don't talk about him. It's been horrible. His sister has stirred up such ugly talk about me that I've become the town pariah."

"Small-town gossip. People will forget." There was the sleek rustle of satin as he pushed the covers down, following the curve of her spine with a fingertip. "I'm going to miss the excitement of hiding with you—a little," he said. "It made life intriguing, all these years."

"You need a wife. You're thirty-seven years old. People are starting to talk about *you.* They wonder if you're normal."

He laughed. "Alexandra, are you proposing to me?"

"Of course. It's what I've been waiting for." She lifted her head and gazed at him. "Orrin, you're a state senator. People expect men in your position to have wives. Don't tease me. You know I'm right. You know you want to marry me."

"Yes. Yes, my randy little go-getter, I do."

She kissed him. They shoved the plush bed coverings aside and made love, heated and shivering in the damp, cool breeze curling off the tide. "Nothing stops you," he said later as they lay propped against the pillows. "That's what's always fascinated me about you."

Alexandra gave him a thoughtful look. "I have to show you what I've done." She climbed from the bed, slipped a long silk robe around her body, and went to a luggage bag atop the room's dresser. She opened it and removed a leather pouch, and from the pouch she took a long necklace of thick gold links.

Humming with contentment, she brought the necklace to Orrin and sat beside him on the bed, her bare legs curled under her girlishly. Orrin examined its odd pendant, running his fingertips over the ornately etched flowers on the surface, weighing it in his palm. "My God, it looks like a pecan dipped in gold. It's, well, *large,*" he offered carefully. "I've never seen you wear anything so flamboyant."

"It serves its purpose." She pressed the edge of her fingernail to the pendant, and an invisible seam appeared. Orrin gave a low whistle as the pendant opened on a hidden, minuscule hinge. Tucked in a gauzy cocoon of fabric was the ruby. "I'll be able to wear it now," she explained. "By God, *I'll* know it's still mine, even if no one ever sees it again."

Chapter
Nine

"*I*s our mom a hippie?" Charlotte asked. Because she'd lost a front tooth, the question had a whistling sound. And because she thought Sam had the answer to every question in the world, she expected an answer. Charlotte stood on a chair at the stove, stirring a pot of oatmeal.

Sitting at the kitchen table of their apartment, Sam put her knitting down. She looked at their matching tie-dyed nightgowns, which Mom had made for them. She looked at the big glass canister of granola on the kitchen counter, and the pots of alfalfa sprouts on the window over the sink. She looked at the IMPEACH NIXON bumper sticker Mom had stuck on the lid of the garbage can, and the astrology books Mom left scattered on the kitchen table every night. "No. Hippies don't wear underwear or take baths."

127

"Good. I want to be just like Mom, but **Daddy** won't let us be hippies."

Since their daddy wouldn't even let them wear pants to school, Sam doubted there was a chance of them turning into hippies. She wasn't interested anyway. One odd person in the house was enough, and Mom filled that bill. Every year since they'd moved to California, Mom had gotten flakier. Four years. Flaky times four. Mom was the manager of a health-food store. Daddy said she worked with fruits and nuts in more ways than one.

Mom was okay, and Sam loved her, but *someone* had to keep their feet on the ground, and Sam had gotten the job. She fingered the irregular purplish rock she wore on a chain around her neck. Mom had had a jeweler attach a gold clasp to Jake's ruby, and Sam wore it all the time. She hadn't seen Jake in four years, so maybe she was as flaky as Mom, hanging on to strange ideas and hopes.

"Good morning, soldiers. *Atteeen-tion!*" They scrambled to the center of the small kitchen as Daddy strode in. He stopped, hands clasped behind his back, looking so handsome in his crisp trousers and shirt, his polished shoes and gleaming belt buckle. Daddy was an M.P. When she was younger, Sam had insisted that stood for *my pop*. He studied them, frowning. "Private Ryder, what's for chow?"

"Oatmeal and chocolate milk, Daddy . . . I mean, *Sergeant*," Charlotte answered.

"Corporal Ryder, have you kept the private up to specs on kitchen protocol?"

"Yes, Sergeant," Sam answered. "She wanted to put cinnamon in the milk again, Sarge, but I nixed it."

He cut his eyes at Charlotte. "Private, you'll make a damned fine cook if you can just stop experimenting." Charlotte giggled. Daddy looked stern. To Sam he said, "Check off the daily assignments for me, Corporal."

"Beds made, clothes laid out, shoes polished, homework ready, Sergeant. Sarge, Charlotte needs a note for her teacher. The first grade is going on a field trip next week."

"File that requisition with your mother, Corporal. She'll be here as soon as she finishes her pretzels."

"Yes, Sergeant." *Pretzels* was what Daddy called Mom's yoga exercises.

"Carry on, then. Good work, soldiers. Dismissed." They saluted. He saluted. Then he squatted down, held out his arms, and they ran to him for a hug. "What you doing today, Daddy?" Charlotte asked.

"I'm flying to Los Angeles to pick up an AWOL. I'll be home tonight." Daddy found runaway soldiers and brought them back; the lowest thing a person could be, as far as Sam was concerned, was AWOL. "I'll keep the troops in line for you, Daddy."

"I know you will, Sam." He chuckled, then kissed her forehead. Sam put both arms around his neck and leaned against him happily.

After he left, Mom scurried into the kitchen, unfolded her astrology charts on the table, and huddled over them with her hands jammed into her hair. "What's the matter?" Sam asked, sidling up to her and peering over her shoulder.

"It's not a good day for your daddy to travel." Mom spread her hands on the star charts as if reading a roadmap. "Not a good day," she repeated with a tremor in her voice.

Sam patted her shoulder awkwardly. "Aw, Mom, let's have some oatmeal. Come on, you'll be late for work."

"Oatmeal," Charlotte added, grinning like a gaptoothed jack-o'-lantern and holding out the pot. "With garlic in it."

Sam groaned and went to fix a new pot.

That afternoon, as Daddy and another M.P. were boarding a helicopter with their prisoner, the man got loose somehow, and grabbed the other M.P.'s gun. Daddy, being the bravest man in the world, jumped in between. And got killed.

Alexandra was in her element. She had a shattered little group to care for, and even Samantha—by far the strongest and most resilient of the three—was coming under her wing. Alexandra looked into the swollen, exhausted blue eyes of her ten-year-old niece and saw herself as a child, already aware that the world was made up of cruel and unfair rules, and that only the toughest survived.

They sat at opposite sides of the modest beige couch of Frannie's living room, with the California sunshine streaming through a curtained window. Frannie was sleeping fitfully in the bedroom, an emotional invalid, with the confused and teary Charlotte dozing in her arms.

But Samantha sat dry-eyed and alert on the couch, her blue jumper smoothed neatly, her hair lying over one shoulder in a regimented braid. Alexandra leaned back, tucking a notepad into a small leather purse, flicking lint off the legs of her tailored slacks. "Am I such a stranger, Samantha? Do you still think of me as a witch?"

"You helped us take my dad to North Carolina," Sam said slowly, staring straight ahead. "You made sure he had a nice funeral and all. You took care of things I couldn't do. My mom is glad to have you around. I guess you're not a witch."

Alexandra sighed with relief and slid across the couch to her. Slipping an arm around the girl's slender, taut shoulders, she said gently, "Your mother and I are very different from each other. We've always wanted different things, and sometimes I sound very, hmmm, set in my ways, I know. But I'm your *aunt*, honey, and I love you— I love you and Charlotte, and your mother, very much. And I want to make you all feel better. I want you to be happy."

"My mom needs your help," Samantha answered, flinching away from Alexandra's arm. "And Charlotte really likes you."

"You could like me, too, if you'd stop thinking of me as the enemy. Because I'm not. You can't let your opinions be colored by what other people say about me. Especially when those people don't know me very well— when they're jealous and mean-spirited without reason."

"You mean Mrs. Raincrow. You mean Jake."

"Yes, honey. Jake's mother never wanted me to marry her brother. I know it's hard for a little girl to understand, but people are naturally suspicious when new people come into their lives, people who have new ideas. They look for things to dislike about the new people and the new ideas. They try to make others dislike them too. They don't want their way of life to change. They're afraid."

"If you explained to them, though, and they saw that you were their friend, they'd—"

"I've tried, honey, I've tried since long before you were born. It hurt me so much for them to say mean things about me. It hurt your uncle William too. My only fear is that they've upset you so much that you won't be able to make up your mind for yourself. You're a smart girl; you don't want other people telling you what to think, do you?"

"No, not anybody."

Alexandra took her hands. "You are so smart, and so talented. Just look at these beautiful little hands of yours. I've never seen hands so perfect. I'm your *family*, honey. That means that I'll always want what's best for you. I want to see you and Charlotte become just as important as you deserve to be. You can trust me in a way you'll never be able to trust outsiders."

"I trust Jake."

"Samantha, I think you have a marvelous capacity to daydream. Every little girl should. But there comes a time when you begin to grow up, and you see people and situations the way they really are, not the way you wish they were."

"My daddy's dead," she said, her voice hollow.

"Poor dear, yes, but now I'm here to help you, and Jake isn't. Understand?"

"Well, yes, I guess, but he *would* help me if he could. He would—"

"He's four years older than you are. He's fourteen. That means that he's interested in girls his own age; he's not a child anymore, but you still are. And when you're fourteen, he'll be eighteen. He'll be old enough to vote, and drive a car, and . . . even to get married. But you won't be. You'll still be growing up. It will be years and years before you'll be anything but a little girl to him, and by the time you're grown up, he'll have a lot of girlfriends his own age, and he won't even remember you."

Sam considered that possibility in awful silence. She thought of older boys, high school boys she'd seen, and how they ignored kids her age. A terrible loneliness settled on top of the aching grief in her chest. Daddy was gone; Jake was some distant, manly stranger, Mother cried all the time, and Charlotte was Sam's needy shadow, someone who always looked to Sam for answers.

"I need someone too," Sam blurted out, looking up at her aunt tearfully. "I'm scared. What's going to happen to us? Where will we go? If you'll tell me what to do, I'll take care of Mother and Charlotte. Just tell me what to do!"

Aunt Alexandra hugged her quickly, then leaned back and studied her wistfully. "I can't convince your mother to move to my house. She wants a home of her own. She's got her own way of doing things. She doesn't want to live with me and your uncle Orrin. I can't change her mind."

Sam didn't want to live with Uncle Orrin either. She didn't even want to call Aunt Alexandra's second husband *uncle*. Aunt Alexandra had brought him to visit during their honeymoon, on the way to Hawaii. He talked too sweetly and was too handsome to be real—a heartbreaker—Mother said after they left. He was a state senator, which meant, Daddy had explained, that he was a damned good liar.

Most of all, Sam remembered how he'd stroked her hair as if she were a kitten, but his constant touching had made her feel nervous for reasons she couldn't explain.

But if we lived in Pandora with Aunt Alexandra, I could see Jake all the time. On the heels of that thought came a darker one. *But he'd be too old, and he wouldn't notice me.*

"I don't expect Mom will change her mind," Sam agreed wearily.

"That's why I have another idea," Aunt Alexandra said. "Your mother is going to work for me. I'm going to give her the money to open a health food store in Asheville. Asheville is a wonderful little city in the mountains, and it's only about an hour's drive from Pandora. And I'll help your mother get a house there too."

"You *will*?" Sam gazed at her in awe.

"Yes, of course. So you see, Sammie? Everything's going to be just fine if you'll let me help and love me as much as I love all of you. Can I count on that, Sammie? Can I count on your loyalty if I give you mine?"

Loyalty. It was one of the words Daddy had drilled into her all her life. Loyalty, and honor, and duty. It meant sticking up for your family, God, the United States, and everyone else who depended on you. It meant keeping your promises.

Daddy had died for loyalty. She wouldn't let him down.

Her throat aching, she whispered, "It wouldn't be loyal to trust Jake too?"

Aunt Alexandra shook her head. "A family has to stick together, Sammie. It would hurt my feelings if I helped you so much and then found out that you still like someone who's been mean to me. Are we friends? Do I have your promise that we are?"

Sam cried silently. Misery and defeat lost out to honor. She had to do right by Mother and Charlotte. What would Daddy think of her if she ruined Aunt Alexandra's plans because of Jake?

But we're married, she told herself.

Idiot, you aren't really married. It doesn't count if you're not even old enough to vote.

"I promise," she told her aunt.

What did he have to say to Samantha now? She was still a kid, Jake realized, part of a time he had outgrown. He shaved the fuzzy bristle on his jaw and upper lip every other morning; his voice dipped into a lower register sometimes, like a badly played clarinet, and his body reacted with distracting salutes about a hundred times a day.

Ellie was the only female his own age he could talk to without thinking of her as a girl. She was in a different category from those puzzling creatures at school who hung out around his locker and reduced him to warm, wordless appreciation.

Like bees to honey—girls couldn't resist a man in uniform, even if the uniform was for basketball and the man was six feet two of nothing much more than long legs, arms, and Adam's apple.

Jake was overwhelmed by his sudden appeal to the opposite sex. He hadn't come to terms with it yet. He could track anything on four legs or two. Word had gotten around about his skill, and he went out regularly for the sheriff, finding lost hikers and runaway kids. Grown men treated him with respect.

He could pry gemstones from mountain bedrock, sink foul shots without half trying, and read Shakespeare without falling asleep. He'd taught himself to speak and write Cherokee as well as any elder at Cawatie. He was a good carpenter, a good mechanic, and he played the dulcimer.

But he couldn't talk to girls.

Caught in that unsettled no-man's land, he struggled with alternating bouts of quiet observation and shyness. And so, when he heard that Samantha and her family had moved to Asheville, he wondered how much good his sympathy would do her.

What could he say to a little girl who'd lost her father? What could he promise her about a future that he could sense but couldn't predict, about years of waiting to see what would happen next?

The shop was in one corner of an old brick building with the fading ghost of a Coca-Cola advertisement paint-ed on one side. The sidewalk in front was cracked, and traffic crawled by with an unending stream of exhaust fumes. The building sat on a slope, with an apron of dingy parking lot that curled down the hill along a base-ment foundation with dirty gray plaster crumbling off the concrete blocks.

It shared the street with salvage shops, gas stations, and a Chinese restaurant with a sagging metal awning. But the windows sparkled cleanly in the autumn sun, and petunias boiled over a clay pot by the neatly painted blue door, and a crisp blue and white wooden sign over the entrance welcomed people to the New Times Grocery and Healthy Living Shop.

Jake scowled over the contrasts as Ed Black guided his truck into one of the slanted parking spots on the slope. A thin cigar jutted from Black's lined mouth, threatening to set the tip of his thick hooked nose on fire, and the smoke curling around his head was as white as his mane of long hair. He punched a button on the radio, cutting Loretta Lynn off in mid-song. The pickup truck's cab was roomy and plush, with leather seat upholstery. Black bought a new customized truck every spring. He owned a restaurant on the main reservation.

"I don't mind giving you a ride to the city," Black told Jake, the cigar bouncing as he spoke. "But I ain't got all day to wait while you do your visitin'. Get a move on."

"I won't be long."

Black squinted at the antique store. "Can't imagine it. You sure your folks want some old thing for an anniversary gift?"

Jake hesitated, sorry to have lied, but certain word would have gotten back to Mother and Father if he'd told Ed Black the true reason for his visit to Asheville. "Mother likes old things. Father likes whatever makes Mother happy."

"Huh. Go on, then. Get a move on."

Jake got out of the truck and climbed lopsided con-crete steps to the street, kicking an empty beer can out of his way. "This is Alexandra's idea of a good place," he muttered under his breath.

No surprise. Alexandra probably wanted her sister to fail. Then Mrs. Ryder would have to come running to her for more help. Alexandra would get Mrs. Ryder right where she wanted her, eventually—right under her thumb. Alexandra would get her claws into Samantha and try to brainwash her. Turn her into a miniature Alexandra.

Not Samantha. Not if I can help it, Jake decided grimly.

A tiny wind chime jingled as he opened the shop door and stepped inside. The place was small, with pock-marked linoleum on the floor and a water stain on the whitewashed ceiling. Bins of fruits and vegetables lined one wall; there were shelves of breads and rolls in homemade wrappings, and other shelves crammed with bottles of vitamins. The smell was ripe and sweet and faintly dusty; a fringe of crystals twisted at the end of strings hung from the fixture of a ceiling fan that stirred the heavy air.

Mrs. Ryder rose from a chair behind a wooden counter with a cash register and a rack of incense sticks. Jake stared at her with pity and vague recognition. She was thinner, and a blue vein showed in the white hollow beneath one cheekbone. Her golden hair hung in a limp clump down her back, tied with a blue ribbon. Her shoulders made narrow bumps under a white T-shirt embroidered with a yellow peace symbol at the center. She wiped her palms on baggy blue jeans and watched him with a slightly worried frown. Then her eyes widened. "I know you, don't I?"

"I'm Jake."

She gasped. "Jake Raincrow? Good Lord, you've grown up."

"Fourteen," he answered, feeling ill at ease. "Ma'am."

"How'd you get here? Are you by yourself?"

"Caught a ride with someone. I, uh, heard about Mr. Ryder. Sorry. Sorry, ma'am." *Where's Samantha?* he wanted to ask.

Swallowing hard, Mrs. Ryder looked at Jake. He didn't need his extra intuition to feel her apprehension. After all, the last time she'd seen him, he'd caused trouble and gotten her daughter in the middle of it.

"Jake, you're nearly grown," she said again.

"Yes, ma'am." His hand itched to touch the knitted square in a back pocket of his brown trousers. Samantha's bug blanket. He had stored it in a dresser drawer and hadn't touched it in years. He felt a little embarrassed about their bond, about a little girl who shared a legacy with him that he accepted but could not yet understand. A legacy no one wanted them to share.

Mrs. Ryder looked as uncomfortable as he felt. "How is your mother?"

"Fine."

"She won't come to visit me, will she?"

"No, ma'am."

Mrs. Ryder's shoulders sagged. "Your uncle's death was the last straw. I'm sorry."

Jake struggled for diplomacy, but gave up. "Your sister stole from her, ma'am."

Mrs. Ryder looked away. "The ruby. I'm sure my sister meant well." Jake said nothing. Her tired gaze returned to him with a hint of hard consideration. "You came here to see Samantha."

"Yes, ma'am."

"Why?" Her voice had an edge to it.

"Just seemed like a good idea."

"Most boys your age have nothing to say to a ten-year-old girl."

He felt heat flooding his face. "It's nothing weird, ma'am."

"I don't know what to think."

"You don't have to worry. I'm not a pervert or anything."

Mrs. Ryder leaned against the counter, never taking her eyes off him. "We have a little kitchen in back, and my younger daughter, Charlotte, cooks. She's only six, but she makes the most incredible bread you've ever tasted. I'll give you a loaf of her pumpkin and sesame seed."

Jake didn't know why she was suddenly so chatty. Mrs. Ryder nodded toward a table. "See those things folded on the table? Shawls. Sam made them. We sell at least one a week. She checks in the produce and makes the vendors leave only the best. She haggles with the people who stock the vitamins, and last week she chased a wino off the front step. In short, she keeps us going. I wander around in a daze, and Sam is my rock. She's grown up too fast, but I can't seem to manage without her."

Jake couldn't help himself. "They around—your girls?"

Mrs. Ryder tucked her chin and studied him. "Charlotte's at a birthday party for a girl in her class. Sam is . . . she's downstairs. Dusting. The owner of the building has an antiques shop. He stores some of his pieces in the cellar."

"Mind if I go down and say hello to her, ma'am?"

She rubbed her forehead. She seemed dazed. *She doesn't have Samantha's tight little hold on the world,* Jake thought. "He's just a boy," she said, speaking to herself in an eerie, lost-in-space way. "What harm could it do?" She looked at Jake. "My sister has been very kind to us. I can't have bad feelings between her and myself. I don't understand your . . . *interest* in my daughter."

Jake winced. "I'm not *interested* in her, ma'am. Not the way you mean it! She's just a kid!"

"I don't believe she's ever been 'just a kid.' Any more than I believed you were an ordinary little boy the day you miraculously got her to start talking."

He started to protest, but her sharp glance cut him off. Jake gritted his teeth and glanced around the store, spotting the top of wooden stairs that disappeared down a narrow stairwell in one corner.

"My sister despises your family," Mrs. Ryder continued. "I wish it weren't like that, but it is, and I respect my sister, and, oh"—she thrust out her hands in supplication—"it's the most terrible thing to remember every second I had with my husband and know that there'll never be any more."

Jake didn't know what to say. A ratty-looking hippie couple came into the shop, and he was enormously relieved for the distraction. Mrs. Ryder turned her bedraggled attention to them, and they asked questions about vitamins. He eased over to the table with the brightly colored shawls. Putting one hand on them, he shut his eyes.

Suffocating. She couldn't breathe. He saw a trunk, a dimly lit room with brick walls, and he felt the weighted struggle of her heart.

Jake swung around, his eyes jerking open. "I gotta see Samantha," he called over his shoulder as he strode to the stairs.

"Wait . . . no, oh, *hell*," he heard Mrs. Ryder say. "All right. All right."

Jake was already at the base of the stairwell, hunching his wide shoulders in the confining space. He shoved open a narrow wooden door and stepped into the cellar. The place was crammed with furniture and junk.

Hands out, he wound his way among the clutter, shoving things out of his way. There was barely room to move. He groaned under his breath. He found one old trunk, the leather bindings gray with dry rot, and planted his hands on the faded wood. Empty. He found another, and another. Empty. He touched them, and knew that.

His heart threatened to explode. Behind a hulking armoire he spotted a fourth trunk. The instant he touched it, he knew she was inside. He jerked at the lid, but the clasp had locked. A rusty iron gate with sharp ornamental spikes leaned against the back of the armoire. He hoisted the gate, jammed one of the spikes under the lid, and jerked upward.

The lid popped. Jake flung it open.

Samantha was crumpled inside, her eyelids fluttering, her face blue. She wore overalls and a thin print shirt. A dust rag and a bottle of spray cleanser were crammed beside her folded legs.

She gasped for air as he snatched her up by the straps of her overalls. Limp, she dangled in his arms. "Breathe, kid, breathe," he commanded as he hoisted her over one shoulder. He saw a heavy wooden door at the cellar's far end and strode to it, pounding her back with his free hand.

Jake slammed the door's handle down with his fist, then pushed outside. He sat down heavily on a concrete stoop facing the back parking lot and an empty, trash-strewn lot beyond it.

Samantha coughed raggedly. He pulled her, face-down, across his knees and shook her. "Breathe. You're okay. Breathe."

"I'm breathing," she said with a little groan. "I'm *full* of air. Stop. Stop."

He pulled her upright by the back of her overalls. She slumped beside him, long blond hair falling over her face. Jake pushed her hair back and scrutinized her, clasping her head between his hands.

Her eyes were half shut. The color was already returning to her cheeks. She coughed again, shook her head, and suddenly he was looking into stunned eyes as blue as fine sapphires. "Say something," he ordered. "What's your name?"

"*Jake*."

"No, that's my name. Say *yours*. Let me know you haven't blown a brain fuse."

"Jake," she repeated. "Don't you know who I am?"

"Shit, yes," he answered, too relieved to think about his language. He'd spent a lot of time hunting with the men at Cawatie, and picked up bad habits. "Yes," he corrected himself. "Samantha, what in the hell—what were you doing in that trunk?"

"Cleaning it." Her gaze flew over his face. "The lid fell shut on me. I yelled, but I guess Mom couldn't hear me." Her darting eyes never stopped absorbing him. "You found me. How did you find me? You found me, just like you said you would. But you're so old-looking."

Breathless again, she leaned back. He dropped his hands to his knees and watched her carefully. His thoughts whirled around the memory of her lying limp in the trunk, and the shock of what had almost happened to her wouldn't fade. She, however, seemed to have put it out of her mind. She was totally focused on him.

He finally found his voice and demanded, "Why do you dust trunks?" That question made as much sense as anything, he supposed. What else could he say? *Hey, kid, what did you expect when you married me? That we wouldn't change?* Jesus, this was strange.

"We get a commission if anybody buys something from the cellar. People like clean trunks better."

"Well, don't crawl inside any of them, okay?" He scrubbed a hand through his hair, trying to forget what would have happened to her if he hadn't found her. If he hadn't come to see her, if . . .

It wasn't pure luck. It's part of some plan, the same plan as always. Nothing has changed.

He looked at her with somber affection. Someday the pieces would all fall into place. For now, he accepted the mystery. "Swear that you won't get inside one of those trunks again."

"I swear." She faced forward and rubbed a shaky hand across her mouth. She was small but sturdy, and her hands moved as fluidly as a ballerina's. It was no surprise that she was a wizard at making shawls. "I'm not dumb," she told him, her voice a thready whisper. "I just wanted to see what it feels like to be in a box." Her voice cracked on the last word. "Like my daddy."

The sadness in her left Jake speechless with sympathy. Finally he said, "He's not in a box. Not really. If you listen, he'll talk to you. When you dream about him, and when you remember him so clearly that you can almost see him, you'll know he's close by."

"Mom says things like that. But I think he's just . . . gone."

"Trust me. Everything and everyone has a soul. Their souls, hmmm, stick to the things that are important to them, the things that are part of them. They don't just leave." He struggled without the eloquence he dearly wished he had. It was easy to have faith, but hard to explain. He had long ago closed off his secret inside himself.

She eyed him seriously. "Then what would my daddy's soul stick to?"

"You. Like . . . music, only you can hear."

"I don't hear anything. Mom says I'm *down to earth.*

I don't float around in the clouds. I grab on to real things, and I hold on. Mom's a floater."

Jake pulled the square of knitted yarn from his back pocket and held it out. "So you figured I forgot you."

She inhaled and looked at it, then him. Her face glowed, and she smiled. Then the smile became uncertain, and he watched her expression wind down like a tired clock. Her back stiffened, and her head rose. She stared straight ahead again. "Please don't tell my mom about the trunk. She'll worry about it—she'll be scared that Charlotte might get shut up in one too. But I'll watch out for Charlotte. Don't tell Mom. She'll get upset and go check her astrology charts. I'm trying to take care of her."

Frowning, Jake tucked the small square of yarn into the pocket of his flannel shirt. "But who watches out for you?" he asked gruffly.

"Me. I do." She pointed to herself. He didn't mention that she hadn't done too well at it today. "You can leave now," she added. She inched away from him, her arms sunk between her legs, as if she were trying to become invisible. "I shouldn't even be talking to you."

He stared at her. "Why?"

"You're a Raincrow." She trembled. "Go away. It's important. And I'm not married to you either. People can't get married before they can vote and have babies."

"Well, I don't recall asking you to do either one."

"People have to stick to their own kind."

"Is that what your aunt told you?"

"Aunt Alexandra is my friend. You hate her, so you're *not* my friend."

Jake carefully put a hand on her shoulder. She shivered and tried to move away, but he held just tight enough to stop her. He felt her fear and confusion, her unhappiness. He saw a thin gold chain peeking between the parted hair at the nape of her neck. Jake caught it with his fingertips and pulled. She grabbed at her chest, but the small stone popped up between the open collar of her shirt.

He remembered the mediocre ruby—not worth five

dollars, he knew now—but a proud treasure when he'd found it. And when he'd given it to her.

She wrapped both hands around it and glared at him. Jake nodded. "You can't tell a lie to me. Don't even try."

Her eyebrows shot up. She gazed at him desperately. "Please, please, go away," she said in a small, fractured voice. "And don't ever come back. When I'm old and have plenty of money, I can talk to you. But for now I have to do what's best for Mom and Charlotte."

The truth was suddenly clear to him. She was caught in the middle of her aunt's twisted generosity, and Aunt Alexandra had made certain she wouldn't stray. "Listen to me," he said, moving around in front of her, then dropping to his heels so they looked at each other on the same level. "You take care of your folks. You take care of yourself. But don't ever think you'll get caught in a dark place where I can't find you. That's just the way it's going to be. I'll come to get you, and there won't be a thing your aunt can do about it."

She shut her eyes and clamped her mouth tight. Jake sighed, stood up, and walked to the corner of the delapidated old building. Mr. Black spotted him and blew the truck's horn. Jake looked back at her. "See you later," he said.

She whipped around and called his name. Jake halted. Her hands splayed on the stoop, she leaned forward and looked at him urgently. For a split second she wasn't ten years old. Like watching a special effect in a movie, he saw an older version of herself superimposed on a small girl's image. It shook him. He knew how he'd feel about her then, and the power of it sank in forever. "When?" she asked.

Jake blinked. The image was gone, but not the memory. He cleared his throat and said as casually as he could, "When you're old enough to vote."

It was new, and bright, and clean. Outside the huge plate windows was a wide covered walkway with wooden benches at regular intervals, and dwarf Japanese maples in handsome stone planters. Next door was a dry cleaners run by a young Vietnamese couple who had brought them a bowl of glazed orange slices as a welcoming gift. On the other side was a bookstore, and beyond that, a florist's shop, a hardware store, and a shop that sold sports equipment. The parking lot was clean, and tall lampposts kept it well lit at night. The busy four-lane street brought a steady stream of customers into the shopping center.

No winos on the doorstep. No dank cellar full of dusty antiques. No exposed electrical wires or giant rats speeding across the kitchen floor.

Frannie sat down on one of the cardboard boxes waiting to be unpacked in the new home of New Times Health Food and Vitamins, and cried with relief. "This is incredible."

Sam, who was placing packages of granola bars on brand-new metal shelves along one wall, stopped working and stared at her worriedly. Charlotte, who had been opening boxes under Sam's supervision, gave a little mewl of alarm and ran to their mother. "What's wrong, Mommy? Did you see a roach?"

"Not even one," Frannie answered, wiping her eyes with one hand and riffling Charlotte's short blond hair with the other. "I can't believe it. I just can't believe that a stranger walked into the old place a month ago and said he wanted a health food store in his new shopping center, and now, here we are. I can't believe the rent isn't a penny more than what your aunt was paying for the other place. I think your daddy is watching over us. I think he sent an angel to help us out."

Sam began stacking granola bars again. "Mr. Gunther doesn't look like an angel to me. He looks like a smart man who had an empty shop to rent." She paused, and for Mom's sake, added, "But maybe Daddy whispered in his ear."

Charlotte leaned against Mom and looked at her earnestly. "When is Aunt Alexandra going to visit us? Doesn't she want to see our new place?"

"I think your aunt's in shock, honey."

Sam jammed a package into place with firm resolve. *I think Aunt Alexandra's not real happy about our good luck.* But she didn't say that, because Aunt Alex was still, after all, paying the rent.

Mom's angel walked up to the glass door and pushed it open with a cheerful shove. "Getting settled, ladies?"

Mom jumped up and said hello to Mr. Gunther, who owned the shopping center. They began discussing an ad Mr. Gunther planned to run in the Sunday paper, listing all the shops and their hours. Sam studied their new landlord furtively while she worked. Mr. Gunther was short and big-bellied, and he wore western shirts with little string ties at the collar, and pants that hung so low on his butt that he needed wide western belts with huge belt buckles to keep his pants from falling down around his cowboy boots. He had thin brown hair, and little gray eyes that disappeared when he smiled, and his stubby little hands were covered in rings made of silver, with colorful stones.

He was the strangest-looking businessman Sam could imagine, but very nice. "Now, where did I leave my notes for the ad?" Mom said, frowning.

"I put them in a file folder and marked it Ads," Sam answered. "On the desk."

"Thank you, sweetie. I'll go copy them for Mr. Gunther." When Mom went into the back room, and Charlotte trailed after her, Sam walked over to Mr. Gunther to study his rings.

"You are one solemn little lady," he said, squatting down on his boot heels and grinning at her.

"I'm running a business," she told him. "I intend to make a lot of money. To pay for the rent and the bills and send my sister to college someday. So nobody can tell me what to do."

"My, oh, my. That's a very respectable plan."

"What do those letters on your pinkie ring stand for?"

He held out his right hand. The ring on his little finger was all silver, and the only ornament on it was

three raised letters that looked like a G, a W, and a Y—
but with curlicues attached to them.

"That's the word for *Cherokee*," he explained. "The
Cherokees are the only Indians who have their own
writing. A man named Sequoyah invented it, way back
when."

"Are you an Indian?"

"Yep."

Her mouth dropped open. Mr. Gunther looked even
less like an Indian than Jake did. Jake had black hair, at
least, and a face that was mostly cheekbones, and deep
eyes, and a tan. Mr. Gunther looked like an ordinary
person. "I have an Indian . . . friend. But you don't look
like him," she said.

"My great-grandmother was Cherokee. Besides,
being an Indian is all up here." He pointed to his
head. "And here." He tapped a ringed finger on the
center of his chest.

"You think you're an Indian, so you are one?"

He laughed and nodded his head. "Something like
that." He cupped his hands, palms up, as if he were holding a ball in them. "If you're an Indian, here's the world.
Every being has a place, and everyone shares. The people, and the mountains, and the trees, and the animals."
He moved his hands apart. "If you're not an Indian, the
people are on one side, by themselves. They've forgotten
how to share. They don't even share with each other."

"So because you're an Indian, you're sharing your
shopping center with us?"

He tapped the tip of her nose the way he'd tapped
his chest. "I'm a bonafide rockhound, and when I see fine
quality stones stuck in the mud, I can't help but put them
where I can watch them shine."

The threads of a question had been scattered in her
mind. Now they came together in a brilliant pattern. "My
friend knows all about stones." Her voice was a secretive
whisper. "He knows where to find them. He gave me
one." She pulled her necklace from inside her sweater
and let the ruby rock dangle between her fingers. "I
bet he could show you where to find rocks. I bet you've

heard of him, since he's an Indian. His name's Jake. Jake Raincrow."

When Mr. Gunther pursed his mouth but said nothing, and just smiled at her, she exhaled slowly.

Mother came back then, waving a piece of notepaper at Mr. Gunther, and he winked at Sam as he stood up.

Sam walked to their beautiful big windows, and stood with her ruby clasped in one hand. Jake had sent Mr. Gunther to help them. Mom was happier now. Charlotte wouldn't be squealing and jumping out of a rat's way anymore. And as for Aunt Alexandra, well, Sam hadn't asked Jake to help them, had she? She hadn't broken any promise to her aunt.

And when she was old enough, and had enough money to take care of her family, so that she owed Aunt Alexandra nothing, she would find Jake, and tell him what she felt right now. *I love you, Jake Raincrow.*

Chapter

Ten

"Pomp and Circumstance" collapsed into chaos the moment the last of the honor graduates—which was Ellie—filed out of the school auditorium into a brightly lit lobby hung with banners celebrating the Class of '79.

The majority of the senior class was still pacing up the center isle, held in check by protocol and the watchful eyes of a thousand family members and friends. As her classmates turned to her with shocked stares and questions, Ellie wished Jake—who was bringing up the rear of the class procession by reason of a respectable but ordinary grade point average as well as a lack of alphabetical priority—would hurry up.

Courage was a lonely thing.

The other honor graduates bombarded her so quickly that she could only stand in grim silence, listening.

148

"What happened to the valedictorian speech you practiced in speech class last week?"

"Are you *crazy*? Why'd you say all that stuff about the new people turning Pandora into their own private playground and turning everyone else into beggars? *My* parents aren't 'smug and condescending.' When my dad was having our tennis court built, he let the whole crew of hillbillies swim in our pool during their lunch break."

"God, Ellie, you *made fun of* Senator Lomax's commencement speech! I saw Mrs. Lomax in the audience, and she looked like she wanted to *kill* you!"

"What was so awful about what the senator said? He was only pointing out that progress is a good thing."

"My mom says we wouldn't have this new high school if he and Mrs. Lomax hadn't pushed the county to build it."

Ellie removed her cap and took a deep breath. "Senator Lomax is a bullshit artist who married my uncle's money to get ahead."

The rest of the class was crowding through the auditorium doors and crowding the lobby, turning it into a black and white flower garden of robes and caps, of stares and whispers directed at her. Ellie looked around for Jake, but couldn't see him.

She made another pivot and came face-to-face with Tim's furious blue eyes. His face was as red as his short-cropped hair, and he had Uncle William's blunt, broad features but none of his gentleness. Her cousin was junior class president, and he wore a sash over his dark blue suit, denoting usher status for the ceremonies. He was tall, thick-necked, with bulky arms and an oversize chest from weightlifting—a menace on the football field, where, over the years, his timidity had evolved into arrogance.

"You stupid cow," he said. "You didn't make a fool of my stepfather. You made a complete, fucking idiot of yourself and your whole family."

Ellie held his gaze without blinking. "What I said is true. I don't call it progress when a golf-course developer flattens the top of an Indian burial mound and turns it into the eighteenth green. Or when Pandora Lake is lined with so many boathouses, the wild ducks barely have a place to nest. Or when the chamber of commerce moves its annual dance to the country club and charges fifty bucks for a ticket. And what Orrin Lomax said about 'wonderful new opportunities' means only that people who drive Mercedes and own quarter-million-dollar homes have the opportunity to do exactly as they damn well please. If that upsets you and him and your cold-blooded mama, too bad."

"My mother turned this backwoods town into something special, and if you had half the sense God gave a rock, you'd be glad."

"Stop using the macho juice," she said softly. "Steroids are rotting your brain."

"I don't take drugs."

She shouldn't say it. She had no proof. But, like Jake, she knew a lot of secrets about their classmates that couldn't be proven. And the heady events of the night were combining with adult freedom to push her over the bounds of caution. She leaned toward him and whispered, "Yes, you do. You use steroids, and amphetamines, and sometimes after a game you're so wired you drive up to Razorback Bald and drink a case of beer to calm down. And when you're like that, you give your girlfriends a couple of slaps if they get on your nerves." Ellie stepped back. "Now, shut your face and go pick on someone who cares what you think."

He grabbed her forearm with one brawny, blue-veined hand. Other students latched on to his massive shoulders, yelling at him to let her go. Ellie jerked back, but he dug his fingers in until she thought they must be touching bone, and she felt his sweaty fear. "I'll break your fucking arm if you tell lies about me," he said.

Suddenly Jake's broad hand clamped down on Tim's wrist. Ellie looked up to find her typically mild-mannered brother's eyes infused with a violent gleam. He'd discarded his mortarboard somewhere along the way, and coppery-black hair fell over his forehead. Years spent outdoors in the mountain weather had given him squint lines and darkened his skin; his eyes were cold green emeralds in that face.

Without a word he twisted Tim's wrist. Tim gave a guttural yelp of pain and let go of her, then turned furiously toward Jake. Humiliation flashed through his eyes, and he glanced around at the eager, horrified audience. "You want to get into it?" Tim asked loudly. "You want me to beat the hell out of you?"

"No," Jake said, drawling the word as if giving it real thought. "But if you put a hand on my sister again, I guess I'll have to risk it."

"You're nothing. You're less than nothing. You're not even going to college. Mother says you'll end up running some crappy rockhound shop and selling cheap garnets to tourists."

"Could be."

Jake's lack of argument seemed only to outrage their cousin more. He hunched his thick shoulders and stepped closer, his jaw thrust out. "Everybody knows you don't have anything to do with girls. I think you're a fucking *queer*."

"I doubt it."

"That's why my mother has kept her nieces away from you. Or maybe you just like *little* girls."

Ellie gasped. Jake stared at Tim without a shred of outward reaction, but his arm brushed hers and she felt the slow, invisible ticking of his patience. Leave it to Jake, she thought with awe, to sort through insults as if they were meaningless pebbles, separating the gems from the plain rocks. "You listen to your mother too much," Jake told him. "She's the one you're trying to prove something to. Not me."

Tim shoved him. Jake took a step back, tall and lean, moving with the practiced grace of someone who'd negotiated sheer mountain cliffs since he and Ellie were old enough for Granny to take them into the high ridges with her. "You probably shouldn't do that again," he warned, his voice never rising.

"Coward," Tim said, and pushed him again. Jake's right arm moved in a blur of motion. The next thing Ellie knew, Tim was sprawling on the floor, blood pouring from his nose.

Parents and other relatives were, by then, pressing into the lobby to find their graduates. There were general shouts of alarm, and people scurrying about, and Mother and Father were suddenly beside them, Father edging Jake, Ellie, and Mother behind him with an outstretched arm. For once, Mother was too shocked to do more than stay behind him, one hand wound in Ellie's robe, the other in Jake's. Father commanded the barricade, but Mother ruled the troops.

Tim sat on the floor, both hands pressed to his ashen face while blood dripped slowly onto his suit.

"Get up." Aunt Alexandra pushed her way through the crowd and stood over him, her hands clenched. Tim's eyes filled with shame. The strained dignity of the dispossessed overtook him, and he clambered to his feet, towering over her with wounded composure that reduced him to scrubbing one hand over his bloody face and wincing.

Alexandra gestured curtly at Father. "Don't shield your flock like some Old Testament patriarch. If your black sheep wants to butt heads, get out of the way. Tim can take care of himself."

"I didn't raise my children to be professional boxers," Father said. "And it seems to me that Tim has already gone down for the count."

"Heard you broke your cousin's nose last night," Joe Gunther said cheerfully, standing in the front yard beside the open door of a car, a large wrapped package in his hands.

Jake walked out to meet him, draping a threadbare towel over one damp shoulder, and trailed by an enormous, half-grown bloodhound still soggy and morose from the flea dip to which Jake had just subjected him. Jake had named him *Bo*—short for bow-legged, not *Beauregard*. Bo wasn't much of a tracking dog, but he was a great actor. He looked serious about the work, and people assumed he was the reason for Jake's success. Jake's reputation as a tracker had spread all over the mountains.

Jake shook Mr. Gunther's hand. "What happened between Tim and me, well, I guess you could call it a philosophical dispute."

Mr. Gunther grinned at him. "Still waters run deep. Never figured you for a man with a temper. Heard Ellie rattled a few cages with her speech too."

Jake shrugged and politely avoided staring at the package, which was wrapped in bright floral tissue paper and topped with a blue bow. Not Joe Gunther's style. Mr. Gunther liked to decorate himself, not packages. Every finger gleamed with a gemstone—most of them found, over the past four years, under Jake's guidance. And in return, Mr. Gunther had looked out for Samantha and her family, and filled Jake in on the peaceful progress of their lives.

"So," Mr. Gunther said. "Where's the rest of your cantankerous crew?"

"Ellie's with Father, working at his office. Mother left for Florida this morning, with Katie Jones. Mrs. Jones works the craft show circuit, selling baskets. She talked Mother into going with her. Mother took some of her watercolors. She's sold a lot of them around here, so she's thinking of branching out."

"How's it feel to be an educated and free man?" Mr. Gunther asked.

"Good. I was never much for sitting in classrooms. Got more on my own, reading whatever I wanted, making up my own mind."

"Wouldn't hurt you to go to college, you know. You could study geology, or something."

Jake waved a hand at the rounded blue-green mountains looming around the valley like sentinels. "I've got teachers."

"Money in the bank, the way you dig into them."

"They share. I don't take too much. We have an understanding."

"But still, college—"

"That's for Ellie. She got a scholarship to Duke, but

I'll help the folks pay for any extras she needs. Besides, if I left, who'd help pay the god-awful taxes on the Cove?"

"So you're stuck to this valley like white on rice."

"Always have been. It's where I belong. I like it."

"You *love* it," Mr. Gunther corrected him. When Jake said nothing, he changed the subject diplomatically. "So what are your plans?"

"Dig a few rocks, do a little tracking for the Sheriff's Department"—Jake looked at the bloodhound, who had flopped on a patch of grass at the edge of Mother's iris beds, dejected—"if Bo doesn't desert me for giving him flea baths every week. As many weeks as I've been dunking him, you'd think he'd get over it."

"A man can depend on the goodwill of a dog." Mr. Gunther studied Bo, who was 100 pounds of loose red hide. "Especially one so ugly no one else would have him." Mr. Gunther cleared his throat. "But there comes a time when a man ought to ask himself if he needs more company. Something with two legs instead of four. Something that smells better than Bo and wears lacy underwear."

"Ellie tied one of her bras on Bo's head once, and he didn't seem to mind."

"Come on, boy, stop tiptoeing around the point. You're a good-looking rooster. I'd bet the bank that plenty of sassy gals have been after you. Words out that you've never, well, you know. Never tossed your bait in the ol' fishing hole, if you get my drift."

Jake folded his arms over his chest and said drolly, "Just waiting for the right fish to come along. Nothing's wrong with my rod and reel."

Mr. Gunther threw his head back and laughed. "Well, I can't fault your willpower." The pleasantries done, he held out the package. "Your little fish isn't so little anymore. She sent you a graduation present."

Samantha. A thread of excitement and curiosity raced through him. He remembered her as the ten-year-old he'd seen four years ago, but his mind's eye had never lost the older image of her—an image that was closing in on reality now.

He took the present with a quick nod of thanks but made no move to open it. Self-protective privacy was ingrained in him—he guarded what he knew, what he felt, and what he shared with other people. Mr. Gunther waited in vain for a minute while Jake pretended to examine the absurdly delicate blue bow. He recalled the silent blond toddler who tied bows even on a cow's tail, and how she'd looked at him as if she'd like to decorate him too.

"Well," Mr. Gunther said finally, "I can see I'm about as welcome as a mosquito. Are we still set for the dig on Traders Mountain next week?"

"Sure thing."

Mr. Gunther set one expensive, hand-tooled boot inside his car, posed in the door frame like a pot-gutted Roy Rogers, and studied him thoughtfully. "You really think some of DeSoto's Spaniards mined emeralds up there?"

Poker-faced, Jake nodded. "That's what the legends say. Mrs. Big Stick told me her great-grandfather talked about it. That before the blight killed 'em he found three-hundred-year-old chestnuts growing at the mouth of what looked to be a collapsed mine shaft."

"Funny," Mr. Gunther said, "how most legends about old mines end up being fairy tales, but you got a knack for knowing which ones aren't."

"Just lucky."

"You know, it could be a sixth sense—the way you find things, and people."

"Nah. I read. I study. It's all logic."

"Okay. Wouldn't want people to think you've got second sight or some such thing. Folks might show up on your doorstep with their tea leaves and tarot cards and ouija boards. Make you feel like a sideshow freak. You'd have to get you a turban and a crystal ball."

"They'd be disappointed."

"Frannie Ryder loves all that silliness. You should see the pack of half-assed palm readers and fortune tellers and what-not who hang out at her store. She collects more nuts than a squirrel. Poor Miss Sammie watches 'em like they might steal the cash drawer." Mr. Gunther eased his burly body into the car and slammed the door. Draping one arm out the open window, he shook his head and sighed. "You know how some preachers' kids get force-fed so much religion that they won't set foot inside a church after they're grown? Well, I suspect your little fish has put up with such a load of flimsy mumbo-jumbo, she'll ask her own shadow for ID before she'll believe it's real."

He drove off up the driveway, waving his hand. Jake stood morosely in the yard, pondering what Mr. Gunther had said. He frowned at the soft, bulky package, moved leadenly to the porch, and sat on the steps with it balanced on his knees. Slowly he unwrapped it, pushing the colorful paper aside with careful fingers.

A quilt. A quilt in dark brown and gold, with a zigzag pattern so distinctly familiar he recognized it as a Cherokee design. He drew his blunt, callused fingertips along stitches so tiny and perfect, he wondered how human hands could have made them. Exhaling softly, awed by the work she'd done on a gift for him, he spread his hands on the soft material and absorbed her warmth. She had made him a quilt to sleep under, to dream under, and she had no way of knowing that wrapping himself in it every night would be like wrapping himself in her life, like sleeping with her.

But she was only fourteen. Chivalry forbade him to think about her that way yet—or at least to try not to think about her that way. He laid the quilt beside him on the porch floor but couldn't resist smoothing a hand over it one more time.

But that last impulsive gesture opened a floodgate, and he jerked the quilt up with both hands, staring blankly at it as her despair washed over him.

"It's all gone. All of our savings. And it's my fault." Mom dropped to the sofa in their living room and stared blindly out a window hung with curtains Sam had made herself, to save money. Just as she'd made most of their clothes, and worked at the store every afternoon and weekends, and done without everything she could for the past four years.

Sam stood numbly in the center of the small room, feeling the dull fury of betrayal, her gaze seguing from one piece of carefully tended flea-market furniture to the next. She, not Mom, had struggled to get them out of Aunt Alex's pocketbook all this time, and even though she hadn't been able to change the fact that Aunt Alex had made the down payment on this small tract house for them, Sam had taken pride in their ability, finally, to take over the mortgage notes.

They'd had ten thousand dollars in the bank. Sam had begun to feel independent and secure, to really believe they'd be free of Aunt Alex's control in a few years, with money for Charlotte to attend college and Mom to pay bills without worrying—free, when Sam turned eighteen, to do whatever she wanted. Free to see Jake.

Charlotte huddled on the couch next to Mom, small and fidgety and infinitely trusting. "Mr. Drury is *gone*?" Charlotte asked sadly. "Why would he do that? He was supposed to start a health food magazine with our money."

"He's a con artist," Sam explained, her stomach twisting. "He talked Mom into lending him money, and then he disappeared. He's not coming back."

"I was so sure of him," Mom said, covering her face with one pale, thin hand. "I studied his charts, I saw good lines in his palms, I—"

"You saw stars and got a line all right," Sam said. Mom's wounded expression made her bite her lip. Her mother was an eternal optimist, and lonely, and deeply, irrevocably unable to tell the difference between sense and nonsense. "I did what my instincts told me to do," Mom said wearily. "You have to trust your faith sometimes, Sammie."

"No, you don't. You have to trust cold, hard facts. And the fact is, Malcolm Drury looked a little like Daddy and talked like a dreamer, and you didn't listen to me when I pointed out that he couldn't take Daddy's place."

"Sammie, don't," Mom said, tears sliding down her face. "I'm sorry. Don't hate me."

Sam couldn't help crying too. "I don't hate you. I hate that you asked Aunt Alex for money again."

"Sammie, your aunt doesn't mind. She loves us. She *wants* to help. It's just a loan. I'll pay her back."

"We'll *always* be paying her back," Sam answered.

Alone at the store the next afternoon, Sam's energy dissolved. Business was slow; no one had come in for an hour. She wandered to the storage room in back and sank onto a rump-sprung couch in front of a narrow window that let in a hot, murky beam of summer sunshine. She kicked off her sandals and sank on the hard vinyl cushion with her legs folded under her and her arms crossed on the couch's back. The vinyl stuck to her bare legs beneath her khaki shorts; the sunlight was fiery on her arms and hands. She tugged uselessly at the short sleeves of her thin plaid shirt. Mom's odd theories even included sunshine. Pollution was eating up the atmosphere, she said, and getting a tan was no better than sticking your head in a microwave oven.

Mom had greased Sam and Charlotte with antitanning lotions and shaded them with umbrellas for so many years that Sam had given up on ever seeing her skin turn a lovely, sunbaked brown. Her hands, when she bothered to notice them, looked as if they'd been molded from fine porcelain, and the perfect oval nails grew so fast, she had to pare them down with clippers every over day. She supposed Mom's insistent regimen of vitamin and mineral supplements was responsible for that.

Resting her chin on her arms, Sam gazed dully at large hills covered in dingy office buildings and busy streets. On the edges of the city the mountains were cool and dark green, and a sweet-smelling bluish mist crept over them in the evenings. But here everything looked gray, even the air.

She wanted their savings back. She wanted to be so much older, and she wanted to believe that a boy she had talked to only three times in her life, a boy whose family her aunt hated, had not considered her graduation present an unwelcome reminder of silly promises he'd made to a child.

"Samantha?" The voice was very deep and rich. She lifted her head but couldn't make herself turn on the couch for fear she'd only imagined it and would look like a fool if she searched for the source. She'd been so engrossed in thought, she hadn't heard the jingle of the door chimes when someone entered the shop. "Samantha?" he said again, and this time she knew he was real. Somehow, he always found her when she needed his help. That wondrous mystery was the one strong, abiding pattern in the fabric of her life.

Her heart in her throat, she turned around slowly.

Jake stood in the doorway.

She wasn't a child anymore—had never really felt like a child before—but now her body had caught up with the plan. A startling new awareness of being female complicated what had been simple devotion. Mother would say she'd discovered the yin and yang of sensuality.

Sam called it biology. And suddenly it was the most powerful force in the world.

He walked toward her slowly, gauging her with intense green eyes hooded with black lashes, as if he had to catalogue her details as thoroughly as she studied his. Sam didn't know where to look first. She saw him through a fog of rediscovery colored with disturbing shyness. He was much taller than she remembered, an inverted pyramid of wide shoulders, thick arms, and lean hips set on long legs. His hair was a soft reddish-black, the color of a hot charcoal ember, and it swept back from his high forehead in a glossy, rebellious mane that stopped just short of his collar. He wore a thin blue shirt with the sleeves rolled up, and thin suspenders with brilliantly colored beadwork on them, and faded jeans just loose enough to make the suspenders look necessary. The jeans were threadbare around the bottoms, which sank into the folds of leather boots that made no sound on the hard floor.

He eased down carefully on the couch, an arm's length away, resting big, rough-looking hands on his knees and regarding her with an unwavering gaze that took her breath away. Dazed, she fumbled inside the collar of her shirt and slowly drew out the necklace. When he saw the thin, tarnished chain with the homely gemstone dangling from it, his face relaxed. He raised one hand toward her, stopped with his outstretched fingers posed near hers, and waited. Sam hesitantly touched her fingertips to his; the contact burned away the awkward moment, and she slid her hand into his. Immediately their hands merged in an intimate grip, his thick fingers weaving gently between her slender ones. She clutched his hand atop the cushion between them.

"You did that the first time I saw you," he said, his voice low.

"What?" Her own voice was a whisper.

"Held my hand like you'd never let go."

They were silent, every second hinged on the next heartbeat and the warm clasp of their hands. "I don't remember that," she admitted sadly. "Did you mind?"

"No. I'm glad you haven't changed."

"I've been called stubborn more than once."

"That's all right. People confuse faith with stubbornness."

She couldn't help herself. She lunged to her knees on the couch, flung her free arm around his neck, and hugged him, turning her face away but pressing her cheek against the warm, smooth side of his neck. Just as quickly she sank back on the couch, but continued to hold his hand tightly. Either he or she—or both of them—was trembling. "Hello again," he said gruffly. "I heard you had some trouble."

She stared at him, amazed. "Where did you hear?"

"News gets around. I keep an ear tuned."

"You must have long-range antennae."

"You could call it that. Tell me what happened."

Before she knew it, she was pouring out the details of

Mom's infatuation with Malcolm Drury, who had invaded their lives with glorious ideas about starting a magazine about herbal medicine, then bolted as soon as Mom invested their savings in his plans. Sam shivered. "We had money in the bank. We were doing fine. We didn't need Aunt Alex's help anymore. But the money's gone. Mom made a mistake with it. I couldn't stop her."

"I know." He said that quickly, then looked as if he wished he hadn't. Sam peered at him, searching her mind for explanations. Of course. She said very carefully, "I bet I know who told you. I bet his name's Joe Gunther. Because you asked him to help us, and he always has."

He seemed, oddly enough, relieved. "You must be psychic."

She flinched. "Please, don't even joke. I live with that kind of junk. Mom's happy to believe in it, but as far as I'm concerned, every self-made guru on the planet ought to be rounded up and shipped to a desert island, where they could con only each other out of money."

A strange, somehow lonely expression crossed his face. "You don't trust anyone. You're afraid to. Even me."

It was as if he'd seen right through her, to the tired, frightened core. Sam bit her lip and stared out the window. She wanted so badly for him to stay. She had a thousand questions to ask about himself. His hand pressed tighter around hers, a disastrous, coaxing gentleness that frightened her because it was so irresistible. Nothing and no one but he had ever made her feel that way. The shock of seeing him again segued into alarm over the consequences. "I decided a long time ago to take care of my mother and my sister. Aunt Alex means a lot to them. Maybe she's the only one I can trust."

"You hate being afraid of her," he said.

That bombshell made her instantly defensive. She couldn't deny it, but how did he *know*? "And you're not?" she asked coolly.

"I'm afraid of what she can do to other people in retaliation. I'm afraid of what she can do to *you*."

A soft *oh* of pleasure melted through her, but couldn't erase the anxiety. "Then why did you come here if you know it might only cause trouble?" He looked away, his eyes shuttered, a muscle working in his jaw. "I'll leave soon. For your sake."

"I—Jake—I don't want you to—I wish . . ." Her voice trailed off miserably, and her shoulders slumped. "You must have a lot of girls," she said finally. "And a car. And . . . freedom." She glanced at him. "You can even vote now."

"You're wrong about the girls."

"Hah. The way you look? You'd be crazy not to—" She halted, wishing she could pull those words back.

"Must be crazy then."

"I could pass for eighteen. I *feel* that old."

"There's no hurry."

"Oh, yes, there is." She thought to herself, *If I were eighteen, I'd go anywhere you asked me to go. I'd stay with you. I'd learn all about you, and I'd do every shocking thing I've thought about since I first read the sexy novels Mom keeps hidden under her bed.*

Jake said something under his breath. It sounded like *Down, boy,* but was spoken in such a hoarse whisper, she couldn't be certain. "What?" she asked.

"Nothing. If you were eighteen—"

"If I were eighteen, I'd—" She stopped. Daydreams faded into reality. "I'd still have to think about Mom and Charlotte. Because Aunt Alex would still control their lives." She leaned toward him urgently. "Can't your folks make peace with her? I *know* she caused hard feelings between your mother and your uncle. I know she feuded with your mother over that—whatever you call it—the ruby your mother was supposed to inherit. But your uncle died a long time ago, and a ruby's just a rock."

A flash freeze couldn't have changed the atmosphere more. His expression hardened. She shivered at the cold, clear glitter in his eyes. "She's a thief," he said through gritted teeth. His voice was soft, but vibrated with some emotion Sam couldn't analyze. Warning, or contempt. Or some sinister brand of respect. "And she's dangerous."

"A thief? *Dangerous?* I can think of a dozen ugly ways to describe her—narrow-minded, and snobbish, and . . .

even Mom admits she's spoiled rotten—*but you make her sound like a monster*. She's not. She has a conscience. It may be a shriveled little thing, but it exists. And she loves her family in her own sneaky way."

He leaned toward her. "You don't know her the way I do."

"Then tell me what you know."

He started to say something, then stopped. Some inner struggle strained his expression; he looked as if he were fighting a hopeless battle. There were such angry, tragic shadows in his eyes that she made a small sound of distress. He sighed heavily and looked defeated. "She made my uncle miserable. She separated him from his family, and she used his money and name to turn our town into a place where money is the only thing that's important. It started when she married Uncle William and took the ruby that should have been my mother's. It's not just a rock."

"It's a very valuable rock," Sam told him. "Valuable enough to make people fight over it. But she didn't keep it—she buried it with your uncle. She made a sacrifice. Can't you? Can't you just forget about it?"

"No. Because I don't think she sacrificed a damn thing. I think she lied about burying it."

Sam stared at him. Her heart sank. "What would have been the point? She couldn't sell a ruby like that without someone finding out; she couldn't wear it."

"Common sense doesn't always tell you what you want to know."

"But it's better than wild ideas you can't prove." She didn't want to argue with him; Aunt Alex stood in their way too much already. "I don't want you to be right about her," she said wearily. "Because you'll always think about that when you look at me."

"*No*."

A terrible new thought occurred to her. *Maybe he sees me as a way to get back at her. Because he knows she doesn't want anything to do with his family. Maybe he's using me to cause trouble.* "Stop it," he said. She stared at him. He was breathing roughly. He searched her eyes, and she couldn't look away. Then he said, very slowly, "I could have left you and your mother and sister to go bankrupt in that crummy shop in Asheville. I could have left you to smother in that antique trunk."

How had he guessed her fears? And was he just saying what she wanted to hear now? She eased away from him, and suddenly her hand felt trapped, not safe, inside his. She tried to pull it loose. He wouldn't let her. "Don't be afraid of me," he said quickly. "That's what she wants. You'll belong to her. She'll use you. You're worth more to her than Uncle William was—worth more than Tim is too. Because she thinks you can be just like her, and she's proud of that."

"Stop talking about her as if she's got horns and a forked tail!"

"I wish she did. You couldn't be fooled, then."

"I don't believe anything I can't see, or touch, or *prove*, or—"

"You have to. *You have to believe*." He almost yelled the words. Sam jerked her hand out of his and stood. "You'd better go," she told him. "Unless you *want* her to find out you came here, to make her mad."

He rose as fast as she had, towering over her, a head taller than she. There was a kind of self-aware control about him that confused her even more, because if he didn't care about her, he could have easily looked intimidating. "Here's another thing you have to believe," he said. "I don't want to draw her attention. Someday I'll have to, but people will get hurt if I'm not careful. So I'll keep waiting. You may be the only one who can stop her. I don't know. But I know that I'd rather die than see you get hurt by her."

Sam cried out and refused to look at him. "I couldn't even stop a crummy con man from swindling my mother."

"Do you have a picture of him? I . . . do some tracking work for the Sheriff's Department in Pandora. I know some detectives."

"We already gave a picture of the jerk to the police here."

"Well, give me one, and I'll pass it along to the people I know. It couldn't hurt."

Bewildered and depressed, she went to a small desk in one corner and fumbled in the drawer. "Here. I had a bunch of copies made. It's a snapshot Mom took of him the day they went to some kind of numerology workshop." She held it out reluctantly, not wanting to touch his hand again. "It's the original. I guess—I hope—Mom won't care if I get rid of it." Jake took the photo slowly, but his fingers brushed hers. "My help," he said softly, "doesn't come with strings attached. I promise."

"You'd better go." She wavered, stared firmly at him, her heart pounding. She couldn't stop the rush of emotion swelling in her throat, then blurted out, "I hope you liked the quilt. Some of the piecework is silk. I thought about the *silk* in star rubies, so I . . . well, it'll last practically forever, it's nearly impossible to tear silk, but try not to spill anything on it, because it will stain. And only dry-clean it—"

"Samantha, I love . . . it. I do . . . love it."

She turned her back, her shoulders hunched in misery and rejection. She heard the faintest whisper of his soft boots on the floor as he left the shop. The chimes jingled with careless charm as the door closed behind him. "I love you too," she whispered.

"Yesterday I drove up to Asheville to see Samantha Ryder."

Wiping his grease-stained hands on an oily rag, Jake told his father in the shadowy privacy of the barn. Blossom had long since gone to bovine heaven; they bought their milk at the gleaming new supermarket on the Highlands road, a few miles outside Pandora. A few years earlier they'd given Grady to a family on the main reservation, where he was teaching a younger generation to respect ill-tempered ponies.

The barn had become a toolshed and garage. Father, sweating in the muggy heat, peered at him over a pair of bifocals and stopped working, one honey-colored hand holding a wrench as delicately as a scalpel. Cars or people—Father liked to fix both. Very little shocked Father. He simply gazed at Jake from under the open hood of the big old Cadillac Jake had bought that spring for five hundred dollars and a promise to tow it out of the owner's yard.

Jake could afford better, but he liked the personality of the big old convertible. It had a solid character that rust spots, sun-faded upholstery, and a badly patched vinyl top couldn't diminish. Father began fiddling with the carburetor again, black brows flattened in a thoughtful frown. "Why?"

"Her mother lost their savings to some guy with a smooth mouth and a gimmick to sell. I had to go."

"Bad timing," Father said, and he didn't mean the Caddy's engine. "Don't mention it to your mother. Not right on the heels of your sister's hell-raising graduation speech and your cousin's broken nose."

"I thought Mother was proud of all that."

"She is. But it stirred up her battle juices." He looked at Jake somberly. "I've kept your secret from her for a while."

"Secret?"

"I treated Joe Gunther for a sprained back last year. He gets talkative after he's swallowed a couple of muscle relaxers. Told me he's been baby-sitting the Ryders for you in return for you taking him to your best gem digs."

"I don't like doing things behind your and Mother's backs, but I had to. It's not disrespect."

"Hmmm." Father popped the carburetor filter out and probed it with the same studious attention he gave to swollen tonsils and broken toes. "A doctor gets a firsthand look at the problems young people get themselves into," Father said casually, continuing to examine the filter. "Drugs, liquor, fistfights, stupid car accidents, idiotic pranks. Young men who show up in my office needing a shot of penicillin for the same reason they needed it a half dozen times before. Girls no older than your sister claiming they've got a 'friend' who needs to know where to go for an abortion."

He paused, turning the filter in his hands as if it commanded all his attention. "And I say to myself, *I'm the luckiest man in the world.*" He raised his head and looked at Jake. "Because somehow your Mother and I were blessed with a pair of Tibetan monks."

"*Monks?*" Jake almost smiled.

"Good-hearted, with good judgment. Smart. Responsible. I keep wondering when you're going to do something to turn our hair white."

"Well, Ellie has always been single-minded about getting a scholarship to medical school, and that didn't leave much time for raising hell." Jake added silently, *And she keeps away from boys because she gets mental postcards from their sweaty little one-track intentions.* Jake had pointed out to her that, in his experience, rampaging females were just as determined, but she stuck to her superior attitude.

"And you?" Father asked. "What single-minded vows have you taken?"

"I'm not interested in bad habits that waste my time."

"I take it Samantha Ryder has never fallen into that category."

"No."

"You ever consider the fact that she's a good bit younger than you? I hate to put it this way, son, but there are laws—"

"They're not half as strong as the laws I judge myself by." Jake was torn between defending his dignity and guarding the private ways that defined everything he felt about her. "She's worth waiting for. I'll wait."

Father exhaled a long, slow breath. "All right." He regarded Jake with a grim smile. "I'll spend the next few years thinking of ways to prepare your mother for the day when you bring Alexandra's niece home. Thank you for the warning."

"Mother won't turn her back on Samantha. That wouldn't be fair."

"No, but your mother's sense of fair play has been strained to its limits a few times too many." Father held up the carburetor. They had temporarily exhausted all manly capacity for deep conversation, and Jake knew it. Jake bent over the engine, and they went back to work. But he had to say one last thing. "I'm going to the Bahamas to look for the guy who stole Mrs. Ryder's money."

Chapter Eleven

Malcolm Drury woke up slowly in the luxurious heat of the tropical sun. He was stretched out on a lounge chair by the faux-rock waterfall of a hotel pool, with a view of the ocean in front of him and a melted rum punch on the table beside him. He lazily scratched a sunburned streak of skin along the edge of his low-riding bikini trunks and considered his good fortune. Then he draped his hand over the lounge's side to fumble for the folded towel that hid his watch and wallet.

His hand collided with another. He jerked upright and peered through expensive sunglasses directly into the steely green eyes of a young man of such considerable height and lanky, muscled build that he was overwhelming even though he had squatted beside Malcolm's lounge, calmly cradling Malcolm's possessions in thick, sinewy hands. In a place dominated by relaxed tourists in

169

bright resort clothing, the intense, blue-jeaned, T-shirted intruder looked entirely out of place, and entirely dangerous.

Malcolm had spent all his adult life profiting from an innate sense for preying on the gullible and avoiding everyone else.

What he saw in the deadly gaze aimed back at him made his skin crawl. "Hey, get the hell away from my stuff," Malcolm ordered, his voice cracking.

"You've spent the money already," the threatening stranger said in a low, thick drawl. "What you stole and what *she* paid you too."

"What the hell are you talking about?" Malcolm snatched at his belongings, and the stranger dropped them on the pink tile beneath the lounge. "Alexandra Lomax," the unwelcome visitor said.

Malcolm's breath rattled in his throat. He lied automatically and well. "I never heard that name before. What do you want?"

"She hired you to wipe out the Ryders' bankroll, and you did it." The stranger stood, leaned over, plucked Malcolm's designer sunglasses between long, thick fingers, then closed his fist around them. The plastic bridge gave a nerve-racking *crack* when it broke. The stranger dropped the mangled sunglasses on Malcolm's oiled stomach. "I thought I could get some of the money back. Too bad."

Without another word he walked away. Malcolm Drury sat in petrified silence, afraid to move or speak, for a long time. When he could catch his breath, he cursed raggedly, grabbed his belongings, and jumped up, scanning the crowded pool patio. The intruder was gone.

Malcolm checked out of the hotel minutes later, booked a room on a cruise ship leaving for the States within the hour, and hyperventilated during the taxi ride to the dock. It didn't occur to him to return to North Carolina and confront Mrs. Alexandra Lomax about her damned carelessness in letting someone discover their little business deal; his instincts had told him from the first that she would chew him to shreds if he crossed her. He was not into confrontation; he was into easy living, and tucked into his luggage was a fist-size bag of cocaine that would keep his lifestyle rolling as soon as he peddled it to the right people in Miami.

At the dock, he anxiously waved off the helpful hands of the lithe, smiling porters and hurried toward a huge cruise ship. Suddenly he was surrounded by lithe, unsmiling customs officials and policemen, and his luggage was pulled away, and Malcolm Drury stared in shock as his belongings were scattered across the gleaming white concrete and the bag of coke was quickly confiscated.

He thought of the brutal Bahamian prisons and drug laws, and his knees collapsed. He sank to the pavement as they were cuffing his hands behind his back, protesting loudly that he was innocent, that someone had planted the drug in his luggage.

As they dragged him toward a police van, he began to cry. It wasn't fair. No one could have known. No one.

They had had many unusual people in the store, Sam thought, but never an FBI agent. He looked exactly the way one should look too—in a dark suit with a small leather folder held open in one raised hand, showing his credentials. Mom stared at him over the cash register and nearly dropped a bag of Charlotte's whole-grain muffins.

"Just thought you'd like to know, Mrs. Ryder," the agent said. "We picked up some information on Malcolm Drury. He was caught in the Bahamas. Drug possession."

Mom sagged against the counter and put her head on the top of the cash register. Sam stepped in front of her and looked up at the agent with unblinking regard. "Do they lock people up and throw away the key down there?"

"Yes, they do."

Good, Sam thought, but didn't say so. "Can we get any of our money back?" she asked.

"I'm afraid not."

"Do y'all think we had anything to do with him buying drugs? That we were going to fence them for him, or something?"

The agent smiled at her as if she were the quaintest creature he'd ever seen. "No, miss, you and your family aren't under suspicion."

Sam nodded. "That's all I need to know then. Oh, except—how did they catch him?"

"Someone made an anonymous phone call to the customs officials."

Dressed in pale gray riding britches and a matching blouse, carrying tall black riding boots and thin socks in one hand, Alexandra breezed down the marble staircase and halted on the landing where, a little more than ten years earlier, William had lain with the life slipping out of him. Bare feet planted cozily on the cool marble tile, she nodded to her secretary, a slender, bespectacled young black woman who was extremely efficient and whose employment added a discreetly open-minded touch to Orrin's conservative political image. North Carolinians shunned nosebleed liberals like the plague, and nutty right-wingers like Jesse Helms stole the national spotlight, but she and Orrin knew the future lay in cultivating the moderates.

Orrin would be governor someday. She was planning the route with unerring attention to detail. "Good morning, Barbara."

Smiling at her over an armful of notepads and mail, Barbara said, "Good morning, Mrs. Lomax. I'm all set. We can get through the day's business quickly. I know you want to get to your horses."

"You know I do." Alexandra nodded greetings to Matilda, a housekeeper she'd imported from England, who scurried out of the downstairs office as they walked to a broad antique desk. As always, Matilda had placed a silver coffee service on one end of the desk, and the secretary poured coffee into two china cups as Alexandra dropped her boots and sank into a damask-covered chair across from her.

Barbara settled onto a chair on the other side and began studying a large notepad, a pen in one hand, as

Alexandra nibbled a bran muffin. "Get Dole Hopkins on the phone today and tell him not to let the DuLanes have the Owl Creek Road property for one penny less than twelve five an acre. I didn't buy that land to lose money on it, and I'm not going to let the DuLanes waddle their rich fannies up here from New Orleans expecting a bargain. If Dole continues to go limp on the negotiations, tell him I'll broker the deal myself."

"Yes, ma'am." Barbara scribbled quickly on her pad.

"I've written Mrs. DuLane a sweet little note inviting her to stay here as my guest during the fall leaf season. Make sure it gets to the post office today."

"Yes, ma'am."

"Call the club and double-check all the arrangements for the brunch next week. I don't want to see even *one* lousy carnation in the centerpieces this time. When I host a flock of dim-witted hick senators' wives, they are going to go home properly impressed."

"No carnations, I promise."

"Tim begins his summer internship with the chamber of commerce tomorrow. Remind Matilda to have his clothes ready. I expect to see him in a suit and tie every morning."

"Jane Treacher left a message that golf shirts and casual slacks would be all right. She said to tell you everyone's casual during the summer."

"A suit and tie," Alexandra repeated. "I set the standards for my son's appearance."

"Yes, ma'am."

"The senator will be back from Raleigh tomorrow. His blood pressure's climbing again and I'm sending him to Dr. Crane's office in Asheville for a checkup. Get an appointment for Monday or Tuesday."

"And if Dr. Crane's already booked? Any alternatives?"

Alexandra thought of the growing community of specialists who'd set up practice among Pandora's moneyed crowd, and of Hugh Raincrow, who was quickly becoming the only general practitioner in town. She'd heard through her grapevines that the new boys eyed Hugh suspiciously and considered him uncooperative. He didn't play golf or charge consultation fees, he still made housecalls, and he refused to refer patients to them for anything less than an emergency.

If Hugh wanted to alienate himself from progress, she was delighted. Indeed, nothing would make her happier than seeing him lose patients to the newcomers. But doctors were clannish, and she couldn't be certain that word about Orrin's unstable blood pressure wouldn't spread among them until it reached Hugh. The less the damned Raincrows knew about her family, the better.

People were still whispering about Tim's broken nose. She had wanted to shake him into a semblance of manly behavior that night, had wanted to see him fight back after Jake hit him.

And she wanted to see Jake humiliated and humbled until he no longer had the power to make her nervous. Alexandra fiddled with the handle of her coffee cup. "Dr. Crane will work the senator into his schedule," she said brusquely. "Tell him I insist."

"Yes, ma'am."

"Let's go through the mail, Barbara. We can finish the rest later."

Her secretary placed a stack of neatly slit envelopes in front of Alexandra. Alexandra shuffled through them, tossing bills into two separate piles. "These are my sister's," she noted, tapping one set. "I'll write the checks tomorrow morning."

"I hope Mrs. Ryder is feeling better."

"She's fine. A little embarrassed over her poor judgment in men, but I've assured her she doesn't have to worry about the money. Oh, I almost forgot—call her this afternoon and tell her I've booked the girls for classes with an etiquette coach in July. A lovely old Asheville lady who used to be somebody."

"And if Mrs. Ryder asks for details?"

"She won't. I've already convinced her that she's been entirely too free-wheeling about their social graces. Charlotte's becoming a flighty little bohemian, and Samantha is apparently in training to become a very dull old woman."

Barbara laughed. "What do you mean?"

"She's an excellent student, but she has no interest in other teenagers or any extracurricular school activities. She practically runs my sister's shop and she, well, in her spare time she *sews*. It's up to me, obviously, to expand all that marvelous strength of character into something a good deal more interesting. Charm, strength, and brains—that's the ticket."

Alexandra laid out the rest of the mail like a game of solitaire. "Invitations," she mumbled, arranging small pastel envelopes according to the prestige of the return addresses. "It's going to be a busy summer."

"A pleasant one too, I'm sure," Barbara interjected.

"Yes, life can be nearly perfect at times." She gave in to a brief, dark thought about never being perfectly secure as long as Sarah Raincrow and her brood existed, but shelved the worry as insignificant. She had control of her own life and Frannie's, and Charlotte's, and most of all, her glorious, promising Samantha.

"What's this?" she said under her breath, lifting a cheap white business envelope with no stamp, no addresses, and only her name scrawled across it in bold, masculine-looking script.

"That was in the mailbox yesterday. I guess someone dropped it off in person."

"That's odd." Alexandra slid her fingers into the envelope and pulled out a second envelope that had been folded in half and sealed. The contents felt flimsy. Alexandra tore the envelope open carefully.

A plain white piece of paper was folded in a large square inside it. She spread the mysterious paper on her desk. Centered on it was a dog-eared snapshot of Malcolm Drury. Her stomach lurched, and she gaped at the photo and then, shock draining her, at the words written beneath it in the same strong, intense hand that had confidently penned her name.

You stole from your sister and her daughters. Don't do it again. Because I'll find out.

"Mrs. Lomax? Are you all right?" Barbara's voice came to her dimly through a buzz of confusion and fear. Had that spineless Malcolm Drury told someone she'd paid him to swindle her own sister—that she'd paid a professional thief to make certain Frannie didn't become too independent? Drury was beneath her concern, conveniently put away by his own stupidity. But some stranger was out there, knowing her secret, watching her.

The way Jake, as a child, had known about her affair with Orrin.

"Yes, yes, I'm fine," Alexandra lied. She covered the message with her hands. "Get out. I mean, we're done. Go on. Leave me alone. *Leave*."

Gaping at her, Barbara hurried from the room. Alexandra forced herself to take several deep breaths, then, with barely controlled panic, ripped the photo, the paper, and both envelopes into bits.

Jake. She refused to succumb to hysterical paranoia about him. Sarah's eccentric son was not going to harass and intimidate her.

But the fear remained, rising up from the deep well of apprehension Jake had created years ago, and it infuriated her and obsessed her until she was convinced he had sent the photograph.

She waited, day after tormenting day, to see if there would be more messages, or some specific form of blackmail. She despised the fear, the uncertainty, the *control* over her thoughts and happiness.

When no more messages came, she felt only a little better. She would have to live with the gnawing worry that Jake knew more about her than she wanted anyone to know. She finally regained a measure of sanity by telling herself it didn't matter—he had no *proof*.

But like his mother, he was a thorn embedded in Alexandra's skin. She could pretend he didn't matter, but she always knew he was there.

"Here, it's going to be right here." Jake nodded at Mrs. Big Stick, then proudly swept an arm at the small clearing marked only by the stumps of a few trees he'd

cut. Massive oaks and sourwoods and hickories still surrounded the knoll, with a thick underskirting of rhododendron, azaleas, dogwoods, and hollies. He would clear
no more than he had to for the house and yards, leaving
the grandest trees. The spring where Granny had taken
him and Ellie so often to sit with their bare feet in the
cold, clear water while she told Cherokee fables was at
the base of the hill.

Mrs. Big Stick, stout and colorful in a billowing red
skirt and oversize print blouse, her scuffed leather walking shoes run-down at the sides from the weight of her
responsibilities, squinted at him in contemplative silence.
A woven bag bulging with her ceremonial materials hung
from one of her shoulders. She hitched it a little higher
and pursed her lips. "Your mother told me how proud it
makes them—you wanting to stay in the Cove. This is a
very important thing."

Jake nodded. A house for him and Samantha. A mark
of his new status, and of leaving Mother and Father's
home. A stake in the Cove's future. A promise to honor
what Father and many generations of Father's ancestors
had fought for and loved. All those sentiments were part
of his decision. "I want to look out the front windows and
see Granny's spring," he added.

"That's good. See? She has never left you."

Without another word Mrs. Big Stick bent and flicked
a cigarette lighter under the firewood he'd piled in the
clearing's center. He watched in satisfied silence, sitting
on a stump at a respectful distance. She nurtured the
fire until it blazed without her help, then pulled a small
tape player from her bag, twisted the volume control, and
pushed a button. Loud, hypnotic drumbeats echoed off the
wall of trees.

Mrs. Big Stick brought out a pouch and sprinkled
tobacco into the fire, then shuffled around the open
space, casting the dried brown bits to the four directions,
chanting indecipherable words as she did. The ceremonial
blessing soothed Jake. He was touching a past as ancient
as the mountains, as enduring as the sun and moon.
When Mrs. Big Stick returned to the fire and stood, still

chanting, with her eyes shut, he took Samantha's quilt from a backpack and spread it on the low branches of a shrub.

Her eyes still shut, Mrs. Big Stick sank stiffly to her knees, felt around for the tape player, and shut it off. Pure silence descended, as if the whole world had been rinsed clean. She continued to kneel, her head bowed. Then, with a firm nod, she sighed, lifted her head, and opened her eyes.

She stared at the quilt curiously. "That is beautiful. It's good to add your own sacred totems to the ceremony," she said. "What does it mean to you?"

"Samantha Ryder made it."

Her deepset eyes widened. Shock and dismay swept over her expression, and she got to her feet with a lumbering speed he'd never expected. Mouth open, she marched to the quilt, halted in front of it, and seared him with a look of horrified disapproval. "You can't. You can't do it. Can't have *anything* to do with her. Oh, this is bad. You should have warned me. I'll have to work on this. I thought you understood. I thought your granny and I had showed you the right path."

"You did." He was astonished and defensive. "I know who I'm meant to be with. I've known since I was a kid. Samantha and I are meant to be together. That *is* the right path."

"No, boy, *no*. Why do you think you lost your feeling for the ruby after your uncle died? Oh, don't look at me like that—I figured out your problem back then. I tried to explain it to you. *When you can't get a feeling from something, it's a warning.* It's something that can hurt you too bad."

"Samantha isn't going to hurt me."

"Not her, maybe, but through her"—Mrs. Big Stick's voice dropped to a whisper—"you don't want any connection to a *ravenmocker*."

"I have to trust what I *know*. It's how I find lost hikers for the sheriff. It's how I find gemstones. It's how I found Samantha—how I always will."

"No, that ruby was trying to tell you the truth, boy. That stone knows more than you will ever want to hear. It was carried by medicine people through times so far past, we can only imagine them in our dreams. *And if it won't talk to you, it's for your own good.* That stone will come back to where it belongs only through pain, and hardship, and terrible grief. *You can't invite it here.*"

Angry and confused, Jake quickly folded the quilt and put it away. "If the stone won't talk to me, I don't need it. I don't want it. I'll listen to my own . . . music."

Mrs. Big Stick groaned and hurried back to her belongings. She shook her head as she shoved them into her bag. Jake watched in tortured silence. "Maybe you're as white as you look," Mrs. Big Stick said. "You don't really believe in the power of a ravenmocker."

"I believe I'd be a coward to let one run my life. And Samantha's."

"You won't be able to stop a ravenmocker with good intentions, boy." Mrs. Big Stick hoisted her bag to her shoulder and marched toward the narrow path that led back to the house.

"I'm not a fool," Jake called. "I have patience. I'm careful."

She grumbled softly in Cherokee, stopped, and turned around. She pointed at him. Doom lined her face. "If you bring Samantha into your family, the ravenmocker will destroy them all."

After she disappeared into the forest, Jake sat down and grimly pulled the quilt between his legs. Mrs. Big Stick underestimated his patience and determination. He would not run from the future, and he would never desert Samantha, and he would never let Alexandra ruin the lives of everyone he loved.

He gripped Samantha's gift in hands that were young and strong and certain. She was as close as his fingertips, and he would wait for her.

Part Two

Chapter Twelve

"Would you like a pillow?" The school guidance counselor asked that question as she closed her office door, trapping Sam in the fake pine and cinnamon scent of a miniature plastic Christmas tree on the counselor's scarred wooden desk. It was too early for Christmas decorations, Sam thought. A lopsided Thanksgiving turkey made of papier mâché still sat on the other corner of Mrs. Taylor's desk.

Sam twisted in a chair beside the desk and looked at her askance. She had no idea why Mrs. Taylor had gotten her out of class for this meeting. "Ma'am?"

"You're famous for falling asleep sitting up," Mrs. Taylor, a big mother-bear sort of person, said without rebuke. She frowned benignly as she sank into a creaking chair behind her desk. "You look pooped even now. If you nod off, I don't want you to smack your head on my desk."

Sam straightened in the chair and tried to appear perky. "I fall over slowly. I don't even make a sound when I hit."

"It's very commendable of you to not disrupt class. But all your teachers are talking about your spontaneous naptimes. They're worried about you—your grades have slipped since last year."

"I'll still graduate at the end of this quarter."

"Oh, nobody's saying you won't." Mrs. Taylor frowned. "I hear you don't intend to come back this spring for the graduation ceremonies. Why, Sam?"

"I'll already have my diploma. That's all I care about. What's the point of marching up on a stage?"

"Sam, get a dictionary. Look up the word 'fun.' " The counselor shuffled through a file folder that had *Ryder, S.* stenciled at the top. "Summer school, heavy course loads, no club memberships, no sports. That's pretty intense. Haven't you heard? You're seventeen. These are the most carefree years of your life."

"I'll be eighteen in January."

"Oh, well, excuse *me.* I didn't realize you were so close to retirement."

"My mom's business isn't doing very well. When we started, we were the only health food store in the city. But in the past couple of years the national chains have opened franchises, and the big supermarkets started carrying things like mineral water and yogurt, and . . . good Lord, now we get guys in three-piece suits complaining because we don't stock five different brands of whole wheat bread."

"Yuppies," Mrs. Taylor said darkly. "The world is being overrun by young urban professionals who vote Republican. I read about it in *Newsweek.*"

"Well, we made a lot more money from Mom's ouhies."

"Ouhies?"

"Old urban hippies."

Mrs. Taylor smiled, but her eyes were shadowed. "I hear you're working nights and weekends at a fabric shop."

"We need the extra money. And after I graduate and go to work full-time, we'll be okay."

"Sammie, do you really want to forego the last part of your senior year? Don't you want to cause trouble and goof off with the rest of the senior class?"

"I really want to make money. And I've never cared much about all that teenage-bonding stuff anyway. I'm not a herd animal."

"Oh? What are you?"

Sam held up her hands. "A spider. If I could spin silk from my fingertips, I'd make my own web and sit in the middle of it. And any uninvited guests would get wrapped up and eaten."

"Hon, if you don't get more rest you'll doze off in mid-spin."

Sam knotted her hands in her lap. "I'll drink more coffee."

"What about college?"

"I'm not going to waste four years when I already know what I want to do."

"Which is?"

"Make money."

"I've got news for you, hon. Clerks in fabric shops drive beat-up old cars and buy their underwear at garage sales."

"I'll own my own business. Custom draperies, hand-made lace, you name it. I'll sell my work through interior decorators. I've got a long-range plan mapped out. You can bet on it."

"Does this plan include five minutes for a social life?"

Sam unconsciously touched a hand to the small, irregular bump made by the ruby under her blouse. "No." The bell rang in the halls outside, and Sam shifted in her chair. "I appreciate you worrying about me, but, Mrs. Taylor, I can take care of myself."

"All right, the lecture is over. Scram." But as Sam hurried to the door, Mrs. Taylor asked drolly, "Hon, have you ever participated in one of those dinner-and-movie rituals where the male and the female learn how to intrigue and annoy each other and the male pays for everything? A *date?*"

"Hmmm. No. That must be near 'fun' in the dictionary."

Sam eased out of the office. For a second she'd been tempted to announce, *I've been married since I was a child*, just to see the dust fly when Mrs. Taylor exploded. But Sam would not explain why she clung to secret, hopeless dreams. She just never let go, as Jake had said the last time they'd seen each other, three years ago.

Aunt Alexandra insisted on giving her graduation dinner in a small private room at the Pandora country club, but all Sam could think about was Jake, with whom she most wanted to celebrate this day but who would never be invited to the elegant club or any other place her aunt controlled. *I'll be eighteen next month. I'm going to work. I'm going to make money. I won't have to worry about Aunt Alex's hold on Mom and Charlotte then*, she told herself.

But that prospect seemed so distant.

Morose and resigned, she sat at the head of a glittering table dominated by a Christmas decoration of holly and red candles laced with gold mesh. She could barely see Mom over it, and just the top of Charlotte's shaggy blond head. Charlotte was bent over the last bite of an amaretto birthday cake—trying, Sam suspected, to determine every ingredient and store the information for her own baking experiments. Mom looked tired and distracted, and the red velvet sheath that had fit her smoothly when Sam made it last Christmas hung shapelessly on her thin torso.

Sam had agreed to this dinner because Mom wanted it.

Orrin, tall and stately, with debonair white wings shading his hair at the temples, sat beside Charlotte, smiling at her as he watched her study the cake. Tim, who did not look pleased to be spending several hours of his Christmas break from the university this way, hunched over a glass of champagne.

Sam wished he hadn't come to the dinner, and assumed her aunt had insisted. He was finely dressed in a tailored suit, but his thick, muscled neck strained at his shirt collar, and a beautiful tie bulged over the collar's gold tie bar. Over the years he had barely spoken to her, and when he did, there was a sarcastic edge to it. She kept catching him staring at her with thinly veiled contempt, and when she stared back, his eyes shifted away quickly.

Aunt Alex commanded the table from Sam's right side, and she looked immensely sophisticated in a gold brocade suit with shimmering gold piping down the front. Her favorite gold necklace, a heavy piece with a filigree pendant the size of a pecan, gleamed in the light from the candles and a chandelier.

"Time to open the presents," Aunt Alex said happily, clapping her hands. A white-coated waiter glided in and removed the last of the dessert dishes. Charlotte darted to a small table in one corner, where several boxes made a rainbow stack of bright paper and bows.

Charlotte made certain her present came first. Sam opened a tiny box with a flattened, lopsided bow. "What a *beautiful* thimble," she said, giving Charlotte a wide smile.

"I know you've got lots of thimbles, but this one's old, and it's made of porcelain. I traded three cakes for it at an antiques store."

"It's wonderful."

"Open Mom's gift next."

Sam nervously took a large, heavy box, recognizing the Christmas paper Mom bought every year from a shop that sold only recycled paper products. It was decorated with fresh pine sprigs tied with a red cloth ribbon. Sam hoped Mom hadn't spent much of their money on the gift. She opened it carefully. Sam sighed with awe as she unfolded yards of downy, white material. "Cashmere," she whispered.

"I knew you'd never buy cashmere," Mom said, her

voice tired and wistful. "I want you to make something beautiful for yourself."

Sam nuzzled the incredibly fine cloth and gave Mom a liquid look of appreciation. "Thank you."

"Mine next," Aunt Alex said. "It's the tiniest box with the gold silk bow. And what, by the way, is that other box beside it? Who brought that?"

Sam eyed the alien box curiously as she plucked at Aunt Alex's gift. "Mr. Gunther left it at the store this morning," Mom explained. "I hid it. I thought it'd be a nice surprise."

Mr. Gunther. Sam's heart pounded. It *could* be from him, or he could be only the courier. Eager to get to it, she barely paid attention as she opened her aunt's gift. Sam looked at the pair of keys dangling from a gold key ring, which bore a handsome gold oval monogrammed with her inititals.

"A *car*," Charlotte yelled. "Aunt Alex and Uncle Orrin gave you a *car!*"

Aunt Alex returned Sam's stunned look with a beaming smile. "There's a powder-blue Mercedes sports coupe waiting for you outside."

Sam's head swam. She couldn't force herself to touch the keys. *I don't want it, it's a bribe*, she thought bitterly. But the gift alarmed her in other ways too. If Aunt Alex could pass Mercedes out like toys, she had more money than Sam had ever imagined. And money in Aunt Alex's hands meant power.

What would she do to Jake if she knew I love him? Sam was dimly aware of the expression in Mom's eyes— shock and wonder mixed with something painful, and she knew that Mom must be comparing the cashmere to a brand-new Mercedes. Sam met Tim's gaze. He looked furious. She remembered suddenly that he'd totaled Aunt Alex's Jaguar when he was sixteen; after that she refused to buy him a new car of his own, and he'd been relegated to a big, embarrassingly sedate Lincoln given to Orrin by a political crony who owned a dealership.

"You'll turn everyone's heads at college," Aunt Alex said.

"I'm not going to college," Sam said. "And I'm going to buy a used van from Mr. Gunther. I need something big enough to carry bolts of fabric and supplies."

Aunt Alex stiffened, and pink splotches marred the perfectly contoured blush on her cheeks. "I'm not going to ruin your graduation celebration with a serious discussion. We'll talk later."

Charlotte flapped her arms, setting off a rippling cascade of swinging earrings and resembling a startled angel in a bright green dress that draped almost to her ankles. "I get my driver's license in two years. *I'll* drive the Mercedes, Sammie! Don't give it *back*!"

"The car is a very generous gesture," Mom interjected quickly. "I'm sure Sammie appreciates it."

Silence descended, and everyone looked at Sam. Sam studied the pleading look in Mom's eyes. "I do," she told her aunt dully. "Thank you."

Aunt Alex settled back in her chair, her eyes slitted, and her mouth set in a thin line. She stroked the pendant of her necklace. "Never settle for less than you deserve," she said. "I'm underwhelmed by your enthusiasm."

Sam said nothing, and tension crept into the atmosphere like a bad odor. Charlotte, deflated, brought Sam the gift from Mr. Gunther. It was a narrow box wrapped in dark blue paper with a matching bow. Sam forced a neutral expression and willed her hands to move casually as she opened it.

Inside, on a bed of tissue paper, was a strange, beautiful hoop. The delicate hoop was wrapped in leather, and strung tightly across was a pattern of woven white string that looked like nothing so much as a spider's web. Several tiny, colorful beads were strung in it. Three long leather thongs decorated with soft white feathers dangled from the hoop.

Her breath caught in her throat. She lifted the dainty hoop from the box. Beneath it was a folded sheet of paper. Sam opened it, scanning the bold, dark script and wondering if it was Jake's handwriting.

"What have you got there?" Orrin asked. "Looks like some sort of Indian gewgaw."

She read aloud in a husky tone, " 'The idea for this

comes from the Oneidas, up north. But even if it isn't a Cherokee custom, it touches the same spirit.' "

"What is it?" Charlotte asked, plaintively fingering the car keys.

"A dreamcatcher." Sam swallowed hard and continued reading. "'Hang it over your bed. It will catch the good dreams and let the bad ones go. The blue bead is a sapphire, for hope. The green one is an emerald, for life. The red one is a ruby, for love and loyalty.' "

It is from Jake. She melted inside, a slow, sensual appreciation for him and his brand of sentimentality. But she felt Aunt Alexandra watching her closely. When she looked at her, Aunt Alex was frowning. "May I see that note, please?"

Sam didn't move. *No* perched on the tip of her tongue, with *Hell, no* behind it.

"Sammie?" Mom's voice had a thready tone of alarm.

Slowly, reluctantly, Sam handed the note to Aunt Alex. Her aunt held it by the tips of her fingers as if it might burst into flame, and studied it with unblinking intensity. Sam swore she saw a slight twitch at the corner of her aunt's left eye. Aunt Alex thrust the note back at her, and Sam took it just as abruptly. "Those are quality gemstones," Aunt Alex said. There was a strained pitch to her voice. "I really think this is an inappropriately expensive gift from someone who's not family. I suggest you return it to Mr. Gunther."

Sam gazed at her steadily, tiny muscles tightening behind her expression, holding back a show of fury that would only upset Mom. "No, I believe I'll keep it," she said evenly. *It's all I can have*, Sam thought. *Maybe all I can ever have.*

"Then I believe I'll keep the Mercedes until we reach an understanding."

Sam pushed the keys across the table to her. "I hope the car dealer takes returns," she said.

Joe muttered to himself about Alexandra Lomax as he drove the winding gravel road through the Cove. The

tips of wintry brown broomsedge stroked the arm he
had cocked on the sill of the car's open window, and
he snatched angrily at them.

Charlotte Ryder was a sweet, lonely kid who desperately wanted a daddy to talk to, and she talked Joe's ears off
whenever he stopped by her mother's shop. Charlotte had
told him about the graduation present Alexandra had given
Sam, and what Sam had done when it came to a choice
between keeping that present or the dreamcatcher.

Joe fumed. He turned off on a dusty new driveway
several hundred yards before the one that went to Jake's
parents' house. The new path curled through deep gray
forest, skirting a massive red oak before it rose along an
incline where dried brown leaves skudded in the cool
breeze. A startled buck bounded across the road; squirrels scattered from the roadway.

Joe's mood darkened even more. This old valley was
a special place, and Jake belonged here like the Raincrows
always had, and for three years now Joe had watched him
labor almost single-handedly on the big log house that
loomed up as the forest opened on the cleared knoll.

It was less grand than his folks' place—one-story,
but sprawling, with wide porches all around and two thick
stone chimneys at either end. The logs were hand-hewn
and square, fitted together at every corner with expert
dovetail joints. Every inch of the house was stamped with
Jake's work and devotion; Joe had watched him build it,
alone, one log at a time, over the past three years.

Bo padded up from the spring ahead of Jake as Joe
crossed a yard dotted with tree stumps and cords of neatly stacked firewood. The bloodhound looked like hell—
muddy and wet, his long tongue nearly dragging the
ground as he panted. Joe distractedly patted the dog's
jowly muzzle and halted, frowning at Jake's appearance.
It would have made a stranger take a step back.

He wore no jacket. His jeans and faded cotton shirt
were stained with sweat and dirt; the shirt hung completely open, revealing muddy rivulets that streaked the
black hair over thick chest muscles. Spring water dripped

from his large, veined hands. There was a tired slump to Jake's shoulders, and a measured fatigue in his stride. His dark hair was slicked to his head, with long shanks of it plastered to the sides of his neck, and the collar of the shirt was drenched. Without a cap of dry, full-bodied hair to soften his features, the angles of his face were too raw, the set of his jaw unconsciously threatening. There was a jaded, troubled look in his eyes.

Joe's gut twisted with apprehension and curiosity, but he knew better than to ask Jake for information. Jake said no more than he had to about himself, and offered details in his own good time. "Nice day for a mud bath," Joe said.

Jake's intense gaze remained on him. "You've got some kind of bad news about the Ryders." The words seemed to weigh him down a little more.

Joe sighed. He'd probably never figure out how Jake sensed these things. "Their business is going to hell in a handbasket. I made up an excuse to cut their rent again, but I don't think it's going to do much good. Even with the money the Queen Bee gives them, they're barely stayin' afloat. I get the feelin' Frannie would cave in and take *more* help from Her Highness, but she knows it would break Sammie's heart. And let me tell you, Sammie's doing every damned thing she can to get them out of the hole. The only young person I've seen work that hard and play that little is, well, *you.*"

Jake raised hands that looked too large and rough to have made something as delicate as the dreamcatcher. He shoved them through his wet hair, then let them drop by his sides. "I've tried every way I can think of to help them through you. I'm tired of hiding."

"I figured a long time ago that keeping your distance is the hardest thing you've ever done. If you'd stepped in the way you wanted to, Alexandra would have cut them off without a penny—cut off her own sister. And I don't doubt she'd have made poor Frannie miserable in other ways to boot. You've done the right thing, because Alexandra is as cold-blooded as a snake."

"She can't keep a hold over them forever."

"I'll tell you what she did when Sammie opened your present. Alexandra didn't know it was from you, of course, but it must have made her nervous. Because she told Sammie it was too nice a gift to take from somebody who isn't family. She didn't want her to keep it. From what I heard, she grabbed your note and scrutinized it like it might be secret code. I'm warning you, she's suspicious."

"What did Samantha say?" Jake never called the girl anything but *Samantha*. He'd decorated her in his own private way, Joe supposed, and Sammie deserved decoration. "She said she wasn't giving it back," Joe replied proudly. "And you know what Alexandra did? She gave Sammie a choice—keep the dreamcatcher or keep *her* gift."

"What did she give her?"

"A *car*. A damned Mercedes." Joe hesitated, studying Jake's expression intently. Jake looked pleased but not surprised. That kind of faith—between two people who'd seen each other only a handful of times—would have seemed foolish if the people hadn't been Jake and Sammie. "You got yourself quite a lady there," Joe added.

"She knows it's me," Jake said under his breath as if talking to himself. "And that means the line's already been crossed."

"Who knows?" Joe asked. "Alexandra? Nah, she's too sure of herself to think you and Sammie would go against her."

Jake frowned, still lost in thought. "It's time. I always said I'd know." His attention was suddenly riveted to Joe again, the meaning of the vague, unsettling words locked inside him. Joe didn't like the uncompromising gleam in his eye. "Don't lose your patience now," Joe told him anxiously. "You don't look like you're in the right mood to make up your mind about anything. You look like you been rode hard and put up wet."

"Bad work." Jake's voice was hollow and slightly hoarse, and once again he seemed to be distracted by other thoughts.

Joe pressed carefully. "You been doin' some tracking?"

"Just got back from Tennessee. Went up to Nashville. Police called me to help find a kid who disappeared from a nursery school playground two days ago."

"Tennessee, huh? You and Bo are gettin' a wide reputation."

"We go where we're needed."

"Find him?"

"Yeah."

From the look on Jake's face, Joe didn't think he wanted to know the details, but he couldn't help himself. He had a grandson in nursery school. "Alive?" Joe asked.

"No. Stuffed under a creek bank. Somebody'd strangled him with a piece of wire." Jake's troubled gaze finally settled solidly on Joe. "His clothes were all gone. He'd been . . . messed with. You know?"

Joe grimaced. "Do they have their sights on the bastard who did it?"

"They do now. I tracked him down." Jake stared into space, as if seeing something no man wanted to see. "Do you believe in ravenmockers?" he asked slowly.

Joe grimaced. "Hell, yes. Some of them have been president."

"I caught one today. He couldn't get away from me, and he couldn't kill me." Jake smiled thinly. "I learned a good lesson today."

Chapter
Thirteen

" **H**appy New Year," Mr. Gunther said the second he walked into the shop. "Sammie, have I got a birthday present for *you*."

Sam, who had been going over the day's mediocre receipts before she left for her night job at the fabric store, peered at him anxiously. "My birthday's not until next week."

Charlotte, halfheartedly working on algebra problems at a table in one corner, perked up at the sight of him. But Mom turned from stacking bottles of vitamin E on a shelf, a pensive expression on her thin face. "Joe, I asked you not to—"

"Aw, this isn't anything that'll raise your sister's hackles. I got Sammie a nice little job, if she wants it. A hundred bucks for about an hour's worth of easy work."

Sam dropped the receipts on the counter so fast they scattered like confetti. "A hundred dollars an hour? How much of my clothes do I have to take off? I'll sew sequins on my underwear."

Mom gasped. "*Sam.*"

"I'm only kidding." Sam looked at Mr. Gunther shrewdly. "I won't go farther than a tight T-shirt."

"You'll have to do better than *that*," Charlotte chimed in. She fluttered her hands in front of the largest bosom in her tenth-grade class. "You were standing behind the door when God passed out big—"

"*Charlotte*," Mom warned.

Mr. Gunther laughed. "The only thing Sammie has to uncover are her *hands*."

Sam frowned at him. "You really are just teasing."

"I'm not, I swear." He plopped down in a folding chair beside the counter, hooked the heels of maroon cowboy boots over the chair's crossbar, and pulled a business card from the breast pocket of his pink western shirt. "I've got a second cousin over in Yonah Lake. Name's Marie Path Walker—well, she was born Marie Walker, but she's a full-blood, and back in the seventies she took up the Indian cause in a big way, so she went back to the old family name—anyhow, then she went out west for a while and studied jewelry-making with the Navajos, and for the past fifteen years or so she's made some of the finest turquoise and silver jewelry you're ever gonna see."

"Take a breath, Mr. Gunther," Charlotte interjected. "Your face is turning red."

He leaned forward, waving his extravagantly ringed fingers like an excited auctioneer. "Now, she's no lightweight, you understand. She sells her work through some of the best stores in New York City and Los Angeles. I mean, *movie stars* have bought her jewelry."

"How about Madonna?" Charlotte asked. Her only noncooking idol.

"Shhh," Mom said.

"Marie needs to put together a real slick portfolio of her best pieces for a distributor over in Europe. She needs somebody to model the rings and bracelets for the photographer. So *I* told her I knew a gal with hands like an angel's."

"That's all there is to it?" Sam asked. "I put on some jewelry and let a photographer take pictures of my hands? And I get a hundred dollars?"

"A hundred dollars *an hour*," Mr. Gunther corrected her. "I did some checking. That's what professional hand models get, and Lord knows their hands couldn't be any prettier than yours. Marie's rolling in money. Didn't bat an eyelash when I told her what you'd cost."

Sam was flabbergasted. "You're serious. There are people who get big money just for modeling with their hands."

"Well, it makes sense when you think about all the ads where all you see is a pair of hands holding something." He gazed at her eagerly. "Marie's got the photographer lined up for next week. She works out of her house, so he'll set up there to do the pictures. Do you want the job, Sammie?"

"I was planning to close the shop on Sammie's birthday," Mom said wistfully. "She needs a day off."

"Mom, I don't need a day off. I need this job. Besides, it won't take very long."

"It's a deal, then!" Mr. Gunther beamed at her.

Sam lifted her hands and studied them curiously. She *was* a spider, and she'd discovered a way to spin gold.

The weather was mild, particularly for January, when cold winds curled between the mountains more days than not. The photographer liked the clear afternoon light outdoors, and had set up his equipment on a stone patio in Marie Path Walker's sprawling, unkempt backyard.

Mrs. Path Walker's house was a huge restored Victorian full of paintings by Indian artists, ceremonial masks, fine English antiques, and Cabbage Patch dolls belonging to her numerous grandchildren. Marie was a tall, thin woman with a flat face, vibrant black eyes, and long black hair shot through with gray. She strode around in loafers, jeans, and a long black sweatshirt.

When Mr. Gunther introduced Sam to her, she examined Sam's hands as if they were disembodied set props and pronounced them perfect but too pale, so Mr. Gunther was dispatched crosstown to the home of a black lady who sold beauty supplies for women with dark skin. He returned with a tube of chocolate-brown foundation, matching powder, and a cosmetic brush. Then he disappeared upstairs to watch television with Marie's husband.

Sam sat on a folding chair on the patio, the tube of makeup clasped nervously in her lap, as she squinted in the bright gleam of the photographer's set lights. Mrs. Path Walker and the photographer scurried around her as if she were invisible, adjusting a blue backdrop strung on a clothesline and endlessly discussing a vast array of beautiful turquoise and silver jewelry laid out on a card table nearby.

It was her birthday. *Eighteen*. The world's definition of an adult finally agreed with Sam's self-image. She was responsible for her own decisions, free as a bird, but not free at all. This work might pay well, but it made her feel restless. She'd never thought of her hands as being valuable merely because of their looks; it was hard to keep them still.

From where she sat she could see the edge of a paved driveway between holly shrubs, and she heard the sound of a car pulling in. *Probably someone bringing neon-pink nail polish for me to wear*, she thought grimly. She scrubbed her damp palms on the legs of her loose black trousers, distractedly running her fingertips over the expertly stitched seams of the pockets.

Neither Mrs. Path Walker nor the photographer had asked her anything about herself—whether she had skills, or deep thoughts, or wanted a glass of water. Apparently, she was expected to sit there like a mannequin, and keep quiet.

A car door slammed. A few seconds later Jake walked between the hollies.

There was a moment of sinking alarm, the recognition of sensitive parts of her body she'd ignored for a long time, and the primal jolt of gratitude and confusion. *Mr. Gunther set this up*, she thought. *My birthday present. The one I've waited for so long. The one I can't accept.*

Jake was brutal-looking, handsome in the manner of big, brawny men who considered a decent haircut a luxury and a bar of cheap soap a cologne. Sunlight glinted on reddish-black hair as glossy as a new penny and long enough to brush his rumpled collar in back. Oddly enough, the hair suited him, making a sweeping counterpart to a serious, straight-edged face. If she drew her fingertips along that face, she'd find angles hard enough to trace a line by. The rest of him would have made an outline of startlingly masculine proportions, a bulge here, a long perimeter there.

He walked toward her with long, determined strides. And then she understood. He'd promised to come for her when she was old enough. *But you can't*, she told him silently. *Not yet.*

She started to turn away, but her eyes were riveted to him. Of all things, a large, ugly bloodhound followed him. The dog had an incredibly long tongue, spilling drool on the neat grass, as pink as a nipple.

Samantha stood, fumbling with the top to the tube of makeup, dropping the top heedlessly, and shooting furtive glances at Mrs. Path Walker. Mrs. Path Walker waved at Jake. "How's your mother, Jake? Sold any more of her watercolors lately?"

"She's fine, thank you. Sold a few."

Now I get it, Sam thought, stunned. *Mr. Gunther knew we'd be safe, meeting here. But nothing has changed.*

Smoothing dark foundation on the unblemished perfection of her hands and lower arms, she frowned and refused to look up, but every nerve was tuned to the approaching sound of Jake's soft, undeterred footsteps on the patio stones.

She heard the photographer ask in a prim tone, "Does that animal always slobber that way? Shouldn't he be put on a leash?"

And Jake answered in a deep, drawling voice that sent waves of warmth across Sam's skin: "You go ahead and try it. The rabies test hasn't come back positive—yet."

Then, abruptly, Jake was beside her. She frowned and continued working on her hands, feeling his gaze on her, absorbing her, making her light-headed with the tension. "You afraid to talk to me?" he asked. "You can throw an expensive present back in your aunt's face, but she's got you so nervous you won't even admit I'm here?"

The tube of makeup clamped in one hand, she turned and stared up at him. There was no moment of polite evaluation. Instead, her gaze locked immediately on his. The sudden intense connection was like hitting a wall and instantly passing through it. Before she could blink, she was inside his territory. "Pretending you don't exist is easier than pretending there's anything I can do about it."

She clenched her fist. The tube gave a rude burp. A blob of foundation shot out, made a neat arc, and landed on his cheek.

His eyes flickered with astonishment. Sam watched him raise a broad hand to his face. A forefinger as delicate-looking as a wooden peg scooped the drop of brown goo off the end of a leathery crease beside his right eye. He rubbed the makeup between his finger and thumb. Their tips were so thick-skinned, the cream stayed on their surface for several seconds. He seemed to be considering the sensation.

As if he could feel anything through those calluses, Samantha thought. She realized she was staring at his fingertips. Hypnotized. Now, *those* were hands that belonged in pictures. Given a good manicure to civilize nails that appeared to have been cut short with a bowie knife, they would cause women to fan themselves. Sam could imagine his hands draped in the lacy cups of an empty bra, offering female magazine readers a dose of fantasy along with their underwear needs. Oh, yes, Jake's hands would look great under her bra. A bra. Someone's bra. Not hers. Oh, God.

"I've seen women who could spit tobacco juice thirty feet and hit a dime," he said slowly, each word like a dollop of honey, his disturbing gaze still locked on Sam's startled one. "But I never saw one squirt her hand lotion."

She dropped her gaze and muttered, "Only for contests."

"You win first prize."

Sam wasn't going to ask what the prize was. "I'm sorry. Would you like a tissue?" She pretended that capping the tube took all ten fingers and the attention of both eyes. She still felt his scrutiny. "No, thanks," he said in a tone that indicated tissues were for cowards. He probably used leftover pieces of sandpaper.

"Jake, I *like* that dog of yours," Mrs. Path Walker announced, eyeing the hound shrewdly. "*He* is an art form." She turned to the photographer. "Let's take a couple of pictures with the girl's hands on the dog's head."

"Hmmm, whimsical contrast," the photographer agreed. "Beauty and the beast."

Jake looked at Sam. His eyes were deadly serious, but the corner of his mouth lifted in a slight smile. "You're not a beast."

Sam's tart reply was stifled by the photographer's bustling approach. "Let's get started then. You need to powder your hands. They're shiny. Sit in the chair in front of the backdrop."

Her lap filled with tissues, the jar of powdered foundation, and a cosmetic brush, Samantha sat down and tucked her loafered feet under the chair's rungs, then began dusting her hands with makeup. Her hands were cold and shaky; she kept her head down and tried to ignore the fact that Jake had walked over next to her and was giving silent directions to his bloodhound. From the corner of one eye she watched the movements of four rust-red canine legs and two denimed human legs that ended in large, scuffed hiking boots. She smelled a pleasant scent. Either Jake or his dog bathed with mint soap. Probably the dog.

"This is Bo," he told her. "If you squirt lotion at him, he'll eat it."

She feathered the brush over her left palm. It skittered like the tail of a nervous hen. "As long as he doesn't try to eat my hands."

"No, the last time he ate anything that clean, it made him sick."

Bo buddied up to her chair. A tail as strong as the rudder on a battleship whacked the back of it, sending small earthquakes through her spine. "He likes you," his owner said. She couldn't be sure, since she wouldn't look up, but from the droll lilt in his voice she suspected he was enjoying the way her brush bounced each time Bo's tail hit the chair.

"I love animals," Samantha answered, hoping to placate him and get through this unnerving event peacefully. "We had a cat once, but it left. I suspect it didn't like vegetarian cat food."

As if pleased to know he was an admired member of the animal kingdom, Bo laid his large head in Sam's lap. She looked down into dark eyes sheltered by saddlebag brows. Jowls as soft as lambskin drooped onto her bare knees. He was irresistible. She dabbed the brush on his wet nose. He sneezed. Tissues and powder exploded in a small cloud.

Sam leaned back, fanning the mist of powder. "He's got a sensitive nose," Jake said. "Sorry." Before she could protest, Jake retrieved her scattered tissues from the grass and began wiping his dog's head, which still remained on her lap. She was inches from Jake's face, close enough to study the sweep of his long black eyelashes and the kind of beard shadow that said he had the hormonal wherewithal to grow a pelt as thick as a bear's on his jaw. And she was close enough to see the lines of serious concentration around his eyes and mouth.

Jake wondered if she knew he felt awkward. True, he'd given Bo a subtle command to put his head in her lap, but the sneeze had been Bo's ad-lib. Having her distracted by Bo had seemed wiser than letting her squeeze the sense out of his brain with her steam-heated scrutiny.

He supposed some men would say her hands were the only thing about her that was beautiful. He noticed them finally, posed like stalled wings in the air over Bo's dusty head, sleek and perfect, with perfect oval nails painted orange—no, *peach* would be the name people who cared about niceties would give them.

The rest of her fell into the category of being simply, wonderfully *Samantha*—not fat, not thin, not flamboyant, not dull—unbreakable, perfect *Samantha*, with a slightly crooked little nose, a small, full mouth, and blue eyes that could make his heart stop.

He finished scrubbing Bo's head and, not quite knowing how to be formal about it, stuffed the used tissues in his shirt pocket. Then, still bent beside her at eye level, the only gentlemanly thing to do was look her in the face again.

He met her eyes, those startling, sad-funny blue eyes that he'd felt watching him the whole time, and received a new onslaught of her direct, arousing appraisal. "Should I dust you off with your brush?" he asked.

"No. And don't wipe my face either."

A patina of powder had settled on a chin that was a bit too strong. She had fine, straight, shoulder-length hair the color of gold, slicked back prettily under a thin white headband. If she wore any makeup, he couldn't tell. Other than the powder Bo had blown on her.

"Good Lord have mercy, let's get the girl cleaned up and get on with this," the photographer said over their shoulders. Jake straightened and motioned to Bo, who drew his head back and leaned against the chair.

"Let me dust you," the photographer said, and began flailing at Sam with a paper towel.

Jake stepped back, frowning, and watched the photographer fasten a heavy bracelet on one of her wrists and place a ring on her hand. She wiped remnants of powder from her face with one of her infamous tissues and occasionally glanced Jake's way with a perturbed look.

The photographer fussed around her and Bo. "Now, put your hands on top of this . . . this *thing's* head. Yes, like that."

"Jake, could you tell your dog to sit up, as if he has a spine?" Mrs. Path Walker asked, huddling over them.

The photographer snorted. "He *must* move away from the chair. The shot will include only his head and the girl's hands. He's positively welded to her side. We can't do it that way."

"He's not a thing, he's Bo," Sam interjected, giving everyone a mild scowl.

Jake added grimly, nodding toward Sam. "And she's not 'the girl.' Call her by her name."

Sam gave Jake a quick look. Bo looked up at him with an expression she suspected had been in her eyes when she gazed at Jake—adoring.

Under the pressure of her hands, Bo's eyebrows sank into more creases than an accordion. She looked down at him and bit her lower lip, then smiled.

Jake felt the quick surge of arousal, a disastrous appreciation for her appreciating a ridiculous dog, an appreciation for everything about her, and the pain of a hope so deep, it made his chest hurt. He had important things to say to her, and wanted to get this public distraction over with as quickly as he could.

"Bo, *move*," he ordered, effectively destroying their camaraderie. She mumbled something about bad tempers and took her hands into her lap. He went over and dropped to his haunches in front of her and the dog, then moved Bo a piece at a time until the whole was separated from her chair by more than a foot of space. "There," Jake said brusquely, and nodded at her.

Her mouth had a breathtaking talent for holding his attention. With a downward tilt of the corners she reproached Jake. "I thought you were a dog trainer, not a dog mover."

He touched the tip of his finger to Bo's nose. Immediately a tongue as long as the interstate between Raleigh and Atlanta appeared. Bo turned his head and wrapped his tongue around Sam's wrist, silver bracelet included.

He simply sat still, looking up at her, his tongue in place. The photographer shrieked. She stared at her wrist calmly. "Now I know how a chicken liver wrapped in bacon must feel."

Jake sighed. Her good humor was more than he deserved. "Bo, suck it in."

The tongue was reeled in, and order restored.

Jake moved a few feet away. The photo shoot began in earnest. Bo sat patiently with Sam's hands cupping his face in various poses, each time modeling a different set of Marie Path Walker's jewelry.

The photographer cooed and praised, a happy man for once. The dog made such a *cute* prop, he kept saying. When he finished with Bo he began tapping his forehead and telling Marie he wanted something with, well, something that had less fur and more sex appeal. "If we could find a man with the right hands, we could do something with a male-female theme," he told them.

"Him," Samantha said suddenly, and pointed at Jake. She was trying desperately to hide how she really felt. "He has only a bit less fur and slightly more sex appeal. But great hands."

Jake stared at her with the look he used to stop police detectives who asked too many questions about his tracking techniques. She shook her head. "I want your hands," she said, and he picked up immediately on the hoarse, wishful undertone. "What would I have to do?" he demanded, realizing it meant a chance to touch her.

The photographer interjected. "Oh, we'll set up a pedestal and arrange your hands with the—with Sam's. Entwined fingers. *Very* male-female. The yin and yang thing, you see. Hmmm, eastern philosophy. Let me see if I can explain it for you—"

"I know my yin from my yang," Jake told him. "And the only question I have is, do I have to wear makeup?"

"Yes, yes," Samantha answered. "Come here and sit down, and I'll fix your hands for you. It won't be painful, and it won't give you any urge to buy pastel boxer shorts."

Jake thought for a moment. "I don't want my name printed in the credits."

"Fine," Mrs. Path Walker said, waving her arms in exasperation.

Samantha stood and hurried to the chair she'd been sitting in before. Self-rebuke mingled with sad awareness. She wanted to touch Jake, wanted to feel his hands in hers for a few minutes. She dropped into the chair and fumbled with a small cloth bag.

"What do you want me to do?" he asked grimly. She jumped. He'd moved over to her while she was lost in thought, and now he was peering into her bag. "Sit down," she told him, nodding toward the ground beside her. "I'm going to give you a manicure. *Sit.* Give me one of your hands."

Jake sat down, cross-legged, and held out a hand. For a minute, at least, they had privacy. When she closed his hands inside hers, he felt both her misery and her happiness to see him. "Why did you come here today?" she whispered.

Their eyes met. "I promised I'd come for you when you were old enough to vote." There was nothing light or teasing about the way he said it.

Sam gave a slow, helplessly satisfied sigh. "And I've always wanted you to."

"Then it's *time.*"

"You know that's not true. I can't walk away from my mom and Charlotte. Aunt Alex pays most of our bills, and I owe her some kind of loyalty, whether I like it or not. I can't support them—not yet anyway."

"I can."

"*Jake.*"

He leaned forward, cupping her hand between both of his, his face taut, his eyes full of unwavering determination. "I have a house. A good-size house. There's plenty of room for them. I have money—not a lot, but enough. I made twenty-thousand dollars last year, selling stones. I help my parents pay taxes on the Cove and send Ellie expenses that aren't covered by her scholarship. But I've saved every dollar I could. We'd be all right."

"You'd do that? You'd take my mother and sister into your house and—"

"*Our* house," he corrected her. "Yours and mine." When she looked at him in speechless shock, he added quickly, "We can make this work, lady. And there won't be anything your aunt can do about it."

Sam stiffened. "Except influence my mother. I don't know if Mom would agree to something that upset Aunt Alex. If I have a sense of honor, it didn't just come from my dad. My mother may be loyal to the wrong people, sometimes, but she takes that loyalty very seriously. And, *Jake*"—she gazed at him sadly—"you can't tell me your parents would accept us. They don't have any reason to want Aunt Alex's relatives in their family."

"My mother's feud is with Alexandra. I've never heard her say a bad word about your mother."

"That's not the same as welcoming her with open arms. And if you think there's bad blood between your mother and my aunt now, just think what—"

"You're afraid Alexandra will try to hurt *me*."

Sam inhaled sharply. "Yes. You and your family."

"The only way she can hurt me is by keeping you away." He hesitated, searching her eyes. "And if there's no way she can do that, then there's nothing to be afraid of."

Sam's mind whirled. She and Jake had been together only briefly, and no more than a half dozen times throughout their lives. Yet he could show up here and invite her—and her family—to move into his house.

And she not only believed he meant every word of it, she wanted to accept.

He was watching her closely. "I know you and me haven't had a chance to learn all the little things about each other. I'm not saying you have to move in and marry me. Or do *anything* that doesn't strike your fancy."

His awkward, gallant hint melted her. "You're forgetting," she replied softly. "We've been married for a long time."

Slowly, his face relaxed. The pads of his fingers moved gently on her palm.

He said nothing else while she worked on his hands. She called the others over and held his hands out in hers, as if she'd created them. "Great. See?"

"To work," the photographer urged. They went to a tall stool he'd covered in black cloth. Mrs. Path Walker handed Jake a heavy silver ring and told him to try it on for size. It would fit only his little finger. He cast curious looks at Samantha, who had placed a smaller, matching ring on her left hand. The symbolism made her giddy.

"Now, pal," the photographer said, stand behind her and put your arms along hers. Yes. Like that. Now, let's see, let's see—"

Sam's back was pressed against Jake's chest, and her hips brushed his thighs. She felt the contact like a magnet. His hands lay over hers. She rearranged them, her fingers through his, and the photographer purred, "*Yes, oh yes.*"

"Take the photos," Samantha ordered raggedly.

"Take your time," Jake countered.

Chapter Fourteen

"**Mom!**" Sam barely had the word out of her mouth before her mother, dressed only in a thin, sweat-soaked T-shirt, collapsed in a pale heap among packing boxes on the bedroom floor. Sam splattered a glass of iced herbal tea across the carpet and bounded to her mother's side, yelling for Charlotte to help her. Because Mom claimed man-made chemicals only insulted her immune system, Sam had been bringing her tea every few hours with a couple of anonymous aspirin dissolved in it.

After watching Mom's flu grow worse for the past three days, Sam was beyond any twinges of guilt over the deception. Mom was sick and in bed already when Jake brought Sam home from Mrs. Path Walker's. Jake, giving in to Sam's urging, had left without Mom knowing he'd been there. Sam decided to say nothing until Mom began feeling better.

Hearing what Jake had proposed would be a shock, she knew.

Charlotte bolted into the room and shrieked when she saw Sam wedging both hands under Mom's shoulders. "It's okay. She just fainted," Sam said with all the false composure she could muster. She was so accustomed to being in charge, she automatically shoved her own terror out of her mind and concentrated on calming Charlotte. "She's okay," Sam repeated. "Help me get her back in bed." Charlotte shrieked again but grabbed Mom's ankles.

Together they hauled Mom's limp body onto the rumbled sheets of her double bed, bumping the bedstead. Mom's strings of quartz crystals swayed from thumbtacks on the pine headboard. Sam scooped the annoying strings into one hand and tossed them over the board, then pulled blankets up to Mom's thin shoulders.

"I thought she was feeling better!" Charlotte cried. "She said she felt better after Ms. Peace-Hope rubbed mint leaves on her!"

Sam clamped her mouth tight to keep from offering the opinion that Mom's "doctor" was a quack who'd do more good rubbing mint on Charlotte's homemade fudge. Sam grabbed a damp washcloth from a bowl on the nightstand and wiped Mom's face hard, as if she could scrub away the bright pink smear of fever on her cheeks. Mom stirred weakly, and her eyes fluttered. Sam knelt on the bed and cupped her hot face. Fear pounded in her throat. "Mom, you keeled over. I'm calling an ambulance."

Mom's eyes opened. She made a wheezing sound of dismay that ended in "Nooo." Her voice was a croak. She panted for air, then coughed. "I'm fine. Just need more time to let my body expel the toxins. Hate hospitals. Call Joy Peace-Hope."

Charlotte, who had been clinging to a bedpost, said, "I'll do it!" and bounded out of the room. Sam gritted her teeth and told Mom, "I'm scared. I'm calling an ambulance. And if Ms. Peace-Hope gets in my way, I'll dehyphenate her."

"Sammie," Mom whispered with weary rebuke. Again Mom coughed with that terrible wheezing sound deep in her chest. "You need more optimism. Good energy. Trust me. I know you think I'm letting you down. I've always let you down, but please . . ." Mom's voice trailed off, and Sam watched her struggle not to cry. Close to tears herself, Sam stroked her mother's damp golden hair and chewed the inside of her mouth until she tasted blood. "You didn't let me down," she lied. "But I'll have a lot more good energy once a real doctor tells me you're okay."

"Guilt," Mom said, and moaned. "That's why I'm sick." Her head lolled from side to side. "Guilt over trusting Malcolm Drury. Guilt over not being able to run a successful business. Guilt over not being able to do what Alexandra can do for you and Charlotte—if you'd let her."

"Mom, you're sick because you inhaled a germ."

"Do you hate me?" Mom's hand fluttered around one of Sam's hands, then clung weakly to it. Choking down tears, Sam looked firmly into Mom's tired blue eyes. "No. Not ever."

"I know . . . my ideas seem foolish to you. I never meant to hurt you. From the day you were born, I made mistakes, but—"

"I wouldn't trade you for a thousand mothers who do ordinary things."

"I should be more like Alexandra. I want you to respect me the way you . . . respect her. She won't let you down."

"Respect?" Sam's voice rose. "It's *you* I've always respected. You and Daddy, and not Aunt—"

Mom began coughing and shivering. The cough became a long spasm. Sam frantically pulled her onto her side and pounded her between the shoulder blades until she gasped for air and the coughing stopped. The skin around her eyes and mouth was bluish-white. The fear in her eyes matched Sam's terror. "I'm calling for an ambulance," Sam said. "And that's all there is to it."

Mom made a hoarse mewl of defeat.

"You let her lie there—burning up with fever and coughing her lungs out—and didn't call me. Why?" Aunt Alexandra asked the question with an air of wounded trust as she stood with her hands on her hips in the center of the small waiting room of the intensive care unit. Charlotte was huddled on a couch in the corner, too tired to cry anymore. Sam stood facing their aunt, so numb with dread and exhaustion, she had to concentrate on keeping her knees locked. Her legs felt rubbery.

Finally Sam managed to say, "I don't like to order her around."

"Well, you'd better learn to. If you'd called me sooner, I'd have insisted she see a doctor before. Frankly, I'm surprised at you for taking chances, honey. You know how irresponsible your mother is. I count on you to—"

"She's not irresponsible. Don't ever call her that."

Amazement, displeasure, and then a kind of grim resolve swept across Aunt Alex's face. She sighed and put an arm around Sam's taut shoulders. "All right, honey. It's just that I'm upset too. Your mother has pneumonia."

Charlotte made a noise. "Is she going to *die*?"

Aunt Alex reached her before Sam could. Enfolding Charlotte in her silk-sleeved arms, Aunt Alex said, "No, of course not."

Charlotte clung to her but peered tearfully over her shoulder at Sam. "Sammie?"

"No way," Sam told her. "People don't die from pneumonia. It's no big deal." She meant that. Her confidence was rising now that they were at the hospital. Drugs and oxygen tanks and neatly uniformed people with stethoscopes around their necks—those were reliable threads she could knit into a solid safety net.

"Come with me," their aunt said gently. "We'll go downstairs and I'll buy you a snack at the cafeteria. Nothing to worry yourselves about now. I'll take care of you."

"Charlotte could use some food, but I'm not hungry. I'll stay here."

Aunt Alex raised her head sharply and looked at

Sam. Command met quiet refusal in an invisible tug-of-war. "I do appreciate your sense of responsibility," Aunt Alex said with an edgy smile. "Directed in the right channels, determination is a wonderful asset. We'll have to talk about that sometime." She took Charlotte's hand. "But not right now. Come along, Charlotte. You and I will visit the cafeteria. Now, cheer up. Your mother is going to be fine, and as soon as she gets out of this place, I'll take all three of you to Highview for a nice rest, and you can make your mother a pot full of chicken soup."

"Mom doesn't eat chicken," Charlotte said wearily. "Not even eggs. Not even when I make eggs Benedict."

"Well, that's going to change."

As Aunt Alex led her from the waiting room, Charlotte looked back at Sam doubtfully.

Sam waited until she was certain they'd entered an elevator down the hall, then strode out of the room. She pushed through the double doors to the intensive care unit. Nurses in white pantsuits looked up from various chores. One of them peered at her over a central desk lined with monitors, each of which reassured her with the steady, pulsing lifelines on their screens. "I know it's not time to visit, but I'd like to see my mother. Just for a minute."

"She's sleeping, hon."

"Could I just go in and hold her hand?"

"Well, all right."

A minute later Sam was alone with Mom in a glass cubicle with drawn blinds. The sight—Mom lying there so pale and still, outfitted with tubes and wires, her lashes making faint gold fringes on the bluish skin beneath her eyes—made Sam want to turn away, to shrink inside her own skin. She moved woodenly to Mom's side and put a hand on one of hers. "I love you very much," she whispered raggedly. "I've never wished you were like Aunt Alexandra."

Mom's lashes fluttered. She inhaled—a watery sound—and looked up at Sam groggily. A wistful smile appeared beneath the clear oxygen tube taped below her nose. "You're as strong as she is. Good. Be strong . . . now. Take my . . . wedding ring."

Dread, the kind she didn't want to name, squeezed Sam's chest. "*No*," she said, shaking her head stiffly, recoiling at the thought.

"It keeps . . . sliding off my finger. Don't want to lose it. Please."

That explanation made sense; Sam could deal with sensible requests. "I'll get a piece of surgical tape from a nurse. We'll tape your ring so it won't fall off."

"No. Please. *Please*." Mom coughed. Sam trembled. "Okay. It's all right. Easy, easy." She put a hand on Mom's forehead and stroked as gently as she could. Mom relaxed. "Your daddy always said you have his mother's hands. She was a nurse at one of the mills."

Sam had heard the story many times, and it worried her that Mom seemed to have forgotten that she knew. "Working with cloth must be in the Ryder genes. But we've never accounted for Charlotte. No great cooks in the family tree."

Mom managed a weak smile. "Charlotte's a new branch." Sam was glad she'd stopped talking about the ring. But her mother moved her fingers weakly under Sam's hand. "Take it," she said. "*Please*. I'll feel better, knowing you have it."

Tears crept down Sam's face. She slid off the plain gold band and clutched it tightly in her palm, absorbing the warmth. "I'll keep it just until you get out of here."

"Look after Charlotte. I know you will. And make peace with your aunt. She loves you. I won't have to worry about my girls . . . being all alone."

Sam froze. "Don't talk that way."

"If something happens to me . . . I put it in my . . . will. She'll be Charlotte's legal guardian."

Sam's knees buckled. Bitter protest failed under the tide of fear. *I have plans*, she wanted to shout. *Jake and I have plans.* Sam braced herself against the bed's metal railing. "Nothing is going to happen to you."

A nurse appeared in the cubicle's doorway. "Time's up, hon."

"Mom, promise me you're going to fight to get well."

"Tired, so tired," Mom answered. "Love you." Her eyes closed. Sam gripped her hand. "*Mom*. Everything's going to be all right. I have something I have to tell you. Maybe it's what you need to hear. *Mom*, we don't have to go on the way we have. Please, wake up and listen."

"Let her rest," the nurse whispered, waving Sam out.

Sam stared at the slow, labored, rise-and-fall of Mom's chest. "It's steady," she said, nodding hard. "You're going to be all right. I'll tell you later. Remember that. I've got something very important to tell you."

When Sam continued to hold her mother's hand, the nurse gently pulled her away.

The next thing Sam knew, she was back in the hall outside the stern double doors, dazed, not quite certain how she'd gotten there, tears blinding her. She had her head down, watching her hands as she rubbed Mom's wedding band between her numb fingertips, as if for luck.

A broad, big-knuckled hand closed carefully over both of hers. She jerked her head up. Jake gazed at her with stark intensity. For the briefest moment his attention flickered to the doors of the intensive care ward. His hand tightened convulsively on hers. The sympathy and alarm that swept into his expression frightened her. Mom was going to be fine. There was no reason for him to look as if he thought otherwise.

She opened her mouth to protest, but the words wouldn't come. The moment had finally arrived when neither of them were children anymore, and all the brief, furtive encounters over the years had always, without rhyme or reason, seemed destined for the stark, nearly desperate way he was looking at her now.

He knows. Somehow, he always finds me when I need him. But I can't need him. Not yet. Maybe not ever.

"I'm scared," Sam admitted. "She's really sick." Her throat worked painfully. "I'm so glad you're here."

Jake exhaled softly and pulled her to him. They stood there, holding each other, her head resting on his shoulder. His lips moved against her temple. "You haven't talked to her about us yet," he said.

"No. I knew it'd upset her. I wanted to wait until she was stronger. I tried to tell her just now—she was saying awful, morbid things about the future—but she fell asleep." Sam drew her head back and looked at him desperately. "She made me take her wedding ring. She claimed she's worried about losing it while she's in the hospital. But the way she talked about it—and, God, she told me to take care of Charlotte, and"—Sam could barely say the next words—"she told me she put a note in her will. *If anything happens to her, Aunt Alex will become Charlotte's guardian.*"

Jake looked shaken. "Your aunt drove your mother to this point," he said urgently. "Why didn't I see it coming? Your mother's got to fight. She's got to do it for you and your sister." He paused, his expression becoming even harsher, more urgent. "Your sister," he repeated. "She's only fourteen." He took Sam by the shoulders. "We can't let her be turned over to Alexandra like property. No judge is going to take her away from Alexandra."

"My mother is going to be *fine*," Sam told him, but his insight had shaken her so badly she knew she didn't sound convinced.

"You don't have to pretend with me. I know what you're scared of, and I'm scared too."

"My mother is fine," she repeated, swaying.

"I'm not going to walk away this time. You won't have to go through this alone."

The nurse shoved a door open and stared at them. "Where's your aunt, hon?"

Sam took one look at the careful expression in the woman's eyes and wanted to bolt past her into the ward. "In the cafeteria."

"You wait right here till she comes up, okay?" The nurse quickly withdrew, letting the door swing shut.

Sam followed her. Jake leapt ahead, pushing the doors open with his shoulder but taking her by one arm.

They stepped inside and Sam halted, horror flooding her. Nurses were hurrying in and out of Mom's cubicle with unfathomable bottles and syringes and implements in their hands. A door opened across the way, and a man she recognized as Mom's doctor strode swiftly toward Mom's room. He gaped at Sam and Jake for a split second. "Out. Out of here, please," he called, but disappeared into the cubicle without looking to see if they complied.

Sam lurched forward, and through a fog of shock and terror she knew Jake was beside her. But he pulled her to a halt just outside the cubicle's door, and when she struggled against his hold, he wrapped both arms around her and pulled her close, her back against his torso. "You can't help her by getting in their way. Let them do their jobs," he said hoarsely, bending his head close to hers. "Hold my hands. Hold on the way you always have, and I'll never let you down."

His voice was the only rational landmark she had. Her fingers were woven tightly in his before he finished speaking. Every nerve strained to its limit as she craned her neck, fixated on glimpses of the medical staff working on Mom. The few words they spoke were all medical jargon; the only thing that registered was the worst. *Cardiac arrest.* She was too numb to care whether her rubbery knees kept her standing or not; but Jake was holding her up, and his cheek was pressed tightly against the side of her face.

She realized she was saying "Don't give up. Mom, don't give up," like a chant.

But after a while she noticed that everyone was slowing down—the nurses, the doctor, all moving slower and slower, and no one was talking any longer, except Sam, who continued whispering, fiercely, brokenly, *Mom, don't give up*.

"Dear God, what is *he* doing here?" Aunt Alex said loudly as she rushed past them. "I left Charlotte in the waiting room. Go try to calm her down." She gave Sam and Jake one tortured, outraged glance before she pushed her way into the cubicle.

"I have to go in," Sam said, and Jake not only let go of her, he propelled her forward, one hand raised in front of her to clear people from her path.

"I'm sorry, hon," the nurse said, putting an arm around her. Sam gave a raw cry of grief. Someone had thrown Mom's pillow aside. Her head lay at a strange, limp angle, and her half-open eyes were empty. She was naked from the waist up, until someone hurriedly pulled the sheet over her breasts.

Crying, Aunt Alex bent over her, cupping her ashen, relaxed face in shaking hands. "Frannie," she said in a broken voice. "*Don't leave me.* You're the only person who loves me no matter what I do. Goddammit, you come back. I mean it. I need you."

Sam moved to her mother's side and clasped her limp, cooling hand. Deep and unstoppable sobs racked her. For the first time in her life she felt sorry for Aunt Alex. She placed her other hand on Aunt Alex's bowed back. "*No,*" Jake said, close by and urgent.

Aunt Alex cried out, then straightened and pulled Sam into her arms. Sam held on to her tightly, wishing she were Mom, clinging to an irrational hope that none of this was really happening. "I loved her so much," Aunt Alex cried. "I'll take care of them for you, Frannie. I'll take care of Sam and Charlotte."

"You've got what you've always wanted," Jake said.

Aunt Alex moved convulsively, sobbing, a sound of rage and shock exploding from her throat. "Get him *out* of here," she told the nurses, pointing at Jake. "Call security if you have to."

Sam wrenched herself away from Aunt Alex. "*No.*" She gave Jake a tortured look. She wanted to be in his arms, not Aunt Alex's. She reached out, then caught herself. *Charlotte. I have to think about Charlotte. Oh, God. There's no way out now.* "Go on. I don't want you here." That lie took all her willpower. *If he stays, it will tear me apart.* "I don't want you here," she repeated.

He reached toward her, and she drew back, but his fingers grazed her cheek gently. His hand dropped to his side. She feared he'd argue, and when he didn't—when

he turned and left without another word—she felt empty
and, this time, so hopelessly hidden inside herself he'd
never find her again.

Sarah hurried into Hugh's office, cold air gusting
in behind her, the brown paper bag containing Hugh's
lunch crushed carelessly under one arm. "Is he free?"
she asked the receptionist without stopping, who nodded
but peered at her disheveled state curiously through the
window of the records area. Sarah had already opened
the door to the suite of examining rooms. She strode
down the narrow hall, jerking at her heavy cloth coat.
The door to Hugh's office stood open, and Sarah rushed
inside. He was standing before a small window with his
back to her, staring into the brick alley of the antiques
store next door, his hair rumpled as if he'd been running
his hands through it. He pivoted, and she saw the troubled expression on his face.

"You heard," she said, unceremoniously dropping the
lunch bag on his cluttered desk and tossing her coat across
a chair. "You already heard about Frannie Ryder."

He exhaled. "Yes."

"It's so damned unfair. She was too young. How
could somebody her age die from pneumonia?"

He shook his head slowly. "It happens. It's a damned
shame, but it does."

"I stopped by the florist's to buy some silk roses
for my table arrangement, and she told me about the
funeral. It was in Durham *this afternoon*. I feel terrible—
we should have gone."

"I doubt Alexandra would have let us within a mile
of it."

"I don't care. I would have tried for Frannie's sake.
Oh, Hugh, what about her girls? Sam must be what—
barely out of high school?—and the younger one's still
just a child. I wish I could say *something* to them."

"I doubt that's ever going to be an option now. Oscar
Talbert came in to have a checkup this morning, and he
said Alexandra already had the girls' belongings packed.

She hired him to go up to Asheville and get them. He was on his way."

"God, she didn't waste a minute. I can't believe Frannie would want it this way."

"I'm sorry, but she did. She gave Alexandra legal guardianship of Charlotte. Put it in her will." When Sarah groaned, he shook his head. "Where else could the girls go? Alexandra is their aunt. It makes sense."

"How can you stand there and look so reasonable when you *know* what kind of 'guardian' Alexandra will be? She turned poor Tim into a swaggering cretin who's so afraid of her that he has to prove his manhood by bullying everyone else. She'll mash those girls under her thumb too." She hesitated, thinking hard. "Sam's old enough to walk away, but I expect she won't do it. She won't leave her sister. *Damn.*"

Hugh came over and took her in his arms. He looked at her with sympathy but also rebuke. "Nobody understands your feelings about Alexandra better than I do. But after William died, you made the decision to have nothing to do with any of Alexandra's relatives. Maybe we could have made a difference to Frannie—we could have helped her some way. Now it's a helluva mess. Are you trying to tell me you want to get involved?"

Sarah shivered and looked at him with defeat. "You're saying it's a little late for me to play Good Samaritan. All right. I feel appropriately lousy. Thank you."

He kissed her forehead. "No, I'm saying you better get your armor on."

Sarah stared at him, mouth open in silent, dawning comprehension. "Hugh Raincrow, you better diagnose this situation for me *precisely*, and don't mince any words. *Why* didn't you call me about Frannie the second you heard?"

Hugh looked at her steadily, as if trying to predict her reaction. "Jake was never cured. He's a chronic case, and there's no vaccine for it. It's highly contagious too. Sammie Ryder's got it just as bad." He gazed at her for another second, then concluded, "Love, I'm afraid."

"Oh, my God." Sarah wound her hands in his shirt and tugged. "Where's Jake?"

Hugh looked away, his expression bearing the regret of the only secrets he'd ever kept from her. "He went to the funeral."

Jake sat on the steps of his empty, dark house, his shoulders slumped. The early winter darkness had an icy edge. Bo lay on the porch close beside him, watching his face. Jake dropped a hand to the dog's head. Bo was puzzled. Why wouldn't Jake leave the cold dusk and take him inside?

"What's the point," Jake said. He was closer to defeat than he'd been since the time Uncle William died, when he'd first understood that knowing the truth didn't always make a difference.

"I don't believe Bo can hear *or* smell," Mother said. Jake raised his head and quickly passed a hand over his damp eyes. Mother stood in the shadows at the end of the porch, hugging herself over a long white shawl. "Both of you let me walk right up."

Jake said nothing. Mother might recognize the misery in his voice and ask questions. She sat down beside him, and he stared stiffly ahead. She touched the sleeve of his black suit. She knew. She knew about Mrs. Ryder, and where he had been, and he didn't feel any anger in her.

"And if that isn't strange enough," she continued, "here you sit, dressed in the last thing I expected to see. When was the last time you wore a suit? Hmmm. Graduation. Four years ago. That's why I took so many pictures. To prove to future generations that my son actually owned a matching coat and pants." She put her arm around him. "And this is a *new* suit too. Should I get my camera?"

Jake cleared his throat. "Father told you about Samantha."

She was silent for a second. Then she said, "Yes, he can't manage to keep a secret for more than, oh, five, maybe ten years, tops."

"Maybe he thought it'd never come to anything." He paused, then added quietly, "Maybe he was right."

"If I could choose any girl for you to love, it wouldn't be one who shares even a drop of Alexandra's blood."

"I know."

"But that's a moot point, I guess. Do you love her, son? I just need to hear you say so."

"I love her."

"No doubt? I mean, does it go way beyond the superficial things, like looks and—okay, you're forcing your ol' mother to take a big, flat, frank step forward—does it go beyond—"

"Sex is only a part of it. I love her the same way Father loves you."

Mother sighed raggedly. "Boy, you know how to settle a discussion."

Jake's head sagged. "I couldn't even talk to her today. Orrin had men around. If I'd tried to get through, there'd have been trouble. I couldn't risk it, not at her mother's funeral. So I kept back, like I've always done. Like a damned helpless coward."

"*No*, like a man who cares more about her feelings than his own pride."

"She wouldn't even look at me. She kept her arm around Charlotte and her head down. She's trapped." Jake clenched his fists on his knees. He shivered, not from the cold. "I talked to a lawyer in Durham. Abraham Dreyfus."

"The same Dreyfus who represented the tribal council in a timber-rights suit against the government?"

"Everyone says he's the best. I asked him what the chances are of me and Samantha getting Charlotte out of Alexandra's custody."

"Oh, sweetie." Her voice filled with sorrow. She patted his back.

"He showed me a picture of his son. He said even if his own son came to him and asked what I asked, he'd tell him he didn't have a snowball's chance in hell. He said no judge in his right mind would tell the lieutenant-governor's wife she can't keep custody of her own niece—especially when the girl's mother wanted it that way."

"I'll never believe Frannie would have made that decision if she'd known about you and Sam—"

"I should have gone to Samantha sooner. I should have seen this coming. Why does it let me down sometimes when I need it most?"

"What, sweetie? Why does *what* let you down?"

Jake silently kicked himself for being careless. "Mrs. Big Stick told me once that I'd bring some kind of curse down on us if I did what I wanted. Maybe I believed her more than I thought."

"Listen to me, son. I respect Clara's ideas, but the *curse* on this family started the day Alexandra married your uncle. Nothing you've done or can do will change that."

"But I'm the one who has to finish it. Samantha and me. I know that much. I just don't know how yet, and it's tearing me up inside." He looked at Mother. "There were people who thought you shouldn't marry Father. What if they'd been able to stop you? What if all you could think about was being with him but you couldn't do it?"

"Oh, no, you're not getting hypothetical sanctions from me, mister. Let's stick to reality."

"You'd have found a way to do it. No matter what that took."

Mother gave a sigh of defeat. "All right. Let's talk turkey." Her voice filled with grim humor. "We'll just kidnap Charlotte and scoot off to Mexico. We'll rent a nice hacienda and hide her until she's eighteen. You and Sam can have a mariachi band at your wedding."

"I won't get you and Father involved. But don't worry—I'll write to you after we're settled."

"Jake!" She craned her neck, studied him with open-mouthed alarm, and shook him lightly. "My Lord, you're serious. Don't even *think* that way."

He got to his feet, hands clenched, wanting to hit something, to punch one of the porch's thick, rough supports until pain drove away all other feelings. "Tim hates her. She's always been his mother's prize, and he knows that. If he gets the chance, he'll hurt her somehow. And if he does that, I'll—"

Mother leapt up and grabbed his fists. "From all I've heard about Sammie, she's not the type who'll let Tim get away with anything. Son, you have to trust that she'll come to you for help if she needs it. Now it's up to her."

Jake lifted his head. The first stars of the January night glittered like small crystals—distant and unreachable. He would sleep under the quilt Sam had made for him. Her grief and fears would never be separate from his.

And if anyone hurt her, God help them.

Chapter Fifteen

"They've been here a month, and all you do is pamper them," Tim told his mother bitterly. "But I come home from school to tell you I've been offered an internship with a judge on the state supreme court and you act as if it were a crayon drawing I'd brought you to pin on the refrigerator."

Alexandra leaned back in a chair in the library and gazed at her son with weary exasperation. "Don't take that air of wounded pride with me. Orrin arranged the internship for you."

"I *earned* it."

"Hardly. Left to your own initiative, you'd fritter away your opportunities. Do you ever think about anyone but yourself? I'm trying to help your cousins cope with their mother's death. Be a man about it."

"I'm always second-class. You've got bigger dreams for *them* than you ever had for me."

"Samantha and Charlotte are handicapped by years of benign mismanagement. I have to concentrate on setting them on the right course as quickly as I can."

"Then send Sam to college. Get her out of here. Why did you let her talk you into staying in town until next fall?"

"Because Charlotte is a weepy little clinging vine, and Samantha thinks she'll wilt if she leaves her so soon."

"Sam is playing you for a fool. She wants to stay here so she can be close to Jake."

"No, we've had some long discussions about that matter. She has absolutely no interest in encouraging him. I think losing her mother made her realize how needlessly difficult and lonely their lives really were. She's ready for something different." Alexandra gave Tim a reassuring nod. "There's room for both of you in my plans. You have a future in law, and then politics. Samantha has an excellent aptitude for business. If all goes as I expect— and it *will*—I'll need her to manage various concerns of mine after Orrin becomes governor. I'll have too many new responsibilities to handle them myself."

Tim appeared only slightly mollified. "What about Charlotte?"

Alexandra bit her tongue. She had no intention of telling him that she saw Charlotte merely as an extension of Samantha, a tool who could be used to keep Samantha's loyalty. Charlotte was endearing and affectionate in the same way Frannie had been, but, like her mother, utterly without serious ambitions. "Charlotte is a born hostess," she told him. "Any family in the public eye needs one of those."

Tim's eyes flashed. "What do you think I'll do— marry some social retard who'll embarrass you?"

"No, because if you ever wanted to marry such a creature, I'd make certain you came to your senses. So far your taste in women has been dictated indiscriminately by your hormones."

"Would you rather people around here whisper about me the way they do about Jake—and Ellie? I had to go through high school listening to kids snicker about my *queer* cousins."

Alexandra frowned. "Jake, unfortunately, has proved he has an interest in the opposite sex. I wish he hadn't chosen Samantha to do it." She waved one hand dismissively. "I won't object to your indulgences while you're in law school. People are suspicious of men who don't have a few youthful escapades to their credit. An overdeveloped streak of virtue implies a lack of know-how—or worse, a lack of interest. But they're equally suspicious of a man who doesn't know when to settle down. Until you're ready to do that, don't whine about my low opinion of your women."

Tim stared at her. "Everything I say and do is just a petty annoyance to you."

"Only when you're in one of your childish moods." Sarcasm tinged her voice. "Competing for my attention against Samantha and Charlotte—as if I'm handing out ice cream cones and you're afraid you'll be overlooked. I won't put up with it. When you're at home, I expect you to be pleasant to them. I *demand* it."

"If Dad had lived, he wouldn't let you—"

"I'm so tired of hearing that. He was foolishly sentimental, and someday you'll thank me for making certain you didn't turn out just like him."

"Someday you'll wish you hadn't treated me like shit." Tim left, slamming the library's massive door behind him. Alexandra picked up the book she'd closed when he stormed into the room. Tim would comply with her orders. He always did.

Charlotte wandered the maze of upstairs hallways, aimless and bereft, trailing one hand along the handsome mahogany molding that kept chairs and tables and people from bumping against the wallpaper. Everything in Aunt Alex's house was protected from carelessness and uncertainty. Charlotte needed that sense of sanctuary, though it churned her grief into frantic regrets.

If only we'd come here sooner. Mom would have been safe here too.

She never said that to Sam, because she was sure Sam blamed herself for not recognizing it in time. Sam never cried in front of Charlotte or anyone else, but at night Charlotte crept into the bath between their bedrooms and listened at her sister's door, hearing terrible sobs even huge down pillows couldn't muffle.

Charlotte continued down the hall, blind with sorrow, guiding herself by the molding. She'd tried desperately to make Sam feel better by telling her she was happy here, because Sam wouldn't have to worry about making money to take care of her, and Mom had wanted it that way.

At the end of the hall were open double doors. Charlotte blinked as if waking up, and stared at them in dull curiosity. Aunt Alex and Uncle Orrin's suite. They had gone to the country club tonight, to play bridge.

She pushed one of the heavy doors aside and stepped into the room. It was large and plush, with the hardwood floors covered in Oriental rugs and good reproductions of the Impressionists on the pale peach walls. The furniture was massive and European; the room had the feel of a fine antiques store. A broad, tall bedstead with handsomely carved posts and coverings of richly stitched satin dominated the room, facing French doors that opened onto a balcony.

Charlotte moved around the room, wistfully touching an ornate lamp here, a tapestried throw pillow there, running her fingertips over crystal boxes on the dresser, and a small ceramic statue of nudes on a table by a draped window. Touching her aunt's beautiful possessions filled her with comfort; Aunt Alex was surrounded by so many pretty things; she was invincible.

She spotted white louvered doors on adjacent walls. Charlotte pushed one open and studied an enormous bath with a sunken tub and twin vanities. Peering around a silk Chinese screen, she scrutinized a peach-colored toilet and matching bidet. She had read about bidets but had never seen one; the strange device intrigued her. She turned a handle and watched a jet of water shoot upward. Amazing. Aunt Alex had to wash her privates, just like an ordinary human being.

There was a single louvered door at the opposite end of the bath. Charlotte eased it open. An elaborate dressing room met her stunned gaze—a small, almost claustrophobic room of deep white carpet, crammed with racks of clothing and shelves filled with shoes, belts, purses—a veritable department store of fine things. She pressed a light switch, and a chandelier glittered softly overhead in the center of a domed ceiling. Along one wall was a long, low dresser before an enormous mirror surrounded by lights. And lined up on the dresser were rows of tall jewelry boxes, gilded and delicate, with tiny drawers.

Jewelry. Breathless with wonder, Charlotte sat down on the satin cushions of a bench at the dresser's center. She slid the tiny drawers out and gazed at an endless variety of earrings, necklaces, bracelets, rings—gold, sterling, and polished gemstones of every color and size. She lifted a pair of clip earrings from one velvet-lined drawer—diamond clusters, sparkling in the light.

Charlotte removed all four of her own earrings—cheap silver hoops and gold studs. She pushed her hair back and fastened the diamond clusters to her ears, then stared at herself sadly in the vast mirror. She thought she looked as invincible as a person wearing diamonds, one of Sam's handmade sweaters, and jeans could look. Satisfied, she scanned the dresser for more prizes. A small gold box was nestled among the bigger cases; she flipped the lid open, then gave a low sigh of awe.

Aunt Alex's gold necklace and pendant. Charlotte couldn't resist. She slipped the necklace over her head and arranged the filigree pendant on the center of her chest.

"What are you doing in here?"

She jumped. Tim loomed in the doorway, dressed in running shorts and a sweatshirt with the arms cut off at the shoulders. He was too large and muscle-bound; she thought of a cookbook photograph, one with diagrams showing the best cuts on a bulky red steer. He was all shoulder, shank, and brisket.

Sam had warned her to avoid him and his sarcastic comments whenever he visited from college; Sam said—and it didn't sound like a joke—that she'd go after him with a knitting needle if he tried to intimidate them.

Charlotte couldn't let anything like that happen. "Just exploring," she told him. She jerked the earrings off and dropped them on the dresser. The pendant felt like a guilty weight over her heart. "I got lost. This house is so big, I need to leave a trail of bread crumbs to find my way back." She was talking too fast, with a high-pitched tone. She sounded frightened when she meant to sound friendly. "I'll make a nice loaf of pumpernickel to carry around with me."

"You aren't lost. You think you can go anywhere in this house you goddamned well please."

Having a cozy familiarity with obscene language, which she had been forced to cultivate at school to parry comments about her large breasts, Charlotte blurted out, "If I tell you I'm lost, I goddamned well *am*."

She regretted that immediately. Fury replaced the sour expression in his eyes. He took one long, quick step into the room, snatched her by an arm, and shook her so hard, her teeth clicked together. "Stay where you belong," he said in a low voice. "And don't rummage through my mother's jewelry. You won't get it. Not any of it."

"Let go of me! I was only admiring it!"

He twisted her arm, grinding his fingers in. She struggled but he wouldn't release her. Charlotte felt light-headed with pain and shock. "I won't come back here again, I swear. Stop it. You're hurting me. Just leave me alone, and I'll leave you alone."

But he bent over her, putting his face inches from hers. "Let's get something straight. You and your sister can pull this accommodating shit on my mother and Orrin, but I don't buy it. I'll make you wish my mother had never brought your little cherry ass into this house."

He grabbed the pendant. The heavy chain sawed at the back of her neck, and Charlotte threw up a hand instinctively. She hit him in the jaw. He gasped. "You little bitch. I'll get that necklace off you whether you like it or not."

Charlotte cried out as he dragged her off the bench. He swept a leg beneath her, and she fell on the carpet. He planted a knee on either side of her and wound both hands in the front of her sweater. She clawed at him, but he pulled the sweater over her head and threw it aside. The necklace clung stubbornly, the pendant sliding under the center of her bra. "Jesus," he said under his breath as he stared down at her breasts encased in the sheer white material. He grabbed her hands and jammed them under his knees. Charlotte was beyond coherence; she made furious and terrified sounds. Her hands felt crushed.

"You think you and your sister can take over this house?" he asked sarcastically. "I'll show you who's in charge." He pulled her bra down and mauled her breasts, squeezing one in each of his powerful hands, bending over her, smiling at her. "I can even do this, and you won't tell anyone, because if you do, I'll say you're lying. A lying little bitch who wants to cause trouble."

Her hands numb, her breasts already feeling bruised, horror shooting through her brain, Charlotte was reduced to strangled groans. He squeezed them roughly again, then snagged the necklace in one hand and drew it over her head. Holding it above her dazed eyes, he whispered, "*Do you understand?* Say it."

"I . . . understand."

He got to his feet and stepped over her as if she didn't exist. He scooped her sweater off the floor and threw it at her. "Get out of here. Keep quiet about this, and stay out of my way when I'm at home, or I'll demonstrate this lesson again."

Charlotte rearranged her bra and pulled the sweater back on with hands that felt like shaking wooden blocks. She wanted to scream. She wanted to kill him. He watched her, his mother's beautiful necklace hanging from his fingertips, the pendant swinging lazily. "Hurry up, Cousin," he said softly. "I'm losing my patience."

She staggered to her feet and ran.

She didn't stop until she was in her room. She huddled on the bed, in the dark, staring blindly out a window. The night—the whole world—was rainy and cold. She was dimly aware of her arm and breasts hurting, and the raw, stinging line across the nape of her neck. She heard movements, and her gaze shifted frantically to the light coming from beneath the closed door to the bath she and Sam shared. This house wasn't safe—Charlotte would never feel safe here again. But where else could they go? She didn't want Sam to give this up for her sake.

Sam knocked on the door, then opened it and peeked in. The fog from a hot shower curled around her robe and the towel wrapped around her head. "I thought you were getting ready for bed," she told Charlotte, sounding concerned. When Charlotte stiffened and didn't answer, Sam padded over to her and sat down, putting an arm around her. There had been so many times like this in the past month, times when they had sat together silently, no words needed to give comfort. Sam didn't suspect the difference this time.

"We'll be all right," Sam said finally, her voice tired and hollow. "Next week you'll start school in town, and I'll start working for Aunt Alex. Life will feel more normal when we're busy."

Charlotte leaned against her, shivering, filled with the one fear she couldn't share.

Clara adjusted a bandanna over her long, graying braids, hitched up the sagging waistband of her voluminous print skirt, smoothed her leather jacket, and padded into the elegant, perfume-scented confines of Naughty Nice on worn brown boots that laced up above her ankles.

"Hello, Mrs. Big Stick. You want some new lingerie for Valentine's Day?"

Clara peered over a rack of lacy teddies. Patsy Jones,

short and thin and well-dressed, with her black hair cut off in a sleek bob, gazed back at her from behind a small gold cash register atop a delicate table painted white and gold. Patsy was Keet Jones's oldest granddaughter, about eighteen. "You know what I came for," Clara answered.

Patsy glanced toward the door furtively, as if someone might walk in and catch them at any second. "You're a few minutes early. She's not here yet. Her shift starts at two." Patsy shifted nervously. "Mrs. Lomax's secretary drops her off and picks her up. I don't think she goes anywhere without Mrs. Lomax knowing about it."

"Hmmmph." Clara wasn't surprised. She glanced around the elegant shop, one of several Alexandra Lomax owned. The ravenmocker had made certain her prize wouldn't stray. Clara's gaze shifted back to Patsy's. "You're a good girl, one who respects her elders and helps when her grandfather asks her to."

"This gives me the jitters," Patsy admitted. "If Mrs. Lomax found out, she'd probably tell the manager to fire me. And I need this job. I'm saving money to go to the university next year."

"What are you going to study?"

"Social work."

Clara nodded politely, though she thought social work was something that just came naturally to people. "That sounds interesting. Plenty of folks around here could use social work."

"Hmmm. I saw Jake Raincrow last week. He came to my cousin's house about a dog. My cousin took it in—it was a stray. Nothing special. He was going to shoot it, but he asked around if anyone wanted a dog. Jake came."

Clara was annoyed at the way Patsy connected Jake and *social work* in the same breath, as if Jake were some kind of community threat. But she couldn't resist looking at Patsy hopefully. "Did he say much?"

"No. Just said he'd find it a home. Cousin Odie told him the dog doesn't act like it's got much tracking sense, but Jake took it anyway. Odie doesn't understand why a tracker would care about a dog like that." Patsy stacked credit card invoices and watched Clara somberly. "Jake's too quiet. He makes people nervous. He doesn't make sense. And lately he's got this look about him—like he's daring anybody to cross his path. People say he might be dangerous."

Clara thrust her jaw out. "If you want to do social work, then you tell people to mind their own business. You tell 'em I said so, because I'm trained to know about these things. Jake's not dangerous—not to those who don't deserve it. When he's ready to take up with the rest of us, he will. Something will pull him out of himself."

"My sister says he didn't have girlfriends in high school. Not ever."

"Seems to me that you Joneses don't have much to do if you spend so much time pondering someone who's going about his own business without bothering anybody."

Patsy ducked her head. "I'm sorry. Didn't mean any disrespect. I forgot, he's from your clan."

"I'm *proud* of him, you hear? There aren't many souls that strong in this world, and the ones that are, they *shine*, you hear?"

"Yes, Mrs. Big Stick." Patsy looked anxious, as if "social work" had gotten her in over her head and she should call for reinforcements.

Clara shook a finger at her. "And let me tell you another thing—" A bell tinkled on the shop's pretty glass door, and Clara clamped her mouth shut. Samantha walked in. Clara had seen her only that one time, when she was little more than a baby, but the memory of that stern, self-assured child was indelible.

The girl didn't seem to notice Clara. She moved with the firm, forward grace of someone much older, and her eyes were tired—with shadows underneath, but hooded with a kind of quiet determination. She was medium height, and her face was pretty in an old-fashioned way, with a blunt jaw and small, tight mouth. Her hair was the deep blond color of old gold, straight, fine, and just long enough to brush her shoulders.

She was neatly dressed to the point of severity in a white cloth coat, a long wool skirt belted at the waist, and plain flat shoes. She carried a huge cloth tote with a wad of knitting sticking out the top, and a brown lunch bag with the top precisely folded. She wore no jewelry except a simple wristwatch with a thin leather band, and she held her belongings with the most beautiful hands Clara had ever seen—boneless-looking and porcelain-smooth, with slender, tapering fingers that ended in the perfect tips of unpainted nails.

Clara liked the no-nonsense look of her and felt bad for her situation. But Clara had to make certain she wouldn't bring doom on Jake and his family. Alexandra was an evil spirit, birthed in a hole somewhere, human in appearance but without human roots. A ravenmocker envied flesh-and-blood people, and used them to work its will.

And poor Samantha would never escape from a ravenmocker.

Clara stepped out from behind a rack. "Make yourself scarce, Patsy. Me and Samantha have to have a talk."

Samantha's head jerked up. She stared at Clara and slowly dropped her belongings on a table. Patsy knew better than to question a medicine woman's directions. She went to the back room.

"You look familiar, ma'am," Samantha said. "Have we met?"

Polite to her elders. That was good. Seemed sincere, not smart-alecky. Clara said somberly, "You talk real well. My medicine worked. 'Course, I think it worked because you couldn't resist talking to Jake, but I'll take the credit."

"Mrs. Big Stick! My mother never let me forget you."

"Your mother seemed like a wise person. Too bad she passed on."

Shriveling grief shadowed Samantha's eyes. "Do you have any other miracles handy?" Her voice was tired, very tired.

"There aren't any miracles. Just faith, know-how, and a keen sense of what's right." Clara studied her somberly. "I don't think you believe in miracles anyhow."

"No, I don't."

"Hmmm. You look into shadows and don't see that it takes light to make them."

Samantha slumped a little. "All I see are shadows right now." She eyed Clara cautiously. "You came here especially to talk to me?"

"Yes."

"Did Jake send you?" The girl winced, and sorrow seemed to weigh every word.

"No. But I came because of him." Samantha scrutinized her with a puzzled frown, and Clara took one of her hands. "I've done my best over the years to warn him away from you—away from everyone and everything that belongs to your aunt. I've got nothing against you yourself, but I want to make sure you understand. Jake's half crazy from worrying about you. One word from you—one sign that you'd risk everything to be with him—and he'll never let go. I know love's a hard feeling to ignore. But he's got to forget it—and so do you."

Samantha's face became a careful mask. Clara felt immediate respect for the girl's ability to shut others out of her feelings. That kind of talent hadn't been learned overnight. This fledgling woman looked as tough as nails— maybe as tough as Alexandra Vanderveer Lomax. Clara thought of poor Jake, of souls that had been so carved and polished by trouble that they gleamed. This girl, she thought, reminded her of Jake a lot.

"I can't stop loving him," Samantha said slowly. "Or stop hoping that someday—"

"I'm sorry for you. Sorry for what you were born into. But the die was cast years before you drew your first breath. Your aunt don't let go of what she wants, you hear? She'll get her way come hell or high water. Oh, you and Jake, you might sidestep her somehow and think you've got her beat, but she'll lie in wait for you. I'm not a crazy old woman. *Hear me, child.* Love Jake all you want, but don't do anything about it. You'll bring ruin to him and his whole family."

Samantha looked away, her eyes shuttered with misery. Clara could see that the girl believed her but didn't want to admit it. Clara looked at her with satisfaction and regret. "Your aunt's evil," Clara whispered. "Don't you ever think otherwise. Don't ever let your guard down."

The girl's tormented eyes shifted back to Clara's. Slowly, her mouth set in a grim line, she nodded.

Chapter Sixteen

Charlotte had been enrolled in Pandora High School for three weeks, and Sam was worried about her. Sam had gained weight—greasy sandwiches, french fries, and candy bars had suddenly developed an angry appeal, as if she wanted to prove that junk food would have kept Mom healthy. But Charlotte, who had always eaten like a starving piranha, and had the padding to show for it, barely ate at all. Her tearful spontaneity had become pale, dry-eyed lethargy, and at Highview she stayed in her bedroom at every opportunity, huddled under the covers with novels that she never seemed to finish reading.

Sam brooded about that, and about Mom, and Jake with obsessive simplicity, and moved through the hours at work in a daze.

"Did you hear me?" Patsy asked. "Hello in there. Anybody home?"

Sam turned from the shop's window, a half-folded silk slip in her hands. Business was slow in the winter, Patsy said. Some afternoons hardly anyone came in. She stood at the window whenever it was like that, her gaze trained on passing cars and bundled-up pedestrians, and she realized she was always, always hoping that Jake would pass by. He didn't.

She looked at Patsy dully. "I'm sorry. What?"

"The weather service says it isn't going to snow," Patsy repeated, frowning mildly at her, "but my grandfather says all the signs are right for a *big* snow. And he usually knows."

"They have computers and satellites at the weather service," Sam told her.

"But they don't have grandfathers who talk to animals."

Sam didn't know what to say to that argument, and was distracted when Aunt Alex's heavy silver sedan pulled into a parking spot by the shop's brick sidewalk. Her secretary and Charlotte got out, Charlotte moving as if her quilted blue jacket and corduroy trousers were lined with lead.

"I picked her up from school a little early," Barbara said as they entered the shop. "The nurse called." Aunt Alex's efficient secretary nodded in Charlotte's direction. Charlotte leaned on the corner of a rack filled with robes and shrugged glumly at Sam. "She went to the infirmary after lunch," Barbara added. "She has a terrible headache. Mrs. Lomax and the lieutenant-governor aren't home from the capital yet, but I gave Mrs. Lomax a call. She gave permission for Charlotte to leave school early today."

"It's the snow weather," Patsy interjected. "It gives people sinus trouble."

Sam cupped her sister's drawn, ashen face between her hands. "I've got some aspirin—"

"Mom never gave us aspirin. I want some herbal tea." Sam looked away, biting her lip and feeling guilty.

"I've got to walk down to the jeweler's and pick up something for Mrs. Lomax," Barbara said, rolling her eyes. "If Charlotte wants herbal tea, she'll have to pick it out herself."

"Then we'll go with you and stop at the health food store," Sam said firmly, and glanced at Patsy. "Okay? It won't take long."

Patsy spread her hands. "I'm not exactly overrun with customers. Go ahead."

Sam got her coat from the back, and they walked out. She tucked an arm through Charlotte's and grasped her hand. It was cold and damp. They followed the perpetually fast-moving Barbara down a sidewalk lined with colorful awnings and leafless shrubs in ornate stoneware pots. The shrubs rattled in an icy wind. "Patsy's grandfather says it's going to snow," Sam said, trying to get Charlotte to discuss something, anything.

But Barbara looked over her shoulder at her, snorted, and said, "He's an Indian," as if that summed up the value of the prediction.

"And you're black," Sam said evenly. "But I wouldn't dismiss your beliefs just because of that."

"I don't need any lessons in racial tolerance, young lady." Barbara looked embarrassed and muttered, "I'm the only black woman in these mountains who owns a BMW and a condo at the country club. Don't you lecture *me* about open-mindedness."

With that convoluted rationale firmly in place, she pushed open the door of a small shop with BECK'S FINE JEWELRY on the glass in gold script. They stepped inside, and Charlotte's hand clenched Sam's tightly. Sam stared at her anxiously. "Your aunt left some things to be cleaned," Barbara said. "Wait here. I'll pick them up and then we can go buy your *tea*."

She marched to a counter and began talking to a short, balding man who greeted her warmly and scurried into a back room while an equally short and balding clerk made small talk about the high quality of Mrs. Lomax's jewelry.

Sam, bewildered and alarmed, stared at the blue vein that had appeared in the chalky skin at the corner of Charlotte's mouth. Charlotte's hand trembled inside hers.

"Let's get some fresh air," Sam told her, and Charlotte nodded weakly. But the jeweler returned with a felt bag that had an invoice pinned to it, and Charlotte froze. "It's such a joy to clean and polish these fine pieces for Mrs. Lomax," he told Barbara, spreading rings and bracelets on the counter under the soft, bright light of a jeweler's lamp. "And this, of course"—he held up the thick gold chain and its pendant, letting the pendant swing gracefully and catch the light—"this is a masterpiece. So heavy, and yet delicate."

Charlotte's grip on Sam's hand relaxed suddenly, her eyes fluttered, and she slumped. Sam caught her under the shoulders the instant before her head reached the floor.

"Go get Dr. Raincrow!" the jeweler yelled to his clerk.

"No, no, *no*," Barbara retorted, dropping down beside them.

"But his office is just down the street."

"I don't care. He's not what Mrs. Lomax would—"

"*Get him*," Sam said, cradling Charlotte's head and staring fiercely at everyone.

The clerk hurried out.

Jake's father was the kind of doctor Sam thought existed only on television: calm, infinitely gentle, and handsome in a solemn, nonchalant sort of way. Stretched out on the jeweler's floor with her head in Sam's lap, Charlotte gazed up at him wistfully as he knelt beside her with his honey-colored fingertips pressed to the underside of her wrist. He studied his pocket watch, which had a scratched face and a tarnished winding stem. "Still ticking," he announced in a low, kind tone, and smiled at Charlotte.

"Me, or the watch?" she asked. Her voice was a shaky croak.

"Both. But you're ticking considerably faster than the watch. Take a deep breath. Now let it out. Good girl." He looked at Sam with warm brown eyes under shaggy brows beginning to turn gray. Sam had not felt like crying until she gazed into his face. Jake had his cheekbones and full, generous mouth. This was a man who had no reason to be kind to Alexandra Lomax's nieces, but there wasn't any hint of dislike in his eyes.

"Are you sure she's all right?" Sam asked gruffly.

"Considering what you two have gone through in the past six weeks, I'd say she fainted from stress and exhaustion." He tucked a blood pressure cuff into the pocket of his overcoat.

Sam kept thinking of the necklace. There was something else going on here, but she wasn't going to ask Charlotte about it in front of Aunt Alex's spy. Barbara was hunched over them, watching Dr. Raincrow unhappily. "Thank you," she interjected coolly. "You may send a bill for your services to Mrs. Lomax."

"There's no charge." For the first time, his voice was less than pleasant. But he looked at Charlotte, patted her shoulder, and his face softened. "Lie here a few more minutes and think about something that makes you feel good."

Charlotte sighed. Tears filled her eyes. "A perfect *soufflé*," she said.

He smiled. Sam choked up and looked away. Dr. Raincrow folded Charlotte's coat and eased it under her head. "Sam, step outside and let's have a talk. You look like you need some breathing room too."

Barbara glared at him. "There's no need for—"

"He's a doctor," Sam said grimly. "I'm going to talk to him." She stroked Charlotte's hair. "I'll be right back. Keep breathing."

"Soufflés," Charlotte mumbled, and shut her eyes.

Sam rose with Dr. Raincrow. He held the shop's door for her, and after they were outside he took her by one elbow and guided her to a wrought iron bench. Sam sat down beside him, her hands knotted in her lap. "She doesn't eat enough, and I don't think she sleeps very well either. She has nightmares. I hear her crying in her sleep, and I wake her up. But she won't tell me what her dreams are about." Sam shivered. "I know she's dreaming about our mother, because I do." Sam looked at him firmly. "She's not pregnant, if that's what you wanted to ask me. She's shy around boys. Besides, we were raised to discuss sex openly. And she trusts me. I'd know if she'd done anything. She hasn't."

Dr. Raincrow cleared his throat and looked at her with fatherly appreciation. "My son is right. You're very honest."

Sam hunched her shoulders and stared at her hands. "No, I'm not. When I can't say what I want, I just don't say anything at all. That's not a wonderful brand of honesty."

"He's down in Georgia." Dr. Raincrow didn't have to say who *he* was. They both knew. "The park service asked him to find some hikers who never showed up at their checkpoint on the Appalachian Trail."

"There's a bad snowstorm coming," Sam said carefully. She knew she was walking a careful line. Discussing Jake might reveal how badly she wanted to see him.

"Hmmm. That's what the old-timers are saying. That's what he thinks too."

"He must be a very respected tracker, from what I've heard."

"He is. His sister has the same talent, but she applies it differently. Now, Ellie"—Dr. Raincrow waved a hand proudly—"she'd take Charlotte's hands for a second, and she'd say, without anyone giving her Charlotte's background, she'd say, 'You're not sleeping or eating enough.'"

"That's kind of eerie." Sam shifted. "That kind of intuition."

"Well, I think it's a matter of having a keen gift for observation. Logic."

"Logic." Sam nodded. "There aren't many mysteries in the world." *Except for Charlotte's reaction to that necklace.*

"I agree." He paused, and she thought he was going to get up and leave. "*If* I believed in meddling in situations I can't completely analyze," Dr. Raincrow said slowly, "*if* I did, I'd tell you that Jake hasn't been fit company for other human beings since the day you and your sister came here to live, and that his mother and I have discussed every way we can think of to change this situation. You and Charlotte would have been welcome in our home."

Sam looked at him with surprise and gratitude she couldn't hide. "Tell him I don't expect him to wait for me any longer. Tell him I don't want him to be unhappy." She struggled with the next words. "Give him this, please." She pulled the thin necklace from inside her blouse, closed her hand around the rough stone one more time, then lifted it over her head and held it out. "Tell him I said good-bye."

Dr. Raincrow frowned and studied the dull, purplish ruby in bewilderment. "He gave this to you?"

"When we were kids. Back when we thought there was nothing we couldn't overcome."

Barbara popped out of the jewelry shop. Sam quickly jammed the ruby into Dr. Raincrow's coat pocket. "Sam, you can discuss Charlotte's condition with Mrs. Lomax's private physician," Barbara said, staring nervously at them. "Let's go."

Sam stood immediately, all business. Dr. Raincrow rose too, and she glanced at his face, then away quickly, because he knew she had no choice, and she saw the anger and something that might be pity in his face. "Thank you," she told him, and held out a hand. "For taking the time to see to Charlotte."

He shook her hand gallantly. "Take care."

Sam hurried back inside, her head up and her shoulders squared, one hand clenched wretchedly over the empty space where she'd always kept Jake's promise.

Charlotte screamed. Sam was beside her within a few seconds, groping for the switch on a lamp by Charlotte's bed, pulling her sister into her arms. Charlotte's hair and nightshirt were soaked with sweat; sobbing, Charlotte wound her hands into Sam's flannel gown and shivered violently. "It's all right, it's all right," Sam told her, rocking her.

"Where am I?" Charlotte moaned, looking around wildly at the pastel prints and lacy trimmings of a room that like Sam's was alien in its very luxury. "Your bed," Sam crooned. "It's safe. Shhh." Sam glanced at a delicate little ceramic clock on the dresser. "It's almost five. I'll stay with you. Try to get some sleep."

Charlotte shivered harder. "I can't sleep. I don't want to see Aunt Alex's doctor this morning. I don't need a doctor."

Sam bowed her head against Charlotte's. "You can't go on this way. Aunt Alex says he'll just prescribe something to help you relax."

"I can't relax. Not in this house. Not—" Charlotte inhaled sharply, wiped a hand across her damp face, then burrowed her head into the crook of Sam's shoulder and was quiet.

Sam's growing confusion and dread had reached a breaking point. She took Charlotte by the shoulders and held her away. One look at her sister's fear-glazed eyes pushed her over the edge. Between gritted teeth she said, "You have to talk to me. *Tell* me what's wrong. You *know* I'll help. You *know* I'll understand."

Charlotte moaned. "You can't help this time, Sammie. I'm okay. I swear. I just have to get used to the way things are here. I won't let you down, Sammie."

"What the—"

"If we don't like living here, we can't just leave. At least I can't. And no matter how much you'd want to take me with you, Aunt Alex wouldn't let you. I know what she could do. I've heard people talk about cases like this on *Donahue*. If I ran away, she could have me *arrested*."

"Charlotte, talk to me, please." Charlotte clamped her mouth shut and shook her head. Sam leaned toward her, holding her tortured gaze with a determined one. "If we can't depend on each other, then we've lost everything. *Listen to me*. The only way you can let me down is by keeping a secret."

Charlotte's resolve evaporated, and she covered her face. And then, in a halting, shame-soaked voice, she told Sam the truth.

Alexandra was half awake, feeling cold and restless in bed, alone. Orrin was at the house in Raleigh, preparing to host a group of foreign investors for the state business commission. She had planned to go with him, until Charlotte's strange affliction intervened. Damn Hugh Raincrow for meddling. Word might spread that her niece had fainted mysteriously, and people would gossip. What if, allowed to run wild by Frannie's idea of child-rearing, the girl had gotten herself pregnant? In a few hours Alexandra would haul her to Asheville and have her examined from head to toe, including a pregnancy test.

And if, God forbid, that was the case, it would be taken care of immediately. Alexandra rolled over and punched a pillow. She dimly heard movements in the hall outside her suite, and as she jerked upright, one of the doors flew open. Light from a hall sconce silhouetted Sam and Charlotte. Sam flicked a light switch. Her face was full of rage. She had Charlotte by one hand, and Charlotte appeared to be terrified.

"A couple of weeks ago, when he was visiting here, Tim mauled my sister," Sam announced. "He cornered her in your dressing room and groped her, and told her not to tell. I want you to call him at school, *right now*, and tell him to come home. Because I want to hear him admit it before I cut his testicles off with a pair of pinking sheers."

"You have to believe me," Charlotte said again. Several hours had passed to that horrified refrain, backed up by Sam's fury each time their aunt countered it with another skeptical question. Alexandra paced the living room floor, a creamy robe fluttering around her bare ankles, her face a mask of rigid doubt.

Charlotte was frozen in a chair at the center of the

room as if this were an inquisition. Sam stood behind her, both hands on Charlotte's shoulders. This was Sam's worst nightmare come true—to be caught between Aunt Alex and her sister, defending Charlotte against their aunt's unremitting insistence that Charlotte was exaggerating Tim's actions or worse, lying about them. "I'm going to ask you one more time," Aunt Alex said, halting and staring down hard into Charlotte's eyes. "Did you make this story up simply to get attention?"

Charlotte moaned, *"No,"* and hugged herself. Sam stepped in front of her and said with barely contained sarcasm, "Is this what you think my mother expected when she left Charlotte in your care? That you'd call Charlotte a liar to save your own pride?"

"Loyalty works both ways. How do you expect me to respond to a lurid accusation about my son—yours and Charlotte's *cousin?* Tim has a temper, I grant you that. It's possible he said something that wounded Charlotte's oversensitive feelings, but that's no excuse for her to concoct an outrageous story in revenge." Aunt Alex slammed one hand onto a table. "I will not have my son's reputation smeared on the basis of allegations by a troubled girl who cannot prove a word she says is true."

"Charlotte isn't a liar. The last thing she wanted was trouble. She didn't intend to tell me or anyone else what happened."

Aunt Alex moved around Sam and bent over Charlotte, suddenly patient and conciliatory. "I'm not going to punish you, I promise. I know it's been hard for you to adjust to losing your mother. I miss her too. I know it's easy to become confused, to want attention and comfort *so badly* that you'll do reckless things to make people notice you." She took Charlotte's hands. "But you have to tell me the truth, and then I'll help you."

Charlotte made a choking sound. "I already did." She jerked her hands away and ran from the room. Sam started after her, but Alexandra grasped her arm. Sam faced her furiously. "I told myself you loved her—that you had her best interests at heart even if sometimes you get them confused with *your* best interests. But you couldn't really care about her—not and condemn her the way you're doing."

"Did Dr. Raincrow put these ideas into your head yesterday?"

Sam recoiled. "You're so bitter toward the Raincrows that you look for any excuse to blame them for your own problems."

"You're the one who's looking for excuses. If you think you and Charlotte can mastermind some scheme to put me at a disadvantage—*if you think* you can cry wolf and leave this house with Charlotte under your self-righteous wing—*forget it*." Aunt Alex released her and, taking a deep breath, stepped back. "I'll fly to Durham this morning and *find* Tim at the university. I'll talk to him face-to-face and get his side of this ridiculous mess." She paused, her eyes narrowing as Sam simply stood, gazing back at her with unwavering contempt. "And when I return with him this afternoon, I'll expect a full retraction from both you and Charlotte, and an apology."

"You won't get either."

Aunt Alex raised a warning hand and pointed at her slowly. "You've heard of 'tough love'? Charlotte needs help. If she doesn't come to her senses, I'll have no choice but to send her where she can *get* that help."

Sam's head reeled. "What do you mean?"

"I mean a private psychiatric hospital."

She is evil. Mrs. Big Stick's words had sounded melodramatic to Sam, but now they didn't. Any small illusions she'd had about her aunt's compassion vanished. She was looking at a woman who would strike viciously, even against the people she claimed to love. And if she'd treat them this way, what was she capable of doing to others? *My God, she really would destroy Jake and his family if I went to them for help.*

"All right," Sam said carefully. "While you're gone, I'll see what I can do. Maybe Charlotte *did* overreact."

Aunt Alex looked surprised. She studied Sam shrewdly, and Sam returned her gaze with unblinking sincerity. Aunt Alex's face relaxed, but her eyes still glittered. "You're a fast learner. I'm proud of you. I was a fast learner at your age too." She breezed past Sam, then stopped at the door and looked at her. "Don't let second thoughts get the best of you. Barbara and Matilda will be in the house all day. I'm afraid, considering the mood you're in, I'll have to ask Barbara to monitor the phones."

Sam didn't breathe. "There's no one I'd call. I take care of my own business."

"Good girl. Once this *misunderstanding* is settled, I'll take you—and Charlotte—to Atlanta for a weekend. We'll spend an obscene amount of money on new wardrobes for both of you."

"I like that kind of bribe."

Aunt Alex stiffened, but smiled. "You *are* a fast learner," she said, and walked out.

The house was quiet. Matilda brought lunch to them. It sat on a tray atop the dresser in Sam's bedroom, untouched. Sam told the housekeeper they were exhausted; they were going to take a nap. Sam accompanied her to the balcony overlooking the grand marble staircase at the front of the house, thanked her for the food, and leaned on the balustrade, watching innocently as the stout woman disappeared through a downstairs door to the dining room and kitchen. Barbara walked through the foyer, a stack of paperwork in her arms, and halted, eyeing Sam uncertainly. Sam realized that neither Barbara nor the housekeeper knew what the trouble was, but like good soldiers, they wouldn't question their guard duty.

"We're going to take a nap," Sam called. "Will you come up and knock when my aunt gets back?"

Barbara looked relieved. "Of course. Oh, by the way, Mrs. Lomax told me to call the shop and say you wouldn't be in to work today."

"Thank you." Sam watched the secretary glide out of sight under an archway to Aunt Alex's office, and thought, *Tell Patsy I won't be coming back at all.*

She returned to her bedroom. Charlotte slipped out of the bath between their rooms. "Are you finished packing?" Sam asked her. Charlotte nodded. "I put everything I could in Dad's old duffel bag."

Sam was extraordinarily calm. She'd made her decision, and she refused to think about it. "I wish I had one." She pulled her cloth tote bag, the one she used to carry her knitting projects, from under her bed. It bulged with clothes. "Get a towel," she told Charlotte then jerked her head toward the tray of food. "Wrap up the sandwiches and fruit."

"Okay." A map of the mountains hung open in Charlotte's hands. It trembled in her grip. "It's *miles* to the next town. Right through the mountains. You really think we can make it?"

"*Yes*. And catch a bus there."

Charlotte pointed to the map, her jittery fingertip making the paper dance. "Sammie, we have to cut close to Raincrow Cove. Couldn't we ask Dr. Raincrow—"

"I'm not getting anyone else involved in this. I won't take the chance that Aunt Alex might find out." Sam went to her and grasped her hands. "Do you trust me? This is going to be hard, but we can make it. We'll go so far that nobody will ever find us." *Not even Jake*, she thought, and it nearly destroyed her. "I'll get a job."

Charlotte straightened proudly. "I'll go anywhere you say." She deflated a little and added, "But what about money? We've got only fifty bucks between us."

Sam turned back toward the door. "I'm going to take care of that right now. Hide everything. Get in bed and stuff some pillows beside you in case anyone wanders up here to check on us. I'll be back in a couple of minutes. And then, little sister, we're climbing out the window of the back guest room and down the jasmine trellis like a pair of human flies." She twisted the doorknob slowly, her heart in her throat.

"Where are you going?" Charlotte whispered anxiously.

Sam looked back at her as she slipped from the room. "To steal a piece of Aunt Alex's jewelry."

Charlotte gasped. Sam tiptoed out. Every nerve alert, she crept through the halls to their aunt's suite, went into her dressing room, and searched each delicate little drawer of the jewelry cabinet until she found what she wanted.

She gripped the gold necklace and pendant in her fist. It felt oddly warm, and made her queasy just to hold it. But she felt no guilt. Tim had used this stupid bauble as an excuse to hurt Charlotte. Aunt Alex had a peculiar obsession with the thing. Pawning it for enough money to fund their escape would be a perfect good-bye.

For a moment grief enveloped her. She'd already said good-bye to Jake, as if she'd seen it coming.

Snow and sleet were falling, making a lacy curtain in the light of a tall lamp beside the open gate at Highview, forming a thin crust on the two Sheriff's Department cruisers parked in the entrance. The snow peppered Jake's slouched, wide-brimmed hat as he strode up to a car and rapped on the window. The gut feeling of anxiety, the need to hurry home, had become a sharp command when he'd seen the cars as he drove past.

A deputy slung the door open. Jake knew the man. "What's the trouble?" Jake asked.

"Where the hell have you been, hoss? Sheriff's been looking for you since dark."

"Ice on the road. I came up from Georgia. Had to detour north of the state line." Jake jerked his head toward the house, where every window blazed with light. There were cars all around it. *Something happened to Samantha.* His legs felt rubbery. "What's going on?" he demanded.

"Looks like Mrs. Lomax's nieces took a hike."

"*When?*"

"We don't know exactly. The last time anyone saw them was around lunchtime. The younger one was home sick from school, and the other was supposed to be looking after her. Mrs. Lomax's secretary checked on them about five, and they were *gone*, man. Looks like they meant it too. Took some clothes with 'em. A back window was open. Must have climbed down a trellis there.

Sheriff has put every man he's got on the lookout, but the damned weather is a problem."

Jake gripped the car door with both hands. *Samantha's too smart to head out in weather like this. Unless she was too desperate to care. What could have made her that desperate?* "Where are you looking?"

"We figure they hitched a ride. Nobody saw 'em walking. No way they'd try to walk far in weather like this." The deputy reached for his radio. "Lemme tell the sheriff you're—"

Jake spun on his heels and ran. As he reached the old Caddy, where Bo was pressing his nose against the driver's side window in watchful excitement, the deputy yelled, "Don't you need something of theirs to give ol' Bo the scent?"

Jake didn't answer. He threw himself in the car, shoving Bo aside, and floored the accelerator.

He slid the car to a stop in the freezing slush beside his porch, and Ellie ran out to meet him, her long hair stuffed under a yarn cap, her hands shielding her eyes from the snow. Home from school for the weekend. He remembered that information vaguely, his thoughts riveted to Samantha. "We heard the news," she said flatly as he ran passed her with long strides, headed for the door. "The sheriff's been calling. Wait!"

"I have to get the quilt she made." He jerked the front door open. "See what I can feel about her." Ellie caught up with him and grabbed his arm. "I have something better." She held out her bare hand. Jake stared at Samantha's old ruby in sick bewilderment. "She gave it to Father yesterday," Ellie told him hoarsely. "Her kid sister fainted in town, and he was there." Ellie curled her fingers over the stone. "I can't feel where she's gone, but I know she wasn't planning to leave when she gave this to Father. Something happened after that. Something that scared the hell out of her."

Jake took the necklace in both hands and shut his eyes. He shivered. "She didn't get in a car. She's still out

there. She's cold. She's lost. She . . . there's a bus station
at Stecoe Gap."

"Oh, my God, that's ten miles from here. She and
her kid sister couldn't be on the road—somebody would
have seen them." Ellie looked at him with grim astonishment. "Do you think she tried to cut through the
mountains to Stecoe Gap?"

He jammed the ruby into his coat pocket and ran
back to the car, jerking the key from the ignition and then
going to the trunk. He opened it, grabbed a backpack and
heavy-duty flashlight, and started toward the woods. "Go
home," he called to Ellie. "Tell the folks where I've gone.
If the sheriff calls, tell him you haven't seen me."

"Wait! Let me call Mother and Father! Then I'll go
with you!"

"Can't wait." He turned at the edge of the forest,
sidestepping toward the inky woods filling with snow.
"They'll freeze if I don't get to them soon."

Then he turned and disappeared into the darkness,
Bo loping to keep up with him.

~~

"We're not lost," Sam told Charlotte again. "We're
temporarily confused."

Huddled beside her in a narrow, dark, cold cave just
big enough for the two of them to sit inside with their
bags underneath their rumps, Charlotte wearily raised
her head, two dangling silver earrings swinging from
each small ear. Charlotte's short, feathery blond hair was
limp with melted snow. "It's all right, Sammy. I'd rather
be freakin' lost and frozen than ever go back to *them*."

"We're not lost," Sam repeated. "All we have to do
is wait until the snow stops, then keep heading north
until we reach the Stecoe road and find the bus station."

"Those big round things in front of us are *mountains*."

"They're not mountains, they don't have names. They
weren't on the map."

"Sammie, that doesn't mean they aren't out there.

We can't move 'em just because somebody left 'em off the map."

Sam gazed miserably into the black wilderness and swirling snow. During the hours before dark they'd had good luck, moving quickly, staying on course. But the modest-looking topographical lines on the map hadn't prepared Sam for reality.

Between them and the Stecoe road was a vast network of steep, criss-crossing ridges, and forest so tall she hadn't been able to see the faint western glow of the sun. By nightfall they'd been exhausted and lost.

They'd moved on, slower, not saying much. Sam wouldn't admit her growing panic, and Charlotte, she knew, was afraid to ask her if they were lost.

When Charlotte spotted the tiny cave, they staggered to it and collapsed. They ate the food; all they had left was a pack of chewing gum that Sam had discovered in the bottom of her purse. Now she tugged the wrapping off with her teeth, tore the gum awkwardly, her fingers numb and shivering, and gave Charlotte half.

Charlotte sighed. *"Bon appétit."*

Sam savored the pathetic morsel. Her thoughts were fuzzy; she shut her eyes and tried to think. When a person studied all the details and made orderly plans, those plans should go right. She scrubbed a damp strand of hair back from her forehead, pulled a stretchy white ski cap lower over her ears, and straightened her white cloth coat. She would look presentable when she froze.

They sat there, shivering. Sam studied her wet feet, the snow melting on her long wool skirt and white socks, little rivulets of icy water sliding down her dirty jogging shoes. Her feet were so numb she couldn't move her toes, and muscles spasmed in her stomach from the chills.

Charlotte, wearing a quilted jacket, army fatigues, and snub-toed leather boots, was better dressed for this blizzard. When they'd decided to run, they hadn't had much time to make plans. Pandora was too small a town for them to just hitch a ride with a stranger. People knew one another there; people talked. And there were only three roads out of the place, all patrolled by the well-fed, overeager deputies of the Sheriff's Department of a ritzy resort town isolated by miles of high mountains. Mayberry on designer steroids.

"I wonder what Mom would do," Charlotte said, rubbing her face with the sleeve of her jacket.

Sam said wearily, "She'd go back to town and consult an astology chart. Wait for Jupiter to jump Venus, or something. Waste time."

Charlotte looked wounded. Sam patted her head in apology.

"They must be looking for us bigtime by now," Charlotte said, her voice high and thready. "God, if we get caught, what'll they do?" Charlotte sucked in a sharp breath. "They can't hold on to you, but I'm only fifteen. They might stick me in one of those *homes* that are really just lock-'em-ups for junior criminals. They might—"

"Nobody's going to find us. Nobody's going to separate us. And besides, you're not the criminal. I am. I made you leave with me."

Sam thought of Aunt Alex's necklace, which she'd tucked in a deep pocket of her skirt. She had always considered herself too good to sink to anyone's level, regardless of what they did to her, but now she was a thief.

A remorseless thief, too.

There was a fine line between being gifted and being cursed, and Jake spent every day of his life walking it like a tightrope. No room for a wrong step, no safety net, no place to rest. He could move only straight ahead, alone, toward a destination he might never reach, fighting a weight that could drag him either way if he held out a hand to anyone else. Alone, he kept his balance.

Samantha didn't know it, but she was pulling him both ways at once. He halted atop an open precipice of granite covered in ankle-deep snow to get his bearings— or, rather, *her* bearings, since he knew the ancient, forested ridges, the hidden hollows, the soaring overlooks and narrow, dark glens of the Cove as well as the backs of his own large, callused hands.

So many generations of his family—both Cherokee and white—had roamed these wild places. The Cove was the only sanctuary he had. And he sensed that Samantha had come into it.

Where? Where was she? And why hadn't she come to his house? She could have found it easily. She should have known he'd do anything, whatever it took, to help her.

She knew. But she didn't want me caught in the middle. She's trying to get her sister away from Alexandra.

He took the old stone from his pocket and rubbed it between his bare, numb hands. *Please, please tell me what I need to know to find her.*

She was nearby. That shook him. He closed his eyes briefly. The caves. That image was strong, certain. His lonely talent would not let him down.

His prayer had been answered.

Charlotte gasped. "I hear footsteps!"

Sam, who had fallen into a lethargic doze, jerked her head up. "Quiet," she whispered. "It might be an animal. A bear." She slid her hand into her coat pocket and made her stiff fingers close around the only weapon she had. A metal nailfile.

She brought it out, then got on her knees with her back to Charlotte, holding the file like a knife. She didn't know what good it would do them, but she wasn't leaving this cave without a fight.

Sam stared out into the curtain of snow. Now she heard the footsteps too—muffled crunches of sound, slow and measured. A pair of long, sturdy legs in faded jeans moved in front of the cave's small opening. They disappeared into heavy hiking boots sunk into the snow. She saw the bottom of a bulky khaki coat. Bo's large wet face pushed inside the opening at a level with her eyes.

Sam sank back on her heels, and her shoulders slumped.

Jake dropped to his haunches, inches from her

outthrust hand, filling the mouth of the tiny cave, trapping them inside, brawny hands draped lightly on his angular knees. The harsh beam of his flashlight glittered on the cave's wet walls.

Her teeth chattered. Sam stared at him grimly. He looked back at her from under the soggy brim of a delapidated fedora, which gave him a jaunty, old-fashioned look in contrast to the rugged coat and jeans. There might not have been a flicker of movement inside him, not even a heartbeat.

Jake gazed back at her with hidden wonder. She was swamped with acres of coat cloth and a sagging brown skirt that puddled around her kneeling body like a tent. A tight knit cap made her face stand out in soft contrast, with wisps of honey-blond hair slicked to her cheeks and forehead.

She looked righteous and fierce, bone-tired and shaky. She looked glorious. "You know I can always find you," he said. He sounded furious, but there was a raw tremor in his voice. "For God's sake, is this better than coming to me for help?"

"Yes." Her hands wavered and dropped into her lap. He reached toward her, but she pulled back. He looked wounded. His hand clenched, and he brought it back to his knee. "Don't ask any questions," Sam begged. Charlotte, ashamed and afraid, had sworn her to secrecy about the reason for their escape. That small dignity was all Sam could give her.

And Sam knew, with tormented certainty, that their only hope was to get as far away as possible. She couldn't let Jake go with them. If they were caught . . .

"We're leaving town," she said with absurd composure, as if announcing a party. "If you could just point us in the direction of the Stecoe road, in the morning we'll move on."

His mouth dropped open. He looked at her as if she'd lost her mind. "By morning you'll be two blond-haired chunks of ice. And if you think I'm going to let you stay here—or let you go on your merry way—your brain must already be full of icicles."

She hadn't expected him to agree. She wanted so badly to take his face between her hands and kiss him for risking his own hide to find them, and for caring. But that selfishness would have sealed his intentions. "We're not going back with you, and you can't come with us," she said.

He looked at her as if he could eat them both alive and spit them out without blinking. "You've got your aunt's nerves."

Sam felt a dreary sense of impending doom. "All I ask," she said slowly, her voice steadier than her sinking hopes, "is that you forget you found us."

He flicked his hand out again. Suddenly one of hers was captured in his big, warm grip. Her stiff fingers convulsed helplessly, and the stupid nailfile dropped to the snowy floor of the cave without a sound. The sound of defeat—silence.

Jake didn't know what to say. He was flooded with too many emotions—her emotions. Anger, fear, *love*. She was determined not to show any of it. Her feelings welled up inside him like a hot tide, until he didn't know whether they were her feelings or his own. "You're doing this for Charlotte," he said. "Somebody hurt her. Alexandra is part of it. But you and me—we can fight back. Don't give up on us. Crawl out of this hole and come with me."

Sam gazed at him, gritting her teeth to keep them from clicking like castanets. "We can't go back. We can't stay anywhere near here. She'd only find us if we did. Charlotte would get hauled back to Highview, and I . . . well, I'm a fugitive now. You can't change that fact."

His grip on her hand was firm but painless; his fingers pressed into her palm without moving. There was a look in his eyes she couldn't quite decipher. Maybe some apology in that hypnotizing intensity. "You're not even a little guilty about it either. She owed you and Charlotte plenty, and you know it. What? What did she do to Charlotte?"

"Don't try to guess how I feel. You always do that, but not this time." She tugged her arm back. To her immense relief, he released her hand. The urge to touch her again was like a fire inside him. One more second and he'd have glimpsed a clue to her thoughts.

But he would never tell her he was a freak of nature, right up there with two-headed snakes and the Elephant Man. The only secret he would ever keep from her, because the fear that she wouldn't believe, that she would be repulsed, was more than he could bear to test.

"Get out of the cave," he ordered. "You've got no choice. I'm taking you to the Cove. It's not very far. Maybe you wanted me to find you. Well, I did, and we'll deal with this problem together. Whether you think that's the best thing or not."

He saw that fact sink into her, weighing her down, as if the mountain had begun squeezing on her shoulders. Tears glittered in her eyes, and she looked away quickly, squinting. She swallowed hard. "If you make us go back, there's no hope at all."

"I won't let her hurt you or Charlotte." His voice was suddenly soft and hoarse. "Trust me. We'll think of something. But I'm not letting you go. Not this time. Not ever again."

Tears slid down her cheeks, and when she looked at him finally, her eyes were dull and grieving. "She'll hurt you too."

He inhaled sharply. "No, she won't." The only tactic that made sense, at the moment, was stubborn command. "Come out of there." He made it sound like a heartless order. "Or I'll drag you both out."

Over her shoulder she said to her sister in a voice that was low and raw, "I'm sorry. He's like the mountains—I can't move him. I let you down."

Charlotte bowed her head. "No, you didn't. You're the only one who's never done that."

Jake watched with silent turmoil as they crawled out stiffly and staggered to their feet. He reached out to help, but both of them pulled back, staring at him angrily. Samantha tilted her head back and looked at him with tired fury. His flashlight illuminated the snow settling on her upturned face, little delicate flakes clinging to her lashes and cheeks, that resolute mouth clamped tight as a vise. She was swamped with clothes—the floppy coat, a long, full skirt, the collars of three different-colored sweaters bulging out between the coat's labels. Charlotte was shorter, flashier, dressed like a cut-rate stormtrooper.

Annie Hall and a stormtrooper. It made him feel worse that they had been hiding in one of the caves where ancestors of his had starved and frozen when the army was rounding up Cherokees. He felt those ghosts. But he reminded himself that some of the people had survived, held on, prospered finally. With the help of the pioneer Vanderveers, they had managed to keep the Cove. It had come down to him through them. Raincrows and Vanderveers. Now Samantha—a Vanderveer by distant association, if nothing else—had tried to find safety here.

"Sammie, we can't go back," Charlotte cried suddenly, losing control. She backed away, sweeping an arm toward the looming forest spreading out around them. *"Run. Let's run."*

"Don't even think about it," Jake said. "I'll track you down like rabbits."

Samantha snagged her by one arm, then hugged her. "He'd probably skin us too." Charlotte cried silently, head bent to her sister's. Samantha stared at him bitterly over her sister's head. "We'll think of something," she said firmly. "I'm not giving up." Samantha held his gaze, the expression in her eyes like blue ice. "I'm not giving up," she repeated. "I'm the only one around here with a clear head. The only one who doesn't depend on miracles."

Her pain was twisted together with his, and with a terrible understanding that finding Samantha was a sign of some kind, that he needed her in some way that was as selfish as wanting to breathe. For now he knew only that he had to hold on to her.

"Why won't you listen to me?" she asked, her voice a groan. "Why do you believe in miracles?"

He turned away from her. "Can't help myself." That was true, but there was more, that childhood superstition that Granny Raincrow had engrained in him. It came back with a potent force. Nothing else mattered. Jake clenched his fists.

I won't give her back to a ravenmocker.

Chapter Seventeen

Don't tell them. Please, don't tell them. Each time Sam looked at her sister she saw that plea in her eyes. The dilemma made Sam sick at her stomach. Wrapped in blankets, she and Charlotte sat on the hearth of the Raincrows' fireplace, but the seductive heat of the fire couldn't penetrate the cold anxiety in Sam's muscles.

Jake's mother hovered over them with maternal alarm, dabbing at their damp hair with a towel. His father stood by a window, watching with a grim, puzzled expression, and Ellie Raincrow hunched on the edge of a chair she'd pulled near the hearth, her long legs and loafers tucked behind the chair's legs, her quiet green eyes boring into them. Jake, melted snow puddling beneath his hiking boots onto a colorful rug, roamed the big, comfortably shabby living room like a caged tiger, and each time he passed near Sam he managed to brush the fingers of one hand over her shoulder, a gesture of concern that made her chest ache with a tangle of emotions she couldn't risk.

She and Charlotte had landed in the middle of a well-meaning and inescapable clan. A mother, a doctor, a doctor-in-training, and Jake—whose mission in life was to find lost souls, whether they wanted to be found or not. Four people imbued with innate compassion and a long-simmering contempt for Aunt Alex. People who would fight her on Charlotte's behalf if Sam told them the truth.

But the Raincrows couldn't do anything about it. They didn't know Aunt Alex the way Sam did. Aunt Alex wasn't just manipulative, she was ruthless. Sam couldn't let them be hurt.

"Please, just take us to the bus station at Stecoe Gap," Sam said again. "No one ever has to know we were here. Just help us get that far, before it's too late."

"I told you that's not an option," Jake said gruffly. She met his apologetic but angry gaze. Sam fought for control and said as calmly as she could, "Then Charlotte and I will end up back at Highview, and there won't be a thing you can do to stop it." Charlotte moaned and Sam quickly put a reassuring arm around her. Her head rising with weary defiance, Sam added softly, "The next time we leave, I won't make any mistakes."

Jake flinched.

Mrs. Raincrow wrung the towel between her hands and dropped to the hearth beside her. "You don't have to explain to *me* that you felt trapped by your aunt, and you were unhappy." She glanced at Jake sadly, then back at Sam. "But something god-awful must have happened to make you take this chance. Can't you trust us enough to tell us why you ran?"

Before Sam could answer, Charlotte blurted out, "Aunt Alex . . . she told me I had to let my second holes grow together." Charlotte nodded wildly, as if that strange excuse were indisputably sufficient. Sam's heart sank.

"What second holes?" Ellie asked, arching a black brow. "I don't recall my professors discussing extra holes in anatomy class."

"Earrings." Charlotte's face turned bright pink. She pointed at the two pairs of flamboyant silver stars swinging from her ears. "She said too many earrings look trashy. But Mom never thought so. She said I had *panache*."

"Charlotte," Sam whispered in warning.

Dr. Raincrow cleared his throat. "Somehow, I doubt Sam would have taken you on the lam just to preserve your fashion style."

Charlotte stared at the floor and chewed her lip. Sam pulled her closer sympathetically. "What difference does it make why we left?" Sam asked everyone hoarsely. She couldn't keep from looking at Jake. He had halted his circuit of the room near the center, and gazed down at her with an agonized expression. "Maybe I lost my nerve," she told him. "I was afraid I'd become what Aunt Alex wanted me to become. Just like her. Someone you'd hate." Slowly, Jake shook his head. She looked away, her throat aching. "So I took the cowardly way out. I ran. Something I was raised to never do. My dad was killed trying to bring a coward back."

"That dog won't hunt," Jake said. "You'd have hung on and fought no matter how bad it was for *you*. I know you left for Charlotte's sake. You've got to tell me why."

"Will everyone stop talking about me as if I'm an undercooked omelet?" Charlotte cried. She turned toward Sam, defeat clouding her eyes. "It was all my fault. I'll say anything she wants me to say. But you can't go back with me. You stole from her, Sammie."

Everyone but Jake stared at Sam in shock. Mrs. Raincrow stiffened. "What?" She looked at Jake reproachfully. "Did you know about this?"

"No," Sam interjected.

"Yes," he said. Sam slumped. She wanted to shake him. She wanted to kiss him. "I know she took a piece of Alexandra's jewelry," he continued. "She needed something she could sell. But stealing from a thief isn't stealing."

"I agree," Ellie said darkly.

Sam reached into her skirt pocket. She pulled Aunt Alex's necklace and pendant out. "I doubt she'll look at the situation the way y'all do."

Mrs. Raincrow held out a hand. "May I?"

"Don't touch it," Ellie and Jake said in unison. Their mother gave them a startled look. They traded an uncomfortable gaze. "Anything that belongs to Alexandra is bad luck," Jake explained, frowning.

"Including Charlotte and me," Sam added. She dejectedly placed the necklace on her palm. Mrs. Raincrow grimaced. "A whore's prize." That remark reduced everyone to silence. She dropped the necklace on the hearth and wiped her hands on her trousers. "We'll bury it in the backyard. Alexandra may insist you took it, but she won't have any proof."

Sam stared at her hopefully. Ellie suddenly moved to the hearth beside Charlotte. Sam swiveled to watch. Her eyes strangely intent, Jake's sister took one of Charlotte's hands between both of hers. Charlotte seemed hypnotized; she looked at Ellie with wary awe. The eerie concentration on Ellie's face grew more intense. Slowly, she ran a hand up Charlotte's right arm, probing. Her eyes narrowed. Surprise and disgust curled her mouth into a grimace. The unfathomable look in her eyes sent shivers down Sam's spine. Sam suddenly recalled what Dr. Raincrow had said about Ellie's intuition. Her breath stalled. *No, no,* she protested silently, and reached over to pull Charlotte's arm out of Ellie's grasp.

"You had bruises," Ellie said, staring into Charlotte's dazed face. "Your hands—this hand, I mean—is still a little sore. Your arm too."

Charlotte made a frightened sound and drew back from her. "I tripped on a rug. Fell down."

"I wonder if . . . someone knocked you down." Now Ellie's eyes were clear and sharp, prying into Charlotte's. Charlotte trembled. Sam waited with breathless dread. She wanted Charlotte to talk, but wouldn't force her. Charlotte pivoted desperately and looked at Sam. "Sammie, what should I do?" Her voice was ragged. "Do you want me to—"

"I promised you," Sam said. "It's up to you."

"I *think*," Ellie continued, "you're afraid of someone there. Hmmm. Alexandra? Maybe, but she tends to get what she wants without beating people up. Orrin? No, he relies on charm. But Tim"—her eyes glittered—"Tim nearly twisted my arm off once."

Something in that confession broke through Charlotte's humiliation. She looked at Sam wearily. "Tell them what happened. I get sick just thinking about it." She put her face in her hands and hunched over.

Her heart in her throat, Sam stared into space and quietly explained what Tim had done and how Aunt Alex had reacted when she heard. When she finished she looked at Jake apologetically. Fury and sorrow gleamed in his eyes. The same expression was on the others' faces as well. Even Dr. Raincrow had a deadly poise about him. "This is grounds for legal intervention," he said. "It's child abuse."

Sarah Raincrow seemed on the brink of violence. She pounded one leg with her fist. "We'll get a lawyer."

"I don't need a lawyer," Jake said. "I need to get my hands on Tim."

Sam jumped up and ran to him. "That's exactly what I was afraid of. Don't you understand? Any of you?" She wound a hand in his shirt but turned to look at the others frantically. "I've thought through the options over and over. What if I go to the authorities and insist my sister has been mauled by our own cousin? What if the social services bigwigs drag their feet and worry about humiliating the lieutenant-governor—so they refuse to believe Charlotte? What if they *do* believe her and take her away? Put her in a foster home or—oh, God—some state institution for teenagers?"

"Marry me," Jake said. "And we'll . . . we'll *adopt* Charlotte."

Her hand convulsed in his shirt. She curled her fingers into the material and against the hard wall of his chest, a quick, adoring caress. But she looked up at him sadly. "It doesn't work that way."

He shuddered. "Then it's settled. We'll disappear and take Charlotte with us." Sam's gasp echoed the small cries of astonishment from his family, and Charlotte. His expression was set. "I'm good at finding people. I can be just as good at not being found."

For the first time, tears slid down Sam's face. "I can't let you do that. I'm not going to turn you into a . . . an outlaw who's accused of kidnapping my sister. Because that's probably what Aunt Alex would have you charged with if we were caught."

He took her by the shoulders. "I'm telling you we *won't* get caught. You don't want Charlotte to go back to Alexandra's. Nothing is more important to you than that."

"Doing what's good for you is as important."

"Then do what I'm asking. Because the only thing that can hurt me is losing you."

Sam strangled on the terrible choice—Charlotte's safety versus Jake's. One loyalty against the other. He saw the torment in her face and pulled her to him, wrapping his arms around her and holding her in a desperate, compelling embrace.

Charlotte was suddenly beside them, crying. Sam reached for her, but she stepped back and looked at everyone frantically. "I'm going to throw up. Where's the bathroom?"

"Down the hall, on the left," Mrs. Raincrow said, shoving her hands through her hair and rising quickly.

"I'll go with you," Sam said, easing out of Jake's arms.

Charlotte shook her head and cupped a hand over her mouth. "No. I can do *one* thing by myself." She ran from the room. Sam hurried to the doorway and watched her disappear into the bathroom, slamming the door behind her. Sam turned shakily. Jake's solid presence behind her—his hands on her arms, his determination to risk his own reputation for hers—slid through her veins like fire.

The unresolved argument strained his parents' faces; Ellie looked calmer, but not happier. "You don't want him to do this," Sam said. "And if I hadn't loved him since I was a little girl, I wouldn't care about anyone's future but mine and my sister's. But I *do* love him, and that's why I won't make Mrs. Big Stick's warning come true. I won't tear this family apart."

Jake's fingers tightened slowly on her arms. "Clara came to see you?"

"Yes. She says I'm bad luck. I didn't want to believe her, but I do." She faced Jake. "It's enough that you want to go with us. I'll never forget that."

"Listen to me. I won't let anyone take you back to Alexandra, and I won't let you try to run without me. If you try to leave with Charlotte again, I'll only follow you. I've always found you, and I always will. Sorry, but you're stuck with me."

She made a garbled sound filled with anger and love and terrible conflict. Jake drew her against him and held her tightly again. She grasped his hands and shut her eyes, trying to think of some other way. Seconds dragged in silent grief.

"You'll need money," Dr. Raincrow said.

Her mouth open, Sam whipped around and stared at him. He was looking at Mrs. Raincrow, who swallowed hard and rubbed a hand over her eyes, then nodded. Ellie, her face a mask of worried contemplation, nodded too. "Let me drive up to town. I'll use my instant teller card. I can get a couple of hundred dollars tonight. When I get back to school on Monday, I'll clean out my account at the bank in Durham. If you and Mom withdraw a large amount of money from your bank in town, people will talk." She looked at Jake. "Call me in a few days. I'll send you the money."

Sam was speechless. His family loved him enough to be part of this deception. To risk everything—to be ruined if Aunt Alex learned they'd aided the plan. "No," she said desperately, pleading. "No, please—"

"I took care of it," Charlotte said. She had returned while no one noticed. Misery crumpled her expression, but she seemed strangely proud. Her eyes darted to Jake. "I guess I never knew how much you love my sister, and how much she loves you. I can't mess up your life. Aunt Alex would kill you, and then where would Sammie be? She's never even looked at another guy."

Sam could barely breathe. "What did you do?"

"I lied about having to go the bathroom. I saw a phone on the table in the hall, Sammie." Her voice was ragged. "I called the sheriff's office and told them where we are."

Jake's mood was black. Never in his memory had Alexandra been allowed in the Raincrow house. Charlotte's well-intentioned intervention had left them with no weapon except words, and he was no damned good with words. He decided, simply and without remorse, that Sam and her sister would be taken from the house only over his dead body.

He placed himself beside Sam, who had an arm around Charlotte again. Sam gripped the back of his shirt with her other hand, and he sensed her fear—the fear that he would do exactly what he intended to do.

Mother had scooped the gold necklace into a drawer of a small lamp table at one end of the couch. Ellie stood near the table, and her troubled gaze went repeatedly to the drawer's knob.

She met Jake's shrewd eyes. *She feels something I don't feel,* he realized suddenly. *Why?* She rested one hand on the table. To anyone else it would have seemed a casual gesture, but he recognized the inward, searching concentration in her eyes. She was listening for answers to some question.

"Let me do the talking," Father warned one more time as Mother reluctantly opened the front door for the sheriff and Alexandra. She and Mother traded cold stares. Alexandra stepped into the living room, her face pale above the luxurious collar of a long fur coat dusted with snow. "What a nice family reunion," she said acidly. "How kind of you to invite me."

"You're not family and you never have been," Mother answered.

"Be that as it may." Alexandra's brittle attention focused immediately on Sam and Charlotte. "I don't want to hear any explanations," she said. "I blame myself for thinking the two of you could easily adjust to your mother's death and to living with me. I should have realized that I hurt you by trying to take her place so quickly. I should have realized that my efforts—no matter how sincere—might seem overbearing to you." She held out her hands. "But I thought you *knew* how much I love the two of you." She turned gracefully toward the sheriff. "I'm sure they think I expect you to drag them back. But this is a family matter between my nieces and me; we simply need to talk for a minute, and then they'll come with me. I'll bring them home in my car. You can go now."

The sheriff looked relieved. He twisted his broad-brimmed hat in beefy hands and nodded. "I figured this was no matter for the law, Mrs. Lomax. I'll just—"

"It *is* a matter for the law," Father said. "Because I've got a fifteen-year-old here who was sexually assaulted in Alexandra's home."

The sheriff gaped at him. Alexandra stiffened. Her hands dug deeply into her collar. She stared at Charlotte, who shivered violently but stared back. Alexandra pivoted toward the sheriff. "I assure you that's not the case. I've heard my niece's story, and I've determined it isn't true. I've already contacted a psychiatrist who'll help her sort out the emotional problems that led her to make it up."

"That's not how it was," Sam interjected. "You threatened to put Charlotte in a mental hospital if she didn't change her tune."

The sheriff stammered incoherently, then said, "Mrs. Lomax, this is a serious thing. I can't just walk out of here and pretend I never heard about it."

"Oh?" Alexandra glared at him. "Neither can you pursue it with no more evidence than the claim of a troubled child. I'm trying to save you the public embarrassment of apologizing to the lieutenant-governor. I'm telling you there's no need for that."

The sheriff blanched. He shot a worried glance at Father. "Did you . . . take a look at her? She got any bruises or anything?"

"I haven't had time to examine her," Father admitted. "But I've questioned her enough to feel convinced she's telling the truth."

Sam leaned forward, straining against Jake's hold on her shoulders. "It happened almost three weeks ago," she said bitterly. "The bruises are gone. But she had marks all over her breasts." Jake gritted his teeth. He felt desperate sorrow for Sam, who had to tell her sister's intimate details to a stranger, and for Charlotte, who mewled with humiliation. Mother strode to Charlotte and put an arm around her. Charlotte seemed to hang inside her and Sam's reinforcing grasp. "No one's going to browbeat this girl anymore," Mother said.

"You saw the bruises?" the sheriff asked Sam.

"Yes."

"That's not true," Alexandra interjected, gazing at Sam as if Sam had disappointed her terribly. "Sam didn't come to me with her sister's story until yesterday. She told me she'd just heard it."

Jake vibrated with fury. "She knows Charlotte didn't lie. You're the one who wouldn't believe it. Wouldn't believe Tim had groped his own cousin." Her eyes flashed. She looked horrified, but beneath it was a lethal warning.

"Tim?" the sheriff repeated incredulously. "I thought y'all meant it was some fellow who works for Mrs. Lomax." He shook his head. "I can't see Tim hurting his own little cousin. He's a grown man. Lord knows, he's never lacked for attention from the girls his own age."

Charlotte gasped. "I didn't make it up. I didn't do anything wrong. I didn't—"

"There's no doubt in my mind that Charlotte's telling the truth," Mother announced. Her livid eyes bored into Alexandra's. "You made Tim into a bully. You've deliberately tormented and humiliated him all his life. He takes it out on any helpless victim he can find. I blame you."

"How convenient," Alexandra answered. She dismissed Mother with a little jerk of her head and looked at the sheriff. "These people, as I'm sure you're aware, will never be character witnesses for me or my son. They are, in fact, so interested in causing trouble for me that they'll say *anything* and *do* anything."

"Now, look," the sheriff said, shifting from foot to foot and gazing at Father somberly, "Everybody knows there's bad blood between you folks and Mrs. Lomax. It is gonna sound like you're meddling in her business just to make a stink."

Jake made a soft sound of disgust. "I've tracked about a hundred people for you," Jake said tersely. "I've worked for you since I was in high school. You've said more than once that you can depend on me more than on your own deputies. And now I'm telling you that Mrs. Lomax wouldn't admit that Tim mauled his own cousin if her life depended on it. I'm telling you she's a goddamned liar."

Sam's hand tightened against his back. He felt her devotion like a warm tide. Father looked at him with a mixture of pride and rebuke. "Thank you," Father said, "for choosing this moment to discover a gift for making speeches."

The sheriff rubbed a hand over his sweaty brow and exhaled. "Jake, I can take one look at the bear hug you've got on Mrs. Lomax's oldest niece and see you're not talking with your brain in gear."

"This is a ludicrous discussion!" Alexandra said. "I came here to take my nieces home, where we can work out our problems and get on with our lives. There's no reason for me to listen to any of this nonsense. Charlotte is my legal ward and I *will* get help for her. Samantha, you're old enough to do as you please, but I'm begging you to do what's right. Don't make me take Charlotte and leave you here. It would break my heart."

Father raised his hands for silence. He leveled an unwavering gaze at the sheriff. "If you don't get on the phone and call social services right now, I'll do it. I've referred cases to them more times than I care to remember, and they know I don't do it unless I'm certain. Every referral they've checked out has turned up true. They'll listen to me."

"I'll get my husband on the phone immediately thereafter," Alexandra countered. "And anyone foolish enough to take your charge seriously will be looking for a new job next week."

The sheriff took a step back, his face flushed. He had wrung the shape out of his hat. "Hugh, you do what you have to do, but I got to let social services sort it out. In the meantime, Mrs. Lomax has the right to take her niece home with her." He looked at Charlotte sadly. "Come on now, girl. Get your things. Nobody's gonna hurt you. Come on."

Charlotte drew back and gazed at Sam desperately. Sam shook her head. "You're not going anywhere."

Alexandra's eyes flashed. "Samantha, don't make this harder than it already is. It would kill me to have Charlotte hauled back to Highview like some sort of criminal. Don't make me do that. I promise you, if you'll persuade her to come home—and come with her—I'll forgive both of you. We can start fresh."

Sam shivered. Jake felt her hopelessness and seethed inside. "We'll go," she said slowly, "if you'll admit right now, in front of everyone, that you believe her story. If you swear you won't send her away. And if you swear that Tim won't set foot in your house again as long as Charlotte and I have to live there."

"You have nothing to bargain with," Alexandra answered. "You stole from me. I'll forgive that too." She held out a hand. Suddenly Jake saw the slightest nervous tick beneath one of her eyes. "Return my necklace. *Right now.*"

Jake stepped in front of Sam and Charlotte. "You're afraid of her. Afraid of me. I'm not drunk, like Uncle William was. I'm not standing at the top of the marble staircase. You can't push me."

Alexandra recoiled, one hand flying to her throat. She whirled toward the sheriff. "Do your job. I want my necklace and Charlotte. I'll expect you to bring *both* to me tonight." She strode toward the hall.

"Wait," Ellie called. "Here it is." Alexandra pivoted, her face strained, her eyes nervous and violent. Ellie leaned on the lamp table and jerked its drawer open. Her hand dove inside. There was a strange harmony about her swift movements. She clenched the pendant in her hand, the thick gold chain of the necklace dangling like a noose. Her eyes were half shut. She swayed. Her eyes widened suddenly, and her expression froze in amazement.

Alexandra lurched toward her. "Give it to me!"

"No!" Ellie grabbed the chain and swung it fiercely. Jake leapt forward to block Alexandra's way. The heavy pendant made a glittering arc and struck the tabletop with a sharp crack of sound.

And popped open.

Jake halted, staring. Alexandra froze in place.

The unmistakable ruby gleamed in a bed of delicate white material. Ellie reached for it, her hand shaking, her face a mask of horrified fascination. Jake's stomach twisted. Old dread and repulsion swept over him. Now he understood. The one thing he could not find, the one blank, self-protective part of himself. Ellie had sensed the stone now, just as she'd known when they were children that it wasn't buried with Uncle William.

It's mine. I'll die for it. Ellie's words that day came back to him, engraved in memories of what he'd seen when he'd touched the ruby, the memory that it was dangerous, that Uncle William had died because of what the ruby had told Jake all those years before.

Don't, he demanded silently. He plunged his hand down to stop her, but she already had the stone between her fingertips. She rolled it in her palm and closed her fingers over it tightly.

"You stole from *us*," she said, facing Alexandra. She opened her hand. The ruby gleamed like blood, its star winking in the light. Mother staggered forward and cupped her hands around Ellie's. "Oh, my God. It *is* my ruby."

Alexandra stiffened. Her head jerked up, and she watched them with unwavering dignity, but her lips were parted in a silent pant of alarm. Mother plucked the ruby from Ellie's palm and faced her furiously. "My brother willed this to me, and you swore you'd buried it with him. But you've hidden it all these years. You've worn it. You've *flaunted* it. And now it's come back to haunt you."

Alexandra looked trapped. "Consider it returned to your care, then."

Mother advanced on her, the ruby clenched in a raised fist. "You're a thief, Alexandra. I should drag you into court and let the whole world hear how the lieutenant-governor's wife cheated and stole from her first husband's family. I'd love every minute of it."

Alexandra backed away, holding up both hands. Mother moved toward her again, both fists raised. Father moved over quickly and thrust an arm between them. The sheriff seemed paralyzed by the drama. Mother pressed against Father's outstretched arm and shook her fist at Alexandra. "But I'll trade you," Mother continued, speaking softly and with deadly calm. "I'll show you more mercy than you ever gave William. This stone will finally accomplish some good. I'll trade you," Mother repeated. "My silence for your cooperation. You walk out of my house and leave these girls alone. Don't even think about taking Charlotte with you—not now, not ever. Tell everyone you've decided to let her live with her sister. Tell them whatever you like. I don't care. But don't *mess* with me, or you'll be sorry."

Alexandra stood her ground, but the twitch below her eye grew worse. Fury and defeat seeped from her like invisible steam. "They are *mine*," she protested. "My nieces. My flesh and blood. I've wanted only what's best for them. Frannie knew that."

"You killed her," Jake said. "You squeezed her down to a shadow, until finally all she could do was disappear."

Sam was suddenly beside him, brilliantly controlled, her chin up and eyes unyielding. "My mother loved you. I wanted to love you too. But my mother never understood you the way I do."

"You're just like me," Alexandra exclaimed. "You could be *just like me*. You're ambitious, and smart, and strong. If you let these people turn you into some pathetic little nobody, you'll regret it. You want what I want—the power, the money, the independence."

"You don't look real independent to me right now," Sam answered. "You look desperate and lonely. I'll never be like you."

"Get out of my house," Mother ordered.

Jake stepped closer. He met Alexandra's blank, pitying stare. "You want Orrin to be governor. That's more important to you than anything else. You won't risk bad publicity."

"I'm not finished with *you*. You may wallow in satisfaction for now, but in time, *in time* . . ." Her voice trailed off. "You don't deserve my nieces," she told Mother finally, her voice hoarse. Then, stronger, she said, "And someday they'll come back to me on their own."

She turned swiftly and walked out. The sheriff flailed his hat at thin air and followed her, his hands out. The front door slammed. Seconds later came the rumble of car engines.

The house seemed to be holding its breath.

Jake felt Samantha's hand gripping his shirt in back again. She didn't realize how much that contact affected him. Besides the obvious—that strong but shivering hold on him—he felt her shock and relief. All that mattered was not letting Samantha down the way it seemed just about everybody else in her life had.

Everyone stood without moving. Jake pretended to listen to the sound of the sheriff's car following Alexandra's up the long driveway to the Cove road. But he was secretly fixated on the ragged cadence of Samantha's breathing.

"Are we safe?" Charlotte asked. "Can we really live here?"

"Yes," Father answered. He took Mother's raised fists and caressed them. She swallowed roughly. "She always had it. And she thought she'd always keep it."

She placed the ruby in his grasp and he studied it, frowning. "I've come to hate this. But it's finally served the purpose it was intended for. To bring people together."

"It's a medicine stone," Ellie said quietly. "It finds its way back where it belongs."

"It's yours," Mother added. Jake flinched. He never wanted to touch the ruby again, and he didn't want Ellie to touch it either. "It's yours," Mother repeated, and went to Ellie. "It should have been yours on your twenty-first birthday. From mother to daughter. I'm a year late, but I intend for the tradition to be kept from now on. Just as it always was, before Alexandra."

Her eyes gleaming, Ellie held out a hand. Mother placed the stone in her palm. Jake met her eyes. Pride. Confidence. She was not afraid of the stone anymore. He told himself that meant something. If there had been a curse, it was over. They had won. He had to believe that.

He turned around slowly. Samantha looked up at him with incredulous hope that slowly changed to grief. "She really did steal the ruby," Sam said in a hoarse whisper. "You were right."

"I don't care. I only care that you're with me. If . . . that's what you still want."

She nodded. Fatigue and weeks of shattering grief clouded her eyes. He touched her cheek and knew she needed time to pull all the pieces together. Time to come back to herself. Time to believe she could be with him without terrible consequences. He fumbled with his shirt pocket and produced her necklace. Its ruby didn't gleam like the Pandora stone. It had no value to anyone but him and her. Her eyes filled with appreciation when she saw it. Jake carefully slipped the tarnished chain over her head. "Welcome home," he said.

Mother gave her and her sister one of the upstairs bedrooms, and reported wistfully over the next few snow-bound days that they slept together, fully dressed, as if they expected to flee again at any second. Mother took a dim view of Jake venturing upstairs to check on Samantha himself; no matter how gallant his intentions, Mother suddenly bristled with rules about bedrooms. She needed to prove all the chaperoning skills he and Ellie had deprived her of testing when they were younger.

Mother, Father, and Ellie discussed the ruby and Alexandra endlessly. Ellie huddled in her bedroom with the ruby in her hands, confiding only to Jake that she felt the history of at least a dozen ancestors who'd conjured medicine with it, and that she was sure, now, that it was a good talisman in her possession.

Jake forced himself to hold it but felt nothing, and the blankness was so foreign and unpleasant, he returned it to Ellie quickly. He had misused it once, and it would not forgive him any more than he forgave himself.

But it had protected Samantha and Charlotte for him, so maybe there was some pattern he could not yet understand. Having Samantha was all that mattered to him.

She seemed reluctant to set foot outside the house, not even to admire enormous icicles hanging from the rough log eaves or the aura of sunlight reflected from tree limbs covered in crystal gloves. Jake watched her from a troubled distance. She was too practical to admit it, but she was afraid she'd break the spell.

"What do you expect?" Ellie asked him. "She lost her mother a couple of months ago, she's been through hell, and she came here with nothing but the clothes on her back and what she could carry in a bag. And frankly, dear ol' socially inept brother of mine, you're always watching her like you want to carry her off to your lair. Lighten up. She loves you. I feel it like a big warm blanket every time I'm around her. But she needs to get her bearings."

Jake retreated. He and Samantha were suddenly awkward with each other, a shyness he'd never expected. Father cautioned him needlessly about the natural aftereffects of stress and grief; her fragile emotions were no mystery to Jake. He was content to sit with her in the company of her sister and his family. Mother found her anxiously scrutinizing a torn quilt as if it were wounded. Samantha was soon ensconced on the living room couch, Mother's sewing kit beside her and the quilt in her expert hands. She had found her therapy.

Charlotte prowled the kitchen, watching Mother cook until Ellie sensed her wistfulness and whispered to Mother that Charlotte needed something to do. The moment Mother handed her a spatula, Charlotte brightened, and from then on the kitchen was her sanctuary.

Jake disappeared the morning the ice began melting and the roads were passable. He returned late that afternoon with the knuckles of his right hand raw and swollen.

Samantha saw him before anyone else, and immediately noticed. "What did you do?" she asked, and for the first time since the night she'd arrived, she took his hand.

"I drove to Durham and found Tim. I hit him only once, but I think I broke his jaw. I told him I'd kill him if he did anything to either of you again."

She didn't look surprised. She studied him, frowning mildly. He knew she was measuring him against the image she loved, trying to decide how much the two overlapped. "You should have taken me with you," she said finally.

Concern blanked out his intuition. For a second he couldn't judge her feelings. "So you could have stopped me?" he asked wearily. "I'm not good with people. I wouldn't have known how to get my point across with words. But I'll try to do better."

"No. I mean so you could have held his arms while I hit him."

She raised his hand to her face and carefully pressed her cheek to his bruised knuckles, looked up at him tenderly, then quickly released his hand and moved away.

Jake was speechless—not an uncommon circumstance for him—but he realized suddenly that the awkward times were only a phase in getting acquainted like regular people, like digging patiently through rocky earth because eventually the pure, sweet prize would find its way into your hands.

They were going to be all right with each other.

Chapter Eighteen

Everything had its place, its harmony, and Jake was wrong to think he could ignore it. Clara muttered darkly as she sprinkled dried horse manure like a tonic among the sleepy green shoots of her spring flower beds.

Clara was mad at him, so during the two months since Sammie's arrival in the Cove she'd stayed away. But others in Cawatie didn't. They were too curious about the Raincrows' crazy behavior, awed by the idea that anyone would openly snatch Alexandra's nieces away from her. How had they managed it? No one knew. Secrets were like new spring plants—people fertilized them with gossip and hoped they'd bloom.

Clara had sorted through the chatter for small, trustworthy clues to the situation. Sarah Raincrow showed off new curtains and drapes Samantha had made for her and proudly said there wasn't an unmended shirt, sheet, quilt, or tablecloth in her house. She said she never had to cook another meal, not with Charlotte in her kitchen. She said she'd never seen two girls more determined not to be dependent on anyone.

Sammie Ryder knows that anything they give her just draws the family deeper into trouble, Clara had decided. *Jake thought she'd move right in and forget my warnings.*

Clara had also heard Sammie had been trying for two months to find a job at the shops in Pandora, but no one would hire her. They gave excuses, but the truth was as clear to Clara as the creek that flowed past her garden.

Alexandra had put the word out. No one in town dared hire her runaway niece.

What had Jake expected—that none of Clara's warnings mattered? That he could thumb his nose at a ravenmocker and then go happily on his way?

She flung the last of the manure on her flower bed.

The world had been put right as far as Sarah was concerned. The tradition that had meant so much to the Vanderveers and Raincrows had survived despite Alexandra; the ruby belonged to Ellie, as it should, and Ellie had taken it back to the university, wearing it in a small leather pouch around her neck.

Charlotte was finishing up the academic year at Pandora's high school, and seemed to have settled happily under Sarah's wing. Sarah liked fussing over her; Charlotte was a typical teenager—full of questions and self-doubt, eager for guidance in ways neither Jake or Ellie, with their unusual aplomb, had never needed Sarah.

And Sammie—Sammie was a strong, quiet, inordinately wise young woman, and if Sarah had had any doubt that Sammie deserved Jake's devotion, getting to know Sammie had erased it.

Sarah wedged the phone between her ear and shoulder and anxiously drummed the tip of a paintbrush on her easel. "Hi. Have they been by the office? Have they called yet?"

"They're buying a used car, not negotiating the federal budget," Hugh answered drolly.

"It's more than a car. It's another twig in their nest."

"If they were buying it together, I might agree with you. But it's Sammie's car, bought from her own savings. I'm afraid I haven't seen much sign of nest-building in the past two months."

Sarah huffed into the phone. "What do you think they do during those long walks they take every day? My dear old boy, do you recall what *we* did when we were dating? We didn't just walk."

"My dear old girl, I have very vivid memories of what we did. And that's why I grilled our son about their nature hikes just the other day."

"Why didn't you tell me?"

"Father-son business," he answered gruffly. "Confidential."

"Well?"

"They just talk. Believe it or not."

"Now, look, I know they're both as prim as old maids, but I've watched them trade too many moon-eyed looks to think they haven't—"

"He says she's still in mourning. That it wouldn't feel right, at the moment, to do more than talk."

"I know how Sammie thinks. She admitted to me that she suspects Alexandra is behind the cold shoulder she's gotten from every shopowner in town. Damn Alexandra's time. I'm telling you, Sammie isn't just in mourning for her mother—she's afraid she'll be a burden around Jake's neck."

"Good Lord, she's got no reason to feel like a charity case. She's mended every piece of clothing we own. She's made new curtains for every window of our house—and Jake's too. She made Charlotte a whole new wardrobe to replace what they left at Alexandra's. She gives Charlotte an allowance and insists on giving you money for groceries." He paused. "You've got to keep Charlotte from cooking for us. It may be good therapy for her, but I've gained ten pounds."

"Sammie wants Charlotte to be no trouble to us. I've seen Sammie poring over her checkbook at night. Her savings are running out."

"I suppose it would be highly old-fashioned of me to point out that women don't have to earn their own livings before they can get married. Jake would take care of her. Jake *wants* to take care of her and Charlotte."

"You are an old Neanderthal, but I love you dearly. *Call me* if you hear from them."

"I promise I'll call." From his tone, she could almost see him smiling. "But you have to promise you'll stop worrying—and that you'll go for a walk with me after dinner. A long walk. We'll mash some daffodils."

"*Hugh.* We've got to set a good example." But she was smiling too. She felt giddy these days.

"*Feel* the gears needing to shift." Jake sat close beside her, one arm stretched across the back of the seat, lying casually against her shoulders. The station wagon was worth every penny of five hundred dollars, and not one red cent more—as Sam had pointed out firmly when its owner wanted six hundred. It was as big as a tank, and it lumbered around the empty parking lot of Pandora's elementary school like a big, paneled beetle in the late afternoon sun. "Feel the vibrations with your fingertips," he added.

Sam pushed the floor shift, and the gears protested like a metallic monster gnashing its teeth. She grimaced. "I need specifics," she told him grimly. "Don't talk about vibrations. Tell me what speed is right."

"It depends."

The gears groaned again. She stamped the clutch and took a deep breath. "I thought machines worked on precise principles. I'd never have bought a stick-shift if I had to learn car psychology to drive it."

"This is a fine old car. A bargain. Your eyes lit up the second you saw all the space in the back."

"I had images of it filled with bolts of cloth. I was seduced. You said it'd be easy to learn to drive." She shifted again, without any better success. "I will learn to drive it, but it may need a new gear box."

He put his hand over hers on the knob of the shift. The contact was warm and strong and helplessly appealing. Sam resisted the urge routinely. For two months she'd held her feelings back, afraid to waltz into his arms, afraid this was all a dream. She couldn't quite name what she was waiting for—the soft *click* of her conscience, assuring her that Aunt Alex couldn't harm him for helping her, an anchor of some kind that would make her believe she couldn't be carried back out to sea, dragging Jake and Charlotte with her to drown.

"You think too much," he said softly. "Just let things slide where they belong. Go with the flow."

He said it with the slightest hint of provocation, but enough to turn her muscles to jelly. Sam met his eyes. She let the car roll, and he eased the gearshift noiselessly into first. It was like a dance; she was hypnotized by the guiding pressure of his hand and the amused intensity in his scrutiny. Sam steered the car in a large circle, glimpsing oaks at the edge of the parking lot as they slid past. She had trouble taking her eyes off him. "Step on the clutch again," he whispered. "Careful. No need to stomp it. Smooth."

"You've got a way with cars."

"It's all in the timing." His hand flexed on hers. She shifted into second. The engine purred. He smiled— slow, approving. "See there? We'll be cruising along in high any minute, before we know what's happened."

Out of control, Sam thought, and jerked her attention to their course. Too late. They had meandered out of the circle and were bearing down quickly on the curb at the lot's edge. She forgot the clutch and jammed her foot on the brake. The old station wagon seized up like an asthma victim just as it hit the curb. The impact tossed her forward, and Jake thrust his arm across the steering wheel. Her forehead bounced on the corded surface of hard muscle.

"See what happens when you don't pay attention to *specifics*?" she said, embarrassed. "You made me run into the curb."

"Me?" He frowned and gestured dramatically with one of his big, suddenly clumsy hands. "I was in charge of shifting. You were in charge of looking out for curbs."

"Well, maybe I like a bumpy ride."

"You're gonna be hell on mailboxes and fireplugs."

A soft laugh burst from her, and she was so surprised to feel like laughing, she couldn't stop. She bent her head to his arm and chortled. Jake leaned closer to her. "I can't promise that I'm good at much else," he said sternly, "but I can damn sure teach a girl how to drive."

"Oh, Jake." She twisted toward him suddenly, lifted her face, and kissed him. It was an awkward attempt, spontaneous and meant to reassure him. She caught just the corner of his mouth, lingered there in a startled daze as a current of long-denied excitement overwhelmed her, then drew back.

She had always known that the moment they opened this door, it would be impossible to close it again. They traded a searing look, his eyes half closed and his face flushed. Slowly, he kissed her back, a straight-on, careful caress, infinitely gentle but hungry.

She wound her arms around him. The scent and taste of him consumed her. He was holding her so tightly, neither of them could breathe, and she was dimly aware of gasping between kisses, and of the sound of his own rough inhalations. Everything was quick and fervent—stroking his hair, catching his face between her hands, arching against him when his fingers slid down her spine, her floppy shorts riding up on one leg as she pressed her leg snugly to his thigh, reveling in the coarse texture of his jeans and the hard, flexing muscles underneath.

She had never been drunk before. Knee-walking drunk was how she felt now, and for the first time she understood why every society since the beginning of time tried to make rules about sex. Wanting someone the way she wanted Jake was a powerful addiction. She drew on the last of her failing willpower and gently tried to push him away but realized it was a halfhearted effort. "I know. I know what's been going on. I'm ruining you. Stop. You're making me forget too much."

He pulled back from her just enough to look into her eyes. His expression was anguished and bewildered. He shook his head warily. "If this is what getting ruined feels like, for God's sake, don't stop."

"*Jake.*" She gripped the front of his thin cotton shirt. "I saw Patsy Jones a few weeks ago, when I was job hunting. *She told me.* None of the jewelers in town will buy stones from you anymore. The sheriff won't ask you to track for him." Her voice was raw. She tugged at his shirt fiercely. "Aunt Alex isn't just trying to keep me from making a living around here, she's after you too."

He gripped her shoulders. His eyes darkened. "Listen to me. There are a dozen people outside this town who'll buy what I bring them. And plenty of tracking work I can do outside Pandora—I don't take money for that anyway. God, I knew you felt guilty and it had something to do with me, but I hadn't figured it out yet."

"I'm making you an outsider in your own town."

"I've never been anything but an outsider. And neither has Ellie. People have always said we're strange."

"I shouldn't have kissed you. You make it too easy to forget everything—"

"I want you to forget about everything but me. Because that's how I feel about you." He sank his mouth onto hers. Sam's argument was temporarily lost in the blindness of need. It was true. She couldn't rationalize against this tidal wave of love and desire, even as fear rose up inside her like a dark taunt. They clung together in silent harmony, but tears slid down her face.

Jake broke away and looked at her, his expression troubled but determined. "I never touched a girl before you. I never kissed one. I always told myself I'd try my damnedest to be everything you wanted without any practice. But all I've done is make you unhappy."

"I'm unhappy because you're so wonderful at it. I don't want to stop."

"Then let's just stop until we get married. Married—

with all the bells and whistles and certificates, so the rest of the world can say it's official. I want it to be perfect."

He had a way of saying just the right thing and making her melt inside. "So do I," she whispered. "I always thought it would be. I thought my dad would walk me up to you, and my mother would be there to watch."

He sighed. Slowly he raised a hand and stroked the back of his fingers along her cheek. "That's the only part of it I can't make right for you." He cleared his throat. "But I can teach you to drive this damned car, and I can help you find a job. And I can keep you so busy, you never have time to look over your shoulder for your aunt's shadow." He rested his head against hers. "Because a shadow can't stop us," he added gruffly. "We've already proved that."

Sam shivered. *She'll wait. She'll always be waiting, and when we least expect it . . .*

She had never forgotten Clara Big Stick's warnings. All that talk about Aunt Alex's evil, about dies being cast, about courting doom—Sam didn't want mystical portents to rule her life the way they'd ruled her mother's, but Mrs. Big Stick had scared her.

"Talk to me," Jake said gruffly. "There's something you're ashamed to say."

She tilted her head back and looked at him in wistful defeat. "Hasn't anybody ever told you that men aren't supposed to figure out other people's feelings?"

"I'll grunt and look dense as a doorknob if you'll do what women are supposed to do—talk."

"All right. I told you Mrs. Big Stick came to see me at Aunt Alex's shop. I didn't tell you everything she said."

"Now's the time, then."

Sam spoke haltingly, studying his reaction. Nothing about it seemed to surprise or distract him. When she finished, he nodded. He got out of the car and came around to her side, moving with swift, purposeful strides. "Slide over. You can practice bumping things later."

Staring at him morosely, Sam moved aside. He settled behind the steering wheel. She tugged at his sleeve. "I'm not saying I believe what she said any more than I believe she made me start talking by dunking me in the river when I was three years old. But I do know what my aunt is capable of doing, and—"

"Oh, you believe Clara," Jake said. He cranked the engine. "And you need to hear her say she was wrong."

"She's not going to drop me bare-butt naked into a cold river again. An icy bath and mystical spirits didn't change my life the day I started talking—*you* did."

"Something special helped us both that day." He gave her a quick glance, loving but determined, as he guided the old station wagon away from the curb. "And it's not going to let us down now."

Clara had a yard full of self-important dogs who barked at the drop of a hat, and their friendly silence was the first sign that someone uncommonly trustworthy had just driven into her secluded hollow.

She left turnip greens simmering on the stove and lumbered through a tiny living room cluttered with old furniture, knickknacks, and piles of books. She stood on the whitewashed front porch of her whitewashed frame house, watching Jake and Samantha walk up the sandy path through her herb garden. The dogs crowded around them in the twilight, looking up at Jake happily and nuzzling his hands.

Samantha carried a large gold box wrapped in cellophane. Clara squinted. Candy. Jake knew about her sweet tooth, and he knew a person didn't show up for conjuring advice without a polite gift to offer.

So he had finally come to ask for her help.

But he couldn't bribe her goodwill with candy. "I already told you what to do," she announced, holding up both hands. They stopped at the bottom of the porch steps. Samantha looked sad. Jake looked respectful but grim. "I told you," Clara continued, pointing at Jake, "a long time ago. You're one of the people. You were taught the right ways by Granny Raincrow. I can't fault Samantha for making mistakes—she's not one of us. She was raised *ignorant*. But you know better, Jake. You know a ravenmocker can't be stopped once it gets its mind set."

"Am I a ravenmocker?" Sam asked wearily. "It doesn't sound very good."

"No," Jake answered. "Not you. She means Alexandra." He looked up at Clara with troubled eyes. "But there's something you don't know. No one outside my family knows. It makes a difference."

"I can think of only one thing that would make a difference," Clara said. "And I told you it wouldn't come back to your family except through terrible suffering."

"But it has come back. Samantha suffered. Samantha brought it."

Clara's mouth dropped open. "The ruby?" she whispered.

He nodded. She listened in shocked silence as he told how the stone had been recovered, how it had stopped Alexandra from taking Samantha's younger sister away. Clara considered the information with amazement. "Come inside," she said finally. "I have to think on this. It may be a trick of hers."

"Of mine?" Sam asked, her eyes widening. "I swear, I didn't know my aunt had it. I didn't know it was hidden—"

"*Hers*," Clara said patiently. "The ravenmocker's."

"No trick," Jake replied. "Alexandra would never have given it up."

Clara made a huffing sound at his confidence. "What makes you think she's given it up? Just because she had to let it go don't mean she's let it go for good."

"Mother gave the stone to Ellie. Where it belongs. Where it will *stay*."

"Come inside." They followed her into the house. Sammie held the box out. "Please accept this gift. And please don't be angry with Jake. He had nothing to do with the reasons I left my aunt's home."

"But he's the reason you ended up in the Cove."

"She didn't want to come to me for help," Jake said. "She tried her best not to get me involved."

"A smart girl. You should have listened. Listened with the gift God gave you." He shook his head slightly and gave Clara a beseeching look. *He hasn't told Sammie about his secret ways,* Clara realized. Because he feared she wouldn't believe? Clara sighed, recalling how Granny Raincrow had guarded the truth too. People were quick to laugh at anything they couldn't understand, Granny had said. Or quick to take selfish advantage.

Watching Sammie, Clara doubted she'd do either. Jake couldn't hide that part of himself from her forever. She waved a hand at Sammie. "Set that box of candy on a table. I've got to check on my dinner."

Clara marched into the kitchen, a small, hot room with bunches of dried herbs hanging from pegs along the walls. Sammie and Jake followed her politely. Clara stirred the pot of turnip greens and pretended to ignore them. But Sammie dropped to one knee on a bright rug that covered a thin spot in the linoleum. Clara stared at her strange behavior.

Sammie's eyes were suddenly bright. Her hands roamed over the rug's intricate zigzagging design. She seemed to have forgotten everything else. "This is *beautiful*. Who made it?"

Clara tried to resist the flattery. "That old thing? I made it. Any old woman worth her salt can weave. The young ones don't have the patience."

Sammie gazed up at her in awe. "This is a work of art. You have a loom?"

Clara jerked her head toward a warped screen door to the back porch. "Out there."

"I've never seen a loom except in pictures. I've always thought of big, dirty mill factories with dozens of mechanical monsters clacking away while tired women turned out bolts of cloth for someone else to enjoy. My dad's people were mill workers. I guess I heard too many stories about how hard their lives were. I never imagined anyone could make something this . . . this personal. May I look at the loom?"

"Help yourself."

Sammie bounded up and ran to the door. She pushed it open and stepped outside slowly, reverently, her attention riveted to one end of the narrow screened porch. Her hands reaching out carefully, she moved with trancelike attention, disappearing from sight.

Jake and Clara traded puzzled looks.

She sat down on the loom's smooth-worn wooden bench. The loom was a confusing contraption to most people, but Sammie studied it as if she'd discovered a new friend. Her hands trembled as she stroked the wooden frame, then ran her fingertips over the bleached white cords of the weft. "You take nothing and make it into something," she whispered. "You start with threads and an idea, and you end up with a piece of fabric that's different from anything anyone else has ever made. Something that's part of you."

Clara was astonished, and secretly pleased. "It's over a hundred years old," she said proudly. "Belonged to my great-grandmother. It's made of chestnut. You won't find another one like it."

"I have to learn to weave." Sammie looked as if she wanted to hug the loom. She swiveled toward Clara. Her eyes gleamed. "Will you teach me? Please?"

Clara felt Jake watching her. She frowned at him, but the urgent expression in his eyes went straight to her heart. "You see?" he said. "It's a good sign."

"Don't tell me about *signs*, mister. I know how to read signs. I'll be the one who decides if this means something."

"It means I have work to do," Sammie said happily.

Clara pondered this development. She never rushed to decisions. But she was beginning to wonder if certain pieces hadn't fallen into place. "It's easy to learn—but hard to learn how to be the best. I'm just fair to middling at it myself."

"I don't mind the work. I can be the best. I'm not just talking, Mrs. Big Stick. I'm not trying to earn your good wishes by pretending to admire what you do."

"I figured that out already. It's the bigger meaning

I can't quite figure yet. You're not one of the people. Throws me off. Wait here." Muttering to herself, she went back into the house.

Jake held his breath. Samantha looked up at him with tears in her eyes. One hand rested on the loom's canvas of straight, regimented threads. She held the other hand out to him. He went to her quickly. They sat on the narrow bench, their heads bent together. "I'll build you a loom," he whispered.

She cupped his head, winding her fingers into his dark hair. The need to touch him had quickly become more desperate than she could resist. Dangerous in its confidence. Unforgettable in its promises. "I love you," she whispered.

Clara sat on her couch, a pair of reading glasses perched on her nose, a hefty, dog-eared Bible open under the light of a chipped ceramic lamp on the end table. She searched the text, thick brown fingertips roaming over yellowed pages. Proverbs. She liked to consult Proverbs. They spoke to her with pure poetry, the wisdom of ancient people who shared a closeness to the earth. There was a passage she couldn't quite recall, something that had teased the edge of her memory when she saw Sammie at the loom.

When she found it, she bent over the Bible, reading silently, her lips moving in somber regard. Then she sat back and shut her eyes, sorting through what Jake had told her. The ruby had come back to them. She'd promised Granny Raincrow she'd look out for Jake and Ellie.

And because Jake loved Sammie Ryder despite Clara's misgivings, she would have to look out for Sammie too. There was evidence that Sammie was meant to be here, meant to be with him.

She hoisted herself up. Carrying the open Bible in her arms, she went back to the porch. They were sitting together on the loom bench, close and quiet, young and hopeful. Clara sighed. It was done. She would heed the advice she had found. "'Who can find a virtuous woman?' " she read slowly. "'For her price is far above rubies. The heart of her husband doth safely trust in her, so that he shall have no need of spoil. She will do him good and not evil all the days of her life.'"

Clara paused, glancing at Sammie in thoughtful wonder. "'She seeketh wool, and flax, and worketh willingly with her hands.'" Clara moved a fingertip down the page a bit, and continued. "'She maketh herself coverings of tapestry; her clothing is silk and purple . . . she maketh fine linen, and selleth it; and delivereth girdles unto the merchant. Strength and honor are her clothing; and she shall rejoice in time to come.'"

Clara closed the Bible. "I'll listen to what the old Hebrews told me about you," she told Sammie. "I'll teach you to be a weaver."

They walked into the house as darkness was falling. Side by side, casting portentous looks at each other, they stepped into the living room. As if by unspoken agreement, their hands met. Jake's formal, intense train of thought relaxed. Samantha didn't have any doubts, and neither did he. All he had to do was make the announcement. Find words good enough to honor it.

Mother was painting at her easel, in one corner. Father turned from his desk. Charlotte sat on the floor, a stack of books and notepads spread in front of her on an old coffee table. She peered at them from under shaggy blond bangs. And her mouth dropped open.

Mother and Father, he noticed finally, looked as if they expected something. How could it be that obvious?

"I've seen this coming for a long time," Mother said. "But you two have got to give us at least a month to make decent plans. Don't march in here a couple of days from now with a justice of the peace and a marriage license."

Father nodded his agreement. "Your grandmother's spring would be a nice place for a ceremony. That's got my vote."

Charlotte waved her hands excitedly. "I'll make the cake for you, Sammie. I've always wanted to try a wedding cake."

Jake felt Samantha's hand squeezing his happily. He

looked at her. Her eyes were warm and pleased. He looked at everyone else. "How did you guess?" he asked.

Mother stood and came to him, reached up, and pulled his head to hers. She whispered loud enough for everyone to hear: "You look like you've been kissed six ways from Sunday."

"He has," Sam added, and smiled.

So Jake would be married. Ellie envied her brother that courage, that achievement. She sat on the back porch in the darkness, braiding her long hair. Everyone else was inside, discussing the wedding plans. She was happy for Jake, happy for Sam, because she felt the loyalty they shared.

Jake had taken a risk Ellie couldn't fathom yet. To know someone the way she and Jake knew people— to sense their fears and selfishness, their mistakes and embarrassments—that brand of empathy kept her from reaching out. She wondered sometimes if she'd ever touch a man and feel anything other than disappointment.

"Ellie?" Sam called her name carefully. Ellie turned and looked up at her, standing behind the screen door to the kitchen, silhouetted by the house's cozy heart of light. Sam was a private person—she respected others' private moments. Ellie liked that about her. Jake had not made any mistake by loving Sam.

"Yes?"

"Can I talk to you a minute?"

"Sure."

Sam slipped outside, closing the screen door so it wouldn't make a sound, then sat down beside her. They sat for a moment, listening to the evening murmurs of insects and watching the first spring fireflies blink across the old field beyond the barn. A fingernail moon was rising over the granite rim of the mountains. "I'd like to get to know you better," Sam said.

"You'll be busy." Ellie said that with a smile. "You and Jake. Making up for lost time. But I'll be around." She put a hand on Sam's arm and gave it a quick, affectionate squeeze. "You're good for him. Don't worry. You're right to marry him. I wish I could find someone . . ." Her voice trailed off.

"You will," Sam said quickly. "I envy *you*. You've got work to do."

"Sammie, you're not much for thumb-twiddling, I know. But you'll do well with your weaving. You've got a lot of talent. Clara told Mother so."

"Mr. Gunther stopped by the other day. He said I should visit a modeling agency down in Atlanta. Take the brochure I did for his friend. See if I can get a contract for my hands." Sam raised her perfect hands in the darkness of the porch as if she were studying them. "What a strange way to use them. I guess I could make a lot of money at it."

"Only if you're willing to travel. You'd have to go away. Jake wouldn't like that. I don't think you would either."

"No. When I posed for that one job, I felt like a life-support system for ten pretty fingers. Kind of a useless accessory."

"Then be patient. Something better will come along. The money doesn't matter to Jake. *You* matter to Jake."

"The first time he took me to see his house, it was like walking into a place I'd seen before." She hesitated, then added wistfully, "My mom would call that déjà vu. I don't know what to call the feeling. But it was *home*. Even with all the empty rooms and bare windows."

"He had you in mind when he built it."

"It couldn't be more right if I'd told him exactly what I like. He's uncanny that way. Amazing."

What he knows about your likes and dislikes is no lucky guess, Ellie thought. She wondered if Jake would ever share that secret with practical, feet-on-the-ground Sam. She hoped so. She patted Sam's arm. Sam loved him enough. More than enough. So much that she was eager to ask Ellie for some delicate type of advice. "Sex," Ellie said as if the subject had already been mentioned, "it's a helluva thing. Designed to be spontaneous and carefree, but surrounded by tricky little responsibilities."

Sam muttered under her breath. "Are you a mind reader?"

Yes, Ellie thought, but only smiled. "What else would you be thinking about a few weeks before you get married?"

Sam eyed her sideways. "If I said *finding the perfect lace for my wedding dress,* you'd know I was full of shit."

That crusty comment from her brother's dignified soulmate made Ellie double over with laughing appreciation. Sam nudged her. "Pardon me, but I talk this way when I'm embarrassed. I'm not embarrassed very often."

"Don't be embarrassed. Think of me as a doctor."

"All right. I know I could ask your father, and it probably wouldn't make him bat an eyelash, and he probably will say something about it sooner or later, which is what I want to avoid. Because there's something about discussing these things with my future father-in-law that would make me mumble like an idiot. That wouldn't look too mature, now, would it?"

"Birth control," Ellie said, nodding. "No, Father may be able to talk turkey with his female patients without a second thought, but not with you. You want to hear *mumbling*? Try to discuss your and Jake's, hmmm, *romantic* details with him."

"That's what Jake said too."

Ellie gave her a thoughtful look. "I suspect there's not much you and Jake can't talk about. That's good. Look, never fear. I can get birth control pills for you, if that's what you want."

"Oh, thank you."

"And discreetly pass along a *case closed* hint to my folks."

Sam sighed. "*Thank you.*"

"But if you're looking for anything that's not clinical advice, you're barking up the wrong tree, kiddo." Ellie frowned and looked away. "I'm the last of the red-hot virgins around here. I probably hold the title in the women's twenty-and-older division."

"You've never—"

"Just like Jake. Strange but true."

"Not *strange*. There's a lot to be said for waiting. I don't care how odd it sounds to everyone else. I'm an expert at waiting."

"Even now?"

"Well, it's getting tougher by the second. But Jake and I agreed." She nodded. "Traditions deserve respect."

Ellie thought of the ruby, and raised a hand to the small leather pouch hanging from a silver necklace under her T-shirt. "Yes, they do."

They heard footsteps on the kitchen floor and turned to look. "What's going on out here?" Jake asked, leaning in the door frame with big-shouldered ease.

"We're talking about birth control pills," Sam answered. "It's all taken care of."

He was silent. He straightened, sank his hands into his trouser pockets, and tried very hard to look casual. Ellie bit her lip to keep from laughing out loud. "I should have stayed in the dining room," he said, then turned and ambled away.

"I better go after him," Sam said. "He'll need me to cover for him until he can talk again." She rose, squeezed Ellie's shoulder in gratitude, and walked inside.

Ellie faced forward, took the ruby from its pouch, and clasped it in both hands. Her amusement faded. She was just lonely and a little depressed, feeling morbid, because that was her nature, she told herself. *Mother and Father and I won't live to see their children grow up. Something is going to happen.*

She refused to believe everything she felt and saw when she touched her own traditions.

Chapter
Nineteen

S am stood in the foyer of Highview, stiff with apprehension and disgust as she waited for the housekeeper to summon Aunt Alex. She glanced at herself in a large mirror that hung over a marble table near the entrance. Dressed in a simple blouse and long blue skirt, she made a meticulous, self-assured picture inside the mirror's ornately gilded frame.

Jake did not know Aunt Alex had written her a note, or that she'd come here to answer it. She wouldn't have the eve of their wedding ruined by Aunt Alex. This confrontation belonged to Sam alone.

Aunt Alex walked into the foyer with quick strides, a pale yellow dress swirling around her, her face composed and pleasant. "I'm very honored you came to see me," she said. "Considering how busy you must be. Most weddings couldn't be organized in only a month's time."

"I had a lot of help. Help from people who don't

have hidden motives. People who want only to make it the nicest day possible."

Aunt Alex gestured toward a sitting room off the foyer. "Please. I have a gift for you. And you know, you and Charlotte left quite a few of your belongings here. I thought you'd want them."

"No. We're starting over. I came here only to make sure you don't have any new plan to take Charlotte back. She's happy with the Raincrows. She's doing well in school. We don't need or want anything from you."

"Don't be too hasty." Aunt Alex gave her a wistful look. "I'm offering you an apology. I've agonized over how I mishandled your trust. I should have treated Charlotte's accusations with more respect."

"That's not the same as admitting you believed them."

Aunt Alex stiffened. She walked with rigid dignity into the sitting room, a place of beautiful pastel fabrics and delicate white furniture. Sam hesitated, anger rising, then followed her reluctantly. Aunt Alex stood at a window, gazing out over the lawn and the lake below, her hands clasped behind her. "I was very unhappy when I came here to marry William," she said. "I was so young—almost as young as you are. My parents pressured me to marry him. He was much older than I, and he drank heavily."

"I heard he started drinking after you married him."

"That's what Sarah wants people to believe. I can understand her protectiveness—he was her brother, a respected man, and she loved him. But it's not true. I knew when I married him that he drank. That he had a violent temper."

Sam studied her warily. "*If* that was true, why did you marry him? It wasn't the Dark Ages. Your parents couldn't force you."

"Oh? They knew I loved Orrin. He had nothing—he was a struggling young attorney. They threatened to ruin him unless I did as I was told."

"My mother married who she wanted."

"She had to leave the country to get away with it.

And she wasn't in love with a man who dreamed of devoting his life to politics. If I'd married Orrin then, he'd never have had his dream. I couldn't do that to him."

The idea of Aunt Alex sacrificing her own happiness for anyone else's was new to Sam. She didn't want to feel sorry for her, or forgive her, but she did want to understand her. Circumstances could twist people's hopes. She had learned that when her parents died. "You didn't have to alienate Sarah and everyone else," Sam said slowly.

"Sarah hated me before I ever acquired her heirloom ruby," Aunt Alex said with a trace of weary resignation. "And I suppose I hated her because she was so free. You can't imagine how painful it was for me to see other people doing what they wanted with their lives, loving whomever they wanted. No one stopped Sarah from marrying a man with Indian blood. I thought she had so much happiness—and I had so little."

"So you didn't feel any guilt about taking something that was important to her."

"I wanted to fit in, Samantha. I *desperately* wanted a measure of control over my hopeless situation. William insisted that I take the ruby. It was the only loving gesture he ever made to me. He knew I didn't love him. That stone came to represent all the pride and freedom I'd lost. I couldn't give it up."

"Was it worth lying about when he died? Was it worth hiding?"

"I thought so, until the day I lost you and Charlotte because of it."

"A *rock* had nothing to do with that. You drove us away. And when Sarah threatened to expose you, you decided your public reputation was more important than your interest in keeping Charlotte and me. That's a strange brand of concern for us."

"You would have hated me more if I'd fought you. I let you have what you wanted, Samantha, because I love you."

"You call it *love* when you pressure your cronies not to give me a job in town?"

Aunt Alex turned. "I've never done that. Whatever you've heard—it's just gossip."

"I don't believe you."

"Samantha, I don't want to hurt your pride. The truth about your problems has nothing to do with me, except for this—I realize, now, that by opposing Jake I made him nearly irresistible to you. I remember how it felt to love someone who was forbidden. The love gets tangled up in a need to prove yourself, to rebel. I was incredibly lucky—what I felt for Orrin was much, much more than a rebellious obsession. Can you say the same thing about your feelings for Jake?"

"*Yes.*"

Aunt Alex smiled sadly. "Of course, that's how you'll answer. He's been kind to you—he's a hero. You want to love him. You think you don't have anywhere else to turn."

"That's not true."

"I'll tell you why you haven't been able to find work at the shops in town. Not because of anything I've done—it's because people are leery of *him*. Jake and his sister have always been peculiar. They're loners. They're troublemakers."

"If that's all you have to say, I'm leaving." Sam turned to go.

"Wait," Aunt Alex called. She walked toward Sam, drawing a slip of paper from a hidden pocket of her skirt. "Here's how much I care about you and Charlotte. Read this. This is my gift to you—the sort of gift I wish to God someone had offered me when I was about to marry William Vanderveer."

Sam shook her head. "Whatever it is, I don't want it."

"I'll read you the contents, then." Aunt Alex halted, opened the folded sheet and read slowly. "A house in your name—free and clear—anywhere you like. Money—a great deal of money—in a savings account under your name alone. And you'll have custody of Charlotte until she's eighteen—legal guardianship."

Sam inhaled sharply. "In return for what?"

"That you walk away from your engagement to Jake."

"God, you don't give up."

"Samantha, I'm making it *easy* for you. You don't have to fight me anymore. And you don't have to marry Jake just to spite me."

"You don't understand. You'll never understand, because you didn't have the guts to do what you knew was right for you when you were young. I think you hated my mother for having that kind of courage. You always wanted to show her how wrong she'd been. Well, she wasn't wrong to marry my dad, and I'm not wrong to marry Jake. You'll never prove me wrong, any more than you could her."

Alexandra stiffened. "I had the courage to *wait* for what I wanted, for what I deserved. And I got it. I always will get what I want, because I know the difference between impulsive daydreams and patient reality. Your mother, bless her soul, died penniless and miserable. She left you *nothing*. And if you marry Jake, that's all you'll ever have—nothing."

"Stay out of our lives. You want me to be like you— fine, in a way, I am. Because I'm willing to do whatever it takes to get what I want, and you'll never stop me, or hurt anyone I love." She spun and walked swiftly into the foyer. Aunt Alex followed, crumpling the paper and slinging it aside. She caught Sam by one arm as Sam reached for the heavy brass handle of the front door. "Pride will ruin you. You'll make more mistakes because of it," Aunt Alex said in a low, brutally calm voice. "And finally you'll see how right I am."

"I have more control over my life than you've ever had over yours," Sam answered just as calmly. "And I didn't have to sell myself to get it. That's what you can't stand." For a fleeting second she saw that truth mirrored in her aunt's eyes. Then it was gone, shielded by fury. "Get out," Aunt Alex said.

"Good-bye." Sam walked out into the bright June sunshine, confident and satisfied, but feeling Aunt Alex's gaze on her back like a claw.

"Where were you?" Jake asked. They sat at the edge of the spring with their bare feet immersed in the cold, clear water. He always called it his granny's spring, and said how much she'd loved it. Sam knew she would enjoy looking down the slope at it from the wide windows of their front room. That room, like most of the house, was empty. But she had plans. A couch facing that window. Rugs on the floor. A tapestry over the stone fireplace.

"Where were *you*?" she asked, squeezing his hand and gazing into the spring innocently.

"I was doing what a man is supposed to do the day before his wedding."

"Buying new underwear?"

"Maybe I don't wear any."

"I'll have to see about that."

"Hmmm. I let you go through my closet already. I've got no secrets." He emphasized *secrets* as if he knew she was thinking of her visit to Highview. But he couldn't know. Sam laughed as casually as she could. "You've got a bunch of threadbare old shirts and jeans with lopsided patches sewn inside them. I can't wait to get my hands on your clothes."

"I'll be glad to sit around naked and watch you sew. The question is, will you be able to concentrate on your stitchery?"

Sam couldn't help giving him a sloe-eyed look of promise. "I doubt it." She feigned an interest in the top buttons of his faded blue shirt. "Look at those button-holes. Torn at the edges. I can't understand how the buttons stay caught in them." She crooked a finger under the first one, and it popped open. "See there?" He watched her with a hooded gaze that was growing more intense by the second. Her fingers lingered on the soft swath of black hair revealed in the open space. Slowly her finger slid to the next button. It popped from its ragged fastenings just as easiliy. "No hope for that one either," she said in a breathy voice. "I've got my work cut out for me."

The forest formed a private hollow for them, a dark green cavern where they could escape the chaos of people and wedding preparations that had taken over his parents' house during the past few days. Visitors from Cawatie were camped all around the main house. Tonight there would be a barbecue over an open pit in the yard, and bluegrass music, and dancing.

They would have to go there soon. This was their last few minutes alone together, before tomorrow. Sam bent her head and, pushing his shirt open, rested her cheek against the center of his chest. "The next time I get to do this," she whispered, "I won't stop at two buttons."

He laughed under his breath. His heart was beating quickly. She felt the accelerated rhythm under her cheek. "You're making our good intentions hard . . . hard to remember."

"This is your bachelor party. Mine too."

"Oh?" She lifted her head as he trailed a hand across her shoulder and toyed with the buttons of her blouse. Her buttons were neatly trapped in place, but then, his large, blunt fingers had amazing abilities. One button slipped quickly out of its moorings. His fingertips felt like fire against her skin. Sam lost herself in his eyes. A second button went the way of the first. She felt the cool forest air on the tops of her breasts. "Two for two," he said in a throaty voice that dissolved her bones. He eased her blouse open, then bent his head. Sam heard herself make a low sound of pleasure as he placed slow kisses just above her bra. He drew back, his face flushed, a tortured half-smile soothing the tight angles of his face. Sam felt one moment of shyness. "I don't have big ones, you know. Nothing fancy. Thirty-four Bs."

He arched a black brow. "If we're going by measurements, I'll get a tape. Maybe you better check all of mine too."

"Oh, I've sized you up. I've got a good eye for estimates."

Both of them were speaking in intimate tones, as provocative as a caress. "Think I'll make a good fit?" he asked.

"The best."

He draped his hands over her breasts, molding his fingers to them gently. "Look at that. My hands are *exactly* size thirty-four B."

The sensation of his palms pressing against her brought a soft cry of delight, and the serious teasing threatened to end in a pre-wedding honeymoon there on the edge of the spring. He put his arms around her and she leaned against him, her head on his shoulder. He was trembling. "Glad we got that settled," he said hoarsely. "But I might have misjudged by a quarter inch or so. I'll have to check again. Better wait until tomorrow. Can't think too clear right now."

"All you want. Everything. I love you so much."

"I love you too." Jake held her tightly, rubbing his face against her hair. He knew where she'd gone today; she kept thinking about Alexandra. It was hell to know it but not be able to ask her.

"I went to see Alexandra," she said. She lifted her head and looked at him with apology. "She sent me a note through Patsy Jones. I didn't want to tell you."

"You know I wouldn't have let you go alone."

"I'm not worried about anything she can do. Not anymore. Maybe I had to prove it to myself today."

"What did she say? What did she want?"

"To give me a house, and money. And legal custody of Charlotte." Sam paused, then added grimly, "And all I have to do in return is give you up."

"Stay away from her. And Tim. Promise me."

"She can't change our lives. I told her so. Do you think I'd leave you? *Ever?*"

"No. But promise me you won't go there alone again."

"I promise." Sam took his hands. "Let's not talk about her anymore."

"I'm glad you told me."

"I didn't intend to. Because it isn't important, and I knew it would make you furious. You *look* furious now. She's my relative, and when I think about you hating her, I feel dirty. Stained. Like I need to wash her out of my blood before I can marry—"

He startled her by scooping a hand into the spring. He brought the water to her face, stroking cold rivulets over her forehead and cheeks. He repeated the strange action on his own face. "You're clean. No need to ever think about it again. Come on. I'll show you what I was doing today."

Without another word he pulled her to her feet. They walked, barefoot, up the hill to the house. It sat atop the knoll like a comfortable log crown, at ease with the forest, the windows gleaming in the afternoon sun. He led her through the bare, woodsy-smelling front room with its high ceilings and massive fireplace, its heart-pine floors, down a hall, past the open door to the large bedroom they would share, to the closed door of a smaller bedroom.

"Close your eyes," he ordered softly. When she did, he pushed the door open. "Now look."

"A loom." She uttered the words in a prayerful whisper.

"I copied Clara's. It's even made of chestnut. I bought the wood from an old man at Cawatie, who was tearing down a barn. The trees it came from stood at the edge of a village. People would pick up chestnuts under them in the fall. The babies slept under the trees on woven mats of cane while their parents worked." When Sam looked at him curiously, he frowned and added, "At least, that's how it could have been."

"It's wonderful." Her hands pressed to her lips, she hurried to the loom and sank down on a smooth wooden bench. He had lined one wall with simple shelves. She pictured them filled with skeins of yarn. During the past few weeks Mrs. Big Stick had taught her how to thread a loom, and she touched the loom's empty frame longingly.

Jake eased over to her and put a hand on her shoulder. "You like it," he said with relief. "It's just what you needed. I thought it'd be a good wedding gift."

She placed her hand over his and looked up at him with stark adoration. "Everything here is exactly what I need."

They were married outdoors, by his grandmother's cool, enchanted spring, on a beautiful June afternoon. A hundred people clustered before the pool of water, making a small path up the center of the group for her. Sam wore a simple white dress overlaid with old lace Sarah had given her, a lace veil floating down her back. She walked up the path alone, carrying no bouquet, her veil drawn back, the hem of the dress moving gracefully around her ankles. She was vaguely aware that the crowd included Mr. Gunther, who was grinning, and Mrs. Big Stick, who sat on a tree stump away from the others, looking solemn. Sarah, Ellie, and Charlotte stood together, and Charlotte cried and smiled at her constantly.

But she could not take her eyes off Jake, who waited for her and held her gaze with an intensity that took her breath away. He wore his beautiful black suit as if he'd always been at ease in such elegant attire, and stood stock-still, his head up, beside his father and a minister from the church at Cawatie. Bo crept out of the crowd as unobtrusively as a huge, baggy-faced bloodhound could. Someone had tied a white bow around his neck. He lay down at Jake's feet. People laughed.

Sam took Jake's outstretched hands and faced him. The world narrowed to just the two of them, a small, intimate space in which nothing mattered but their certainty and faith. The minister, his brown face glistening with earnest perspiration, his gray hair pulled back in a long braid, read the ceremony in Cherokee and then English, and through a haze of emotion Sam heard herself repeating the vows, and Jake echoing them.

They traded plain gold wedding bands engraved with their initials and the date. The minister reached the *I now pronounce you* moment, and Jake said, "Wait."

Sam stared at him, bewildered. His hands tightened on hers. "Your sister is my sister," he told her. "Your parents are my parents."

Sam choked up. "Your sister is my sister," she replied. "Your parents are my parents."

"Your home is my home."

"Your home is my home." Bo chose that tender moment to rise from behind Jake's feet, edge over to Sam, and lean heavily against her legs. Sam staggered, glanced down at him, then back at Jake. "Your dog is my dog," she added.

Jake smiled. "Now, that's love."

"I pronounce you husband and wife," the minister intoned. "Kiss her quick, Jake, before Bo knocks her down."

They stood in the shadows, quietly watching the party that had spilled out of Sarah and Hugh's house after dark. Sam's thoughts shimmered with the newness of it all—the anticipation, the unspoken intimacy between her and Jake. He had one arm around her shoulders, and she had hers around his waist. It was time for them to go back to their own house, alone, for the first night. She hadn't quite decided how to mention it, and she dreaded the coy looks they were going to get when they told everyone good night.

Lanterns were strung in the trees, casting pools of light under the dark, huge limbs. The bluegrass band had closed up shop at midnight. But people were still dancing; someone had brought an enormous tape deck and speakers. The music varied wildly—country, then rock 'n' roll, then pop. No one seemed to notice. The old people did their two-steps; the younger ones bounced around as if the dewy grass were a disco floor. The sleepy ones, and the drunk ones, were snoring in the porch rockers and along the perimeter of the darkness, propped limply against tree trunks.

Sam smiled. "When we lived in Germany, my dad took us to Oktoberfest one year. I'd never seen so many grown people sleeping under shrubs before. It looked a lot like this."

Jake laughed. "The last time I went in the house, Charlotte was asleep in a chair next to the cake table. With a spatula in one hand."

"Do you want to go now? You've been so quiet. I thought you might be . . . well, nervous."

"I wanted to shoo everyone away and carry you off right after the ceremony."

"And do what, after that?" Her heart was pounding, and the question held breathless mischief.

"Sit on the bed awhile and look at you. Pretend to be suave. Try not to gawk and wink."

"Oh, you stole my plan."

They bent their heads together and laughed softly, the tension momentarily broken. "Samantha Raincrow," he said slowly, as if tasting the name and liking it. "Let's go say our good nights, and then let's go home."

She kissed him.

Our house, she thought with awe as they left the forest path and walked, holding hands. The porch light was on, but the rest of the house was dark. The only soft sound was whippoorwills calling to each other. "Who turned the light on?" Sam said under her breath. "I think we've been ambushed."

"They've been here," Jake answered. "Ellie and Mother and Charlotte. I saw them sneaking this way during the party."

"Well, your mother, at least, wouldn't tie tin cans to the door or spray 'Just Hitched' on the kitchen counter in whipped cream." She hesitated. "But Charlotte would."

They reached the front door. "Hold on," Jake said when she put a hand on the doorknob. He pushed the door open, then picked her up.

"Oh." She smiled at him sheepishly. "I'm not thinking about proper customs."

"I forget why people are supposed to do this," he admitted, carrying her into the dark, quiet living room. "But it feels right."

"Everything feels right," she whispered.

He carried her into the bedroom, and she fumbled for a light switch near the door. A small brass lamp lit the room with luxurious delicacy. The bed was king-size, and it had been turned down, with the quilt she had made for him years ago folded carefully across new white sheets. Several huge new pillows in lace-trimmed cases had been arranged in artful poses along the bed's plain pine headboard, and white rose petals were strewn across them.

Jake lowered her to the bed. They sat side by side. She winked at him. "That was my job," he said solemnly.

"I hope it didn't look like a nervous twitch."

He sighed. "Nothing wrong with being jittery."

"Are you?"

"Me? Why, it's never crossed my mind. I'm an old pro at this kind of stuff."

"Scared stiff," she said.

"Stiff, and scared," he corrected her. Sam collapsed into soft chortles. He grabbed her hand. "We'd better check the rest of the house."

"Oh, yes." Relieved, they hurried through the rooms, turning on lights, gazing around, turning lights off. They found a note on the kitchen counter. "Food" was scrawled in Charlotte's looping hand, with an arrow pointing to the refrigerator. Sam opened the door and gasped at the array of bowls and casserole dishes, the whole cooked turkey, and the ham. "They must expect us to do nothing except eat and . . . well, not a bad idea, actually."

"Look," Jake said. The sink was full of ice. A bottle of champagne nestled in the center of it. Two beautiful crystal champagne glasses sat on the counter with a card propped against them. He opened it. "Love, Ellie," he read. "Well, I guess Charlotte did the food and Ellie did the champagne and Mother did the bed. I'm glad she didn't leave a note on it."

Sam nodded weakly. "That's not a place you want to find a note from your mother. Well, we can eat, drink, or—let's have some champagne."

"Good idea." He took it from the ice and studied the foil-wrapped top intently. "I've never had champagne before. I'm not much of a drinker." Sam leaned close to him. "Me neither. But I believe you unwrap the foil and push the cork up with your thumbs. And point it at the ceiling so we won't get beaned when it pops."

"I don't even know how to uncork a bottle of champagne," he said with disgust, shaking his head. "It's gonna be a helluva night."

Sam placed her hands over his. "Just be careful where you point your cork, and we'll be all right."

He began to laugh again, and looked at her with so much appreciation, she blushed. "Now I'm pink," she said jauntily. "I hate being pink."

"Your face looks wonderful pink."

"You should see the rest of me."

That stopped the teasing. Suddenly they were quiet again, but it was an electric silence filled with strong needs and emotions. "We could drink the champagne later," he offered.

She nodded. "I don't think I can swallow right now anyway."

They turned off the light over the sink and walked back to the bedroom. He put a hand on her shoulder, and she jumped. "I think," he said loudly, as if announcing the idea to a crowd, "I think we should just get undressed and lie down, and turn off the light, and . . . talk for a while."

"You read my mind."

He said nothing, but looked at her wistfully. "I bet you made a special nightgown."

"Satin with lacy trim. With a matching robe. And I made you a pair of matching pajama bottoms." She looked at him somberly. "No lace."

"Thank you."

"It's all under the mattress. I put everything in place when I was here by myself one day, measuring for curtains."

She bustled around, folding the sheets back, feeling under the mattress, pulling out shimmering white material and laying it all on the bed neatly. Then she reached under the mattress again and drew her hand out with something else cradled lovingly in it. "My dreamcatcher," she said, and hung it on one post of the headboard.

The look they shared melted the uneasiness. His eyes shining, he took a step toward her, his hands out. Sam gave a small cry of welcome and moved quickly into his arms, planting fervent kisses all over his face, receiving his eagerly.

A few minutes later, her wedding dress and his suit joined the satin gown, the robe, the pajama bottoms, on the floor. Sam lay in his embrace, rose petals clinging to her hair, the night dissolving into feverish caresses and whispers, and nothing in her whole life was easier to do than loving him.

Alexandra moved through the quiet, dark rooms of Highview, her glorious, gabled, stone sanctuary—won in marriage to William, preserved in the fifteen years since his death, expanded in moneyed splendor of her own making—historic, dignified, elegant, empty.

Orrin was at their second home, in Raleigh. She'd sent him away. He didn't understand her misery, her obsession. He was tired of hearing about her rebellious nieces, tired of negotiating a semblance of civility between her and Tim, whom she had banished from Highview since his disgusting breach of common sense regarding Charlotte.

Orrin was secretly glad, she suspected, that Samantha's wedding to Jake had finally occurred. He thought it would put an end to a petty crisis that distracted her from their goals.

But the wedding had only turned her defeat and disappointment into black rage.

The front of her sleek green robe was flung open, red streaks showing on her breasts, where she'd clawed heedlessly. She carried a thin black riding whip in one hand, and slashed at everything in her path.

In the foyer, a crystal vase filled with flowers crashed from her blow, scattering in silvery chunks across the Italian tiles.

Jake was touching her cherished Samantha, dirtying her, taking her further and further away from the life she was meant for, the life Alexandra had wanted to give her.

Alexandra strode into a front room, slapping an invaluable Tiffany lamp from a black marble table.

In the dining room she smashed delicate dewdrop crystals in the lower tiers of the chandelier, slung porcelain figurines from the heavy teak sideboard, sent an eighteenth-century sterling tea set clattering to the hardwood floor.

In the library she jerked leather-bound volumes out of the bookcases, leaving them strewn behind her.

She knelt on the floor of the master bedroom upstairs, surrounded by torn portraits of her and Frannie as young girls, surrounded by broken lamps, ripped lingerie, scrapbooks of Tim's lackluster childhood and adolescence—her life, her failures spread around her on the large Oriental rug in the center of the room.

She had never been beaten. She would not be now. She would wait, and think, and plan. There would be some way to punish Jake for all he and his family had taken from her.

Chapter Twenty

"You know," Father said, wrapping one hand around the handle of Jake's ax, "I'd rather not have to hunt for your fingers and sew them back on."

Jake glanced vaguely at the enormous pile of kindling and the small stack of logs waiting to be split. He hadn't realized he was working quite so fast. Bo, he noticed, lay under the porch, eyeing him curiously.

Father had come over to keep him company, and he couldn't understand the problem. He drew a deep breath of cool October air. The forest around the house was brilliant with autumn foliage; it was a perfect day for chopping firewood, and he had visions of a long winter in front of a warm fireplace with Samantha. He hadn't built a second fireplace in the main bedroom for no reason.

"Considering the mood you're in, you need a safer pastime," Father continued, laying the ax on a chopping block made from a tree stump. "Maybe we can find a bear for you to wrestle."

Jake slumped down on the stump and brushed wood chips from his jeans. "I want to be in town. I keep wondering how it's going. Maybe she needs cheering up. What if she doesn't sell anything? She worked all summer to get ready for the art show. She calls it her *debut*. I don't want her to be disappointed."

"Son, I know you're an old married man with four months' experience, but I have to let you in on a little secret: When a woman is worried about being embarrassed, the last thing she wants is her husband there, watching. Makes a woman testy."

"But she let Mother and Charlotte go with her."

"Your mother had paintings to sell. And nobody could keep Charlotte from shopping for earrings. It's almost six. They'll be back any minute. Relax." Father pulled a pipe from the pocket of his flannel shirt, and sat down calmly on the ground, cross-legged. He fiddled with his pipe and studied Jake from beneath graying brows. "Sammie does wonderful weaving. Even Clara says she's a natural. Your mother says it's quality work too. But Sammie won't make a reputation for herself overnight."

"I just hope she sells *something*. It's important to her. Important for her to know I'm not the only one who can make a living for us."

Jake thought of the enormous throw pillows Sam had made for their new couch, their delicate silk and satin coverings like tapestry, and the rugs so beautiful, he took his shoes off before he walked on them. He'd never seen anything as fine as that. If ignorant people ignored her work, he'd . . . he didn't know what he'd do. Their life together during these months had been more perfect than he'd even imagined. He left her reluctantly in the mornings with his mining tools slung in a pack on his back, and all day he thought of her the way he'd last seen her, sitting at her loom, her face still flushed from the things they did in bed after they woke up. And the nights, God, the incredible nights.

Father sighed. "Life was less complicated when your

mother and I got married. I expected to bring home the money, and she expected to spend it."

"But I remember the first time Mother sold one of her paintings. She went around humming 'I Am Woman,' under her breath for about a week." Jake stood up suddenly. "They're coming."

Father looked over his shoulder, frowning at the empty tunnel of the driveway as it disappeared into the bright gold and red of the autumn woods. "I must be getting old. I don't hear the car."

Jake busied himself setting a new log on the chopping block, then reached for the ax again. He didn't want to look as if he'd been waiting on pins and needles all day. The old station wagon rolled up the driveway a few minutes later, and he casually leaned on the ax as he watched.

Mother and Charlotte got out of the passenger side, their expressions unfathomable. Charlotte, a neon-pink sweater draping her from neck to thighs, pink tennis shoes peeping from under the legs of her baggy jeans, pointed to a new set of silver baubles swinging from her ears. "Great stuff. And I made friends with a lady who's opening a dessert shop in town. We traded recipes. She said she might have a part-time job for me when I turn sixteen next spring."

Jake nodded vaguely and watched as Samantha climbed from the driver's side. Her face was somber. She leveled a glum gaze at him and walked up to him slowly, a long gray skirt swinging around her legs, her arms crossed over a striped sweater. "Well, I'm not going back tomorrow," she said dully. "It wouldn't be much use."

Jake dropped the ax and draped an arm around her shoulders. She wasn't depressed. She was teasing him.

He stared at her hard, and she lost control. Her eyes gleamed, and a smile lit her face. "Because I sold everything today." She threw her arms around him and kissed him boisterously. "*Everything.* Throw pillows, wall hangings, rugs, the whole kit and kaboodle."

Mother burst into laughter and bent over Father, pounding his shoulders with her hands, making his pipe bounce in his mouth. "I've never seen anything like it. I swear, a couple of times I was sure women were going to whack each other with their Gucci purses. They'd snatch Sammie's things from under each other's noses. And get this, honey—a few of them were friends of Alexandra's. But they couldn't resist."

Jake exhaled with relief but wagged one blunt forefinger at Samantha accusingly. "You little poker-faced—"

"I wanted to surprise you." Her smile softened. She reached into a skirt pocket and produced a small bag woven in a Cherokee design. She unzipped it proudly and showed him a neatly folded wad of bills. "A thousand dollars," she said, her voice awed. "I'll put a down payment on a washer and dryer. And a sewing machine. The rest goes into our savings account."

He couldn't feign exasperation any longer. He picked her up by the waist and swung her around. "As long as you're happy, I'm happy."

"It's not much money for a whole summer's work," she said, a little wistful and breathless. "But it's a start. I took orders for a lot more. I'll stay busy all winter." She thumped his chest lightly. "Next spring we can buy furniture for the living room, and I'll put some money away for Charlotte's college—"

"I'm going to cooking school," Charlotte said firmly.

"You're going to college first, pink petunia," Sam answered.

Charlotte scowled. "Is making money going to turn you into Aunt Alex? So you know what's best for me without asking me?"

Everyone stared at her. Jake felt Sam's immediate guilt and alarm. He squeezed her shoulders gently. She looked up at him, her expression chagrined, then turned toward her sister. "I suppose I did sound like her just then."

Charlotte chewed her lip. "Aw, Sammie, I shouldn't have said that. I'm sorry."

"No, you're right. You decide what you want to do, and I'll help you."

"*We'll* help her," Jake corrected her.

Sam gazed up at him tenderly. "It's good to be home."

Alexandra tolerated the holiday rituals of a politician's spouse in the same stoically determined manner with which she survived the other endless polite duties—the ribbon-cutting ceremonies, the boring dinners, the speeches to civic clubs. They were the dues she paid to get herself and Orrin into the governor's mansion someday. She had perfected the art of the seamless smile, the pleasant expression of attention and concern, the warm handshake.

Afterward she would retreat to the Tudor house on the outskirts of Raleigh, or to Highview, or the nearest posh hotel room—whatever was closest that day—and drink a double brandy.

"Happy Thanksgiving," she murmured for the hundredth time, moving down the line of people to press grimy outstretched hands. They were like patient ants waiting their turns to snatch crumbs at a picnic. The open door of a tractor-trailer was their destination, where volunteers from some charity group handed each a cardboard box packed with a turkey and canned goods. A cool wind blew in from brown hills dotted with sturdy wild cedars. Alexandra wished for the comfort of her furs, but had to settle for the prescribed humility of a down jacket and tailored slacks.

The shabby line stretched across the cracked gray pavement of a parking lot of a run-down shopping center somewhere in a nameless part of the state; she had slept during the drive, accompanied by two of Orrin's assistants, and she barely knew or cared precisely where they had deposited her.

Like an actress with a traveling road show, she played the same part wherever the stage was set. Set Orrin's assistants to work with the volunteers so it wouldn't appear she had bodyguards by her side. Shake hands. Pass out a few boxes. Pose with the volunteers for a photographer from the local newspaper. Leave as quickly and as tactfully as possible.

She had posed already, handed out boxes already. Now she had only to finish the ritual, call the aides over, and go. "Happy Thanksgiving," she said to the next faceless charity case.

A hand touched her shoulder. Stifling a frown at the presumptuous contact, she turned.

Malcolm Drury gazed at her with teary-eyed regard. "Hello, Mrs. Lomax." Shock and distrust poured through her. Alexandra managed to keep a gracious expression welded to her face. This living ghost had been consigned to a Bahamian prison years ago. When she'd thought of him at all, she'd assumed dead.

But he wasn't. He was free, and here, though the past few years had obviously not treated him well. The dapper, sleek, spinelessly ingratiating con man who'd served her purposes was pale and thin, with receding brown hair and dark circles under his eyes. He was dressed in stained brown trousers and an army jacket with torn elbows; he smelled faintly of sweat and illness.

"Excuse me, do I know you?" she finally managed to say, her voice carefully polite and puzzled.

"I forgive you," he said in a grating whisper only she could hear, and offered a pitiful smile. His teeth were stained; a front tooth was broken. But his eyes were cagey slits. "I'm dying. When I got sick, they let me out. I'm working as a janitor for a church in Raleigh. They got me a little apartment. And an old car. It's hard. I'm at peace with myself." He paused. "But life is hard."

Alexandra quickly took his arm and steered him away from the line of people. "I'm sorry, but I don't know who you are."

He coughed—a raw, racking sound, thready with dismay. "It's all right, Mrs. Lomax. I can't hurt you. After what I went through down there in prison, I can't hurt anybody."

Alexandra bent her head close to his. His stench and his pathetic, untrustworthy groveling made her head swim. "What do you want?" Her voice was soft and lethal.

"Just to say I forgive you for what you did to me."

"I didn't do anything to you. And if you think you can coerce me with your unprovable accusations and false piety, you're sadly mistaken."

"You didn't have to make sure I wouldn't hurt you. I didn't tell anyone about our deal. I got your sister's money, and I left. I was minding my own business."

"You pathetic fool, you were no threat to me. Not then, not now."

"I know that," he said, a whining undertone to his voice. "Why did you send someone to cause trouble for me? Why did you want me to suffer in a place where I wasn't even treated like a human being?"

"I never—" She halted, her thoughts racing. "What do you want?" she repeated, distracted, considering the options.

"I just don't want to die in a crummy hospital with the welfare types, Mrs. Lomax. That's all."

"Let me think about it. Perhaps I can make some arrangements. Discreetly. It all depends on your willingness to keep your mouth shut."

"Oh, Mrs. Lomax, that would be wonderful." He pressed a slip of paper into her hand. "Here's my address."

"I'll tell you who's responsible for what happened to you. It certainly wasn't me. I didn't know anything about it at the time. I learned later."

His faded, watery eyes glittered. "Who?"

She leaned close again. "It was the man who married Frannie's eldest daughter. Jake Raincrow is his name. He lives in Pandora. He's the one who tracked you down. And, no doubt, he's the one who instigated your trouble. He's the reason you were searched for drugs and sent to prison."

Malcolm mouthed the information slowly. A sickly flush rose in his gaunt cheeks. He trembled. There was no mistaking the rage that seeped into his eyes.

Alexandra couldn't stand him a moment longer. Her mind reeled with the consequences she might have set in motion. She took his hand as if gripping it kindly. Her fingernails dug into his sweaty palm, and he winced. Alexandra leveled a warning stare into his pained and angry eyes. "He's married to my niece," she repeated. "You have no quarrel with my niece."

"Oh, I don't have any quarrel with anyone," Malcolm answered. "I'm not a vengeful person."

He turned and staggered off toward a ramshackle sedan, nearly running.

Alexandra watched him as he drove away, wondering just what he'd do next. "Mrs. Lomax? One of Orrin's aides was beside her. "Any problem with that god-awful character?"

"Oh, no." She said it sadly and shook her head. "He just wanted to tell me how much he admires my husband. Poor soul, he was so shy. I never even got his name."

Sam was tired and thoughtful and proud. The washer and dryer had been delivered while she and Jake were taking a shower; in her hurry to scrutinize them, she'd pulled on nothing more than one of Jake's fresh T-shirts and a robe, then excitedly peered around a doorway as Jake and the delivery men wrestled the gleaming new appliances down the hall to the laundry room.

Jake had managed a little more decorum—jeans and a crookedly buttoned flannel shirt.

They connected the pipes and electrical lines, played with all the knobs, and stood in pleased silence, as if they'd become parents. Cozy afternoon light filtered through white curtains on a window above the appliances, and yellow leaves drifted past the windowpanes. The laundry room's log walls filled her nose with a pleasant piney scent. Their light gold surface seemed to reflect the warm sunshine. The day was golden.

"I never had my own washer and dryer before," Sam said, her tone bittersweet. "Mom and Dad couldn't afford them, and Dad said they'd get torn up if the army moved us very often, and then after he died, well, Mom wanted to buy them on credit, but I talked her out of it." She hesitated, then added sadly, "We started a separate savings account to save up for them. But then Malcolm Drury showed up. He took everything—even the money in that account." Sam looked at Jake miserably. "I wish she'd gotten her washer and dryer."

Jake stroked a hand over her damp hair. "It wasn't your fault. She was lonely. She trusted him. You couldn't have changed her mind about him."

"I think about him sometimes. Buying drugs with the money we slaved for. I like to picture him sitting in prison down in the Bahamas. I hope they have rats in the Bahamas. Big man-eating rats. I hope he never gets out."

"I expect he's dead by now. He liked to keep moving. Trap him in one place and he'd claw his own skin. That kind of fear probably did him in." When she looked at him oddly, Jake added, "From what you've told me about him." Suddenly he pulled Sam toward him, cupped his hands under her elbows, and lifted her atop the washer. "There, queen. Test your throne. Stop thinking about rats. Think about baked turkey and dressing. Think about the belt-popping amount of grub your sister is cooking for Thanksgiving."

She gave him a subdued smile. He shook his head at her mood, reached around her, and fiddled with the washer's dial. "Let's put it on the spin cycle."

"Why?"

"Just to tickle your fancy." The machine hummed and began vibrating. Her eyes widened. "Hmmm."

"Now, wait a minute. Don't enjoy it *that* much."

"Come closer. See for yourself. It's like a massage." A small rakish smile curled one corner of her mouth. Sam wrapped her legs around his hips and pulled him to her, then draped her arms around his shoulders and kissed him. "I need you," she said wistfully. "I need to stop thinking."

"I know."

"Let's have a little dedication ceremony." She reached between them and unfastened his jeans. "This is the only room we haven't, hmmm, *dedicated* yet."

He held her tightly. "Let's take care of that right now."

Jake looked around the table as everyone settled in their chairs for Thanksgiving dinner. This was contentment—the family gathered peacefully under the soft glow of an old chandelier, the table decorated in Mother's best lace cloth and china, platters and bowls and casseroles crowding one another for space, wonderful aromas rising from them. Ellie had come home from medical school for the holiday. Father wore his traditional Thanksgiving sweater—a moth-eaten relic Mother had given to him on the first Thanksgiving after they were married. Mother wore a necklace of garnets Jake and Ellie had made for her when they were children.

Charlotte sat beside Samantha, perusing the food with an authoritative air, as if daring any of her creations to disappoint her.

Samantha took Jake's hand under the table, and her warm, loving grip made his contentment complete. Father pulled the turkey platter to him and lifted a serving fork. "Thank God for antacids," he said. "Let's eat."

"*Hugh.*" Mother eyed him with amusement and mild reproach. She gazed from him to everyone else, her eyes shining. "Thank God for this family."

"Yes," Ellie said, her voice soft, her eyes pensive. "Please, God, let there be a lot more times like this."

Everyone looked at Jake, waiting. He frowned. They continued to wait. "God knows what I'm thinking," he said finally.

Samantha squeezed his hand and rescued him quickly. Her head bent slightly, she closed her eyes and said, "Take care of my mom and dad. Let them know they aren't forgotten. Tell them their daughters will always love them. Tell them we have wonderful people around us. Thank you."

Leave it to Samantha to give God directions. But Jake met her misty eyes and nodded gently. Charlotte cleared her throat. They turned toward her. Tears slid down her flushed cheeks. "*Ditto,* God," she said.

Sam put an arm around her. The two of them gazed at Mother, Father, and Ellie. "We love all of you," Sam said hoarsely.

Mother was crying too. Ellie wiped her eyes and smiled. Father answered gruffly, "Well, *ditto.*"

Everyone laughed. Sam looked at Jake again. The serenity in her expression completed his thanks.

"'Night, El." Jake stuck his head inside her bedroom door. "We're heading home. See you tomorrow. Happy Thanksgiving."

She sat in a small wicker chair by the window, hooded by the dim light of a lamp on her night table. He had caught her with a look of distant sorrow in her eyes; she looked away quickly and smoothed a hand over her face. The simple chain necklace hung from her other hand, and the narrow leather pouch swung like a dark pendulum. Jake stepped into the room. "It's making you unhappy. I'm glad you took it off. Put it away."

"I am." She dropped the necklace on the windowsill. "It's old. So old. I read somewhere that there are people like us who feel ancient history in the things they touch."

"I've read that too. They say strong emotions are left behind, like pictures that never quite fade. But I don't feel that too much."

"You look at the here-and-now."

"Not always. I just try to concentrate on what's important to *me*. Tracking people. Finding stones. Trying to understand how people think. What's dead and gone, well, I don't need to know."

She opened the pouch and pulled the ruby from it. "Everyone who's owned this is dead—except me. And Alexandra."

"She never owned it. She took it for a while. She was never meant to keep it." He looked at her solemnly, teasing a little, trying to change her mood. "And, El, maybe you haven't covered this in medical school, but . . . everyone dies eventually. It's a fact, ruby or no ruby."

Ellie lifted the ruby, holding it between her thumb and forefinger. It caught the light, a bloodred drop of memory. "You remember the stories Granny told us about the Uktena?"

"Hmmm. Kept me checking under my bed at night for years."

"The terrible dragon-snake, with the crystal in its forehead. And after a man killed the Uktena and took the crystal, he had to protect it, and honor it, and hide it in a special place. If he didn't care for it well enough, it would fly away and search for the Uktena, and kill people in revenge." She laid the stone back on the sill and wiped her hand on her jeans. Jake said lightly, "I haven't seen any flying crystals or Uktenas around."

"Maybe we just don't recognize them."

"Put it away, El," he said again. "You'll have a daughter someday. Save it for her."

"I won't have any children."

He was surprised and a little angry at her for talking that way. He started to tell her so, but the phone rang in the hall, and he heard Father walking out of the living room to answer it. "We'll talk about this more tomorrow," Jake told her. "You've let that damned stone confuse you."

"Son," Father called. "It's for you. The sheriff's office over in Cloudland Falls."

Frowning, Jake went to the phone. Samantha came out of the kitchen as he was talking, a box of neatly wrapped leftovers in her hands. He waved her over and peered into the box distractedly, the phone wedged between his shoulder and ear. She watched him with a worried frown, her head tilted to one side. Mother, Charlotte, and Father joined her. "All right," he said to the caller finally. "I'll meet you there in about an hour."

When he put the phone down, Samantha scrutinized him hard. "They can't expect you to come out at night, on Thanksgiving."

"I gotta go. An old man wandered away from his granddaughter's place this afternoon. He's not quite right." Jake pointed to his head. "They think he took a walk and forgot the way home."

"I'll go with you," Samantha said immediately.

He shook his head. "Your being there would confuse Bo. He'll think we're on a picnic."

She wanted to argue, he could tell, but she bit her lip and studied him with resignation. "Sometime I'm going with you when you track people. I want to see how you do it."

Can't tell you that, he thought. *You'd think I was crazy.* "Be cool, Sammie," Charlotte interjected. "I'll spend the night with you. I've got a brownie recipe I want to try. We'll eat brownies and watch TV."

"The girl cooks nonstop," Father said. "Incredible."

Samantha sighed. Jake cupped a hand beneath her hair and rubbed small, reassuring circles on the nape of her neck. She was thinking about a different kind of dessert, a recipe she and he kept testing enthusiastically. "I'll probably be home by morning," he said slyly. "Save something sweet for me."

She cast a furtive look at the others, who bit their lips and tried not to smile. Then she lifted her chin and gave Jake a slit-eyed look. "I'll make it a Thanksgiving tradition."

They gathered their coats. He kissed Mother's cheek and gave Father a quick hug, then looked in on El again. She had returned to the chair by the window, the ruby lying on the sill near her outstretched hand. "Put it away," he called in a low voice.

She looked at him wearily, and nodded.

Sam woke and sat up in bed. The darkness was deep and chilly; she pulled the quilts up to the soft collar of Jake's huge flannel shirt that she slept in. She rubbed her eyes and squinted at the digital clock on the dresser across the room. Three A.M.

This was the first night they'd spent apart since their marriage, and she was lonely. She kept thinking of him and Bo out in the frosty November night, working their way through inky woods with only a high white moon for company. She thought of the elderly man who was lost, hoping—knowing—that Jake and Bo would find him and glad that sheriffs in distant places were calling Jake to help them. Maybe soon the sheriff in Pandora would stop fearing Aunt Alex's opinion and ask Jake to work for him again.

Sam slipped into a heavy terry-cloth robe she'd made for Jake and tiptoed into the front room. They'd purchased a squat-legged old couch and two matching armchairs at a salvage store; Jake had refinished the ponderous wood frames, and they'd had the pieces upholstered in a warm shade of blue. With an assortment of other lovingly refinished old furniture, the rugs Sam had woven, and a few funky lamps they'd collected from junk shops, the room had taken on a friendly, comfortable feel.

Charlotte was asleep on the couch under a jumble of blankets, with a half-empty pan of brownies on the floor near one dangling hand. The last embers of the banked fire glowed weakly in the fireplace. Sam adjusted her sister's blankets, then wandered around the room, trailing her fingertips over the furnishings, feeling proud and protective of her and Jake's home.

She headed down the hall to her workroom, thinking that weaving for a while would settle her. She loved the methodical and precise rhythm of the loom.

But the steady wooden clacking would probably wake Charlotte. There might be a new round of brownie eating, and Sam already felt stuffed.

Grumbling under her breath, she returned to the front room, slipped her feet into the scuffed loafers she kept there, then carefully unlatched the door and stepped onto the porch. Frost sparkled on the leaf-strewn yard and the small hollies they'd planted at the porch's edge. The forest slept peacefully, with moonlight dappling the ground beneath the bare limbs of the trees. At the base of the knoll, Granny Raincrow's spring reflected the pale light like a mirror.

Sam exhaled peacefully, then took a deep, invigorating breath. And smelled smoke.

Chapter
Twenty-One

S he ran into the yard and turned urgently, studying the fat stone chimneys. But the cooling ashes in the front room's fireplace couldn't produce such a vivid scent, and she hadn't built a fire in the bedroom at all. The roof seemed fine.

Sam swung around, scrutinizing the forest in all directions but seeing nothing unusual. Still, she smelled smoke, and the scent was growing stronger. She told herself the fire could be miles away. The wind easily channeled smoke and fog through the narrow mountain coves.

She faced the wall of forest that separated their homesite from Hugh and Sarah's. They might tease her about her city-bred nervousness if she woke them up, but she'd take that chance. Better to make a quick phone call and get razzed for it than to stand out there, worrying.

She started inside, but glanced in their direction one more time.

A boiling cloud of smoke rose above the treetops, the moonlight filtering through it. Sam raced into the house and yelled Charlotte's name. Charlotte bolted upright. Sam grabbed her by the shoulders and shook her awake. "There's a fire at Hugh and Sarah's! Call them, then call the fire department! I'm going over to the house!"

Charlotte lurched off the couch, hands splayed. Sam pushed her toward the phone on a lamp table, then ran out the front door. To her horror, a tongue of orange flame curled above the trees. She raced down the path into the woods, stumbling on roots, clawing the whip-thin branches that sliced at her, leaving one of her shoes behind and kicking the other off so she could run faster.

Smoke met her, billowing through the forest, acrid, flecked with glowing bits of debris, a hot cloud that choked her and stung her face. Sam covered her nose and staggered, panting, into the yard. The roar of the fire filled her ears; there were sharp popping sounds as the aged logs surrendered. The sight of the house—engulfed in a sheet of flames, smoke belching from the upstairs windows—wrung a guttural scream of horror from her.

They must have gotten out. Her mind refused to believe that Sarah, Hugh, and Ellie were inside the inferno. She staggered forward, her arms shielding her face. A suffocating wall of heat drove her back. She punched the air. Screaming their names, she circled the house, falling over the stone edge of Sarah's flower beds, crawling, shoving herself up again.

They must be here somewhere. They must have gotten out. *Oh, Jake. We can't lose them. I won't let them die.* She stumbled through a hedge of evergreen shrubs along the backyard, then fell to her knees beside a spigot and a coiled hose. Sam wrenched the spigot's handle and dug her hands into the hose, grabbing the free end triumphantly. She lunged to her feet and pointed it at the rear porch. Flames burst under the roof, and the roof collapsed with sickening metallic shrieks as sheets of tin ripped from the rafters.

Sam heard her own shrieks of fury and despair. Not a drop of water came from the hose. She shook it, cursed it violently, then realized with galling defeat that the well pump ran off electricity from the house.

The upstairs roof caved in, and shards of burning wood rained down on her. Sam covered her head and stumbled back, coughing, blinded by smoke. She fell again and crawled until the air cooled and she could breathe. Rolling onto her hands and knees, she stared at the house and beat the ground with one fist.

"*Sammie!*" Charlotte collapsed beside her, shaking her. "They didn't answer the phone! Where are they?"

"Inside. Oh, Jake, *Jake*. I can't get them out!"

Charlotte clung to her, sobbing wildly. Sam sank back on her heels and rocked, one hand latched in Charlotte's nightgown, the other clawing at the silent scream in her own throat.

Somewhere in the distance the high, thin wails of sirens began.

Jake fell against a sheriff's car, his knees buckling. He was covered in sweat, weighed down by a horror he couldn't comprehend. The glare from portable floods and the headlights of a dozen police and emergency vehicles pierced his dazed vision.

Someone clamped a hand on his shoulder. There were people around him, talking loudly. He'd burst from the woods at a run with Bo galloping beside him. "What's wrong with you, son?" Jake braced his arms on the car's hood and stared into a deputy's florid, worried face. "Found him," Jake said, shuddering. "He's all right. Left him asleep beside a creek. About a mile back." He gasped. A band of unfathomable terror squeezed his chest. He knew only that something was wrong, something terrible that had closed in on him as he stopped to let the bewildered, exhausted old man lie down to rest. He had to get home.

"I need a phone," he said loudly, pushing himself away from the car, swaying. "Goddammit, give me a phone."

"All right, son, whatever your problem is, come on. We got a mobile unit."

Jake was dimly aware of the hustle of startled men around him, of pushing ahead of the deputy, of lunging inside a van and grabbing the phone someone held out to him. He called Samantha first. He shook the receiver as if it were lying to him as he listened to their phone ring repeatedly with no answer. Neither Sam nor Charlotte could sleep through so much. He choked back the bile rising in his throat and called his folks' house next.

That line was silent. Jake fought an urge to slam the receiver against the van's floor. "What is it, son?" the deputy asked. Jake barely heard him. He knew the number at the sheriff's office in Pandora, had memorized it years ago, when he began tracking for the department. His fingers shaking, he punched it into a console. The moment the dispatcher's familiar voice answered, he said, "Get somebody down to the Raincrow place. *Now.*"

"Jake? Is that you?" The woman's maternal voice was a moan of tearful recognition. "*Yes.* Send somebody down there. I can't explain. You've got to—"

"They've already gone. Everybody's gone down there. Oh, hon, get here as fast as you can. I don't know how bad things are yet. But there's a fire."

Jake dropped the phone and lunged out of the van. He ran to his car, not daring to think about anything. Bo leapt ahead of him as he slung the door open.

Samantha was all right. He could feel that much, that certainty.

But the rest was a terrifying blank.

This was how hell looked. How it smelled, and tasted, and sounded. Fire trucks and ambulances. Police cruisers. Pickup trucks and cars. Plumes of water shooting from hoses into the hissing, smoldering ruins of the house. The glare of headlights and huge portable lamps. People hurrying around in no apparent order, shouting at one another. Strangers everywhere—no, some of them were people she knew, friends of the family—but when they tried to hug her or talk to her, she stared back at them without responding. She couldn't take her eyes off the house. The roof had caved in, flattening the upstairs bedrooms. The upper walls had collapsed inward, and the wide roof of the front porch tilted crazily to one side. The windows of the bottom level had shattered, and smoke boiled out of them.

The front door was still shut. Smoke curled around its edges, outlining it in obscene detail, as if taunting her to open the door and find what waited inside.

Which she could not think about anymore. Not if she wanted to keep her sanity. Sam knew she was covered in soot and dirt, that embers had burned holes in her robe, that her bare feet were bleeding. But shock had taken over—a surreal and emotionless stupor that let her stand on the edge of the chaos, dry-eyed and unflinching. A paramedic had placed blankets around her and Charlotte's shoulders; Charlotte sat at her feet, staring blankly into space.

Only one dread could penetrate the haze in Sam's mind. The thought of Jake coming home to this.

Sam stiffened as several firemen approached the porch gingerly, pulling shields over their faces, their axes raised. The blanket slid, unheeded, from her shoulders. *Please, let this only be a nightmare. Please let the house be empty. Please let me wake up. Please don't do this to Jake.*

"They went somewhere." She heard Charlotte's voice, hollow and pleading. "They got up and drove to the all-night diner in Owessa. Sure. We did that two or three times. To get waffles. Sarah says it's an adventure to eat when everybody else is asleep."

Sam fought an urge to scream. *The cars are still parked in the barn. I checked.* "Yes, I bet that's where they are. Eating waffles." She shuffled forward. Charlotte grabbed the bottom of her robe. "Where are you—don't go. I'm telling you, they're eating waffles." Her voice broke. "Don't go over there, Sammie."

The firemen ducked under the lopsided porch roof.

One of them swung his ax at the door. The heavy old wood refused to give. He slammed the ax into it again. The sound nearly shattered Sam's control. The door swung inward. The firemen disappeared into the house.

Sam distractedly pulled her robe away from Charlotte's anxious grip, then put a hand on her sister's bowed head. A group of women converged on them, tugging at Sam's arms, urging her to stay put. Sam shrugged them off. "I'll be back in a minute. Stay with my sister, please."

"Oh, Sammie," Charlotte moaned.

Sam walked toward the house slowly, bumping against the fenders of closely parked vehicles, her gaze riveted to the open door. She edged past a crowd of men in the yard, who were watching and waiting so intently, they didn't notice her. Sam halted near the firemen controlling the hoses. There was now nothing to block her view.

She was a dreamcatcher. The weave of her web was unbreakable. She would catch this nightmare before it reached Jake, and when dawn came, the sunlight would whisk it away.

The first fireman backed out the door, his movements labored. Sam hunched over, desperate to see under the sunken porch roof and know what heavy weight he pulled.

He dragged his burden by its blackened arm.

"*Keep her away*," Sam yelled. Her voice was a raw groan. She huddled on the ground beside the three bodies and slung her hands fiercely. People had stopped trying to lift her up. "Keep my sister away from this! I don't want her to see them this way!"

Sam hugged herself and rocked slowly, forcing herself to look, wishing she were blind. She had to see what Jake would see, as if she could make it easier for him by knowing first.

Each second left its brutal mark.

I can tell them apart.

They're still wearing their bed clothes.
They didn't burn.
They suffocated in the smoke.
They choked to death in the heat and the smoke.

"For God's sake, get the sheets over them," someone ordered. The sheriff spoke close to her ear gently. "It's not your sister we're worried about. The women got a hold on her. You come on now. Get up."

"No."

"Jake's here," someone said loudly.

Sam lurched to her feet and pushed through the crowd, searching the confusion of vehicles and people for him. He appeared from behind an ambulance, dodging everything in his path with the frantic grace of an athlete. When he saw her, the stark agony in his face tore her apart.

Sam threw herself at him, making incoherent sounds of pain and comfort. She wanted to hold him back. He gripped her around the waist and carried her with him, lodged against his side. People leapt out of their way. Sam put her arms around him and held him with all her strength.

A terrible raw shout of despair came from him when he saw the bodies. He and Sam sank to the ground together. She wound her arms around his neck, trying to shield him, trying to hold him so close, his pain would flow into her.

His hands convulsed in the back of her robe, and he shuddered against her. Like everything else about him, his grief was a private torture only she could share.

Crying, Sam pressed her cheek against his hair. Nothing she could say would reach him. *We'll get through this somehow. I love you. I love you. We can survive anything together. We always have.*

Clara Big Stick's misgivings suddenly loomed in her mind, blacking out everything else, making her retch helplessly against Jake's shoulder.

What if Clara's original warnings were true? *No, I don't believe, I never seriously believed . . .*

She and Jake couldn't have brought this on his family.

The funeral director was a short, puffy woman who looked as if she'd learned to do her own makeup by practicing on corpses. Talkative and eager to please, she led Alexandra down a somber hall. Their footsteps made no sound on the deep beige carpet. They were alone—except for the dead, and the dead couldn't listen.

"Mrs. Lomax, it was the saddest thing I've ever seen," the director said. "That young man and your niece coming in here to see his loved ones before the coffins were closed. They stayed long past our visiting hours, and I finally peeked in on them to say I really must lock up for the night. Your poor niece had to beg him to leave. He said something very strange, something about witches stealing from the bodies, and she looked absolutely heartbroken."

"Witches are an old Cherokee superstition," Alexandra explained, giving the woman a meaningful glance that dismissed such things.

The director nodded sadly. Then, leaning closer as they walked, she whispered, "I checked the caskets after he and your niece left. He'd put all sorts of little mementoes in each one. It is so tragic."

"I appreciate you opening the house a little early today so I can pay my respects in privacy." The director seemed pleased to be commended. She led Alexandra to a half-shut door. Alexandra smiled sadly at her. "I won't be long." With that she stepped inside and closed the door behind her.

Draperies shut out the morning light. An amazing number of flower arrangements crowded the spaces between the caskets, which were positioned along three of the walls. A subdued chandelier cast the elegantly simple room in soft shades of light.

Alexandra stood in the center a moment, stunned at the triumph she'd accomplished by merely waiting until circumstances favored her. There was no doubt in her mind that Malcolm Drury had started the fire. Jake had paid for his interference in her life. And most perfect of all, she was guilty of nothing but letting his foolishness follow its own course.

She went around the room, studying the cards on each flower arrangement and making a mental list of the people who had sent their condolences. She wanted to know who thought highly of the Raincrows. There was an astonishing variety. The tribal council at the reservation's offices at Qualla. The agent from the Bureau of Indian Affairs. Abraham Dreyfus, the respected lawyer from Durham, who had done considerable amounts of legal work for the tribe, a man she and Orrin considered an arrogant Jew. All the physicians in Pandora who'd insisted to her over the years that they considered Hugh Raincrow a laughable country doctor. The mayor. The sheriff. The woman who chaired the arts league Alexandra had created and still generously supported. The dean of Ellie's medical school. Sheriffs from all over western North Carolina and the states bordering it.

And, most irritating of all, flowers from several of Alexandra's closest friends, women who inhabited the fine homes around town, women who stupidly assumed Alexandra had not heard how they'd purchased Samantha's weaving and avidly placed orders for more.

Ungrateful fools. The Raincrows didn't deserve this homage. It was she who'd turned Pandora from a sleepy nothing of a town into the beautiful, interesting place they loved. She who'd endured Sarah's bitterness, she who'd lost the treasure that proclaimed her place in the Vanderveer legacy.

And she would not be satisfied until she got it back. Alexandra went to a casket, glanced furtively toward the closed door, then lifted the lid. Grimacing, she looked at Hugh. A stethoscope and an aged, fire-ravaged copy of *Tom Sawyer* were tucked inside one of his arms. A spray of eagle's feathers had been inserted between the lapels of his suit, covering his tie, placed directly over his heart. Alexandra reached down slowly, cringing at the thought of touching his cold, hard skin, and felt inside the collar of his shirt for a necklace. Finding nothing, she quickly shut the lid and went to the next casket.

"Well, Sarah," she whispered, "it's clear who won, isn't it? Look what your incessant cruelty to me has accomplished. I've taken far more from you than you ever took from me."

Alexandra was beyond any sense of repulsion now. She quickly checked under the lacy neckline of Sarah's green dress, hoping to feel the cool metal of a chain. Disappointed, she toyed contemptuously with the artist's brushes that had been placed under Sarah's folded hands, then frowned at the magnificent square of satiny red-and-silver material that had been arranged on the white pillow beneath her old enemy's red hair.

Alexandra stroked it with a fingertip. The threads were extraordinarily delicate, woven with such care that the silver seemed to float among the darker background.

Samantha made this for her. Samantha loved her enough to honor her in a way she'd never honor me. Alexandra drew back, furious.

She pulled the lid down and strode to the last casket. Ellie concerned her less than Hugh and Sarah; Alexandra wasted no time mulling over the whimsical items that had been placed with her and pushed apart the narrow scalloped V at the neck of her gold dress. No chain. No chain bearing Alexandra's ruby. Of course, it could be hidden elsewhere on the bodies, but Alexandra decided it was not.

Jake had it now. So retrieving it was only a matter of time and patience. She had proved the wisdom of both, hadn't she?

She closed the casket and smoothed her coat, then turned to leave.

Clara Big Stick stared at her with glittering, hateful old eyes.

Alexandra gasped involuntarily. Somehow the fat, dreary old woman had managed to slip into the room and shut the door again without her noticing. A bulky cloth bag hung from one of her shoulders. She clenched the strap of it with one beefy brown hand and pointed the other at Alexandra, then advanced slowly.

"In the cold land where you live, O red spirit, we two have fixed your arrows for the soul of the Night Goer," she chanted. "We have them lying by the path. Quickly we two will take her soul."

Alexandra backed up, overwhelmed by the eerie words and the old crone's sinister, commanding voice. Clara marched onward. "Listen, O purple spirit, in the cold land where you live. Quickly we two have fixed your arrows for the soul of the Night Goer. We have them lying by the path."

"Stay away from me," Alexandra said. She took another step back and felt a soft wall of flowers blocking her retreat. The old woman halted, her unwavering finger stabbing directly at Alexandra's face. "Quickly!" she said. "We two will cut her soul in two!"

"Stop this, you babbling old fool."

Clara's hand dropped. She nodded. "It is done. When the arrows fall on your head, you will die. The great stone will find you, and you will die."

Alexandra made a sound of disgust, but even to her ears it sounded nervous. Clara laughed. It was the most chilling thing Alexandra had ever heard. She skirted the old woman with as much dignity as she could muster, then nearly ran from the room.

Chapter Twenty-Two

$\mathcal{E}$ ach thing he touched brought him no closer to an answer, but he couldn't give up until he had one. Jake moved through what remained of the house—the first floor, with its blackened and water-damaged furnishings, the piles of debris that had once been his home. Jagged, sooty timbers crushed the hall staircase; shards of glass from the hall lamps crunched under the soles of his lace-up boots as he sidestepped a fallen painting of Mother's, the canvas burned beyond recognition.

Rain drizzled outside and found its way through cracks in the ceiling. He stared up at it, cursing weakly. He was covered in dirt and soot, and exhausted to the point where misery receded into a dull throb behind his aching eyes.

He stopped outside the door to Ellie's bedroom. He hadn't been inside her room since the day after the fire, when he'd forced himself to dig through the scorched jumble until he found the ruby. Sam had been with him that day, horrified and confused by an obsession he would not discuss with her.

He had clenched the stone in his hand and, feeling nothing, slung it into a jar that he kept on a shelf in their bedroom. When they lay in bed at night, sleepless, he would catch her staring across the room at the jar, and when he held her he felt her questions, her fear, her loathing for the morbid value she thought he gave the stone.

He hated it too, because it might hold some clue to the fire but would not help him.

A state arson inspector had turned up nothing; he and Pandora's fire marshal concluded that the fire started in a stack of old newspapers stored in a cardboard box by the wall under the window eaves. They'd found the ash bucket nearby, and when Jake had recalled Father cleaning out the fireplace Thanksgiving night and carrying the bucket to the porch, they speculated that some exploring raccoon or 'possum had knocked it over after the family went to bed. A live ember must have rolled against the box.

Jake moved down the hall, running his grime-streaked hands over the log walls. He could not hear screams or feel his family dying; he wouldn't let himself, because he'd never sleep again if he did.

"You in there?" a male voice called. "Jake?"

Jake emerged from the house, blinking even in the gray December light, furious that someone had interrupted him.

Joe Gunther stood in the ravaged yard, steel-gray cowboy boots mired in the mud and charred leaves, rain dripping from the brim of his western hat onto a gray slicker. The older man frowned at Jake's filthy, gaunt appearance. "Hadn't been to see you since the funerals," Joe said, his face grim. "Sammie called me today. Asked me to talk to you. She's worried half out of her mind."

Jake shivered. Thoughts of Samantha's misery weighed him down. He knew what she feared, what scared her so much she wouldn't even say it. He, too, lived with the terrible thought that Clara's predictions had been right in the first place. During the funerals, Clara had only shaken her head at him when he'd tried to talk to her.

Which was why he came here every day, alone, and tried to learn the truth.

"You've got to let go of this," Joe said, sweeping a jeweled hand at the house. "You're making yourself sick."

"I've got to know exactly what happened here."

Joe looked at him sadly. "An accident, Jake. A god-damned, senseless accident. Now, look, I know it's hard, but the best thing you can do is clear all this out. I can have bulldozers and dump trucks down here in the morning. We'll scrape this spot clean."

"*No.*"

"You've got Sammie to think about, and poor Charlotte too. You weren't even at home to help Sammie set up a bed for her. You've got a wife and a teen-aged sister-in-law who are grieving their hearts out, and Sammie would feel a helluva lot better if you'd grieve with her instead of prowling around this god-awful place by yourself."

"When I'm done, you can send bulldozers."

"Done with *what*, man? Done making yourself and Sammie so crazy, neither of you'll ever get over it?"

"*When I'm done,*" Jake repeated between clenched teeth.

It was almost dark, the dreary day sinking into a wet dusk whipped by the wind. Huddled miserably in a thick coat, Sam sidestepped piles of scorched timbers, broken glass, and ruined furniture. Bo walked beside her, his tail and head low. Jake had ignored him for days.

She knew how Bo felt.

Jake had shut her out, and that made the horrible aftermath so much lonelier. She had her hands full with Charlotte, who had lost another set of parents, another home. Visitors came by the house every day, shy people from Cawatie, who brought small gifts of food and asked how Jake was doing.

What could she tell them? That he came here every morning and stayed all day, then sat by himself on their porch at night, until finally she coaxed him to bed, where he held her with wordless, almost savage intensity, and they both pretended to sleep.

She wanted to cry when she saw him now, coatless, hatless, his shirt plastered to his broad back, mud streaking his jeans. He was picking through a pile of refuse near the ruins of the back porch, wet, dirty, pulling each bit of soggy cloth, each broken dish out of the pile, holding it a moment, then dropping it by his feet and reaching for the next.

"Jake." He straightened and turned wearily. Sam moved up to him cautiously, unable to read his bleary, hooded eyes. She took her coat off and put it around his shoulders. Sam could barely speak past the sorrow in her throat. Finally she said, "I'm not letting you come here alone anymore. Whatever you're doing, I want to help. Please, please don't shut me out."

"You can't help." His voice was hollow. He shrugged her coat off and draped it around her. His hands lingered near her face. Slowly, gently, he cupped her jaw. Sam gave a helpless sob. "*Say it.* I'd rather hear you say it than go on this way. You think we caused this somehow. If you hadn't given me a home, if we hadn't gotten married, if you didn't love me—"

He jerked her to him and wound his arms around her, stroking the back of her head, pulling her face deep into the crook of his neck. "I'll love you forever," he whispered. "I don't know what happened, or why, and I have to find out. But *we* didn't cause it."

Sam trembled with relief. "I keep thinking that I should have stayed here that night. That maybe, with more people in the house, one of us would have smelled the smoke in time."

"And I keep thinking that I could have saved them if I hadn't gone to track a stranger."

She moaned. He had never confessed that private torture before. "No, *no*. The house burned too quick.

Everyone says so. The logs were so old, so dry. Oh, Jake, don't blame yourself." She raised her head and looked at him desperately. "Don't blame anyone. I don't believe in curses. I *won't*." She shook her head wildly. "If you believe in them, it means you think my aunt had something to do with this."

He grasped her by the shoulders. His face was hard, his eyes full of pain. "I don't know what to believe yet. I can't even think. Because when I do, and when I fall asleep and dream, I see my parents and Ellie waking up in smoke so thick, they couldn't see, couldn't breathe. I see them trying to find each other and get out together, while the house burned up around them."

"Don't you think I see that too?"

"Not the way I do."

"Oh, Jake."

He released her and stepped back, holding her away as if it took all his willpower. "Go back home. Charlotte needs you."

And you don't, she thought with despair. "What are you looking for? Tell me, and I'll look too."

"I don't know what I'm looking for. Or if it's even here. But I can't stop looking, and you can't do it for me."

"I can do one thing—I can get the ruby out of your sight. I can make sure you don't lie awake, staring at it at night. You're thinking about it. You're thinking about all the bad blood between your family and Alexandra because of it. That's why I hate it, and I wish you'd let me take it to the highest cliff around here and throw it away."

His hands tightened fiercely on her shoulders, then quickly relaxed. He looked more beaten than angry. "It's the only thing that survived."

Sam stared at him. "*We* survived." Crying, she pulled away from him. "Try not to forget that."

He wanted to go home to Samantha. He wanted to kiss her and tell her that the night of the fire, when he was driving home frantically, he'd been thinking of her more than anyone else. That when he arrived and saw her he felt he could bear anything else since she was safe.

And that no matter what he learned now, he would never believe that he had doomed his family by loving her.

He crawled in the rainy, cold darkness on his hands and knees, searching among the wilted shrubbery, digging his fingers into the flower beds of the backyard, where cars and feet had churned Mother's careful winter mulch into sludge. He wouldn't be satisfied until he'd gone over every inch of ground, maybe every inch of the Cove. He shivered; he was cold to the bone, soaked. Every muscle ached, and his fingers were numb.

He didn't know what time it was when he finished with the yard. He found himself at the edge of the dirt lane, swaying with fatigue and battered by loneliness. He fought a desperate need to be inside Samantha's arms, to feel the soothing warmth of her incredible hands on his skin. To forget his pain, if only for a little while.

He threw his head back. "Talk to me, Ellie. Help me. Tell me what I'm looking for. I don't care if it hurts. I'll listen. Because not knowing is worse."

Emptiness. Only the sound of wind soughing through the bare branches of the forest and the patter of rain. He slumped. His twin was gone, the one person who would have understood without question. She had seen this time coming, but not well enough to avoid it. The ruby had warned her. It would not, however, help him. Because he had misused it once and caused their uncle's death.

Defeated, his legs numb and weak, he concentrated on getting to his feet. He reached down with one hand to brace himself. His hand sank into dripping grass at the road's edge.

His fingers closed on something small, a soggy rectangle of material that crumpled in his grip. The familiar, trancelike rush of sensation jerked him upright. Instantly his mind filled with images. An emaciated but familiar face capped with thin brown hair. A huge, stately brick building with its name marching across a dignified marble marker on the lawn. The words *Durham First* disappeared behind an enormous magnolia tree.

The face. The *face*. It belonged to someone inside a car that had sat here on the road. It turned toward him, illuminated by the greenish lights of the car's dashboard. A hand flung something out the window. The something Jake held in his hand now.

Jake fumbled a flashlight from his back pocket and posed it over the mysterious object. In the bright beam he saw a matchbox.

In his mind he saw the face transformed into one he recognized without doubt. He bent his head to his hands and groaned.

Malcolm Drury.

Sam paced the living room, every nerve tuned to the light tattoo of rain on the roof and the ticking of a mantel clock that had belonged to Jake's grandmother. The clock chimed loud and long as its hands met at midnight. She hurried, barefooted, down the hall and shut the door to Charlotte's bedroom, peeking in briefly as she did. Charlotte, her face wan and sad even in sleep, turned fitfully in the twin bed Sam had bought for her, then settled again.

Sam sighed with weary relief and walked back to the living room. Bo rose morosely from a rug before the couch, padding to her and sticking his jowly red face into her hands. "If he's not back by twelve-thirty, we'll go after him," she told the bloodhound. Sam knelt and gave him a sympathetic hug that she was certain helped her feelings more than Bo's.

Suddenly Bo scrambled out of her embrace and galloped to the door, his tail wagging madly. Sam jumped up at the sound of footsteps on the porch. She ran to the door and pulled it open.

Jake looked the worst she'd ever seen him, his shirt and jeans filthy, matted to his body, water dripping from his dark hair, and the expression on his face . . . her hands rose to her throat in alarm.

Haunted. Tormented. Something dark and urgent had wiped out the young husband she knew, yet he stared at her as if he'd never needed her more. Without a word he picked her up and kicked the door shut. Nameless dread trapped Sam in her own silence. She sank her hands into his drenched, gritty shirt and felt the ragged pulse of his heart. He carried her to their bedroom, shoved that door shut too, then lay down with her on their bed in the dark.

Instantly his mouth moved over her face, kissing her fiercely, his dirty, wet cheeks leaving streaks on her skin, his hands shaking as he dragged her robe off her shoulders, then finding her breasts under her nightgown. She responded to his agonized frenzy with a soft cry of compassion.

They took each other frantically, half-undressed, wound together in a breathless tangle with her hugging his head into the crook of her neck. Afterward they continued to hold each other, his shivering body pressed deeply inside hers, his arms wound tightly around her back and waist.

Sam was afraid—for him, not herself. She tried to talk to him, but he dragged his mouth back and forth over hers, repeating *I love you*, in a raw, desperate tone until she murmured plaintively and pressed her fingertips over his lips. "I know. I love you too. Be still now. Let me take care of you." She searched with one hand until she found an edge of the damp, jumbled quilt and pulled it over them.

A long time passed before he moved just enough to lay beside her, facing her. She burrowed into his unrelaxed grip and rubbed his back desperately, trying to impart warmth and comfort to the inflexible column of muscle and sinew. Finally she felt a slight giving. "I want to sleep," he said. The pleading tone in his voice brought a ragged murmur of agreement from her. "I'll get you a dry shirt," she told him. "And fill the bathtub. You can soak, and I'll wash your hair for you—"

"No. Please. I just want to stay here and forget about everything but the way it feels to be with you. I wish I could sleep the rest of my life."

"Shhh. Don't talk that way. Just . . . sleep, for now. I'll hold you. I won't let go. I never have. I never will."

"Don't let go." His voice faded. Sam stroked his hair, dried it with a corner of the quilt, and hugged her bare leg over his hips. She wanted to wrap him a cocoon so safe, so dreamless, he'd wake up with the old serenity in his eyes. "Promise me you won't go back to the house site tomorrow. Just try to stay away from it for one day. Rest. *Please*."

"I promise." His breathing slowed. He slept finally. Sam rose on one elbow and rested her cheek against his head. The rain stopped and faint moonlight eased through the windows. It reflected off the glass jar containing the ruby, on the dresser. Sam stared at the intruding glimmer defiantly. Aunt Alex's bitter feud with Sarah because of the ruby, a feud that had separated Sam from Jake for most of their lives. The day Tim had assaulted Charlotte when he found her admiring his mother's necklace. The fear and anger in Aunt Alex's eyes when Ellie had discovered the ruby inside that necklace. Jake's bewildering obsession with it. The sight of him searching for the stone in the shambles of his sister's room, and his look of revulsion after he found it.

Her nerves were strained to the limit; otherwise, she would never have allowed the bitter, senseless thought she had before exhaustion overcame her.

She would never feel safe with that ruby in their house.

Sam woke with a start, alone. Sunlight streamed through the windows. She bolted out of bed, her cotton gown stiff with dried water and grime from Jake's clothes, looking around for him wildly. The bedsheets were a dirt-stained shambles; she ran a hand over Jake's empty place, alarmed when the cool sheets told her he'd left some time ago.

She threw her robe on and dashed to their bathroom, hoping she'd find him in the shower. When she didn't, she ran through the house, calling his name. Bo met her in the hall, whining. Charlotte, sluggishly contemplating a bowl of cereal at the kitchen table, stared at her anxiously. Sam gripped the table's edge. "Have you seen Jake?"

"No. I figured he went, went *there*, you know." Charlotte's head drooped. She had trouble talking about Sarah, Hugh, Ellie, or their house. "Like he does every morning."

He promised me he wouldn't go. Sam hurried outside, dread and disappointment twisting her stomach. Frosty air bit into her bare legs and feet. Her station wagon still sat in its spot at the end of the driveway, but his enormous old Cadillac was gone.

Maybe he'd driven over. She dug the keys from under the station wagon's front seat and followed his tire tracks down the narrow, winding lane to the little road that ran through the Cove. Sam slammed on the brakes and got out, shivering. His car tracks turned left, out of the Cove, not toward his parents' house.

She was dizzy with confusion and fear. Where had he gone without telling her? There had never been any important secrets between them; now he left on lonely missions without even bothering to explain.

Shaking, she returned to the house. Charlotte stood on the porch, wringing her hands in the bottom of her pink sweatshirt. "Where is he?"

"Gone. Somewhere. I don't know." Sam walked inside leadenly and went through each room in a daze of worry, as if her aimless wandering might turn up clues. When she ended up in their bedroom, she sat on the bed's edge, staring into space.

Her gaze shifted angrily to the jar atop their dresser. The ruby was gone too.

I did it. I paid that bastard back but good, and no one will ever find out. Malcolm reveled in his accomplishment with endless satisfaction. He had nothing left but that one victory, and it consumed him. He trudged up the last flight of echoing metal stairs to his third floor apartment, his ragged, syrupy breaths eased by the thought that he had elevated himself from dying petty con artist to dying arsonist and murderer.

Flush with new confidence, he decided he'd visit Mrs. Lomax and insist she provide him with a nice condominium and job-free security as well as medical expenses. He really didn't deserve to spend the remainder of his life as a church janitor, living in a shabby apartment building with no elevator.

Smiling, he unlocked the dented metal door to his apartment and stepped inside. The fading light from a sliding glass door to the balcony obscured the dingy furniture. He pictured himself lounging in a plush recliner in his new condo.

A powerful arm circled his throat from behind. The door clanged shut.

Malcolm made a gurgling sound and struggled. He was thin and weak; his unknown attacker towered over him and seemed to be built of unyielding granite. Silently the man dragged him across the small living room. Stangling, Malcolm flailed his arms and legs. One hand fumbled in a pocket of his dingy khaki jacket and grabbed a knife. But he had never been adept when it came to physical survival; his skills lay in the more refined art of emotional manipulation.

He pressed the release button on the switchblade, and stabbed himself in the side.

Malcolm's pained screech was choked off by the crushing arm around his neck. A second later he was sprawled facedown on the thin brown carpet, his knife snatched away from him, his arms pinned behind his back with bone-crushing force.

"You killed my family," a deep voice drawled. Shock and disbelief reduced Malcolm to gasping sputters. The identity of his violent visitor was as clear to him as the sharp pain in his side. How was this possible? To be hunted down by Jake Raincrow *again*, when there was no trail, no proof . . .

Mrs. Lomax told him about me. She played both sides. She wants me dead now.

"You set the fire," that same lethally calm voice continued. "*She* told you who I was and where to find me. But you made a mistake. You didn't get me. The worst mistake you'll ever make."

Malcolm squirmed helplessly. Bile surged into his mouth, and a coughing spasm shook him. His eyes clamped shut. He was dragged to his knees. A thick-fingered hand closed tightly under his jaw. He stared into a rough young face and eyes as merciless as an animal's.

I should kill him, Jake thought. *For my family, for me, for Samantha. Kill him. Never tell a soul I did it, or why.*

Samantha. The truth would haunt her the way it haunted him. His family was dead because of her aunt's schemes.

And all he had to prove it was Malcolm Drury, a piece of shit in a human skin who'd served time in the Bahamas for cocaine. Any homicide detectives worth their pay would doubt Malcolm's story—a story that linked the lieutenant-governor's wife to murder, a story that would sound like bizarre lies concocted by a sick, desperate man.

Justice would be surer if Jake strangled him and walked out.

But then what? Live with the knowledge that he could never prove Alexandra was to blame for it all? Prowl the edges of her life looking for ways to punish her?

Or slip inside Highview some night when he knew she was alone and choke the breath out of her the way the fire had choked his parents and Ellie.

Murder two people. He, who had given up hunting and fishing years before because he knew what his prey felt as it suffered and died.

Could he kill Samantha's flesh and blood and not feel her soul in his hands? Could he look into Samantha's peaceful, unsuspecting eyes every day and night for the rest of their lives and believe with all his heart that he'd saved much more than he'd destroyed?

"I'm not going to hurt you anymore," Jake told Malcolm slowly. "If you tell me what I want to know." Jake vaulted to his feet, lifted Malcolm by the shoulders of his jacket, then set him in a sagging armchair. Malcolm hunched over, moaning, sweat sliding down his face. "You're going to tell me everything," Jake continued. "And then I'm taking you to the police. And you'll repeat it for them."

Malcolm seemed on the verge of hysteria. He rocked back and forth, his mouth moving soundlessly.

"*Talk*," Jake commanded with soft contempt. He wound a hand into the collar of Malcolm's jacket. "If you don't, I'll break every goddamned bone in your body."

The sudden, unmistakable sound of footsteps climbing the stairs seeped through Malcolm's fog of panic. He sagged with relief. Jake absorbed every vivid thought.

It was Monday. Bible-study night. Members of the congregation took turns bringing him dinner and salvation once a week. Well, tonight they had brought the only brand of salvation Malcolm wanted. All he thought he had to do was stall until a knock came at the door, then scream for help.

Jake pulled a faded bandanna from a pocket of his jeans, pried Malcolm's mouth open, and stuffed the bandanna into it. He clamped a hand over Malcolm's lips and shook his head when Malcolm gagged. "No, you won't scream," Jake told him.

Malcolm's eyes rolled back. His chest heaved. Jake jerked him to his feet. "You're not going to strangle on your own vomit. Not until I'm done with you anyway."

Jake dragged him to the glass door, slid it open, and tugged most of the bandanna from his mouth. He rested his hand on Malcolm's throat, his fingertips pressing carefully into the skin. "Make one sound and I'll rip your windpipe out."

Malcolm's head moved weakly, and he inhaled. Jake tried to measure the footsteps against the background noise from the street below the balcony, where men's voices rose in a loud argument over the price of a motorcycle.

The footsteps halted on the landing outside the apartment door. Someone knocked lightly. Malcolm's eyes settled in their sockets, and he stared at Jake, the bandanna hanging from his lips like a long red-checkered tongue. "Mr. Drury?" The visitor's voice was muffled by the door. "Malcolm, it's Harold Johnson. From the church. I'm your prayer partner this week. I've brought a pizza. Malcolm?"

The knocking started again. Malcolm shuddered and moaned. Jake tightened the pressure on his thin neck. The pulse beat wildly against his palm. Repulsed by the pity he suddenly felt, Jake looked away from him.

A minute later the visitor called out, "All right, Malcolm, I saw your car in the parking lot. But I'm not going to force pizza and fellowship on you. If you're hiding in there, I just want you to think about God's disappointment, not mine. Good night."

The footsteps retreated. Jake sighed with relief and rewarded Malcolm by moving his grip to the back of Malcolm's coat.

That small show of mercy doomed him.

Malcolm lurched forward on the narrow balcony and clawed the bandanna from his mouth. "Help me!" he screamed. "I'm being murdered! Help me!"

Jake yanked backward just as Malcolm took another desperate leap. Malcolm's baggy, unzipped coat slid off.

And the same fateful momentum that had propelled Malcolm Drury through life carried him over the balcony's rusty iron rail.

Jake was at the rail in one quick step, hands out, the coat dangling from one as if he could net his prey in midair. He watched, stunned, as the man he had decided not to kill plunged headfirst onto the sidewalk three floors down.

The men who had been arguing over the motorcycle gawked at the limp body and the blood-speckled concrete around Malcolm's head.

Then they looked up at Jake.

Chapter
Twenty-Three

This couldn't be happening. Not this, after the fire, the funerals, the endless grief. She could not be following a deputy down the narrow, too brightly lit hallway of the Durham city jail, leaving a shell-shocked Charlotte and Joe Gunther in the lobby.

Jake couldn't belong in this place, charged with killing a man who was supposed to have disappeared permanently into a Bahama prison.

How had Jake discovered he'd come back to the States? And why, God, hadn't Jake told her he was going to find him?

"Here you go," the deputy said, not unkindly, as he stopped before a thick metal door and inserted a key in the lock. She wouldn't have been allowed to see Jake tonight if the sheriff hadn't given special permission. Jake had tracked for him.

She had to get permission from a sheriff to see her own husband.

Sam forced that thought out of her mind. She was operating on numb disbelief and adrenaline; any break in her concentration would make this all too real, and she'd fold up like an accordion.

She jumped at the sound of the lock turning. The thought of Jake behind a locked door made her sick. The door had a small peephole of a window reinforced with crisscrossed wires. This was a place where windows meant someone was always watching.

Stop thinking. You can let yourself think only about how to get Jake out of here.

Her legs shook. She stepped into a small bare room with no other windows, a metal table, and two chairs. A merciless fluorescent light fixture made spots dance in her vision.

And the sight of Jake facing her across the room, his tall, lean body encased in a prisoner's baggy white shirt and trousers, made the spots converge into a black haze. She staggered and gripped her forehead with both hands, fighting the darkness with a furious surge of willpower.

Jake caught her by the shoulders and held her up, but resisted when she tried to hug him. She stared at him with torturous confusion.

Jake wanted nothing more than to have Samantha's arms around him, but he fought the selfish need with every ounce of strength. Clara Big Stick's premonitions had come true, because he refused to take them seriously, because he'd thought he and Samantha were invincible when they were together. That damned confidence had made him blind. The evil he'd respected as a child had never been conquered; it had waited, a ravenmocker laughing in the darkness.

Now his family was dead, his future belonged to strangers who were convinced he'd killed a man, and no one stood between Alexandra and what she wanted. She wanted control of Samantha and Charlotte. She wanted the ruby back.

He'd had time to think through the consequences
and decide what he had to do. The gift he'd lived with
all his life had never seemed more like a curse. The truth
that only he knew, and how he knew it, would sound
crazy to a jury. And maybe to Sam, no matter how much
she loved him.

His worst fear was that she *would* believe him. If he
told her why he'd sought out Malcolm Drury, and what
her aunt had to do with it, she'd go after Alexandra.

Alexandra would eat her alive.

He had to get Samantha as far away from her as he
could. But there was only one way he could make her
leave him. By driving her away.

Sam locked her hands into his shirt and continued to
search his face desperately. His expression was stiff, his
gaze agonized and strangely unwelcoming. He released
her and dropped his hands by his sides.

"Are you all right?" she asked. An absurd question,
but rational thought had deserted her. She ran her fingertips over his head and chest in a frantic examination,
reduced to searching for invisible injuries as if she could
erase the real one that way.

Jake stepped back and caught her hands as if he
didn't want her to touch him. "You're the only one I'm
worried about," he said.

"Why didn't you call me instead of Joe? Why did I
have to hear about this from someone else?"

"Because I know how bad it sounds. I wanted someone I trust to be with you."

He was the one in jail, but he was worried about
her. Sam said in a choked voice, "You found out Malcolm
Drury had come back, and you had to make certain he
wouldn't bother us. You were so afraid something else
would happen. Isn't that it?"

"Yes."

"I should never have told you about him." Her voice
shook. "I despised him for stealing from my mother. I
wanted something terrible to happen to him. It did.
He was stupid enough to smuggle drugs, and someone
pointed him out to the police in the Bahamas, and they

caught him. Case closed." Shame washed over her as she realized she was berating Jake. She bowed her head. "You didn't kill him. Joe told me what you said. He fell. It was an accident."

"That's not how it looks. There's not a chance in hell a court will let me walk away from it."

"Don't you *dare* stand there and tell me you're giving up before we've even started fighting! You're not going to prison!"

"Yes, I am." He said it with a kind of eerie certainty that frightened her so badly, she gagged. She turned her face and cupped a hand over her mouth, shutting her eyes, struggling for control. He pulled her against him with a convulsive sigh, pressed his face into her hair, and held her fiercely. She felt his tears slipping down her cheek, and cried with him.

Alexandra crossed the parking lot of the Durham motel with eager strides. She was pleased with herself—amazed at the way one, small push had started a perfect chain of events.

Malcolm Drury was dead, taking any threat to her with him. Sarah and her brood were gone. Jake was as good as dead. Orrin—dear, loving Orrin, who thought she was distraught over the events—had studied the evidence against Jake and sadly confirmed Alexandra's hope. No jury was likely to acquit Jake, and a murder conviction carried a long prison term before any chance of parole.

Samantha was only nineteen. She'd get on with her life and forget about him. All Alexandra had to do was take advantage of the situation. She searched the line of numbered doors and nodded with satisfaction when she found the one she wanted.

Alexandra laughed. Wasn't fate undoubtedly on her side? Who would have thought her problems could solve themselves so beautifully, with no liability to her and very little effort on her part?

She knocked softly. The door opened a crack. Charlotte stared at her from beneath the guard chain. Her eyes were more startlingly blue than Alexandra remembered, and there was a hard edge to their unflinching gaze.

"Let me in, dear. Samantha asked me to come."

"I know. I tried to talk her out of it." Charlotte opened the door. Alexandra saw no sign of Samantha in the small, efficient room. The door to the bath was closed. She heard the muffled sound of running water.

Stepping inside, Alexandra gracefully removed her tailored coat and draped it over a chair, feeling Charlotte's eyes watching every move suspiciously. Alexandra had dressed in casual slacks and an old blazer, thinking it made her appear unforbidding and sincere.

She appraised Charlotte's bare feet, tight jeans, sloppy pink sweater, and shaggy blond hair with hidden dismay. Unlike Samantha, Charlotte had a trashy streak. Apparently, the Raincrows had encouraged it. "Let me tell you something," Charlotte said, sliding plump, stubby hands into the back pockets of her jeans. "If you upset Sam any more than she already is, I'll rip your fucking head off."

This unbridled aggression was a surprising change. Alexandra suppressed an urge to pop her in the mouth. There would be plenty of opportunity to squeeze Charlotte down to size. "I'm only here to help," she replied patiently. "Believe it or not, I feel terrible about everything that's happened. As much as I disliked the Raincrows, I never wished to see the family end up in ruin. Sarah was my sister-in-law at one time. Jake and Ellie are my son's cousins. As children, they were his closest friends."

Charlotte slammed the door. "You're only worried about your and Orrin's reputation," she shot back. "Because the news people keep mentioning that Jake is married to your niece."

Alexandra glanced furtively toward the bath, wishing Samantha would come out. Her patience was slipping. "If I cared about public image, I'd distance myself from this whole situation. But I'm here to support you and Samantha in every way I can. And that includes doing my best to help Jake."

Charlotte eyed her uncertainly. The bathroom door opened suddenly, and Samantha hurried out, a towel draped around her slender shoulders, her hair wet and slicked back, her face swollen and pale. She wore a black terry-cloth robe of such oversize proportions, it must be Jake's. She moved with a kind of dogged determination, her eyes dull. "Thank you for coming." Her voice was hoarse.

"I'm glad you called me."

Charlotte snorted. "Sammie, I'm going outside and sit on the curb. But only because you asked me to split when *she* got here." She grabbed a coat and walked out, slamming the door again.

Samantha gestured to a chair. Alexandra nodded and sat down, noting with pride that her niece maintained a strong, shoulders-back posture as she settled on the end of the room's bed. "I doubt you want to hear any sympathies from me," Alexandra told her.

"That's right. I need money. I've got to hire a good lawyer."

"Do you have anyone in mind?"

"His name's Ben Dreyfus."

Alexandra suppressed a frown. "I've heard of his father. Abraham Dreyfus is a very respected attorney."

"I wanted the father, but he's sick. A mild heart attack, I heard. So . . . Ben said he'd talk to me." Sam's shadowed eyes met Alexandra's. "I'm going to need a lot of money for legal fees. The trial." Her voice faltered. "And if . . . the worst happens, then for appeals. I'm not putting Jake in the hands of a court-appointed lawyer."

"Hmmm. That's a wise decision. Don't worry about the cost. I'll pay for everything."

"It's only a loan. I'll work it off. Work for you. Do whatever you want."

Alexandra marveled at the offer. There was no doubt in her mind that Jake didn't know Samantha's plans; Jake would never have agreed to them. Nor she did doubt that Samantha hated asking her for money and had been driven to this point by desperation. Samantha's devotion to him, her sacrifice for his sake, was troubling. Prying her away from Jake would be a delicate and lengthy business. But worth the effort.

"I'll give you the money—no strings attached," Alexandra said.

"No. I couldn't take it as a gift."

Which was exactly what Alexandra had known she'd say. "I'll be delighted to have you back on speaking terms with me, whatever the conditions. Let's forget about the past. We've both said and done hurtful things, but we can start over. I promise."

"There's only one promise I need. That you'll leave Charlotte out of this. She'll live with me. She'll be my responsibility. You won't expect us to come back to Highview. We'll stay in the Cove. It's home. And I don't want anything to do with Tim. I don't want him near Charlotte."

"You have my promise."

Sam looked at her with grim astonishment. "I didn't think it would be this easy."

"That's because you don't really know me. I hope we can change that. I'll start by saying how pleased, really pleased, I am about your weaving. I've seen the work you've sold. If you'd like to continue with it, then let me be your partner. I'll find, no, *we'll* find a very nice place for you to set up shop in town. Someplace with lots of display space. I'll introduce you to interior decorators."

"I'll pay you back. Every penny you loan me."

"Oh, we'll discuss that later. You have too much to worry about already." Alexandra stood. Timing was everything. She intended to be the very model of selfless generosity. All the odds were in her favor now. "Is there anything I can do for you today? Visit this lawyer with you? Book a room at a good hotel for you and Charlotte? I'm sure you want to stay in Durham, close to Jake." Alexandra eyed the crumpled pizza box atop the television set, and the empty cans of soda. "You need to eat well and try to rest. Room service would be a blessing."

"No . . . thank you. You've done enough."

Alexandra bit back an argument. "What about Jake's dog? Can I send someone to the Cove to feed him?"

"Joe Gunther is taking care of him."

"Oh. Well. Call me after you meet with Ben Dreyfus.
Just tell me where to send a check."

Samantha rose stiffly. "Thank you." It was clear she
felt honor bound to offer some humble show of gratitude—a hug or at least a handshake. And it was clear
she didn't want to give either. Alexandra quickly slipped
into her coat and said, "That's that, then. I know nothing
can make you feel better at the moment, but just don't
think you have to struggle with this awful situation alone.
I'm a, well, a changed woman. Wiser. I sincerely hope we
can bring Jake home to you, and that maybe, just maybe,
he'll see that I'm not an enemy."

Samantha said nothing. The mention of Jake's name
seemed to weigh her down. Alexandra paused at the door,
a tide of merciless interest overwhelming her. She damned
the compulsion, but it was too powerful. Alexandra said
carefully, "I'm not asking this question for any selfish
reason. I simply want to know that an heirloom that
meant a great deal to the Vanderveers as well as the
Raincrows is safely stored away. Do you know what's
become of the ruby, Samantha?"

Samantha leveled a somber, unwavering gaze at her.
"I saw it only once. Sarah didn't tell Jake or me what she
did with it. We didn't ask."

Alexandra's composure nearly failed her. Lost? Sold?
Hidden? The thought that even now Sarah might count
the last coup was unthinkable. She steeled herself. "It
belongs to you and Jake now. It's worth a small fortune.
It should be located and insured. But . . . well, I'm certain
Jake will find it when he comes home. He has a remarkable talent for finding things."

Samantha didn't blink. "When he comes home," she
said.

Jake paced the cell, sweating. The nights here weren't
quiet or dark. The barred wall that faced the corridor let
the yellow security lights reach into the cell. Guards
patrolled the corridor regularly, and he could never

tune out the rhythmic click of their hard-soled shoes, or the snores and nightmarish cries of other, sleeping prisoners.

Everything he touched made him recoil. The bare cinderblock walls, the toilet, the sink, the metal bunk, its blanket, sheets, and pillow. Everything whispered excruciating information about the men who'd been there before him. He was immersed in their lives, their bitterness, their fear. The acts they'd committed crept into his mind in vivid detail.

He was drowning. He had to shut them out. He had to wall off the part of his mind that worked that way, even if it meant shutting out Samantha too. It was the only way he'd survive. Handicapped. Soulless.

He concentrated on the sound of his own feet hitting the smooth concrete floor. Blood had been spattered on this floor more than once. And every other fluid a human body could produce. *Shut it out.*

"You better learn to sleep, man. Sleep is the only time you get to go where you want."

Jake halted. A big, fleshy man with a shaved head lay on his stomach in the bunk across the way, his chin propped on bulging forearms. He was black, and seemed to merge with the shadows around him. He laughed tonelessly. "I see new ones like you all the time," he continued in a low voice. "Dragging their asses around the floor day and night. Ain't learned to get inside themselves yet and stay there."

Jake moved to the bars, stopping close to them, careful to keep space between them and his body. "How do you do it?"

"Comes with time. Lots of time. I was in for five years once. I learned. Figured I could hold on to the outside if I thought about it enough. My wife, she said she'd wait, but she didn't. She got lonely, run off with somebody. My kids were calling him Daddy by the time I got out. Hell, that was a good thing anyway. A man does much time, he ain't the same anymore. Might as well be dead."

"You made it."

A quick, brutal laugh echoed softly from the bunk. "Yeah, and here I am, fucked up again." More laughter, trailing off into a hiss. "You got a wife?"

"Yes."

"You won't have her when you get out. And even if you do, you won't be fit for her. You ever see a dog that's been chained in a yard all his life? Chained up and left alone so much that he don't know anything else? You let that dog go, and he'll either run out in front of car like a fool, or he'll just creep around, like he's always waitin' to hit the end of the chain again. He don't even know how to act around other dogs. And they don't want nothing to do with him."

Jake walked to his bunk. Slowly, he sat down. "That's right," the other man called, chuckling. "Settle down. Don't look no farther than the end of your chain."

Chapter
Twenty-Four

Sammie Raincrow was pale, desperate, prettily blond, and gritty as sandpaper. Ben Dreyfus liked her from the moment she walked into his small, luxurious office at Dreyfus and Dreyfus, carrying a lined yellow notepad, a dog-eared pamphlet about the trial process, and a wad of twenty-dollar bills. "I need a lawyer who'll stick with my husband for the long haul," she said immediately. "If you haven't got what it takes, tell me today. I'll pay you for your time and move on."

"I'm afraid, from what I've learned about the case, I can't do anything spectacular for him."

"Are you tough?"

Ben launched defensively into his résumé, feeling like a fool. He had, after all, a law degree from Harvard, and he came from a very old, rich, and hardworking family of lawyers who had instilled in him a dedication

364

to doing every task, no matter how small, thoroughly and well. He had a brother on the state supreme court and a sister in cardiology at Johns Hopkins. His father, Abraham, had not made him a junior partner in the family law practice just to keep him off the streets. Besides all that, his mother was president of the ladies' auxiliary of Temple Beth Tikvah, serving greater metropolitan Durham. *So there*, he added silently as he finished.

She stared at him across his desk and said, "How old are you?"

"Twenty-seven," he blurted out. Then, recovering, he arched a brow and grunted, "A child genius." He smoothed a hand over his leather suspenders, silk tie, and natty dress shirt. "I've been told I have the presence of a young F. Lee Bailey."

"I was thinking of Dustin Hoffman. In *The Graduate*."

Ben had heard that before too. "I have much better hair," he said grimly.

"I'll be honest with you."

"Please, I don't know if I can take anymore."

"I wanted your father to handle this. Everybody knows him. He's done a lot of good work for the Cherokees. Joe Gunther says he picks his clients on principle, not just to make a buck. Is that how you operate?"

Flustered, Ben waved a hand at a stuffed bass on the paneled wall. "Well, I did inherit the Dreyfus *fishing* gene. I suppose I can dredge up a little integrity too."

"Do you believe, really believe, my husband's innocent? Because I won't have a lawyer who isn't one hundred percent on his side."

"Look, it's my job to see he gets a good defense, not write him a letter of recommendation to the Boy Scouts."

"That's not good enough."

"Give me a chance. I haven't even talked to him yet."

"All right. Talk to him. But if you don't believe him, don't take his case."

"Okay, we have a deal."

"Good." She sank back in the leather chair as if some of the invisible strings that held her up had snapped. Her face ashen, she curled one incredibly flawless hand over her mouth. "You have to understand something." Her voice was muffled, weak. "I don't quit. Whatever happens, I'll keep fighting for him. I'll expect you to do the same." She swallowed hard. "Excuse me. Where's the bathroom?"

Ben stood anxiously. "Down the hall. Second door on the right."

She staggered out, covering her mouth. He followed as gallantly as he could, keeping one eye on the Oriental rugs and hoping she'd make it to the ladies' room before she threw up. She did. He sighed and walked into the small office next to his. The paralegal, a crusty woman who had worked for his father since dinosaurs roamed the earth, stared at him over her word processor. "Raincrow," she barked. "Whadd'ya think?"

"Odds are he's a goner. Poor bastard—first his family fries, then he goes nuts and slaps around some pathetic jerk who romanced his wife's mother out of her nest egg a few years ago. The jerk decides to take a flying lesson off a balcony." Ben shrugged. "What the hell. I like a challenge. And Dad wants me to take it."

"Is this gonna be a freebie?"

"Oh, no. I've got house payments. Women to impress. A Porsche to support."

"You crummy shit." Ben blinked at the paralegal. No, even she wasn't *that* crusty. She nodded toward the door to her office. "Say hello to Sammie Raincrow's sister. Charlotte."

Ben turned around reluctantly, wishing he were in court, where he was much better at not offending people unless he intended to. Sammie's baby sister glared up at him, and he gazed back with undeniable intrigue. She was shorter, rounder, younger, and not nearly as even-tempered, which was saying a lot. The term *baby sister* evaporated from his thoughts. *Lolita* came to mind.

"You crummy shit," she repeated. "You're just interested in money."

"I'm a lawyer. I always talk that way. It's nothing personal. But I apologize."

"*Right*. Where's my sister?"

"Here." Sammie walked up, wiping her face with a damp paper towel, hoisting a bulging, handsomely woven tote bag over one shoulder of a slender wool coat. She looked at Ben hopefully, and he felt like a snake. "When can you meet with my husband?"

"Tomorrow. I'll call you."

"I'll be at the jail. I sit in the lobby as much as they'll let me."

That tragically devoted image bored into Ben's mind permanently. Lolita grabbed her gentler kin by one arm and pointed at Ben. "He's in this just for the money. I heard him say so."

"That's not true," Ben said dryly. "I'm a masochist, and I enjoy working for people who verbally abuse me."

Sam shook her head at her sister. "He's a lawyer." As if that both excused and condemned him. "He's a good lawyer, I hope. That's all that matters."

She gave Ben one last look, tired and sad and more than a little wishful. Her pet tigress joined in with a slit-eyed appraisal. "You can count on me," Ben told them both. He was suddenly righteous and determined to see this thing to a happy conclusion, regardless of how long it took. To please the noble Sammie Raincrow and wipe that look off her sister's cocky, luscious little face.

Sam stood across the bare little room from Jake, the same room where they'd been allowed to talk before. She had run up to him as soon as the guard closed the door behind her, putting her arms around him, drawing his face close and scattering small kisses over it. He'd surrendered for a second, half out of his mind with love and desperation, kissing her, tasting her tears in his mouth.

Until he sensed Alexandra's presence around her and how hard she was trying to hide it. Rigid with alarm, he stepped back from her and moved away. Her eyes filled with anguish and bewilderment. "Jake?"

"Did you get it from the sheriff?" he asked bluntly. "Did you do what I asked you to do—get the ruby?"

She nodded vaguely and looked even more upset. "I've got it. They let me have all your things, to take home. But what, what—"

"Then what are you afraid of? What are you ashamed of?" His voice was accusing.

"What . . . what do you mean? Is this about Ben Dreyfus? Do you want me to interview another lawyer?"

Ben Dreyfus was solid, dependable. Jake had sized him up quickly by picking up the gold fountain pen Ben had laid on the table during their brief meeting. Ben Dreyfus's most sentimental possession—an engraved pen his grandfather had given him at his Bar Mitzvah. A map of Ben's life, with all the moral landmarks Jake needed to judge him by. "No. He'll do." Fear washed through him like an acid. "But we don't have enough money to pay him for long."

"Don't worry about that. I've got work. I'll—"

"You're hiding something from me. I've always known when you do. It's about money."

"Oh, no. Joe Gunther has offered to help. And other people have—"

"That wouldn't take care of things, and you know it." He paused, bitterly holding her agonized gaze. "You asked Alexandra for help."

She went very still. The battle between guilt and honesty was painfully clear to him. He wanted to slam his fists into a wall. Alexandra was already after her, and Samantha didn't have an inkling of what that really meant. "We need money," she said finally. "It's just a loan. I'm going to work for her and pay it back. She's changed, Jake. She promised she wouldn't try to take over. She'll leave Charlotte alone."

"Oh, *God*." He trembled with fury and dread. "She didn't waste any time. She slid right back into your life as soon as I was out of her way. And you let her."

Sam held out her hands, pleading, angry. "Listen to me," she said in a low voice. "It'll be months before your case comes to trial. I'm sure I could work out something with Ben about his fees, but I can't stop bill collectors. I can't send the government an IOU for taxes on the Cove. I won't let pride stop me from doing whatever it takes to help you and keep hold of everything that's important to you."

"This is how you do it? By running to her when you know it's the last thing I want?"

"Can't you understand? I'm doing this for your sake." She trembled miserably. "You're here because of me."

Hurt her. Make her go. Because the farther she is from you, the safer she'll be. Loving her isn't enough to make a difference. You know that now.

They had no future until he finished with Alexandra, until she paid for what she'd done. "That's right," he said, dying inside. "So, by God, do what I tell you to do. You owe me."

It took all his willpower to form a lifetime of devotion into a weapon, to ignore the shattered expression dawning in her eyes.

The nightmare was complete. Sam stared at him in despair. He had confirmed her worst fear. Moving as if in a trance, she staggered toward him, reaching for him. He grabbed her by the shoulders and held her away. The hard look in his eyes cut to the quick. "You really do believe in curses," she said. Sam's voice was thready with alarm. "And that I've brought you bad luck."

"I've hurt everyone—my family, you—by believing what I wanted to believe instead of what I should have *known*," he said slowly. "I've made a lot of mistakes. I won't make any more."

"Is loving me one of those mistakes?" Her voice was a bare whisper filled with dread.

Say it. Lie. Say it for her sake, because you've never loved her more than you do right now. "Yes."

The small, devastated sound she made ripped into him. He released her and stepped back, fearing his courage would fall apart if he didn't put some distance between them.

Sam couldn't think, couldn't breathe. His logic, so warped and incomprehensible, was clear on only one point. He believed that somehow he'd destroyed his family and himself by loving her.

Dimly she heard the lock rattle. The door to this, this *cage* opening. The deputy's voice telling them time was up.

Time was up. A whole life of unswerving loyalty had come to an end. *No*. He might not want to love her, but he did. And she would never, *never* give up. "What do you want me to do?" she asked Jake, surprised at how calm she sounded.

He did not, would not, turn to face her. The boy, the man who had never turned away from her before. His shoulders were rigid. His head rose. He stood like a condemned man waiting for the gavel to fall. "Take Charlotte," he said in a voice as falsely calm as her own. "Get as far away as you can. And don't let Alexandra find you, because she'll try to take over your life. And I won't be there to help you." He paused, then added, "Take care of the ruby. I'll want it back when I get out."

"You're afraid Alexandra still wants it. That's what you care about. That she'll get that damned stone away from me."

"She will. You'll let her talk you out of it the same way you gave in to her behind my back."

"That's not how it was!" Her voice was raw, disbelieving. "Don't you trust me?"

"I don't trust anybody anymore."

"*Jake*."

"All I need from you is the promise you'll keep the ruby. It doesn't mean anything to you. It's important to me. That's all you can do for me now."

His words slammed into her. Sam took an unsteady breath. "I'm not leaving you. I'm not going to let you give up on us. I'll make everything up to you somehow."

He turned violently toward her. "Get this straight. Clara Big Stick was right. We aren't meant to be together. You're bad luck. *I don't want you anymore. I don't want anything to do with you.*"

"Time's up," the deputy repeated, less patient now.

Sam sank her hands into Jake's shirt. He had broken her. "Please," she begged. "*Please* don't hate me."

He wrenched her hands away. "Go on. Get out."

She staggered back. "I'll never leave you."

"You will. Goddammit, I'll divorce you."

Those words jerked her to attention. Her stunned expression slowly jelled into an unyielding mask. "No, you won't," she hoarsely. "Because I'm the only one who can take care of your precious rock for you."

Jake cursed weakly. He hadn't thought of that. Yet he felt an undeniable sense of relief which he despised as cowardice. He would have divorced her to cut the man-made evidence of a sacred bond that could never really be broken. Another way to let her go, to make it easier for her to survive in a world where Alexandra would never stop hounding her.

"You couldn't divorce me anyway," Sam said in a low, toneless voice. She had retreated behind a wall of shock. Grim determination had taken over. "I don't need a piece of paper to tell me we'll always be married."

"That's all, let's go," the guard said. He took Samantha by one arm. "Come on, ma'am. You know the rules."

"I'll be back to visit you tomorrow," she told Jake. "And every day after that. Every time they'll let me."

Jake stared past her. He felt empty. "I won't accept visits from my wife after today," he told the guard.

"Fine," the guard grunted, dragging gently at Samantha's arm. "It'll save me from wrestling with her."

Sam broke away from him and lurched toward Jake. She put her arms around him, shivering, tearing him apart with the violent, silent sobs racking her body. He pushed her into the guard's grip. "Good-bye," he said. His voice failed, and he turned away, struggling to keep his head up and shoulders squared.

She moaned. "*Jake, I love you.*"

He heard her scuffling footsteps as the guard pulled her out of the room. He relaxed when the door clattered shut.

He had reached the end of the chain.

Clara waited. She sat at her loom on the cool back porch, a heavy sweater drawn around her hunched shoulders, brown hands lying still on the warp threads, an old print skirt tucked warmly around her arthritic knees. She listened. The car door slammed. She heard footsteps on her front porch, and the creak of the screen door pulling back. She left the doors and windows of her house open except in the nastiest weather; she liked the air, and had no fear of unwelcome visitors.

She had expected Sammie to come sooner or later.

Clara studied her solemnly when she stepped onto the back porch. The girl's blue eyes had always been old. Now they were ancient, worn with care and loneliness. Her coat hung on her slim shoulders like a mantel of mountain bedrock; the lace on one of her tennis shoes was untied, and her golden hair was carelessly tied back with a faded bandanna, probably one of Jake's. This was not the orderly, eager-faced young woman Clara had come to cherish during the past months. This was a lost soul.

Sammie dropped to her knees and laid her head on Clara's large lap, sitting very still and tired. "He told me to leave," Sammie said slowly, her voice hollow. "He wants me to take Charlotte and go. Anywhere. He said it was a mistake for him to love me."

Clara patted her cheek. "He's right about one thing. You and Charlotte got to get away from here. Get away from Alexandra. I heard she's telling people how bad she feels for you, how she's goin' to help you and Jake. Don't you believe it. She's smackin' her lips over you. Thinks you're hers now."

"I am. Because I'll do anything to get the money I need for Jake's defense, and to pay bills at the Cove."

"It's not about money. You wallow with pigs, you'll get dirty."

"I'm already dirty." Sammie shivered. "When I came to the Cove I was convinced my aunt would take revenge on Jake if I kept loving him, if I stayed with him. I thought she was the only person we had to worry about. I was wrong. She didn't do a thing. *I'm* the one who hurt him. I didn't mean to, but I did."

"No," Clara answered grimly. "You're not evil, child."

"I let him down the night of the fire. He went off to help a stranger, and I should have taken care of everything while he was gone. *He* would have gotten the family out in time if he'd been there."

"You did the best you could that night. Jake knows that."

"He changed after the fire. He shut me out." She paused, her shoulders slumping even more. "And then, out of the blue, he went after Malcolm Drury. It makes no sense, except to Jake."

Clara sighed. "I was a fool. I read the signs wrong. I should have known the ravenmocker wasn't done with Jake."

Sammie shivered. "It's me. I'm the ravenmocker."

"Nonsense. Girl, witches change shape to look like anybody they pick. You can't figure 'em out. I couldn't, and I'm good at it."

Sammie raised her head and looked at Clara miserably. "He doesn't want me anymore," she repeated.

The truth was obvious to Clara. She took Sammie's face between her gnarled hands. "Hear me now. Trust what I'm saying. It's not easy to hear, but you've got a long, hard road ahead of you, so I'm telling you how to walk it. Jake don't blame you for what's become of him and his family. He blames himself."

"*Why?*"

"Because he let his guard down. He let the ravenmocker slip right past him."

"My aunt?" Sammie frowned and shook her head. It was clear that the subject was beyond her limited understanding of witches. "She had nothing to do with—"

"Them witches, they're sly. Who's to know what part she played?" Sammie was silent, a polite, strained silence. Clara knew what she was up against. Sammie thought this was foolish, superstitious talking. Deep down, Sammie didn't want to so much as even wonder if her own aunt could have stolen the life from Jake's family and lured Jake into terrible trouble.

Good. That was good. Sammie couldn't fight the ravenmocker alone. Neither could Jake. They needed each other. "There's only one thing you got to believe right now," Clara continued patiently. "You can wish it weren't so, and you can call it wrong and superstitious and feebleminded—anything you want to call it—but you can't ever forget it's how Jake feels."

Sammie's expression became urgent. "Tell me."

"A ravenmocker is after him. And after everybody he loves. It's got the rest—he's afraid it'll get you too. He can't stop loving you, but he can keep his distance so the ravenmocker won't hurt you."

Sammie got to her feet. Her shoulders stiffened, and her head came up. "Then it's up to me to prove to him that no such thing exists."

Clara considered that vow in troubled silence, then nodded. Sammie would be with him, fighting beside him, until finally he would realize he couldn't fight a ravenmocker without her. That was all that really mattered, all that would save them.

Sitting at a kitchen chair with her head on the table, Charlotte drowsed. She didn't like being left alone in the Cove. Sammie had promised to hurry back from seeing Clara Big Stick. Charlotte had wanted to stay in Durham, but Sammie insisted she go back to school. Christmas break was only ten days away. They'd return to Durham then.

Christmas in a motel room. Christmas spent trying to get Sammie to eat and sleep enough. Keeping Sammie company in the lobby of the jail, where people whispered to Charlotte that it was no use, that the poor little thing's husband didn't want to see her. How could Jake stand himself, telling her to go away, blaming her for what he'd done?

And Ben Dreyfus, the elegant, charming jerk. He would meander into the lobby every day, pretending to be worried about Sammie, when all he cared about was money and publicity. He was always offering Charlotte sticks of gum as if she were a kid. He commented on her earrings, said she could transmit radio signals with that much metal. He had a way of teasing Charlotte that reduced her to sputtering.

Charlotte shifted in the chair, half-awake, pushing Ben Dreyfus out of her thoughts. She wasn't going to end up like Sammie, loving one man, getting hurt.

Murky, painful dreams crept through her mind; she walked through the woods and saw the Raincrow house standing, good as new, as old. *Nothing happened,* she thought, and ran inside. *I'll say hello to everyone, and then I'll go tell Jake and Sam. Jake will be home now. Sammie'll be so happy.* But her shoes mired in wet soot, and the house became a dark cavern of blackened walls. Cold wind whistled around her. Horror clawed at her throat; the charred doorway to the living room pivoted of its own accord, and Charlotte's fledgling scream faded into amazement.

Ellie stood in the rubble, looking at her like a sad, beautiful statue, long black hair floating in the air. *Wake up,* Ellie told her. *Tim's in the house.*

The strange dream evaporated as Charlotte jerked her head up. Every nerve vibrated. She looked wildly around Jake and Sammie's big, sunny kitchen. The house was eerily quiet. *Oh, jeez, Sammie, hurry and come home. I'm cracking up. Oh, Ellie, I wish you really could talk to me again.*

She heard a footstep in the front hall.

Sam drove down into the Cove, through the deep, familiar forest. All the leaves had dropped; fall was slipping into winter. A new season.

Ellie and Sarah and Hugh are dead. If you go past your own driveway, you'll turn off into the muddy, ruined yard of the old house.

Jake was in jail for an accident provoked by his obsession with her past, her family. He didn't want to see her again. He blamed her, he blamed himself for loving her. Because he believed they'd brought a curse on his family, and him.

Those thoughts tugged at the veil of shock around her. She pushed them down, covered them, guided the station wagon up the close, woodsy lane to her and Jake's house.

She drove well. Jake had taught her well. They had taught each other about marriage, about friendship, about the sweet, hot intimacy of sex.

And now he wanted 'her to forget about him. To leave.

Sam glimpsed the sleek black sports car in the yard. She squinted, not recognizing it at first. Her breath caught as she realized it was Tim's car.

Charlotte's alone with him. Sam stomped the accelerator. The bulky station wagon careened into the yard. Sam slid it to a stop near the porch steps. The front door was shut, but a window to the front room had been pried up. One length of her smooth blue drapes had been pulled backward through the opening.

Sam bolted from the car, holding the ignition key in front of her like a tiny knife.

Before Sam could reach the door, it burst open. Tim glared at her, big and deceptively debonair-looking in a white sweater, leather jacket, and creased trousers. His face flushed darkly beneath his close-cropped red hair. "Where is it?" he demanded, apparently unconcerned at being caught.

Sam wanted to strangle him. "Where's Charlotte?"

"Hell if I know." He dismissed her with a contemptuous stare, then turned and walked to a small table inside the doorway. He jerked its shallow drawer out of the frame. Roadmaps, batteries, and other small items scattered on the floor. Sam bolted inside. He slung the drawer against a wall. "My mother doesn't give a damn about you," he told her. "She wants the ruby back. I'm not going to put up with you and your lying bitch of a sister. You can't crawl back under my mother's wing and alienate her from me again. I came here to find that stone."

Sam clenched her fists. *"Get out of my house or I'll kill you."*

"You've been taking murder lessons from Jake?"

Sam lurched at him, swinging the hand that held the key. She caught him along the jaw, plowing a jagged furrow as he whipped his head back. He yelled in pain and pinned her against the wall, digging his hands into her arms, lifting her to her toes. "Jake's not coming back," Tim said, his spit flecking her face. He shook her. "Who are you going to run to now? Hmmm? Who'll come after me this time? My mother *owns* you, and Charlotte too. I can do whatever I want. *Now, where's that stone?"*

Sam's long wool skirt was wrapped between her legs. She squirmed. He slammed her against the wall. Her teeth clicked on her tongue, and she tasted blood. She got one leg free and jerked it up, catching him between the thighs. He gagged, staggered back, and dropped her. His face contorted. He drew back one fist.

Sam ducked as his fist grazed the top of her head. He grabbed the front of her coat and wrenched her into place, pulling back his hand again.

Charlotte's warlike scream filled the hallway. She appeared with the full force of a small tornado, launching herself at him. Sam glimpsed the silver flash of a long kitchen knife next to Tim's head.

He fell back against the facing wall, groaning. Blood poured down his neck. He clutched the side of his head and stared at Charlotte, who raised the carving knife to stab him. "I'll make sure you never touch me *or* Sammie again," she shrieked.

Visions of Charlotte killing him propelled Sam forward. She pushed between them and grabbed Charlotte's wrist. Charlotte wrestled blindly with her, but Sam pried the knife out of her clenched hand and faced Tim. He leaned against the wall, dripping blood, his face chalky. Sam jabbed the knife toward his throat. "Move," she yelled.

He backed out, Sam advancing to match every step he took. Blood spurted between his fingers. When he reached the porch steps he turned and stumbled down them. Sam followed him to his car, Charlotte beside her. Sam clutched Charlotte's jacket sleeve with one hand and kept the knife posed in front of them.

Tim staggered to his car, crimson streaks staining the collar of his white sweater, blood speckling the car door as he jerked it open. "She's *crazy*," he yelled, flinging his free hand toward Charlotte. "This time we *will* get her locked up. You can visit Jake in prison and *her* in a mental ward!"

"You're not going to tell anybody the truth about this," Sam answered smoothly. "Because you'd have to admit you were here. And you don't want your mother to know that."

He gaped at her, and she knew she'd made a point he couldn't deny. He cursed viciously and threw himself into his car.

Her feet braced apart, Sam stood in the driveway with the knife raised until he was out of sight. An eerie silence descended. She heard only the sound of her own ragged breathing, and Charlotte's. The knife and her hand were covered in Tim's blood.

Charlotte inhaled sharply. "I fileted him."

Sam pulled her toward the house. They halted inside the hall, staring at the grisly spatters of blood on the wooden floor and log walls. Charlotte yelped and fell to one knee, pointing to a small bloody object on the floor. Sam's stomach twisted when she realized what it was.

Charlotte looked up at her with shaky triumph, then whispered, "I cut off the tip of his *ear*." She scooted back, her hands rising to her throat. "I cut off his ear," she said louder, with a hint of hysteria. "Sammie, I cut off his—"

"*It's done*. Shhh. It's all right." But Sam was already thinking of the consequences.

"It's not all right," Charlotte cried. "I just did a *van Gogh* on him." Sam pulled her to her feet and hugged her. They were both shaking. "Tim won't tell anybody the truth," Sam said.

"Even if he doesn't, he won't just *forget* what we did, what I did. He'll come back."

Sam cried out, overwhelmed by decisions that ripped away the last shred of hope. She pushed Charlotte down the hall. "Go on. All we can do right now is *run*. Grab all the clothes you can carry. I'll get mine. *Hurry*."

Charlotte swung around and stared at her. "We ran once before, and you hated doing it. Sammie, this is your *home*. And Jake—what about Jake?"

Sam's teeth chattered. She wanted to sink to the floor and cover her head, curl up like a child and cry until there was no pain left in her. "He doesn't want me. You understand? I've brought nothing but bad luck to him and his family. He went to see Malcolm Drury because of *me*. He's in jail because of me. He's going to prison because of—"

"He loves you! He wanted you to come here and marry him, and you made him happy—everybody said so! You didn't cause the fire, and you didn't ask him to find Malcolm!"

"It doesn't have to make sense. It hurts too much to make sense." Sam shook her lightly. "Listen to me. We'll go away. We'll go to . . . to California. Aunt Alex can't find us there. I know how I can make money— a lot of money." She thrust her hands into her sister's startled face. "With *these*. These are all I'm worth right now. These will earn a living for us, and pay Jake's legal fees, and the taxes on the Cove."

"But, Sammie, it'll *kill* Jake if he thinks you deserted him."

"He told me to go. I said I'd never do it, but he was right. I have to." Sam's hands fell limply to her sides. She threw her head back. Sorrow overwhelmed her, and she made a guttural sound of defeat mingled with his name.

If you break down, you'll be no good to him, or Charlotte, or yourself. Sam took a deep breath and looked around her with brutal resolve. She would not think of the loom Jake had made for her, of their wedding night in this house, of all the days and nights since, when they'd believed nothing could intrude on this small, contented world of theirs. "Get your things," she repeated. "We're leaving."

Charlotte ran toward her bedroom. Sam walked blindly into hers and Jake's. She threw armloads of her clothes onto the bed, then gathered them inside the beautiful quilt she'd made for him years earlier. Every second was laced with despair. *I'm not deserting you*, she heard herself saying out loud in a hollow voice. *I'll find some way to take care of everything. I swear*.

She thought of the ruby, safely stored in the car, inside her purse. She had brought it to the Cove innocently, and now, not innocent anymore, she was taking it with her. Or it was taking her. And someday she'd come back. So would Jake.

Whether there would be anything left of his love for her, anything for them to share except that stone, she couldn't say.

Before she walked out, she lifted the dreamcatcher from its place on the bedstead's post, kissed it, then put it back.

A part of her was lost forever. She was only nineteen years old, but when she locked the front door behind her and Charlotte, she left the last bit of her young self inside.

Joe Gunther had the keen, disquieting feel of watching a train wreck in slow motion, wanting to stop it but helpless to do anything. There was too much he didn't understand, and what he did understand came from a grandfatherly conviction that he hadn't misjudged the love between two young people he'd known for years.

Sammie hadn't up and run off because she wanted a new life now that Jake was going to be locked away for a long time. It was a hard thing to live with, her knowing Jake was in this mess for something he'd done on her behalf, tracking down the man who'd conned her mother out of money. But Sammie wouldn't have left out of shame. She'd stand up to it, and try to make everything up to him.

Joe had spent too many years watching Jake's uncanny way of finding stones and people not to believe that Jake had some kind of sixth sense. Jake had known when Sammie left.

Joe sat across the table from him in the spare little visiting room, staring at Jake's taped, swollen hands, trying not to think about Jake slamming his fists into the concrete wall of his cell. Joe told him quietly, "I don't know where she was when she called. She said she'd let y'all's lawyer know soon as she and Charlotte get wherever they're headed. She's afraid Alexandra wants to get her hooks in her and Charlotte, with your folks out of the picture, and all. I don't know what made up Sammie's mind. She just said she'd been a fool to think her aunt would let her alone."

Jake's large, hooded eyes met Joe's with a haunted coldness no one could breech. "I told her to go. I told her I didn't love her anymore."

"That's a lie, man."

Jake's big, broken hands flexed hideously on the table. "She'll be safe now. I trust you and Ben Dreyfus to keep it secret—you make sure Alexandra never finds out where she is."

"She said she'll be sending Dreyfus money. And letters. For you."

"I don't want her letters. I'll never give her a reason to come back."

"Are you *trying* to break her heart? You'll be free someday. She'll be waiting. I don't care how long it takes. *That gal will wait for you the way she always has.*"

"It won't be safe for her then either."

Such strange talk reduced Joe to silence. Jake seemed bent on self-destruction. There was something terrible and lonely in Jake, something no one could reach.

*Which of us has not remained forever prison-pent?
Which of us is not forever a stranger and alone?*

*O waste of loss, in the hot mazes, lost, among bright
stars on this most weary unbright cinder, lost! Remembering speechlessly we seek the great forgotten language,
the lost lane-end into heaven, a stone, a leaf, an unfound
door. Where? When?*

*O lost, and by the wind grieved, ghost, come back
again.*

THOMAS WOLFE
Look Homeward, Angel

Part
Three

Chapter
Twenty-five

*T*en years. And all he wanted from her was the ruby.

Sam cried with the kind of helpless defeat she'd never allowed herself to show anyone while he was in prison. She hated losing control. This was not the best she could do. She would not stand there, sobbing, in a beautiful hotel suite she'd selected so carefully, paid for with such pride, and filled with letters and photo albums and her weavings to show him she'd had no life besides her work and waiting for him.

Sam drew on the gritty determination that had saved her from falling apart so many times during the past decade. She wiped her face brusquely and turned around.

Ten years. A small, tormented lifetime had left its mark on her and Jake. She saw it when she looked at her face in a mirror, and when she looked at him now.

She was twenty-nine and he thirty-three. Still young, but withered and untended deep down where it counted, and that showed in their eyes. She grieved for him as well as herself, but sympathy wouldn't get the job done.

If her tears had had any effect on him, she couldn't tell. He watched her with a harsh, haunted expression, as if remembering how loving her had tangled him and his family in a prophecy of destruction. She forced herself to speak calmly to that memory. "I can't change what happened to you because you tried to protect me from Malcolm Drury, but I *will* spend the rest of my life proving that you have something worth coming home to."

Jake stood there, aching inside, wishing he could tell her his worst fear had been that she'd come back while he was still in prison, that Alexandra would find her and take her away from him forever.

I'll always love you, he promised her silently. But if he made one wrong step, if he drew her close to him, he'd lose sight of everything but loving her and wanting to be with her. That blindness would let the old evil slip back into their lives and finish its work.

He never wanted her to know the truth. He could live with it for both of them, but he had to take care of the past first.

The need to hold her, to lose himself inside this sleek, beautiful woman who'd waited for him the way no other woman on earth would have, was so painful, he could barely breathe.

But he'd learned how to ignore pain. He disguised it under layers of quiet rage. Even the hardest bastards in prison had left him alone because he'd given the impression he was too goddamned *calm* not to be dangerous. "This is what you wanted," he said slowly. "I'm here."

That empty vow, delivered between gritted teeth, sank into her like a slap. Sam searched his face, praying she'd find some hint of the husband she still loved, the man she had to believe still loved her. But all he let her see were the changes—the lines deepening around his eyes and mouth, the heavier mantle of muscle on his shoulders, a body that had filled out without an ounce of fat, the unsparing shield of solitude around him.

She held out her hands, inviting him to look at her from head to toe. "You sent me away. You tried to keep me away from you for ten years. But I was always there, paying the bills, working with Ben to get you out, taking care of the Cove—taking care of the ruby. I made a lot of money in California. I paid Charlotte's way through college and sent her to one of the best chef's schools in the country. She's got a great job with a restaurant group in L.A. Alexandra never found us—as far as I know, she doesn't even know I've come back." Sam spread her arms wider. "*Look at me.* You don't have to take care of me anymore. You don't have to fight my battles for me. I'm *not* bad luck." Her voice rose bitterly. "*There is no curse on us.*"

"I have things to do," he said. His voice was low and tight. "All I want is for you to stay out of my way."

If she'd been on shaky ground before, now she had no balance at all. She found herself reaching for the table beneath the room's wall mirror—anything to hold on to. The unbreakable thread of faith stretched back as far as she could remember, and she could be cruel in its defense. "I'm still your wife," she said. "And I have the ruby. When you come back to your senses, I'll give it to you. Not before."

The invisible vibration between them, the war of thready self-control, reached its limit. From the look on his face, she had the horrible feeling he might rip the suite apart, drag her to the bedroom without a shred of affection, or simply turn and walk out. Nothing, at the moment, would surprise her.

"I owe you," he said. "You took care of everything that's important to me. So let's go home. You can pretend the last ten years didn't happen."

A homecoming with a stranger. She loved him so much, she'd hang on no matter what he did or said to her.

≈

"Is he here? Where is he? Where's Sammie?" Charlotte called in a furtive stage whisper, glancing around grimly. She left her rental car sitting under one of the Cove's ancient gnarled oaks and strode to the house, where Ben lounged on the wide plank porch, a baseball cap pulled low on his forehead. The sight of him made her angry and confused about *why* she was always angry at him. She had seen him only a few times in the past ten years, when he'd fly out to L.A. to meet with Sam. But without fail he managed to get further under her skin. Thank God, he didn't treat her like a kid anymore, but now it was worse. He seemed to find everything about her worth commenting on, and not in a good way.

"Calm down," he answered. "The last thing we need around here is a perky little Julia Child bellowing questions." His voice was one of those elegant lowland drawls, the province of old Carolina gentry, as smooth as bourbon. "I thought you swore you'd stay in California. Didn't want to taint Jake and Sam's reunion with your cynical muttering."

He peered at her under the cap, looking like a dapper deadbeat, his legs stretched out, rumpled khaki trousers outlining stocky, muscular legs with bare ankles and polished loafers. He lay with his back against a porch post, his hands folded lazily over a white golf shirt with the collar splayed widely. Dark chest hair peppered with gray peeked between it, making a bed for a tiny gold Star of David on a slim chain.

Only her worry about Jake's arrival kept Charlotte from strangling him. She stopped at the porch steps, hands on hips, armored in a low-cut pink sundress that dared him to stare at her cleavage. "Their reunion?" she echoed with disgust. "What kind of reunion is it when all he can do after ten years is heap more misery and blame on my sister? I called Sammie at the hotel this morning. She sounded like *shit*. When I found out he wouldn't even let her drive him home—that he'd walked out on her, I caught the next plane to Asheville." Charlotte jabbed a finger at Ben. "*You* drove him here, and my sister had to follow—alone—in her own car. Mr. Matchmaker. Mr. Confident. Hell, why don't you just collect the balance of your fee and get out of our lives?"

Ben flicked the brim of his baseball cap up and stared at her with angry gray eyes. His offbeat, ugly/handsome face had never looked more serious. Tremors scattered down her spine. "Get this through your stewbone skull, Chef Ryder. I'm a *friend*, all right? I'm trying to help two people I admire and care about. Two people who have a helluva lot of empty years to overcome. Nobody said it was going to be easy. At least I'm in there pitching for them to be happy. That's more than you've ever done."

"I watched my sister live like a *nun* for ten years," Charlotte replied, her voice simmering with tension. "I watched her write letters to Jake and put them away because he wouldn't even *read* them. I watched her organize her life into a narrow little framework so she'd have no room for close friendships, or temptations from other men, or vacations, or anything else that might have made her life easier—all because she didn't want to have a comfortable life of her own as long as Jake was in prison. She put herself in her own prison." Charlotte's voice rose. "But he didn't *care*. He wouldn't have anything to do with her. He let her suffer."

"You didn't talk to him. You didn't see the look in his eyes every time I mentioned her name. He doesn't blame her for anything. But no man survives prison for as long as Jake did without shutting out a part of himself he loves. And he can't just turn it back on like a water faucet."

Charlotte flung a hand out dismissively. "He could at least manage a drop or two of appreciation."

"Face it, kid. You've got a big emotional investment in this because of your own fears. You don't want to come back here, and you don't want Sam here either. I know why. It has a lot to do with your aunt."

Oh, he knew how to hit home. Charlotte felt every miserable knot twisting inside her. "Our aunt," she said slowly, "has tried to get her clutches into us as long as I can remember. And if you think she's finished, you don't know her the way we do."

"So what is she going to do—creep out of the governor's mansion and descend on her errant nieces like a vampire?" He shook his head, and his eyes narrowed as if he were considering the scene. "The wife of a governor who's being talked up as a candidate for vice president two years from now. The mother of a state senator. Oh, yes, she's going to swoop out of her cave, ready to sink her fangs into a nasty little personal feud that brings up questions about her and the governor's relatives. Trailed by a herd of newspaper and television reporters eager to dig up gossip. Countess Dracula and her untrustworthy tribe of Renfrews. No, I don't think so."

"You don't have the vaguest idea what I went through with her. You don't know everything. Don't lecture me about my feelings. You're pushing forty, and you've never even managed to find a wife. You're no model of emotional maturity."

"Perhaps my role in life is solely to torment you. You seem to think so. Well, fine. I intend to make it very difficult for you to screw up Sam and Jake's chance for happiness with your sincere but misguided bleats about the past."

"I hate you."

"There's a fine line between hate and love."

"*Where are Sam and Jake?* That's all I want to know."

"He headed into the wilderness as soon as he set foot from my wicked chariot," Ben answered dryly. "Sam gave him a ten-minute head start, then followed him like the diligent trooper she is. I hope they're on a mountaintop making mad, passionate love."

Charlotte whirled around and stared at the forbidding forest, her hands clenched. "She'll get lost, and this time he'll let her *stay* lost."

"Sit down and corral your sinister imagination. I've never known two people less likely to lose each other." He waited a beat, then added, "Except for us. A fact which gives me heartburn."

Charlotte sank onto a porch step and decided, shakily, not to speak another word to him.

Sam was no tracker, not like Jake, but she had poignant memories that were better, she hoped, than her tracking skills.

She followed a deer path through dense, old-growth forest just beginning to fill in with spring greenery. Nothing was too absurd for her tortured mind today, not the hope that he was headed for a place that had been special to them, not even the idea that he'd be secretly pleased if he discovered her following him.

Not even if she looked foolish in her yellow, crisply tailored jacket and skirt with sweat soaking her silk blouse, her hose shredded by briars, and her hands covered in heavy leather work gloves. *Oh, yes, I have to protect my hands. They're worth a fortune.*

She congratulated herself for having traded her pumps for jogging shoes. Small evidence of sanity, but she'd take it.

Sam halted suddenly, halfway up a crest where the mountain's stony backbone protruded in great hummocks of granite streaked with white quartz. Her foggy concentration had almost let her clamber right up to Sign Rock. She skirted the crest and climbed through a gnarled rhododendron thicket on its sister ridge. From that vantage point she could look down on the jutting ledge of Sign Rock. *And spy on him,* a weary inner voice rebuked. *I have to know if he went there,* she answered.

Her hair slithering from her neat French braid in tangles around her neck, she crept to the edge of the thicket and scrubbed a gloved hand across her face. Sign Rock was a wide ledge of stone jutting from the mountain's side, with a view of blue-green mountains stretching below it to the horizon. Ancient hands had carved messages into it; mysterious, crisscrossing lines blurred by centuries of patient rain.

God, yes, he was down there, close enough to hear if she gave in to the painful urge to call his name. He stood with his back to her, long legs braced apart among the faded lines, as if he were surveying the edge of the world to prove that there were no more walls in front of him.

Jake had told her the lines pointed the way to the great mother towns of the old Cherokee Nation. A traveler could stand there and see his way home. Towns that were ghosts now, under highways and shopping centers, carved apart by state lines. Towns that had been forgotten except as vague notes in anthropology books.

He had known the name of each one, and she'd listened, fascinated, as he'd described them. It hadn't mattered to her that he was weaving the details only with his imagination. He loved this place, and he had brought her there because he loved her too.

She prayed he'd come there today because he wanted to remember that.

Her breath stalled when he suddenly pried his shoes off and began unbuttoning his shirt. He shrugged it off and tossed it aside, never taking his eyes off the misty ocean of mountains before him. Sam clawed the heavy rhododendron branches aside with drunken, agonized intrigue. She wanted a new imprint of him in her mind, every new mark, every muscle, every inch of skin.

There was something, some dark splotch on one of his forearms. She leaned forward, breathless, straining her eyes to decipher it.

He stepped closer to the rim of the ledge. Terror washed over Sam. Going home. Seeing the way. Remembering. *He wouldn't step off the edge of the world, would he?*

She started down the steep slope, shoving at branches. One whipped back soundlessly and caught her cheek. She recognized the pain only because it made her eyes blur with tears.

Jake pivoted and stared up at her.

She hadn't needed to call his name. He couldn't have heard her movements. But the instant she *hurt*, he'd turned around and looked straight at her. And now she saw the tears on his face.

Sam didn't have time to analyze another mystery on

a day that made no sense. She scrambled down to him gracelessly, sliding on her well-dressed rump the last few inches and collapsing on Sign Rock with her legs folded under her. She tilted her head back and gazed up into his bleak expression. He towered over her, his hands clenched by his sides. Maybe he was furious. Maybe he thought she was pathetic. Maybe he didn't care either way.

But she did. "I was afraid you were going to jump." Her voice echoed. The mountain was throwing her fear back at her.

"If I wanted to give up, I'd have done it in prison." His voice, deep and raw, poured through her. All she could feel at the moment was relief. She shut her eyes and bent her face into her trembling hands. "Thank God."

"I've forgotten what it feels like to make choices. To go wherever I want to. To live without always being watched. I don't want you following me."

She raised her head and looked at him wearily. "There's a part of you I've never understood. I let you keep it to yourself because I thought it didn't hurt anything between us. You used to go off without me. You wouldn't let me watch you track people, or go with you when you dug for gems. You wouldn't let me help you search the ruins of your parents' house—you wouldn't even tell me what you were looking for. And then you went after Malcolm Drury without telling me. I'm not going to let you shut me out again. It *did* hurt us."

"It will hurt more if you don't stop."

"Nothing could hurt more right now. Nothing could hurt more than wanting to touch you and knowing you won't let me."

He dropped to his heels. The look in his eyes made her shiver. She thought of animals who had been caged apart from their own kind in the old zoos. Put them with a mate and they became dangerous, their courtship rituals forgotten in a frenzy of violence or shy bewilderment.

"I thought about you and clawed my skin at night," he said slowly. "To make me stop thinking."

"That's the one thing about your life in prison I understand *perfectly*. Because I've gone through it every night with you." She hesitated, weighing every word. "It could be a starting point now. There doesn't have to be anything pretty about it at first."

"Oh, it wouldn't be *pretty*," he answered with a bitter edge. "And it'd be over faster than you can blink."

"I'll blink slowly and often."

"Tell me the rules, Samantha," he said abruptly. "What do I have to do to earn my keep? How many times a day, and what do you want me to whisper in your ear to make you feel good about it?"

His brutal words numbed her. "I don't think you can get away with it," she whispered tightly. "I think you *know* you'll crack like an oyster the second you touch me. And, mister, when you open up, I'll go pearl hunting."

"You'd come up empty-handed." But that vow didn't register in his eyes. She'd struck a chord, and suspected he knew it. Sam searched his eyes desperately. He *is* still in there, she thought. The man I knew is there. It was the first real victory in a terrible day, the first evidence she wasn't operating on blind hope alone. She had new strength. She could move this mountain. She felt dangerously giddy. Sam jerked her bulky gloves off and held up her hands. "These are good for a lot more than posing for pictures and working at a loom. These can turn you inside out. I've reduced strong men and their cameras to dewy-eyed delight with these hands, without so much as laying a finger on them."

Sam reached out boldly. He flinched but didn't draw back. It was as if he were testing himself. Her fingertips floated a sparse inch from his chest, brushing the fine black hair, trembling, moving across his heart, begging him to lean forward and prove her right. He didn't. But there were invisible tremors in him, a heat wave rising off his skin, making her drunk and reckless. Her hand reached the waist of his trousers, and for one urgent moment she considered unfastening them. No, too easy.

Cruelly easy. She wanted to feel his hand in hers, needed to complete the old circle they'd begun the day a solemn little boy had reached down to a girl who could answer only by taking his hand.

She drew her fingers to his arm. Afraid some flicker of anger in his eyes might break the spell, she followed the course of her hand. Olive skin stretched over sinews and thick muscle, softened by downy hair.

And scarred by that strange new mark she'd tried to decipher before. Sam's fingers curled into her palm. She stared at a blurry blue tattoo. It covered an area the size of her fist. Four lines of Cherokee script, welded into his skin.

Sam raised her startled eyes to his. "Why did you do this to yourself?"

"I had the time." His voice was raw and thready. "All it takes is time and an ink pen."

And the courage to stand the pain, she added silently. He looked away from her and started to reach for the shirt he'd thrown nearby. Sam grasped his wrist. Her fingers reached only halfway around it—a useless manacle if he wanted to pull away. But he froze. The connection held them both in speechless misery. His eyes were riveted to hers again, this time with an intensity that seemed to melt into her. "What have you done?" he whispered, not with accusation. With terrible surrender.

Sam felt dazed. She clung to his arm and forced herself to look at it. One small step at a time. "I . . . did everything that would make me feel closer to you. I am . . . your wife. My name is *Raincrow*. I belong to you. I belong to the people who left their signs on this ledge. I wanted to be able to speak and write their language."

She bent her head over the tattoo. A second later she gave a soft cry and looked up at him again. "*Proverbs*," she said hoarsely. "It says, *Proverbs 31:10*." Sam took his hand in both of hers. "You never forgot. Clara quoted it the day you asked me to marry you. It was the blessing she gave us. The day we knew everything would be all right. '*Who can find a virtuous woman?*'" she recited. "'*For her price is far above rubies.*'"

Whether he realized it or not, his hand curled around hers like a vise. Sam leaned toward him urgently. "If you still believe that, nothing else matters. I'll never forgive myself for what happened to you, but I won't give in to the idea that you'd be better off without me. We had so much to look forward to, and we can have it again."

"You can start by giving the ruby to me. You're wrong if you think it's the only hold you've got on me." When she looked at him hopefully, he added, "I owe you for taking care of the Cove while I was gone."

Sam felt as if he'd slapped her. "It always comes back to the damned stone," she said wearily. "And I'll never understand why. But the answer is still no."

The rest of the answer lay hidden inside her. She would never voice any thought that played into ridiculous fears about forces beyond their control. But the thought was there, taunting her.

The stone was the only thing that could start trouble between them and Alexandra again. Sam could keep it away from her. And her away from Jake.

Give the stone back, and he'd stay because he *owed* her. Keep it, and he'd stay because he *owed* her. Either way was an empty victory. Her way, at least, would protect him from more horrors. Alexandra had not caused his family's death, of course, though Sam felt certain her aunt didn't mourn the tragedy. Alexandra hadn't put Malcolm Drury into Mom's life, hadn't put him in Jake's path finally.

But Alexandra might feed off the past and use it to advantage. Jake had already suffered so much. The fear that he could be drawn into new trouble, this time by Sam's own flesh and blood, overrode everything.

He drew his hand out of hers slowly, and she let him go. Her heart stopped as he brushed his fingertips over her bruised cheek so lightly, he seemed to be drawing the pain out. But the strange mixture of emotions that compelled his sudden gentleness ended when she reached for his hand again.

He rose and stepped back quickly. There was nothing gentle in his face. "You have your rules, I have mine.

Believe this one, because I won't give you a second chance if you break it. There's only one thing that'll make me leave you. And if you do it, I *will* leave, by God, without a backward glance."

Still drugged from his small caress, Sam nodded weakly. "What is it?"

"Don't touch me again. Not for any reason."

He watched her for a moment as if making certain the words had registered. Oh, they had. So strongly, she remembered how it felt to have no voice, to be trapped inside her own small world with nothing but her hands to talk for her.

Now he had even taken that away.

She was on display, and being on display made Alexandra rise to the occasion with expert charm. She believed in the traditional role of the political wife—smile, be a gracious hostess, tirelessly promote her husband's issues, stay in the background, and quietly control far more than the public ever suspected. *She* had paved the yellow brick road to Oz. Orrin was governor because of her work behind the scenes. And Tim, well, Tim was a manageable liability.

She knew how to handle the prowling, eagle-eyed scouts from party headquarters too. The plump-faced man sitting beside her looked impressed. "How long have you had your pilot's license?" he asked over the drone of the Piper's engine.

"A year. Getting it was one of the goals I set for my fiftieth birthday." Alexandra banked the tiny two-seater plane skillfully. "Look to your right. You can just glimpse Pandora in the top of the mountains."

"The governor is very proud of you. He calls you his inspiration."

Alexandra smiled. "Herb, I've been telling you people for years that we're a perfect couple. It's no pretense. No skeletons in our family closet. The party won't find a more promotable family for any, well, let's just say any *special service* the party has in mind." She threw a jaunty glance Herb's way.

The wretched little fanny-kisser gazed at her thoughtfully. "You know we don't enjoy prying into personal backgrounds. It's just that we want to avoid surprises. It's not enough for a potential candidate for national office to measure up politically. The media is so damned *vicious* about digging up gossip. My God, the next thing you know, they'll be doing exposés on the candidates' *pets*. 'Candidate Admits Dog Bit Mailman, Denies Cover-Up.'"

Alexandra laughed. "I have only horses, and they wouldn't *dare* bite the mailman." She brought the Piper closer to the rounded, cloud-shadowed peaks approaching Pandora. "It's a wonder any worthwhile public servants survive the scrutiny. But Orrin and I will, I assure you. Don't pull any punches with me, Herb."

Alexandra didn't wait for him to answer. She wanted to drive her point home with smooth confidence. "Your people have questioned me about my son before. I'll tell you what I've told them. He's doing a good, solid job as a state senator—he's outspoken and aggressive, so yes, he makes enemies. Any good legislator does that. His opponents envy him—I mean, after all, he's a Vanderveer, and that name carries a lot of respect in this state."

"Alexandra, I didn't—"

"I know what they say about him—the lurid stories they pass around about his ear. People are rarely eager to believe the truth when lies are so much more interesting. But the truth is simply that ten years ago he was assaulted in a dark parking lot by two garden-variety thugs looking for a wallet to steal. When Tim refused to cooperate, there was a fight. They ran, and the police were never able to locate them. His poor ear is an honorably won urban battle scar as far as I'm concerned. He keeps his hair long enough to cover the tip. No one even notices it."

"Alexandra, please, I'm not interested in—"

"And as for his failed marriage a few years ago, well, it was a well-intentioned mistake. His wife was a smart young woman from a good family, but she simply didn't realize how much she'd have to put her own ambitions on hold in order to further Tim's." Alexandra sighed. "You can't have two chiefs in a political tribe." Taking a deep breath, Alexandra added quickly, "Tim was heartbroken, but he learned from the experience. He'll remarry. In the meantime, yes, he *is* cutting a wide swath through the female population, but there's nothing notorious about *that*. To be bluntly honest with you, Herb, the media won't catch my son with his pants down."

Herb coughed awkwardly. Alexandra congratulated herself. Just the right touch of earthy honesty tended to assuage his type. "Almost home," she announced cheerfully, pointing toward a tiny airstrip nestled in a mountain plateau. The metal rooftops of several small hangars glinted in the sunshine, and a small private plane ascended from the runway as they watched. "Have I ever mentioned that there was no airport of *any* size between here and Asheville until Orrin and I organized a business coalition to build one? You'll meet some of our VIPs at dinner tonight. They fly in from all over the southeast to spend summers in their homes here. We have quite a social season. Now—any more questions, or have I put your mind at ease about my rambunctious son?"

The man's uncomfortable silence set her nerves on edge. He fiddled with the crease in his tailored slacks. "Alexandra, I didn't come here to ask you about Tim. I came to ask you about your nieces."

She jerked the control, and the Piper bounced on a wind current. "My nieces? Isn't that delving unnecessarily far from the trunk of the family tree?"

"Not these days, I'm afraid." He hesitated. "It's my understanding that your nieces left your home while the younger one was still underage. And that you were her legal guardian. You haven't seen either of your nieces in ten years. I also understand that the older girl married your nephew, and that her husband is serving time in prison on a manslaughter conviction."

"Good Lord, *Herb,* you make it sound as if I've got a hidden batch of incestuous hillbillies. My eldest niece was infatuated with my first husband's nephew. They weren't *blood* cousins."

"Of course, I know that. But—"

"Despite everything I could do to dissuade her, she married him. He was a rough character—part Indian, I suppose that gave him an exotic appeal my niece couldn't resist. I knew it was a mistake, I *knew* the family was unstable, but what could I do about it? Samantha was eighteen; I couldn't stop her. I pleaded with her; I offered her every alternative. But she married this boy and took her younger sister with her. I had a choice between allowing the girl to live with her new in-laws or locking her up like an unmanageable animal."

"But how did circumstances end up—"

"There was a fire. My niece's in-laws were killed. Her husband lost what little common sense he had and immediately became involved with some low-life drug peddler. He killed the man. Orrin and I were, of course, determined to take my nieces under wing again, but they disappeared. We hired detectives, with no luck. Losing contact with them has been one of the great sorrows of my life."

Alexandra hoped the explanation was enough. The truth wouldn't do—the truth was that she'd let Samantha and Charlotte slip away, let them hide, distanced herself from them, so questions about the past would be forgotten.

But those questions were creeping into her life, now.

"Your niece divorced her husband?"

"She's had no contact with him over the years, thank God. I learned that much. He's still in prison. I can't imagine that she's waited for him all these years. She was so young. They'd been married less than a year when he was sentenced."

Alexandra's stomach was in knots, her palms sweating on the plane's controls. It was unthinkable that Jake and Sam could resurface together and pose any threat to her neatly manicured family history. "Herb," she said as casually as she could, "are you telling me the party might have second thoughts about Orrin because of some old family notoriety concerning my nieces?"

"I'm saying only that we're a tad paranoid about even the smallest possibility of character assasination. We're looking for *saints*, Alexandra. That's what it takes these days to keep the political wolves at bay and the party's extremists happy."

"Tell me what you want. Give me your best-case scenario."

"A warm reunion with your nieces. The loving aunt welcoming back her only sister's children, who've put their youthful rebellion behind them and now see the light. And no convict nephew-in-law. People can sympathize with your niece's impetuous marriage—and with her divorcing her husband after he killed a man."

"If that's what you want, that's what you'll get. I've got two years before the ninety-six convention. I promise you, I'll get it done. Excuse me, I've got a plane to land."

Alexandra was glad to end the conversation. She had no idea how she'd locate Samantha and Charlotte, but felt confident she'd think of something. And as for Jake—she had dealt with him before successfully, and if any threat still existed, she'd deal with him again. She brought the Piper in for a smooth landing, gliding to a stop near the limousine she'd ordered.

Barbara, elegant and helpful as always, her dark face marred by worried eyes, hurried over and greeted them. "My longtime personal assistant," Alexandra said to Herb with watchful aplomb. She might have disreputable nieces but, by God, she had a politically correct secretary.

As the chauffeur took Herb and his luggage to the car, Alexandra drew Barbara aside. "What's wrong? Tell me quick, before that nosy little *troll* wonders what we're whispering about."

Barbara looked morose and fearful. "Jake Raincrow was released from prison today."

"Why? How?"

"Time credited for good behavior, or something like that."

"Oh, my God," Alexandra said under her breath. "Well, it's for the best. Gives me more time—"

"Mrs. Lomax, I hate to tell you the rest."
Alexandra stared at her. "What?"
"Samantha is back too."
Alexandra's hands rose to her throat. "And?"
"They're together at the Cove."

Chapter Twenty-Six

"*Are you stalking me? Is this how lawyers get their jollies?*"

Charlotte's voice rang out with tired exasperation as Ben closed the door of a customized Jeep and ambled into her patch of yard, stepping lazily through neat, manicured rows of brightly blooming azaleas. She bit her tongue immediately and looked around angrily, as if the class police might march out of the forest and haul her away. There was probably a rule against yelling like a street whore from the doorway of a pricey condominium. People in this resort development on the outskirts of Pandora yelled only when the golf pro was late for their lessons.

He scowled at her. "I set my hook. Now I'm letting you play out the line."

He fit in with the surroundings far better than she, with his khakis and golf shirts, though he wore a dingy fishing cap with a lure pinned to the crown. He was, in fact, disastrously appealing. She glared at him from her doorway, wearing tight white leggings and an oversize T-shirt with the Cordon Bleu emblem on it. "Does your family know your hobby is fishing for heathen women?"

He halted on the cobblestone before her entrance and studied her with half-shut eyes, his head tilted back, the cap's brim pulled low. "At this point in my nearly middle-aged bachelorhood," he drawled in his dignified way, "the Dreyfus dynasty would be ecstatic if I reeled in anything short of a Palestinian terrorist."

"Wait a second. I'll get out my flattery meter and decide whether that registers as a compliment. What are you doing here?"

"I know all, I see all," he intoned. "Sam said you'd come here this morning to sublet a furnished condo. I realized immediately that you were setting up a base of operations from which to spew wisdom. That decision requires my attention. Hah! Thought you'd slip away from me, did you?"

She gritted her teeth. "Look, you jackass, I don't need your permission to stay around here."

"Oh, I'm glad you're staying. It's one of my fondest nightmares come true. I simply want to know what's draining through that sievelike mind of yours. What you're up to."

"Taking a little vacation. Sam didn't want me to stay at the Cove—she's trying her damnedest to have private time with Jake. And God knows I didn't want to stay there. Not with Jake camped out in a *tent* at the old housesite. I thought nothing could go worse than it already has, but seeing him turn his back on my sister—again—is more than I can take."

"I don't like it either," Ben admitted. "But at least they're within shouting distance of each other."

"That's too close." Charlotte's stomach twisted. She was being bitchier to Ben than usual, because she was upset. "He *hit* her when she followed him the other day, Ben. I don't care what she told us—she's got a black eye!"

Ben gaped at her. "Oh, for the love of—he'd never hit her. You think your sister would lie about something like that?"

"I think she's so desperate to pretend he still loves her that she'd lie down and let him walk on her if he asked."

"He does love her." Ben stared at her pensively. "Take it from a man who recognizes repressed emotions. But he's got to have time to work out whatever it is that happened between them. I don't know everything he's thinking. But I've watched him suffer for ten years, and I don't doubt that he's where he needs to be, and where he wants to be."

"*Alone*," Charlotte retorted. "Alone in a tent on the spot where Sarah and Hugh and Ellie died. It's the most morbid—Ben, he wants to wallow in the past. And he wants Sam to wallow with him. He's punishing her. It's like he wants to break her heart because he'd gotten hurt for defending her honor. As if Sam asked him to go toss our mom's shitty boyfriend off a balcony."

Ben was shaking his head before she finished, his mouth open in a grimace of disgust. "You just don't get it, do you? It doesn't matter what you believe about his motives. All that matters is that Sam is hanging on to their future by all ten glorious fingernails. You could do so much more to help her if you'd stop fighting the situation. You're the most vividly passionate person I know. Full of energy. Creative. Fiercely loyal." He frowned and looked away, as if verging on a compliment disturbed him. It certainly disturbed Charlotte. She felt too vulnerable when he talked this way. "Put your talents to good use, blondie," he added gruffly. "Don't spit in your sister's stew."

So much for compliments. Charlotte squinted at him, then waved a hand at the handsomely furnished living room behind her. "I set up a refuge for her. A place she can come to whenever she feels lonely. Which is most of the time. *I'm on her side. I'm a realist.* All you've ever done is encourage her to believe in something that doesn't exist anymore."

"I doubt she'll seek consolation and advice from a sister whose experience with affairs of the heart wouldn't fill a demitasse."

"I've had plenty of experience."

"Oh, yes? Sam confided to me once that your conquests favor middle-aged *sous-chefs* who are harmless enough to bully."

"I like men who are mature enough to be——"

"Harmless," he repeated. "Grateful. As pliable as an egg custard."

Charlotte turned and reached for the door to pull it closed in his face. "I'm *so* glad you took the time from your busy schedule to drop by and lecture me—again."

"Just fishing," he said smoothly.

"I hope you wade into a pool of piranhas." She had the door half shut when a golf cart rumbled up to the cobblestone sidewalk and the resort manager, dressed in tennis whites, waved at Ben. "I've got your keys, Mr. Dreyfus. Sorry to keep you waiting."

Keys? Ben took them from the woman with a small, gentlemanly nod. He held them up like a fine trout he'd hooked, and smiled at Charlotte. "Hello, piranha," he said drolly. "I'm taking a little vacation too. I've leased the condo next door."

The clatter of the loom hypnotized Sam, and she needed the easy, productive rhythm. It should have felt so *good* to be home again, to have the dust and cobwebs cleared out, the electricity on, the curtains and linens and rugs washed clean of mothball scents. It should have felt wonderful to work at the loom Jake had made for her and know she was picking up the threads of their lives.

But the month since Jake's homecoming had only proved how frayed those threads were. Now she and Jake were hermits living in separate caves. Apparently he didn't want to venture out of the Cove or into her sight. It had hurt more than she could put into words when he'd given Ben a list of supplies he wanted, including a tent. Chills ran through Sam every time she thought of him sleeping where his family had died. He wanted to be close to ghosts, not to her.

And if she touched him, he'd leave. She didn't doubt it.

When she heard the rumble of a car, she jumped up with nervous expectation. Charlotte and Ben visited every day, but Charlotte morosely kept to the kitchen, as if cooking were the only support she could bring herself to offer. Ben, carrying fishing tackle and a reel, wandered over to see Jake, but reported nothing more helpful than the size of the trout that eluded him in the Saukee. He fished, and Jake let him. No revelations there.

But today was different. She knew who was coming to visit, and it wasn't Charlotte and Ben.

Sam removed the thin cotton gloves she wore when she worked at the loom—calluses had to be avoided—wiped her sweaty palms on her jeans, and ran to the porch. Goose bumps rose on her arms beneath her plain white shirt, not from the cool spring afternoon.

Joe Gunther's big luxury sedan purred into the yard. The sight of his jowly, friendly old face brought tears to Sam's eyes. And Clara peered out the passenger window stoically, her long hair gone completely white now, her brown face an accordion landscape of wrinkles, her dark eyes peeking out among the folds like polished brown marbles.

Sam ran to Joe as he lumbered around the front of the car, his beefy arms spread. He still dressed like Roy Rogers with a jewelry fetish, a silver and turquoise bolero at his collar, every finger flashing a ring. Sam returned his hug, struggling not to cry. She had never known any of her grandparents. Joe and Clara filled that place in her life.

"Well, Miss Sammie," Joe said gruffly, stepping back from her and studying her with misty eyes. "You got him home, just like I knew you would."

Sam cleared her throat roughly. "He's not really home," she admitted in a small voice. "But at least he's nearby."

"I'd have traipsed down here sooner if you'd given the go-ahead. Me and Clara."

"I know. I was trying to give him some . . . some settling time. But it looks like he's as settled as he's going to get." She nodded toward the forest. "He's over there. He stays over there."

"Aw, Sammie, it won't be for long. He's just got to get his lungs full of fresh air. Remember how to breathe."

"I hope you and Clara can help." Sam opened the passenger door, stepped closer, and dropped to her bare heels. Clara was as solid and round as the mountains, a loose denim shirt flowing over her long, flower-print skirt. Somber affection glowed in her eyes. She raised a hand from her broad lap and stroked Sam's hair. "You're a grown woman inside and out now," Clara said gently. "It suits you."

"Oh, Clara, I don't feel grown. I just feel older." Clara touched the purple streak along her right cheekbone with her skilled, soothing old fingers. "He didn't do it," Sam said evenly. She glanced over her shoulder at Joe, who was also studying her face worriedly. "Prison hasn't turned him into that kind of man."

Joe sighed and looked relieved. Clara spoke softly. "It ain't you he's at odds with. It never was."

"I wish I believed that. If it's not me, then what is he afraid of?"

"Ravenmockers," Clara whispered.

Sam bit her tongue. There was no point in arguing with Clara. Rising to her feet, she offered Clara an arm. "Let me help you out of the car."

"I'm not that old." Clara peered at her shrewdly and hoisted herself from the seat. "You seen your aunt yet?"

"No. I suppose we'll cross paths eventually."

"Oh, you will."

"Look who's here," Joe said in a hushed tone.

Sam turned quickly, her heart in her throat. Jake walked out of the woods. She had seen him so little since his first day at home; all the hours of waiting, of thinking about him, welled up inside her like a painfully hungry dream. If she wanted him too much, she'd wake up. He wouldn't come to see *her*, but somehow he'd known they had visitors.

"He's a sight for sore eyes," Clara whispered to her. "Even if he moves like there's still bars around him. Look at him, Sammie. Don't never let him forget you're on the other side of them bars. He'll find his way out."

Joe moved forward and met him, extending one hand. Sam's heart broke at the strained expression on Jake's rugged face; it was as if he feared he'd wake up too. Slowly he grasped Joe's hand. Joe had tears in his eyes. He pumped Jake's hand, then abruptly slung his other arm around Jake's shoulders and hugged him.

Sam's breath caught. Jake stiffened inside the older man's awkward embrace, his jaw worked, and he turned his face away. Joe cleared his throat and stepped back. When he did, Jake looked at him with a flash of affection that was gone as quickly as it came.

"Let me at him," Clara snarled under her breath. She shuffled over with ponderous speed, her gnarled hands rising. Jake glanced at Sam, and for one second, as their eyes met, she was certain she saw some of the old tenderness. Then it was gone, and he was gazing down at Clara, who took his face between her hands.

Jake was glad for any distraction that eased the overwhelming pull Samantha had over him. And desperately glad for an excuse to walk into this yard and be with her. *Do you still love your wife?* Clara whispered to him in Cherokee.

Jake nodded slowly. Clara, of all people, should understand. *With all my heart. I stay away so she won't get hurt by what I have to do.*

You need her. You can't fight a ravenmocker alone.

I have to. There are reasons.

Then I'll sit by your fire later, and you tell me.

I will.

Clara patted his face, then moved her hands down his arms, squeezing, studying him shrewdly. "Strong," she announced in English, nodding over her shoulder to Samantha and Joe. "They fed him well."

"Looks like you been lifting weights," Joe said gruffly. He nodded to Samantha too. Jake thought with fragile amusement that they seemed eager to confirm, for her, that his spirit must have survived safely inside such a hard cocoon.

But Samantha made a soft, distressed sound that nearly tore him apart. "They used him like a trained animal. They hauled him out every time a sheriff needed a tracker." Jake flinched. Her anguished gaze settled on his with apology. "I know. Ben told me."

Jake struggled with emotions he had subdued for years. He didn't want to share those empty years with her—he wanted to forget them. Instead, he wanted Samantha to fill him up with every detail of her time alone. "I find people," he said brusquely. "It's what I do."

Joe interjected quickly, "Don't see how you accomplished much without old Bo."

Sam remembered the other reason Joe had come today. She whirled around, staring at the car. "*Bo.*" She jerked the rear door open and stared inside. "*Bo.*"

"He's not dead. He's asleep," Joe called. "He's an old dog. He sleeps most of the time. And snores too."

Sam knelt by the open door. Bo was stretched out on the plush leather seat. When she called his name again brokenly, he raised his head. His jowly face was brindled with gray. He had a cataract on one eye, and he tilted his head, studying her with groggy disinterest with his good eye. She couldn't find a shred of recognition in it. *He won't recognize Jake either*, she thought. Her heart sank.

Suddenly she was aware of Jake's footsteps behind her. The knowledge that he was standing there, his denimed leg almost brushing her shoulder, made her want to wrap her arms around his knees and beg him not to expect too much from an old dog who'd never been very alert anyway.

"Hello, old friend," he said. The hoarse sound of his voice ripped into her. She would give anything to have him speak to her with that much welcome.

Bo lurched upright. His long, thick tail wagged madly, swaying his lanky, arthritic body. He bounded past her, whining, and landed in an undignified heap on the ground in front of them, knocking into Sam. She sat down hard. Jake dropped down beside her. Bo scrambled into Jake's arms and began licking his face.

Tears slid down Sam's face as she watched Jake pet him. She couldn't be jealous of an old dog, not when he'd brought the first glimmer of a smile to Jake's mouth. But, oh, how she wanted to take Bo's place then. "You can trust Bo," she said. She scratched Bo behind one floppy red ear. "Bo didn't forget you either."

Jake looked at her over the dog's head, his eyes sad and intense, searing her. Did he realize how he was looking at her—how openly greedy it was? She clung to the sight, hypnotized by the vivid hunger, the intimacy, unable to do anything but absorb him as he was absorbing her.

Her hand was inches from his, reaching toward his fingers as if he were a magnet. *Don't touch him. Don't give him an excuse to leave.* She jerked her hand back and looked away, trembling, miserable.

Jake did the same.

Smoke curled upward from the campfire and mingled with the blue-gray cloud around Clara's head. Seated on a wide, low stump with her skirt spread around her in queenly style, she puffed on a long-stemmed pipe, cradling its smooth soapstone bowl in her knotty fingers. With her other hand she guided the fragrant tobacco smoke over her head.

Jake sat cross-legged next to her, staring into the fire. She handed the pipe to him and he copied her. With this ancient sacred ceremony he was calmed and strengthened, welcomed home by dreams the smoke carried into the invisible stream of past, present, and future. He breathed his promises into those currents.

Clara took the pipe again, emptied the bowl into the fire, and watched the flames. "Tell me what you've kept secret all these years," she said. "Tell me what you know."

"Alexandra killed my family. She sent that man here. He hated me, and she knew it. I was the one who found him and sent him to prison. I knew he'd stolen from Samantha's mother. Alexandra sent him to do that too."

Clara's eyes narrowed. She absorbed the startling information in troubled silence, as if nothing surprised her. "I see," she said finally. "And you learned these things the way you always have."

He nodded grimly. "Without any way to prove them. And wishing they weren't true."

Clara sighed. "They would break Samantha's heart."

"Yes."

"But they are breaking yours already. Hatred and revenge are ravenmockers too. They'll eat you up."

"If revenge were all I cared about, it would be easy. A gun. My bare hands." He looked at her with deadly calm. "I've lived with murderers. Killing is easy when you don't love anything or anyone, including yourself."

"Hmmm. But you do love."

"I love Samantha. I want our life back. Without shadows over it."

"Then tell her what you know. And how you know it."

"Ask her to believe in something that would shame her the rest of her life, something I can only *feel*?"

"You're not so afraid she wouldn't believe you. You're afraid she *will*. Because she couldn't rest until she punished her aunt. But ain't that her right? You can't take away the shadow over her. Only she can do that."

"You told me, more than once, not to draw a ravenmocker's attention," he said, his voice low and strained. "I learned that lesson finally. I've learned how to use my . . . *gift*. It cuts both ways. I can use it to hurt people, and this time I will."

Clara drew back, looking angry and alarmed. "You learned nothing. Why do you think the stone stopped talking to you when you was just a boy? You do what's right—you open your heart to your wife, and she'll do right by you too. She's wise to keep the stone away from you. When your mind is clear, she'll give it back. Then you can listen to it. It will speak to you. Then you'll know what to do."

"I already know what to do. I've had years to work on it. Other things speak to me."

Clara shook her head furiously and gestured toward Bo, who was stretched out, asleep, on Jake's sleeping bag beside the fire. "You're as bad as old Bo. Only seeing with one eye. Only seein' what's straight in front of you. That's not enough."

"The fucking hell it isn't." Jake took a deep breath and shut his eyes. Shame twisted his stomach. This was how much he'd changed. Talking this way to an elder, a medicine woman. He bent his head to Clara's knees with silent apology.

She sighed heavily and patted his head. "That was prison talkin'. My brother give me a VCR a few years ago. I rent movies. I've heard worse."

"Not from me before. Not ever."

She took him by the chin and raised his head as if he were a young boy. He opened his eyes and found grim sorrow in her watchful scrutiny. "I told Granny Raincrow I'd look out for you and Ellie," she said. "I ain't done a very good job of it. If you're set on doing something crazy, I ain't goin' to turn my back on you."

"I need your help." He reached behind him and pulled a thick brown envelope from a backpack. "I want you to mail this for me."

Clara bent over and eyed the address in the firelight. "What business you got with the big newspaper in Raleigh?" Her mouth worked silently, mental wheels turning as she glanced from the envelope to him. "Your granny used to get feelings off of pictures in the paper. Like who was lying, and who was scared, and who had something to hide. She always went over pictures before she'd go to vote."

"It works," Jake answered carefully. "Real well."

Clara stared at him, then at the envelope again. "Ain't got a return address on it."

"Or anything else that will tell where it came from. Or who."

She took the envelope by her tobacco-stained finger-tips that had coaxed babies into the world, healed the spiritually wounded, and waved witches away from help-less souls. "If you're messin' with Alexandra and her folks, she'll find out."

"There's no way she'll find out." Jake leaned back and looked into the fire with bitter satisfaction. Hidden and treacherous. Not a proud revenge. Not one that would clear his name or tell the world what Alexandra Vanderveer Lomax had done to him and everyone he loved. But one that would quietly strangle her with her own ambitions. When he finished with her, she wouldn't be a threat to him or Samantha anymore. Samantha would never find out he'd been involved, or why.

And then they would have a future.

Chapter
Twenty-Seven

"This is such an *honor*. I was so thrilled when you agreed to drop by and discuss your work. I mean, having a member of the governor's family sell her creations through my gallery—well! It would be quite a coup." The brightly dressed woman fussed around Sam as if the mere sight of her would swell the gallery's reputation.

Sam smiled vaguely, twisting her hands around a thick portfolio until her knuckles ached. So the word was out. Whether she liked it or not, the well-heeled social set in Pandora valued her for her connection to Alexandra and Orrin. Alexandra was influencing her life again, though Sam still hadn't seen her.

"You never explained how you heard about me," she told the woman carefully.

"Oh? Didn't I mention that your aunt has been raving about you? She's so proud of you." The woman smiled at Charlotte. "And you also, of course." Charlotte stood beside Sam, wearing a shapeless pink jumper, her attitude hidden behind black sunglasses. Charlotte carried a second photo album. "I bet," Charlotte answered dryly.

The gallery owner looked at her askance. Sam shot Charlotte a warning look, and Charlotte clamped her mouth shut. Aunt Alex, *raving* about them? That made no sense, and worried her. Sam turned her attention to the woman again. "I assure you, my tapestries will sell on their own merits."

The large shop on Pandora's main street was filled with paintings and sculptures. Sam glanced around at the polished wood floor, demure, creamy walls, and delicate track lights overhead. The place was filled with paintings and sculptures. No cracker-barrel work by local artists, no farm scenes painted on logging saws, no ceramic cookie jars in the shape of Santa Claus. No, this was *fine* art, which meant plenty of indecipherable watercolors and porcelain blobs masquerading as nude studies. A cool, spotless, whispering sort of place that made her skin itch under her jeans and silk blouse. *I should have worn overalls and a tractor cap,* she thought grimly. *Just to cause more gossip.*

But she needed an outlet for her work, needed to settle into a semblance of a new life here. It was another way of showing Jake that their lives could return to normal.

"Well, dear," the owner said, "what kind of little weavings do you do?"

Charlotte leaned in front of Sam. "*Little weavings?*" she repeated darkly. "Lady, her *little weavings* are one-of-a-kind collector's items. The list of people who own her *little weavings* includes more than a few names you've seen in movie credits."

Sam jostled Charlotte out of the way. "I had a loyal following in California."

The woman looked flustered. "Why, I . . . I knew only that you were some sort of model." Her eyes skittered over Sam's face and body with a furtive assessment Sam had encountered often over the years. The kind of scrutiny that said *They must perform miracles with lighting and makeup*.

"I'm a hand model," Sam explained wearily. She raised one hand, which was covered in a white cotton glove. "Commercials and print ads. A few films. When an actress has stubby fingers with chewed nails, I'm called in to substitute for her hands in closeups."

"That's amazing! The only thing they photograph are your hands?"

"I'm a spare part. It's a living." Sam tapped the portfolio. "This is my real work. What I hope to concentrate on now."

She started to launch into a list of interior decorators who'd represented her tapestries in Los Angeles, but the shop door opened.

Alexandra walked in. Sam froze. Dimly she heard Charlotte's sharp inhalation, an anxious hiss of surprise.

Their aunt had weathered the years well. Her Barbie-doll face had softened except for the cool, shrewd blue eyes. She was thicker around the waist and hips, but still trim. There was the look of well-preserved youth about her, an athletic elegance under her pale green jacket and straight-legged trousers. The honey-gold scarf tucked smoothly under the jacket's plain neckline matched the color of her shoulder-length hair. Everything about her breathed money and style, pride, self-assurance.

And she'd ambushed them.

"Surprise!" she said happily, smiling. "I thought I'd come by and talk both of you into having lunch with me."

Ten years, a history of ruthless manipulation, no love lost between them, and she acted as if nothing had happened. Stunned, then instantly wary, Sam studied her speechlessly. Alexandra waltzed over to her, slid a slim arm around her shoulders, then smiled at the gallery owner. "I'm hijacking them, Darla. Forgive me."

"Oh, certainly, Mrs. Lomax. Samantha, just leave your albums. We can talk later. I don't have the slightest doubt that we can do business."

Sam handed her the portfolio, took the other one from Charlotte's stony clutches, and set it on a table. "Thank you." She turned to Alexandra, meeting her inscrutable blue gaze with one just as unswerving. "Yes, let's do lunch."

Alexandra smiled wider. It didn't reach her eyes. "Marvelous. Come along. I have a driver waiting." She glanced toward Charlotte. "There's a first-class little restaurant on the lake. You'll love it."

"Sammie," Charlotte said, her voice vibrating with anger.

"We'll follow you in my car," Sam said.

"Oh, no, that would be pointless. Please—"

"I'm short on time. I told Jake I'd be back soon." A wistful, unremorseful lie. Jake disappeared into the mountains beyond the Cove every day. He didn't know or care where she went, or if she ever returned.

Alexandra's smile hardened at the edges. "All right," she said slowly. "I wouldn't want to upset Jake."

She had left the front door unlocked. The instant he touched it he'd sensed that she always left the door that way for him.

Jake moved through their house, the house he'd built for Samantha, for the children they should have had by now, the unknown children who whispered to him when he slept. He hoped they were more than dreams. He couldn't see the future.

This was the first time he'd set foot in their house since he'd come home. Like Samantha, it brought him too close to surrender. He'd waited until she'd gone up to town. Just this once, alone, he would indulge the raw, desperate hunger to share her life.

He went slowly through each room, running his hands over the familiar furniture, remembering the sight of her sitting at her loom, of her stretched out on the couch wearing nothing but one of his thin T-shirts, of her standing by the windows in the big front room, delicately silhouetted by sunlight. Of shy mornings at the kitchen table, when they had glanced at each other and then away, smiling.

He walked into their bedroom but couldn't bear to touch the bed. The quilt she'd made for him long before they'd married was neatly arranged on it. The dreamcatcher he'd made for her still hung on one rounded, knobby bedpost. His hunger was painful, a frenzy that broke cold sweat on his face. He lay awake at night and thought about her here, in their bed, dragging her hands over her body in the same bereft, frantic way he touched his own.

He glimpsed himself in a full-length mirror beside the dresser and stared. He saw a stranger with haunted eyes under unkempt black hair, high cheekbones sunken and shadowed by beard stubble, a hard face. He saw big shoulders hunched in an attitude of perpetual intimidation, a sweat-soaked gray football jersey with the sleeves torn out at the shoulders, thick arms that ended in big-knuckled hands, the crude blue tattoo. He saw dirt-stained jeans stretched tight over a blatant, rigid outline.

This was how Samantha saw him too. But she still left the door unlocked.

He turned and left the room, feeling his way blindly. When his head cleared, he was standing before the closed door of a spare bedroom. Closed doors made him feel restless, angry, even when he was outside them. He shoved the door open.

The small room was crammed, floor to ceiling, with cardboard boxes. She'd left narrow aisles between the stacks; he had to angle his shoulders to slide between them. She'd labeled the contents of each box on one side, with methodical care, in thick black marking pen. On one side of the aisle he counted a dozen marked Sweaters, and five marked Shirts—Casual.

He felt troubled, bewildered. This clothes hoarding was something new, something she'd never done before. Of course she'd had a comfortable life in California, one he'd spent the years trying to picture with endless dedication. What had he wanted—for her to live like a nun in his honor? No, he'd wanted her to survive, to be happy.

But he hadn't pictured her going on shopping sprees.

Angry at her, angry at himself for condemning whatever had given her pleasure, he pulled a box from the top of one stack, dropped it unceremoniously, and squatted on the heels of his dusty hiking boots before it. Nice boxes, with removable lids. Frowning, he pushed the lid aside. *Sweaters*. He spoke the word under his breath as if it were nasty, then sank both hands into the careful folds of a luxurious black pullover with a wide band of gold around the shoulders.

The instant he touched it, he knew. It was for him, not her. A vivid scene flashed in his mind. One of those expensive shops for men's clothing, her standing at a darkly paneled counter with this sweater in her hands. Christmas garland on the counter's edge. Her eyes sad and tired. Buying a Christmas present she couldn't give to him, pretending he was with her.

And he had been, even if she didn't know it. His throat ached. He closed the box and put it back in place, then moved among the rest, pulling them down, opening them with shaking hands. Trousers. Jeans. Ties. A leather jacket. A camel-hair coat. Boxes filled with colognes. Boxes filled with belts, suspenders, handkerchiefs. Even socks and underwear.

Ten years of clothing for an invisible man.

"She set us up," Charlotte said again as Sam parked the car in the graveled lot before a delicate whitewashed house huddled in a grove of tall firs by the lake. Their aunt's sedan already sat by the entrance. A driver in suit and tie held the car door for her. Alexandra rose gracefully from the backseat, then looked over at them.

Sam gritted her teeth. "I know she did. She wanted that woman to think we're one happy trio. As if this isn't the first time we've seen her since we came home."

"This isn't *home*." Charlotte slung a large leather purse over one shoulder, jerked her sunglasses off, and stared at Sam hard. "It stopped being home the day the

Raincrows died. We never should have come back. She won't let us alone. You'll always be caught between her and Jake."

Sam gripped her hands. "I don't want any more trouble. The past is finished, you hear? We're not kids now. She has no control over either of us—no control over how I lead my life, or over Jake. I'm going to put an end to any doubts about that. I'll do as I please and be perfectly civil to her whenever our paths cross." Sam tugged at Charlotte's steely fingers. "I'm not going to worry about Tim either. He's got too much at stake in his political career to risk stirring up an old feud. I know you're afraid of him. He won't bother us. I promise you."

Charlotte sagged a little. "Sammie, I came back here because of *you*. You're the only family I care about."

"Then help me move forward. I can't fight everyone—you, and Alexandra, and Tim, and Jake too. The past can't hurt us. Jake has to believe that, or we'll never—" Her throat ached, and she had to stop.

"Okay, Sammie, okay." Charlotte squeezed her hands worriedly, but looked over at their aunt with narrowed eyes. "I hope you're right."

"Well, ladies." Alexandra leaned back in a wicker chair and studied them. Her voice had a measured tone, as insidious as acid etching its way into glass. The time for a reckoning had come. They were alone in a room that overlooked the lake, at a table set with linen and crystal and a bouquet of jonquils in a bud vase. "The last time I saw you, we'd made a rather nice truce. I thought we had some peaceful times ahead of us. But then you left without a word to me. Was it that hard, Samantha? Was the idea of accepting my help so repugnant to you, really?"

Sam thought of the day they'd left, of Tim, of scooping the tip of his ear into a plastic soup bowl and tossing the bowl into a dumpster along the road outside town. And she thought of Jake's anger when he'd heard about her deal with Alexandra—of Jake rejecting her, sending her away with his beloved ruby in safekeeping. A lot of murky water churning under the bridge that day.

"I decided I'd try to get a modeling contract in Los Angeles," she answered smoothly. "I couldn't go without taking Charlotte, and I knew you had a . . . responsibility . . . to keep Charlotte with you."

"Did it ever occur to you that I was worried *sick*? That I had no way of knowing if either of you were all right? You could have ended up in a gutter somewhere."

"But we didn't." Sam removed her gloves and spread her fine-boned hands on the white tablecloth. "The day we got to L.A. I walked into one of the biggest modeling agencies in the country. I showed them the jewelry brochure I'd made. They took one look at my hands and offered me a contract. Call it dumb luck, but that's the way it happened. They advanced me the deposit for an apartment. I went to work and made five thousand dollars the first *month*."

"You could have stayed in Pandora. I told you I'd pay your bills. You could have been near Jake in prison—I'd have had Orrin speak to the authorities. Conjugal visits, special privileges. Didn't you ever think of that?"

Since Sam wasn't going to tell her how things stood between her and Jake, she didn't answer. Charlotte had been twisting a napkin as if trying to wring blood from it. She smoothed it on the table. "Jake understood," she said sweetly. "He wrote to Sammie every day."

Sam stiffened. Alexandra looked at her skeptically. "And how is Jake?"

"As fine as a man can be after spending ten years in a cage."

"I'll tell you what I think." Alexandra stroked one fingertip along the table's edge, as if outlining her thoughts. "I believe you left because you were ashamed of him."

Sam leveled a harsh gaze at her. "No."

"Oh, I know you're a very loyal person. You wouldn't divorce him. You wouldn't admit that his recklessness and his violence frightened you, that he'd ruined your life, your reputation. So you fled to California, hoping he'd forget you." She leaned forward. "Samantha, you don't have to stand by him now. He's a free man. He can take care of himself."

It took all Sam's willpower to continue sitting there. *I want peace*, echoed through her mind. *No more hard feelings. No more old feuds.* "I love him. And he still loves me. The day he came home was the happiest day of our lives."

One unerring truth, one ragged hope, and one enormous lie.

Alexandra's eyes bored into her. "I heard that you were seen in town not long after he returned. With a bruise under one eye."

"I had an accident."

"Did you?"

"Jake didn't hit her," Charlotte said evenly, though she looked out the window as she said it. Her gaze swung back to Alexandra's. "She's like me. She'd never put up with a man who treats women that way."

The pointed reference to Tim wasn't lost on their aunt. Her face tightened. But she continued to train her attention on Sam. "You've made a great success of your life. I'm very proud of you. You have the look of a woman who has good taste, and class, and *substance*, a woman who's grown accustomed to certain refinements. And what have you come home to? A log house in the middle of a wild cove, and a husband who has a criminal record. A husband whose closest companions have been murderers and rapists and child molesters. A man who will never quite be clean again. A man who has quite likely been damaged in ways that no one, not even you, can overcome."

Sam struggled with the frayed limits of her patience. A cruel inner voice taunted her. Maybe it was true, that Jake would never be the same again. But she couldn't believe that, couldn't let her aunt's insight weaken her determination. "I won't even try to explain why you're wrong about him. But you *are* wrong. You can't change me. You can't change my decisions. If that's all you've been waiting for, you're going to be disappointed."

"Can you honestly tell me you never looked at another man while Jake was gone?"

"Oh, I looked. But that's all I did."

"Ten years. The prime of your youth. Without intimacy, without companionship, without children. Has Jake made that up to you? Can he *ever* make that up to you?"

"He already has, just by coming home."

"Samantha, don't misunderstand me. I want you to be happy. I'm afraid pride is holding you to a husband who no longer exists. *I'm on your side.* I will help you discreetly extricate yourself from this marriage and start a new life here."

Nothing had changed. Sam's stomach twisted sickly. There would never be any compromises with Alexandra. Only a battle of wills. All Sam could do was keep Jake out of it. "I understand you perfectly. You're worried about Orrin's political image. A niece who's married to an ex-con doesn't fit in with the Brady Bunch platform, does it?"

Cold rage segued into Alexandra's eyes. "You can't harm what I've created. And when Jake leaves your life in shambles again, I'll be there to pick up the pieces. Just as I did with your mother. Because I seem to be the only person in this family who can distinguish between hard, cold reality and wishful thinking."

"In other words, the end justifies the means."

"Precisely."

Sam stood. Charlotte followed, scowling from her to Alexandra. "This was a nice reunion," Charlotte announced. "Let's do it again in about a hundred years. Bring Tim next time. I've got a set of carving knives I want to show him."

Sam took her by one arm with a warning grip. "What is that supposed to mean?" Alexandra demanded, posed on the edge of her chair.

"Nothing," Sam answered. "Leave us alone. Leave *Jake* alone." Her mind whirled. She had to play by their aunt's rules. "You've had a score to settle since the day you married Judge Vanderveer—the day Sarah saw you for what you are. You feed off other people's lives; you took her brother's goodwill, his good name, even the *respect* that had existed between the Vanderveers and the Raincrows for generations."

The words fell like small bombs, ripping away all pretense of civility, clipping the last of the polite veneer from her aunt's expression. Sam looked down into that dangerous vortex—the pride and anger, the humiliation and the hatred for being humiliated—and she knew she should stop, retreat, think this through rationally.

But it was too late. Years of loneliness, then being pushed to the edge of despair every day since Jake's tormented return, had found a channel. "That's why the old ruby has always been so important to you—it's a medal you can wear. It represents your claim on a history you never earned or even understood. Without it you'll never forget you come from a family of ambitious mill bosses who used you to pull themselves up the social ladder."

The silence that followed resonated through the room with chilling effect. Alexandra didn't breathe; she radiated eerie calm. "What claim do you have on righteousness, Samantha? Your husband killed for you. You deserted him. I had people in place, watching, waiting. He never wrote to you. He wanted nothing to do with you. I suspect he doesn't want you now. You don't have the courage to admit that. You say hateful things to me because you know I'm telling you the truth. You have nothing."

"I have the ruby. I've had it since I left town." Her aunt's eyes flickered. It was a naked, predatory flash of interest. "I'm the only one who knows where it is," Sam continued. "And if you do anything, *anything* to interfere in our lives, I'll make certain it disappears for good."

She walked out, Charlotte trailing her with quick, urgent strides. Sunlight dappled them through the graceful firs as they crossed the parking lot in numb silence. "Sammie," Charlotte said finally, her voice strangled. "I'm so proud of you."

Sam leaned on the car and put her head in her hands. She wasn't proud of anything she'd said. She had wanted to weave a safety net for her and Jake. Instead, she'd created a noose.

Behind the closed doors of the conference room of one of the state's most powerful newspapers, a long table was strewn with coffee mugs, soft-drink cans, and photocopies of the anonymous handwritten notes. Excitement seeped into the air like the scent of blood. After much debate, two news editors, the executive editor, the publisher, and one of the newspaper's lawyers traded a tacit look of agreement. The executive editor nodded her permission to the reporter who sat across from them, watching the interplay avidly.

"We're going to keep this investigation close to our chests," she told the reporter. "You check out every detail as quietly as you can. What you've got may be nothing more than half-baked rumors or outright lies. Either your *pen pal* has incredible access to the governor's family, or he—she?—is a malicious crank with a vivid imagination. We're not printing one *word* unless we have some solid evidence."

The reporter smiled thinly. "The person who dropped this dynamite in the mail went to a lot of trouble to name specifics. I think it's legitimate. But I'll be careful. And when I'm done, we'll have plenty to back it up."

The lawyer cleared his throat awkwardly. "Why do you think this person singled you out? You're not the only reporter who covers politics for this newspaper. No offense, but there are veteran reporters here who should have seemed like a better choice to an informant. Do you think this informant may be black?"

The reporter eyed him sardonically. "You mean I was chosen because *us black folks gots to stick together*?"

"Don't be offended, I said. But to be frank, yes, I—"

"Maybe," the publisher interjected, "the person picked Bob here because he—or she—likes the fact that Bob is homegrown. Born and raised in North Carolina."

"A homeboy," Bob added dryly. "I doubt it had anything to do with my awards for investigative journalism."

"Leave my reporter alone," the executive editor said, smiling. "I can think of about a dozen politicians who shiver at the sight of his by-line. Our mystery informant obviously knows Bob's reputation."

"Good enough for me," the publisher said. "Run this stuff up the flagpole and see who salutes. Or who races for cover."

On that note, the meeting ended. After the others filed out, the exec shut the door again and looked at the wiry young man who was staking his professional pride on a sheaf of notes sent by a stranger. "Bob, God help us all if this is a crock of shit."

He looked pensive. "I'd like to think this character, whoever he-she is, was impressed by my ass-kicking journalistic credentials." He tapped the frayed manila envelope on the table. "But I've got to tell you something—there could be a personal reason why I'm the one this is addressed to."

"If you've got a hunch, now's the time to share it."

"It's a long shot. Something damned few people would know, or take the time to learn." He shook his head, puzzled.

"*What?*"

He frowned. "My parents were tenant farmers. I was born on a farm outside Pandora. Mrs. Lomax was still married to her first husband then. Judge Vanderveer. The Vanderveers ran that town."

"Aw, jeez, Bob, that's ancient history."

"Not to me. The judge was our landlord."

"Oh, *shit.*"

"I was just a kid when all the tenant families were evicted off Vanderveer land." He paused, choosing his words carefully. "There was no good reason for the eviction. My old man never got over it."

"You think your mystery correspondent believes you have a grudge against the governor's wife because she used to be a Vanderveer?"

"My old man said Judge Vanderveer wasn't to blame.

My old man said the judge's wife was behind it. She divided the land into estate tracts and sold it to her cronies." He smiled bitterly. "So, yeah, you could say I have a grudge against Alexandra Vanderveer Lomax."

"I'm going to pretend you never told me any of this."

"Don't worry—I'll give you a story that'll stand on its own merits." He held up the notes and the envelope. "But let's just say that somebody out there knew I was the perfect choice for the job."

Chapter
Twenty-Eight

J ake walked out of the woods weighed down by a
muggy June morning, his thoughts, and the backpack slung over one shoulder. He carried a good
twenty pounds of rock he'd dug from the base of a waterfall. Twenty pounds of mountain bedrock that no one
else would have given more than a passing glance. But
when he finished chipping it apart, he'd find something—
specks of color, the gleam of perfect crystals. His knack
for mining had faded over the years; that had worried
him. But the intuition was growing stronger every day.
He could make a living the way he had before. That
much, at least, consoled him.

Bo padded along, wheezing. "Old dog, you shouldn't
follow me," Jake murmured gruffly. Telling Bo to stay
behind was useless.

Samantha followed them both some days. When she

could catch them before they left. Jake always knew when she was nearby. Thinking about her watching him was a key reason he couldn't concentrate on his work—didn't want to concentrate. It was pitiful and agonizing—the two of them slipping around in miserable secrecy, glad to be within sight of the other, unable to say so.

He crossed the clearing where his parents' house had stood, where they and Ellie had died. He mourned them as if their graves were still fresh, and he listened for their voices, tried to feel the breath of their shadows. Sometimes he was certain he did, but bitterness and grief—unsettled business—made him ashamed to answer.

His black mood gave way to wary surprise. A knitting needle protruded from the red-clay earth before his tent. A slip of notepaper had been taped to it, fluttering in the soft breeze like a small flag of surrender. Or a challenge. Samantha's way of leaving a message and a point.

He scooped it up. *Someone called. A tracking job. I have the details. I'm going with you. No arguments. You can't drive—you haven't renewed your driver's license.*

He shut his eyes and laughed humorlessly, rubbing the tip of the knitting needle along his lower lip as if he could taste her through it. He'd served time for killing a man, and that didn't repulse her, but, by God, she wasn't going to let him get as much as a speeding ticket.

Whale music. Sam sat in the middle of Granny's spring, in cold water to her waist, dressed in white shorts, a white T-shirt, braless, with a boom box perched on the shallow bank beside her, listening to a CD of mournful instrumental music that evoked images of large, solitary mammals calling to their lost mates in dark waters.

A little eccentric, to say the least. She didn't care. It suited her mood these days. Every time she thought about her encounter with Alexandra, she felt angrier at herself, and more depressed.

Lost in black thoughts, she splashed the cold, clear spring water to her face and let it splash heedlessly down her thin shirt. There was something to be said for ritual bathing. If she sat here in Granny Raincrow's spring, maybe she'd rinse away her failures.

"It's not a birdbath," Jake said behind her.

She twisted quickly and stared up at him through a length of damp blond hair that slid seductively in front of one eye. He stood at the edge, his feet hidden in a thick fringe of ferns, as if he'd been planted in their midst. His presence charged the cool, shadowy air. His shuttered gaze dropped down her body, where the water had plastered the thin cotton to her breasts. The look in his eyes made her dizzy. She shared that raw and barely restrained hunger. But she could only provoke him, and he would only keep away.

"Okay, so I'm a bird," she said. She flashed a look at her chest, then back at him with challenge. "A yellow-crested titmouse."

The whale music rose to a haunting crescendo. He scowled at the big portable player as if searching for distractions. "You wanted to talk to me. I can't talk with that fish opera going on." He moved quickly to the boom box, dropped to his knees, and jabbed one blunt finger against a delicate button. The music continued, but the cassette berth opened. He stared at the player, his expression growing darker. He balled his hand and smacked the top of the player. "How do you turn off the damned radio?"

Sam gaped at him. "Don't whack my boom box. That's not the radio playing, it's . . ." Her voice trailed away. He wasn't familiar with compact discs. The world had moved on without him for ten years. Compact discs, VCRs, fax machines, portable computers, car phones. Cable television. A thousand small changes waiting to remind him that he'd been left behind.

Her throat aching, Sam scrambled over to the player and pressed a control. The music ended abruptly. Beneath a small window on top, a shiny disc spun to a stop. His eyes narrowed as he watched, and understood. A muscle flexed in his jaw.

Sam was close enough to hear the soft intake of his breath and see the brief glimmer of humiliation in his large, hooded eyes. She ached to reach for him, to hold him protectively. Their eyes met. Sam struggled to hide the tenderness he might mistake for pity. "The important things haven't changed," she said hoarsely. She gestured toward herself. "No strange new equipment *here*. Push *my* buttons."

"*Samantha*." He spoke her name with warning. He spoke it with a raw undertone of desperation. She leaned closer, drunk on the sound. "I haven't heard you say my name in ten years. Please, say it again. I sit on the porch at night, wrapped in nothing but a blanket, praying that you'll walk up and say my name, and slide your hands under the blanket, and—"

"Stop it." His voice was ragged. He vaulted to his feet and walked a safe distance away, his big shoulders hunched. "You said I have a tracking job. Tell me the details in the car. You got your wish—you're going. We're wasting time."

For a moment she was too grief-stricken to answer. The connection had been so strong. If he felt the same helpless, overwhelming need, how he could turn away from her? "If I were a man who hadn't had sex for ten years," she said wearily, "I don't believe I could turn down an offer. For any reason."

"That doesn't say much for your opinion of men in general and me in particular."

"No, I'm saying I must rank somewhere below lepers and sheep."

He was silent and deceptively still, as if paralyzed by too many conflicting emotions he couldn't describe or release. Then, slowly, his expression softening enough to bring tears to her eyes, he said, "At night you sit in the rocking chair nearest the steps, and sometimes after you fall asleep your arms relax, and the quilt slides down around you. When the moon sets, its light comes under the porch roof. First on your hair, then your face, then on down, letting me see just a little of you at a time. The rest is always hidden in the shadows. It's a kind of torture. I spend the night trying to put you together, but I never can."

Sam felt drugged. The breath soughed out of her. She could only look up at him in silent, dazed wonder, the way he was looking at her. He shifted as if groggy, scrubbed his hand over his face, and the mask slipped back into place. "We're wasting time," he repeated. "Change your clothes. I'll get Bo and wait at the car. How far do we have to go?"

"A long way." She hadn't recovered enough to offer practical details.

"Then move it." He pivoted quickly and strode up the knoll.

A long way, she thought. *But another step closer.*

Charlotte had a bad case of the creeps. She didn't like being alone in the Cove—at least, she thought she was alone. Sam had gone somewhere—the house had been locked when Charlotte arrived, and Sam's car wasn't in the yard. Jake, of course, was nowhere to be seen, but that didn't mean he wasn't prowling the woods like a bear with a thorn in his tail.

It wasn't like Sammie to take off without letting her know. And it wasn't like Sammie to forget Charlotte's daily visit.

The house had been closed up for so many years that Sam still hadn't quite rid it of a musty scent. The smell was too forlorn to Charlotte; it reminded her of the incense their mother had burned, and of the decrepit, antique-filled cellar beneath Mom's first store. Gray light filtered through the window curtains over the kitchen sink. The afternoon was dark and rainy, playing on her gloom. Thunder rumbled occasionally in the distance.

She threw open a back door in the kitchen and latched the screen. Trying to distract herself, she set the kitchen radio to an oldies station and cranked the volume up. Maybe the Beach Boys and Little Richard could drown out her bittersweet memories of Hugh, Sarah, and Ellie. She hoped her nagging worries about Aunt Alex and Tim couldn't compete with Diana Ross and the Supremes.

Humming stoically, she removed containers bulging with food from a cardboard box. Cooking created order in the midst of chaos. It was an anchor—proof that any problem, no matter how terrible, could be chopped, diced, or whipped into submission.

Our problems don't amount to a hill of refried beans in this crazy world. Charlotte arranged her day's concoctions in the refrigerator with grim resolve. *Casablanca.* If Rick had been a chef, he'd have said *that* to Ilsa.

One of her problems called her name and rapped imperiously on the screen door. She jumped. Ben peered through the screen at her. He was the only man she'd ever known who looked debonair wearing rumpled khakis, a faded chambray shirt, rubber boots, and a camouflage fishing vest with a rubber worm peeking out of the breast pocket.

He wandered over to the patio of her condo every evening, armed with a can of peanuts and a bottle of good wine. Charlotte wanted to ignore him but couldn't resist. He would settle in a lounge chair and entertain her with anecdotes about his law practice and his interesting, close-knit family. She told herself she tolerated him because she had nothing better to fill her time. And because he brought her fresh trout to cook almost every day.

Now the sight of him filled her with relief. She couldn't brood about much of anything while Ben was around. Charlotte turned the radio down and hurried to the door. "Did you get rained out, fisherman?"

"Hmmm. The trout were holding little umbrellas. I decided to call it a day."

She held the screen door open and eyed him drolly. "So you decided to trail the evil sister and see what she was up to?"

"Of course." He left his muddy rubber boots on the back porch along with his vest and stepped inside. He had a pink rosebud in one hand. He tucked it under the fastener on one shoulder strap of her white overalls. She wore only a pink tube top under the overalls, and his fingers brushed the bare skin of her shoulder. "I've become so accustomed to your ill temper that I actually invent excuses to see you. But today I have business to discuss with Sam and Jake."

She was silent, thinking about the rose and his touch, feeling absurdly pleased and more than a little warm. "Sammie's not here," she said finally. "I don't know where she's gone, and that worries me. Jake—well, he could be anywhere. There's only one sure bet. He's not with Sammie."

"Hmmm. I need to talk to them about Dr. Raincrow's old offices."

Charlotte felt a pang of sorrow. Sam had asked Ben to manage the tiny building for them over the years. He'd arranged for its upkeep and handled lease agreements. Sam had insisted that the offices not be turned into yet another specialty shop. *I don't want Jake to come home and find someone selling mink-trimmed poodle collars and gourmet cat treats in there,* she'd said.

But that hadn't been a problem. Several of the town's doctors had competed avidly for the lease, as if they could acquire Dr. Raincrow's reputation just by occupying his space.

Ben sighed. "The tenant won't sign a new lease unless we remodel. He wants skylights. Says the lack of ambiance makes his patients think he's cheap."

"Skylights?" she repeated contemptuously. "Dr. Hugh didn't need any stinking *skylights* to keep his patients happy. What next? A wine bar?"

Ben gave her a pensive look. "I've been thinking," he said slowly, "that I'd like to move here permanently. That maybe Sam and Jake would let me lease the building for my law office." He cleared his throat. "No skylights or wine bar, I swear."

Charlotte stared at him. He was tossing a tempting lure in her direction, but she was too skittish. She'd mastered the art of scooting under logs. But the gleam in his eye was a lure she couldn't easily ignore. She'd circle it. "Why in the world would you want to give up the bright lights of Durham and stay *here*?"

"You know why."

Charlotte backed away. "I'm not staying very long.

I . . . I have a good job back in L.A. A *very* understanding boss who let me have time off to help Sammie get resettled. I have my sights set on wooing the rich and infamous with my culinary magic. I intend to hook up with some show-biz types who have money to invest in a restaurant. That's my goal—to own my own restaurant. Chef to the Stars. I'll get my picture in *People*."

Ben's expression had become darker with every word she spoke. "Cooking for Zsa Zsa," he said sarcastically. "I can't imagine a higher calling." He moved toward her. "Stop running away. If you've got a problem with *me*, have the guts to tell me exactly what it is. Drop your act and be honest with me."

"What an ego! You think you make me *nervous*?"

"I think most men make you nervous. Why?"

"I've had *plenty* of men." She refused to take another step back. Instead, she turned blindly toward the kitchen counter, dragging more containers from her box. "I'm a magnet for men. Me and my big cantaloupes. You're not any different." What a terrible lie, and she knew it.

"Oh? Miss Irresistible Melons." He took her by one arm and made her face him. "If all I cared about was your *produce section*, I'd have taken my shopping list to a friendlier grocery store a long time ago. I've come close to doing it. But then I get another glimpse under that steely rind of yours, and I'm hooked all over again."

"Ben, I'm *afraid*. I have a knack for causing trouble. It was my fault the trouble started between Sammie and our aunt. It was mainly because of me that Sammie couldn't stay here when Jake needed her. Somehow, without even meaning to, I'll cause trouble for you too."

"I'm a lawyer. I'm Jewish. Dealing with trouble is my specialty. What are you talking about?" She felt trapped. She shook her head wildly. "I don't want you to deal with it! I've seen what happens to people who try to solve each other problems! Look what that's done to Jake and Sammie!"

Her strained logic snapped his patience. "You can't love people without wanting to fight their battles for them," he yelled. "*And I love you!*"

"That's my point!" she blurted out. "I love *you*." The last three words echoed in her ears. She couldn't believe she'd said them. Worse, she admitted for the first time that it was true. But she'd never tell him why men frightened her. She'd never tell him about Tim. Charlotte gave a garbled moan of defeat.

A second later they were in each other's arms.

After fifty-four years of hard, joyful living, Detective Hoke Doop of the Durham police department knew where to put his faith.

He believed in the power of an old-fashioned preacher to scare the hell out of sinners, and the messy, majestic power of the law to punish sinners who wouldn't get scared. As a young man, he'd stuck a foot inside the barely open door to the city's all-white police force and become, against all odds, what he'd wanted to be since he was a kid watching cops-and-robbers movies from the colored section in the balcony of a Durham theater: He became an officer of the law.

He believed in the awesome love of his fat, sassy little wife, Louetta; the fine qualities of their four grown children, and the innocence of their six grandkids. He believed that hot fried catfish and cold beer could soothe any man's troubles, and that Elvis had been the only white man who could sing gospel music with true soul.

And he believed Elvis was really dead—no small feat in these parts.

Hoke was nobody's fool.

Which was why he didn't feel like a fool for trusting Jake Raincrow's God-given gift. Being equipped with a touch of the same thing, he had figured Jake out years earlier. He suspected that Jake knew he knew.

They leaned, side by side, against the fender of an unmarked police car. Hoke had trouble concentrating on business. His attention kept returning to an amazing discovery.

Jake really did have a wife. She wasn't just a rumor. She was a sturdy, picture-pretty blonde with big smart blue eyes that had a few hard miles at the corners. She favored old jeans and fancy hiking boots and a long-sleeved work shirt with the tail tied in a dandy little knot that impressed him. Her hands were hidden inside two pairs of gloves. After smiling at him and shaking his hand with her overpadded mitt, she'd taken old lop-eared Bo off aways and was now bent over him, rubbing his saggy shoulders as if he were a prizefighter she had to loosen up for his comeback match.

Behind her, the junkyard made an eerie sight at the end of a weedy, rutted dirt road through the woods. The rusty hulks of old cars were lined up in neat rows draped in vines and briars. Pine saplings dotted the spaces between them. They resembled nothing so much as a forgotten cemetery. Thunderheads had rolled into the June sky; the wind was rising, and the air smelled like rain.

Hoke relit his old brown pipe, sucked on it for a minute, and glanced at Jake, who was as quiet as a sphinx and nearly as still, a rumpled, wide-brimmed hat pulled low over his eyes. He couldn't seem to stop looking at his wife either.

Hoke was eager to get going, but he knew better than to rush things. Jake needed time to meditate, or some such thing. Might be an Indian attitude, might be the silence of a man who'd spent a lot of years locked up, with nobody worth talking to, until talk became unnatural.

The damnedest thing was, this dude could find things, and people too. He'd proved it over and over to the guards. They'd take him out on convict road crews to clean up the state parks, and he'd show the forest rangers where to dig wells for drinking fountains. It had been a game to them, but not to him. After word got around that he was a dowser, the warden had brought him over to his farm to see whether he could locate a gas tank that had been buried so many decades before that nobody in the warden's family could remember where it was.

So the story went, Jake found the old gas tank, a slave graveyard, and the warden's missing car keys. After that they'd hauled him all over the state—to find lost hikers in the national forest, to track down runaway kids, to puzzle out where bodies had been dumped after a killing.

Hoke snorted in disgust. They'd probably have kept him in prison for ten more years, just for the free lost-and-found service.

"You got a nice wife," Hoke said finally. "Should of brought her along before. Before you went to prison, I mean. This is something, her waiting all these years for you to get out. She must be a helluva fine woman."

Jake stirred. He looked at Hoke without batting an eyelash. "She is. Let me borrow your handcuffs."

All right, she was here. One small step. Maybe Jake hadn't spoken ten words to her during the hours in the car, but at least they were together. She would get to watch him and Bo work. Jake would have to let her into this part of his life in a way he never had before. No more blind spots.

She would keep her distance, and act nonchalant, and dote on Bo, while secretly absorbing every fascinating detail. She walked over to Detective Doop's car, Bo shuffling along beside her, yawning.

Bo was long past retirement age. Jake didn't want to admit that, she thought, because it was one more reminder of the lost years. They needed to have this day. Soon Sam would find some way, very gently, to discuss getting a young dog.

She halted in front of Jake and Detective Doop. "Bo's awake and eager to work," she said.

The detective squinted at him. "How can you tell, ma'am?"

"He's just a little rusty." She avoided looking at Jake, afraid he'd recognize her strained optimism. "What are we looking for?"

Detective Doop's puckish expression faded. "A child, ma'am. A little girl."

She felt the blood drain out of her face. "I thought . . . I assumed . . . you didn't explain—"

"Didn't want to upset you, ma'am."

"Hoke didn't expect you to come with me," Jake interjected.

Sam inhaled sharply. "Be that as it may. Why are we the only ones here? Doesn't a lost child rate more people power than this?"

Hoke Doop nodded grimly. "They're all congregated on the other side of town, hunting through a stretch of woods along the highway. But I got a hunch that baby's body is around here."

"*Body?*"

Doop sighed. "All right, folks, here's all seven yards of it. There's a bunch of apartments 'bout a mile from here. Woman kicked her no-account boyfriend out. He come back to her place last night, beat her up, then run off with her baby. We picked him up just short of the state line this morning. No baby. He's not talkin'. Everybody figures he most likely killed her and tossed her along the interstate. I don't think he waited that long. I think he come over to this godforsaken stretch of nothin' and dumped the baby in the woods. Just a hunch."

Just a hunch? Sam felt sick, then furious. This man had dragged Jake here without good reason. Oh, yes, call Jake Raincrow on a whim. Toss him into a grisly scenario as if he had no feelings. But Jake seemed unfazed. She swallowed the scorching words she wanted to say.

Doop pulled a heartbreakingly small pink T-shirt from his coat pocket and handed it to Jake. "What do you think?"

Motionless and apparently lost in concentration, Jake held the shirt in both hands. "Your guess is as good as mine." Sam searched his face. Jake didn't make flippant statements. Something didn't jibe here. If he were a weaver she'd say he and Detective Doop were deliberately skipping a few threads in the warp. "Shouldn't you be using something that the *man* wore? I mean, if this monster carried the baby into the woods, what good does it do to give Bo the *baby's* scent?"

Jake straightened, tucked the tiny shirt into the waist of his jeans, then reached into his back pocket. "Good question. I haven't got time to answer it. I'm going. You wait here."

She stared at him. "I didn't come with you to be left behind now. I won't slow you down. I *am* going with you and Bo."

"Hmmm. I figured you'd say that." He held out a hand to her.

Was he going to pull her along behind him like a straggling hiker? All right. She wouldn't debate small insults. Sam thrust her gloved hand into his.

He brought his other hand from behind his back and snapped a cuff around her wrist. Before the gasp of protest cleared her lips, he pulled her wrist to the side mirror of Doop's sedan and snapped the cuff's partner around the mirror's shank. "Sorry," he told her gruffly. "Hoke'll keep you company."

Then he walked away, gesturing to Bo to follow him.

Sam jerked frantically against the manacle. "This isn't fair!"

He kept walking and didn't look back.

Ben looked as if he'd been stirred with a whisk—dark hair disheveled, bare legs tangled in the quilt, one arm dangled around her shoulders, his head barely anchoring a pillow that hung half off the bottom corner of the bed. Charlotte suspected she looked the same way. She was splayed across his chest with the entire sheet wadded atop her naked rump like a giant dollop of whipped cream, her chin propped on her forearm, her forearm crooked on his chest. It was peaceful chaos. Each of them kept one hand free to explore all the newly discovered territory.

She wasn't certain how long they'd been in Sammie's spare bedroom, but the murky afternoon light was beginning to fade. Charlotte found herself listening for Sammie's car. Reality crept back, and she started asking herself what in the world she'd done.

"You're losing your dewy-eyed reverie," Ben noted gruffly. He trailed his fingertips down her spine. "Don't stop looking into my eyes as if I'm a great recipe you've discovered. I like it."

"Sammie and Jake should have been the first ones to do the horizontal two-step in their own house."

"They were."

"No, I mean, after Jake came back."

"We'll be their inspiration, then."

"I'm not telling my sister that we went nuts and used her spare bedroom for a motel." Charlotte sat up. Ben's hypnotic gaze dropped to her breasts. "I'm trying not to stare lecherously," he told her. "But they *are* impossible to ignore."

"I don't mind. You're the sweetest, most gentle man in the world." She looked away, blushing. Hiding behind wisecracks was much easier than telling the truth.

"Tell the aliens they can keep her."

"Who?"

"The impostor they were trying to foist off on me before this afternoon." His expression became mischievous. "How did they do it? Mind-meld? Cloning? Did you notice a large larvaelike pod under your bed one night? *Never* fall asleep when a large pod is waiting to metamorphose into your exact replica."

"I have a large larvaelike pod in bed with me right *now*." She hesitated, then added softly, "But I wouldn't change a thing about him."

"I promise, I'm the real McCoy."

"The McCoys had a Jewish branch?"

"The McCoybergs. They shortened it at Ellis Island."

"I see." She searched his eyes seriously. "You realize, of course, that I'm a religious handicap."

"Funny, I don't feel culturally disabled. In fact, I feel blessed."

She made a soft sound of pleasure. "You sure you want to be one of the shiksa-challenged?"

"I'll decorate Christmas trees if you'll cook the seder dinner." Charlotte frowned and looked away. After an awkward moment Ben added, "I can't believe you'd turn down an opportunity to cook."

"It's not that. I'd be happy to cook the seder dinner every night and twice on Sundays."

"I believe," he said coyly, "that once a year is all

that's required. Think of it as Thanksgiving with kosher wine."

"We're avoiding the real issue. You think I've forgotten about going back to California."

"No, I think you were never serious about that." He cupped the back of her head, splaying his fingers into her hair and rubbing small, seductive circles. Charlotte trembled. "We're on a high plateau, Ben. I'd like to stay put awhile and catch my breath. Adjust to the altitude. Not look back, and not look forward either."

"Just wait for a strong wind to push you in the right direction," he said sardonically. "All right, I'll huff, and I'll puff and I'll—"

"Hyperventilate. Rest your case, Perry Mason. Your briefs have a hole in the them."

"I haven't forgotten our earlier conversation either— though it feels as if it happened in another lifetime, arguing with that alien." He sat up. He searched her face somberly. "Your aunt bullied you. You've got some bad memories. But that was more than ten years ago, and you're a grown woman now. There's no good reason for you to feel threatened."

Shame and bitterness rose in Charlotte's throat. She didn't want the man she loved to learn that she'd been mauled by her own cousin and called an emotionally disturbed liar by Aunt Alex. Her memory of the lust on Tim's face when he'd grabbed her breasts still made her feel confused. An endless cycle of self-doubt stayed with her. Was she provocative in some way she didn't recognize? She'd read dozens of books about incest, consumed the reassurances of every therapist who discussed the subject on TV talk shows, but deep down she still felt there was something wrong with *her* too.

Ben knew she was quirky. But he didn't know she was capable of slicing off ears with a carving knife.

She lifted the corner of the quilt that covered his thighs. Nodding toward their jaunty centerpiece, she said brusquely, "That key is *very* useful, but there are some doors it won't open."

He scowled and started to reply, but she scrambled

out of bed. Their clothes were scattered everywhere. She found her overalls and tube top in a corner. "R and R is over, soldier. Help me square this place away. It's back to the front lines. I'm going on a reconnaissance mission."

"You can't evade my questions forever."

"I've shown you all the good stuff." She dressed quickly and gazed at him with all the nonchalance she could fake. "Save your energy for what matters. I'll get some clean sheets for this bed. Then let's find Jake, so you can discuss the office lease with him. Then we can traipse back to Condo World and toss a coin to see whose sheets we're going to wrinkle next—yours or mine."

"Don't try to distract me with dessert when I'm still waiting for the entree."

She went to the door, looked back over her shoulder, and forced a smile. "I never promised you a full-course meal."

"Good Lord," Doop muttered under his breath. He seemed shocked, too, standing there with her locked to his sideview mirror. The grizzled, stocky detective looked at Sam as if he were embarrassed and didn't know what to say. She pounded her free hand on the car's fender. "You have a key, don't you? Unlock my wrist."

"Ma'am, I . . . I've seen a lot of strange things, but nothing quite like this. I depend on Jake. Trust him. Feel bad for what happened to him, 'cause I think he got a raw deal. I figure him for a man who does things for good reason."

"Not this time. *Please* unlock this cuff. You don't understand. You've never met me before because even when Jake and I were first married he never let me go on tracking jobs with him. It was the only part of his life he shut me out of. I don't know why. But I know that if I hadn't let him do it, I'd have been with him when he really needed me. He wouldn't have gotten into trouble. *I can't let him shut me out again.*"

Doop shifted uneasily. "I'm no good at playin' marriage counselor, ma'am." He scowled. "You settle down now. If it starts to rain, I'll give you a tarp to hold over your head."

Sam strained her eyes toward the woods, then twisted toward Doop. "I can tell that you respect my husband, and he respects you. But you're not helping him this way. He's got something bottled up inside him. He's always been that way. I've got to find out what it is so it can't hurt him again."

Doop waved his hands soothingly. "Well, of course, havin' the *touch* can set a person apart. At least, when it's as strong as it is with Jake. It's like one of them genius kids who starts bangin' out songs on the piano without a lesson. They get it by the grace of God, but people treat 'em like they're some kind of freaks. They got to take care with the gift, ma'am. I figure Jake learned that early on. You wouldn't want him to go paradin' the grace of God around like it was a prize at a turkey shoot, would you?"

Sam drew back against the car's fender and eyed him nervously. Jake wouldn't have left her alone with a lunatic. She'd humor Detective Doop if that was what it took to win his sympathy. "So you believe Jake's . . . gift . . . is the reason he's secretive?"

Warming to the discussion, Doop leaned his thick-set body against the car and nodded fervently. "You see, ma'am, I have the touch too. Oh, not like Jake has it. Just my good, solid hunches." He sighed. "If I could do what he does—if I could figure people out—find 'em, know what they're thinkin', feel whether they was dead or alive—if I could do that just by handling a bit of something they'd worn—why, I'd probably have made captain by now." He wagged a finger at her. "But I'd probably keep my ways to myself, just like Jake. Because regular people get edgy about things they don't understand."

Play along. "I see your point."

"Now, you being Jake's wife, you believe in him and respect his gift, and you probably think everybody else should too. But it just don't work that way, ma'am."

Don't chew your tongue off yet. "Would you say he's a bonafide psychic?"

Doop grunted happily. "Bonafide, certified, gold-medal-winning hall-of-famer."

Enough was enough. Every astrologer, palm reader, crystal gazer, and self-styled mystic who had played on her mother's need for reassurance floated through Sam's disgusted thoughts. Mom's good-hearted faith in bullshit artists had primed her for Malcolm Drury. Sam would never look for easy answers that way.

She drew a deep breath and stared Doop straight in the eyes. "Sir, Jake's parents and sister burned to death in a house fire. If Jake were psychic, he'd never have let that happen."

Doop's pleased expression faded into troubled confusion. "It don't always work that way, ma'am. Nobody bats a thousand. And maybe we're not supposed to know everything. Only God sees the big picture."

"Jake was away from home that night. Tracking a stranger, just like today. Helping other people. Doing what he was asked to do by men like yourself. He lost three people he loved dearly, and where they went he couldn't follow. He couldn't track them, and find them, and bring *them* home safely. He was never the same after that. He was so bitter and hurt, he couldn't think straight. He saw threats everywhere. He went looking for them, and he's *still* looking."

Sam grasped the detective's coat lapel with her free hand. "Don't make him look alone." Her voice was hoarse, pleading. "Don't add a dead child to the heartbreaking memories he has to carry around by himself."

She lowered her hand and sagged against the car, trembling. She couldn't tell whether she'd made a dent in the detective's bizarre ideas about Jake. She'd failed at so much.

"I can't read you the way he can," Doop said grimly. "But I can damned sure see why you're special." He clamped his pipe between his teeth, pulled a key from his coat pocket, and unlocked the handcuffs. "Go on."

Chapter
Twenty-Nine

J ake and Bo had vanished. Twenty minutes of hopeless
 wandering made her understand the panic a person
 lost in the woods must feel. Rain began to fall—at
first in slow, fat droplets that barely found their way
through the canopy of forest, but now with steady force,
soaking her. Sam wiped her eyes as she picked her way
among muscadine vines that hung like soggy garlands
from the smaller trees.

She climbed a hill, pushing through dripping huckle-
berry shrubs and briars. The sound of rustling leaves made
her halt, searching anxiously. A fallen poplar sprawled
across the hill's crest, its ripped base propped precariously
on the rotting stump.

Bo peered at her from a narrow shelter beneath its
trunk. He was curled up. With rainwater running along
the creases of his skin, he looked like a red clay sculpture
in danger of dissolving. All he could manage to move

was his long red tail, which wagged among the matted leaves.

Frowning, Sam dropped to her heels and stroked his droopy ears. Where was Jake? How could he work without a tracking dog? *Unless Bo's only a prop. So people won't suspect the truth.* Sam ignored that ridiculous thought.

Bo had run out of steam, she decided, and Jake had been forced to leave him there. He'd probably circled back toward the junkyard. He was probably there now, telling Hoke Doop they'd need one of the police department's dogs, a stretcher for Bo, and a less soft-hearted guard for *her* next time.

"I know you're tired," she told Bo. "But can't you follow Jake's trail at least? Come on, Bo. Get up." She tugged at his collar. "Try, okay?"

Blah blah blah, Jake, blah blah was undoubtedly how Bo interpreted it. But *Jake* was enough to get him on his feet. He sneezed, then shuffled stiffly down the hill, nose to the ground.

Sam followed right behind him. Her breath caught in her throat. He was leading her farther away from the junkyard.

He was close. He could feel it. But he didn't know what awful scene he'd find, and he tried not to think about that. At least he'd prevented Samantha from seeing the worst. And from seeing how he worked. He'd realized before they started that Bo was too old to keep up with him.

Maybe he could have convinced Samantha that *he* was the one with the extraordinary sense of smell.

Jake followed a muddy ravine. The familiar sensations stole over him, a trance of déjà vu that lingered. He recognized the ravine as if he'd seen it before.

Around the next bend a gnarled crabapple would be clinging to an undercut lip of clay. The crumbling hulk of a radiator would protrude from a bed of ferns. A pock-marked metal sign with GILMAN'S AUTO SALVAGE fading into rust would be lying in the ravine's narrow bottom.

The search would end there.

"Jake!"

Samantha's voice. His concentration evaporated. He halted and turned unerringly toward the sound, then watched, amazed, as she and Bo came up the ravine behind him. Her face was flushed. She squinted at him with unrepentant determination, rubbing rain from her eyes as she dodged roots and slipped in the mud.

A shattering combination of admiration, anger, and dread filled Jake's chest. "What did you do?" he demanded. "Pick the cuffs' lock with a fingernail file?"

She staggered to a halt in front of him. "Detective Doop listened to reason. He let me come after you." Bo collapsed at her feet, his sides heaving. "Good thing he did," she added, her puzzled gaze boring into Jake. "You lost your dog."

"Go back. Turn around and *go back*."

"*You left Bo behind*," she insisted with rising intensity. She stared up at him as if she were afraid of his explanation, as if she desperately needed to hear a logical answer. Her eyes flickered to the baby's pink shirt, clutched in one of his fists, then back to his face. "How can you—" she swallowed hard—"how can you track the baby if you don't use Bo?"

She was hammering at the only door he didn't want her to open. They'd known each other almost all their lives. He couldn't suddenly reveal a side of himself that would change her whole idea of him. *There're a few things you've never known about me, sweetheart. I like to watch soap operas, and brussels sprouts make me choke. And, oh, by the way, I've got a psychic phone line to the astral plane.*

When he said nothing, she made a hoarse sound of alarm. Her hands darted forward. She snatched the baby's shirt from him and knelt by Bo. "Here, Bo," she said urgently. "*Please*. You can do it. I know you can."

Bo snuffled the shirt, wheezed, then dropped his head to his paws. "Please, Bo," she said. Her voice was ragged. "Jake can't track people by-guess-and-by-God. That's not possible."

A low groan curled from Jake's throat. He bent over and pried the shirt from her viselike grip. She refused to let go. They froze, locked in a tug-of-war that threatened her most basic understanding of him, their past together, their future, and all of her self-protective commitment to common sense.

Suddenly, as if the vivid emotions between them had called up something equally strong, he knew exactly what he'd find around the bend of the ravine. *Life*.

He left the shirt in her hands, whirled around, and ran to find it. Dimly he heard her startled cry and the sound of her hurrying after him.

Jake squeezed himself between an overhanging ledge and the gnarled roots of a massive tree. Sam stumbled up behind him. She gasped.

Jake knelt on one knee. A tiny girl dressed in a diaper and a dirty T-shirt lay curled up, her eyes closed, atop a rusting sign that said GILMAN'S AUTO SALVAGE.

Jake reached out, his large, brutal-looking hand posed over the child's drenched hair. He touched his fingertips to her cheek.

She stirred, mewled softly, and opened her eyes.

Samantha scrambled through the opening and fell to her knees beside Jake. She made small fervent sounds, cooing to the little girl. Jake leaned back, removed his shirt, and handed it to her. She wrapped the baby in it and quickly cradled her in her arms. Jake watched in bittersweet anguish.

Maybe Samantha would forget about the rest.

Tears slid down her cheeks. She looked at Jake over the baby's head. "You *found* her. It's true. Oh, my God, it's true, isn't it? Hoke Doop says you have a gift." Terrible sorrow hollowed her voice. "I've loved you since a time when I wasn't much older than this baby. Why couldn't you tell me?"

He didn't feel the cold rain on his bare shoulders and chest. He didn't feel anything except the strangling sense of doom crawling through him.

He got to his feet. His knees were weak. "I don't know what you're talking about," he said between gritted teeth. "I'll carry Bo back. You follow with the kid." He left her sitting there.

She knew. And all he could do was lie to her, because every question she'd ask would bring her closer to learning what he knew about her aunt.

"He's not here. No surprise." Ben said it morosely. They stood at Jake's campsite. Charlotte concentrated on not thinking about the pitiful clearing where the old house had been. The oaks hovered around it like courtiers to a missing king.

Gray clouds blanketed the sky so deeply that the granite head of the distant bald was hidden in them. Evening mist rolled across the pine forest that had overtaken the old pastures. "There used to be a barn over there," Charlotte said, pointing wearily. "A few years ago Joe Gunther called Sammie to report that the roof sagged and the walls were covered in graffiti. He said the local kids had decided the Cove was irresistible. Haunted. A wonderland where they could find arrowheads and gemstones. He was worried about the barn collapsing on one of them. Sammie told him to bulldoze it. She told him to send her a piece of board from the walls."

Ben frowned. "A piece of board?"

"The day it came in the mail, I found her sitting in the living room of her apartment. She'd had most of a bottle of wine. She was hugging the damned chunk of wood. Told me she had to save it for Jake." Charlotte stared grimly at Jake's empty tent. "I don't think he cares."

Rain began to pour down. Ben took her by one hand, then ducked into the small tent. Charlotte refused to follow—considering her attitude toward Jake, it didn't seem right to take refuge in what passed for his home. Ben scowled up at her and tugged. "Wet and cranky or dry and cranky," he called over the sound of the rain. "It's your choice."

She scrambled inside. They sat side by side on a sleeping bag atop an air mattress. She shivered, and Ben put his arm around her wet shoulders. "Relax," he whispered. "Think about what I'm thinking about. It'll warm you up."

Charlotte gave in and leaned against him. "That's an understatement. We might start to steam."

She glanced around with gloomy curiosity. A lantern hung from the center of the ceiling supports. Various belongings of Jake's—a mining pick, clothes, canned food—protruded from small canvas bags. She spied a closed bag.

She dragged it into her lap. It was enticingly bulky. She fiddled with the knotted ties. "What are you doing?" Ben asked sternly.

"I'm an inspector for the Boy and Girl Scouts Alumni Association." She pointed to the ties. "Now, I'd say this square knot doesn't meet our standards."

He clamped a hand over hers. "Scouts don't tamper with other people's private possessions."

Charlotte met his reproachful stare. "You're right. It's disgusting." After a steely pause she added, "Unless it's for a good cause."

"*Charlotte*," he said in a warning tone.

"Maybe there's some clue to Jake's behavior in this bag. *One* hint that he still loves my sister. Something I could tell her about that would cheer her up. Doesn't she deserve that?"

Ben sighed. "That noise you hear," he said slowly, "is my conscience being throttled by situational ethics."

"You're a wonderful man, Benjamin. Remind me to massage your conscience later." She quickly unfastened the bag and opened it. "Okay, one dog-eared Bible. Spiritual reading material. That's a good sign." She laid the Bible on her knees. "One package of pipe tobacco. One long-stemmed stone pipe . . ." Charlotte's voice trailed away. She cradled the pipe in her hand, gazing sadly at the ring of tiny garnets that circled the base of the bowl.

Ben leaned closer. "What?"

"This belonged to Dr. Raincrow. I remember it."

"Another good sign," Ben said gruffly. She laid the tobacco pouch and pipe atop the Bible. "One . . . whatever this is." She studied a wrinkled manila envelope that bulged with soft contents. The metal wings of the fastener had broken off from repeated use. She eased a folded sheaf of glossy magazine pages out. Like the envelope, they were rumpled from much handling. Each bore a tattered edge where it had been torn from the magazine binding. "Ah-hah. Let's see what interested him so much that he'd swipe pages from the prison magazine collection." Her pulse thready, she unfolded the stack.

She and Ben peered at the page on top. Ben grunted. "An ad for denture cream? I believe Jake has all his own teeth."

Charlotte froze. "Those are Sammie's hands holding the tube." She and Ben traded an incredulous look. "How could he know that?" Ben asked.

Charlotte shook her head. She flipped through the rest of the pages. An array of products, everything from fine jewelry to monkey wrenches, each posed gracefully in Sammie's hands. "*All* of these are ads with Sammie's hands in them!"

Ben took them from her and went through the collection again. "There couldn't be too many hand models in the country. The odds are good that Jake would come across ads with Sam's—"

"But there's not *one* in here that isn't her." Charlotte poked a shaky fingertip at the bottom of the pages. "And look at the dates. He started collecting these right after he went to prison." Her voice choked up. "Oh, *Ben.*"

Ben folded the pages gently and slid them back into the envelope. "However he knew it was her work, it doesn't matter. What matters is the reason, and that reason doesn't surprise me. I told you he never stopped loving her." Ben laid the envelope in her lap. "Any more doubt?"

Charlotte sagged a little. "I don't know what to think. If he loves her, why is he treating her so badly? Why won't he tell her how he feels?"

"I don't know that myself." Ben hesitated. "But then, I waited a long time to tell you *my* feelings." He cleared his throat. "And I have menus from every restaurant you ever worked for."

After a stunned, melting moment, Charlotte kissed him. "I stole one of your personalized notepads and a handful of your business cards. I still have them."

Ben looked delighted but shocked. "How did you manage to get that? You came to my office only once—the day we met. The day Sam hired me."

She nodded somberly. "Yeah. That was the day. I was just sixteen. Jailbait. It was a good thing you didn't suspect." She paused. "I didn't understand it myself."

Ben leaned his forehead against hers. "I tried my damnedest to treat you like an obnoxious kid sister. But the *sister* image never took, *kid* dropped out of my mind a few years later, and then—"

"I was just *obnoxious*, hmmm?"

"Too late. I was already hooked."

"Me too." She put an arm around his neck. "We better get out of here because I'm awfully tempted to wrestle you to the mat again. This *ain't* Jake's spare bedroom. It's his whole house."

Ben kissed her. "I'll race you home."

They eased apart and looked at the items jumbled in her lap. "I'll tell Sammie about the magazine pages," Charlotte said softly. "It'll mean a lot to her."

"You win. Prowling proved to be justified. This *once.*"

Charlotte tucked the envelope back into the bag, then realized something else still remained in the bottom. "Remember you said that." She pulled a thick file folder out. Ben groaned. "Enough. Don't look at it. I mean it—"

"Hold your conscience down for a few more seconds." She flung the folder open. A mound of newspaper articles met her startled gaze. Some were yellowed with age; some were just text, the black ink smeared by Jake's fingers. Others included photographs. She flipped through them. Dread and shock washed over her.

Every one of them concerned Aunt Alex or Tim.

Ben forgot his protests and bent over them. "What the hell?"

Charlotte began to tremble. "He's keeping track of them. He doesn't trust them. I'm not the only one who thinks they'll never leave us alone. Oh, God, maybe that's why he acts the way he does toward Sammie."

She looked at Ben frantically. Even he seemed troubled. "I'll talk to him."

"No. You can't tell him we went through his things. It might make him less inclined to explain, and that wouldn't help anything. And don't tell Sammie what we found. *Please*. I'm going to see what I can learn about this—quietly. Maybe this time I can solve a problem for her instead of *being* a problem."

Ben touched her face soothingly. His eyes darkened. "All right. But you have to let me help you."

"No, *no*—"

"It's too late to shut me out again. That plateau you wanted us to perch on just turned into a cliff."

He wasn't going to relent. She'd keep tiptoeing around her secrets as long as she could. Hopefully, forever. Charlotte bent her head. "Any ideas where we should start climbing?"

He fanned the articles across his thighs. "Look at *this*."

It was a group photograph taken at some charity ball. Orrin, and Alexandra, and Tim. And beside Tim, holding his arm and looking at the camera with a tight smile, was his wife. Ex-wife now, Charlotte recalled.

Jake had drawn a circle around her.

Jake hadn't said a dozen words to her during the long ride back. Most of the time she hadn't even been certain he was listening. Sam was still in shock. There was a huge blind spot in what she knew about him—and obviously a blind spot in what he knew about her.

They'd loved each other since childhood. He'd trusted her with everything but the part of himself that defined him more than any other. Why?

Since he wouldn't tell her what she desperately wanted to know, she'd decided to tell him every detail

about her life during his time in prison—a nonstop mono-
logue that had gone on for hours. She hoped he'd heard
the unspoken message in it.

I don't have anything to hide from you.

The night was bleak. The Cove closed around them
like a dark, rainy tunnel. Sam drove slowly along the
narrow gravel road, dreading the trip's end. Jake would
disappear into the night without admitting anything.

Bo, curled up in the backseat, gave a raspy cough.
"Bo's catching cold," Sam announced. "And he moves like
the Tin Man with a bad case of rust. You shouldn't take
him to the tent with you. It's too wet and cool."

Jake stirred as if waking up. "He can stay with you
tonight."

"Good. But you know how Bo is. The second you
leave, he'll start clawing the door." *I might do the same
thing,* she added silently. Sam took a deep breath. "Your
clothes are damp and dirty, and you haven't slept on a real
mattress in weeks. It would make sense for you to stay at
the house too." She added quickly, "The bed in the spare
room is already made up."

"I'm used to the tent."

She turned the car up the drive to the house. "We
haven't eaten any dinner. You can't heat a can of pork and
beans over a wet pile of logs. I expect Charlotte made
her daily food run while we were gone. Remember what
I told you about the way I pigged out for a few years?
Please help me plow through a few surplus casseroles. I
don't want to get fat again."

"No reason to think you will. No point in it anymore.
No pretty-boy models to worry about."

Sam mulled over that strange comment. "I don't
recall telling you I had a reason for gaining weight."

He shifted in his seat. She could almost feel him
frowning. "Well, did you?"

"You tell me. Tell me how you determined that I
stuffed myself to keep men from flirting with me."

"Watched a few million *Oprah* shows in the prison
TV room," he tossed back. "Picked up a lot of female
psychology."

They reached the house. Rain drizzled from the eaves. He had not given her an answer about staying the night. She cut the engine and turned toward him. "Look, Dr. Freud, I'm offering you a hot shower, a good meal, and a dry bed. Any ulterior motives are in your own over-*Oprah*ed imagination. Bo needs a decent night's rest. He won't rest unless he knows you're within licking distance." She paused. "And all right, I promise not to regale you with any more passages from my oral diary. We have a big house. You can pretend I'm not around."

"I doubt it. I couldn't when you were on the other side of the country."

He didn't give her a chance to respond to that bone-melting statement. He got out of the car and opened the back door. Bo grunted but wouldn't budge. Jake carried him to the porch.

Sam hurried after them and unlocked the front door. Excitement made her giddy.

He was going to spend the night.

Jake stepped into their darkened house with her for the first time in ten years. The air seemed to vibrate with expectation. *He's home. He's really home now,* Sam told herself. She flicked the hall light switch and looked up at him happily, but there was no surrender in him. "I'll take a shower," he said without a trace of emotion. "And stay until Bo's sound asleep."

He used cold water. It numbed the outer sensations but couldn't chill the turmoil inside him. Just being inside these walls again, feeling every old desire and warm memory, tormented his willpower.

It was good to be home. It was good to be with Samantha. Too damned good. He was sinking quickly.

He dried himself with a huge white towel that had been one of their wedding gifts. He stood on a bath rug she'd woven during the first few weeks of their marriage. Even this narrow little bathroom off the guest room was hard to take. If he'd let her talk him into using the shower off their own bedroom, he'd be kissing the walls.

Jake shivered. He'd felt less threatened in prison baths, surrounded by men with nicknames like *Sweet-heart* and *Dong*.

He walked out of the bathroom in a hurry to get dressed. Damp, dirty clothes were an armor he needed. He'd left them in a pile in the floor.

They were gone. A long, luxurious, burgundy robe lay across the turned-down bedspread.

Just a robe.

Maybe he'd be angry. Maybe he'd take the hint. Either way, Sam was through playing easy-to-ignore.

Bo was stretched out on an old blanket in front of the fire. Sam prodded him gently with her bare toes. *Wake up. Look restless.* He snored.

She leaned back on the couch and tried to appear relaxed, though every nerve was on alert. A log sizzled and popped. On the coffee table sat two glasses and a bottle of champagne in a stoneware cooler filled with ice. The bottle shifted noisily in its melting bed. The fluorescent bulb of the lamp on the end table gave off a low humming sound along with seductive light.

There were only two silent hot spots in the whole house. The guest bedroom, and her body.

She was holding her breath. She'd jumped in over her head. She wore the white silk nightgown and matching robe she'd made for their wedding night. It would be either a life preserver or a cement overcoat, depending on his reaction.

She heard him walking swiftly up the back hall. Since she'd swiped his boots too, his bare feet made mellow thuds on the smooth wood floor. She hoped the rest of him was mellow.

"Samantha, *goddammit*," he called loudly on his way into the living room. He strode through the doorway. The robe fit beautifully. Oh, how it fit. "Get my clothes—" he began. That was as far as he got. He halted, staring at her. So many emotions merged in one paralyzed moment. She wasn't drowning alone.

Sam rose as gracefully as she could. Her legs shook. She moved toward him, hands clenched by her sides. He would have to touch her first. That was the only rule she wouldn't break. "We never got to the champagne on our wedding night," she told him in a ragged whisper. "Let's forget about it tonight too."

He was shaking as badly as she. He raised an arm across his chest, the back of his hand turned toward her. It was a far more self-protective gesture than threatening. Sam stopped close enough for him to slap her. She could barely speak. "You could hit me, but you'd never do that," she told him. "I know it. Nothing you've hidden from me, nothing you think I can't accept, can change what I know best about you. I love you. I will *never* stop loving you. And all I really need to know is that you still love me too."

Ten years of separation shattered in a heartbeat as he pulled her to him.

The morning sun drew water from the soaked earth and turned it into a shimmering mist above the forest floor. Jake sat by his grandmother's spring, blanketed in the floating silver haze, his bare arms propped on his knees. He wore only his jeans. He should have been fully dressed. He was sitting there as if the night had never happened, when he should have walked deep into the mountains. He should have bathed the heavy tenderness from his muscles, washed Samantha's wonderful scent from his skin, her taste from his mouth. But he hadn't.

He had broken promises to himself and to her, though she didn't know it. The old, harsh voice inside him said nothing had really changed. They weren't safe until the past was finished.

What line could he walk now? Half in darkness, half in light, unable to give up either one. Jake put his head in his hands.

He heard the front door slam open. He heard her shout his name brokenly—once, then again, agonized and searching. She thought he'd left her again.

He bolted to his feet and ran up the path. She was crumpled on the porch steps, the white silk robe sliding down her naked back and shoulders, her face hidden inside one tightly curled arm. She beat one fist against the porch floor. Her body shook with silent sobs.

The light was too strong now. He couldn't do this to her.

She jerked upright at the sound of his footsteps. Jake fell to his knees and wrapped his arms around her. The relief in her eyes made him give a hoarse cry of apology. She took his face between her perfect hands and kissed him.

Wedged between the bottom of the sun-warmed steps and the cool, steaming earth, they held each other and rocked slowly, balanced for now, at least, on faith.

"Let go of my . . . hmmm, all right, don't let go, but I *am* going to call Sammie this time." Charlotte willed one hand away from the back of Ben's head and searched for the portable phone again. It was lost somewhere in his bed. One of his more provocative activities made her take a quick, helpless breath and arch against him. Her shoulder pressed down into hard plastic, and the phone beeped shrilly.

"I shouldn't have bought a model with a paging feature," Ben grumbled. He raised his head from the general vicinity of her navel and squinted at her with mild reproach. "It's not even eight o'clock. You'll wake her up."

Charlotte frowned and tapped a fingertip against his lips. "Here we are, going at it like wild bunnies, and I don't even know if she came home last night. If she doesn't answer the phone this time, I'm heading over there. Besides which, we've got to get out of this bed and talk about what we're going to do. About those newspaper clippings of Jake's."

"We can discuss them in bed."

"My dear Mr. Dreyfus, we've said maybe *two* coherent words to each other since we got here yesterday."

"Well, *more* and *yes* are two of my favorite words."

She smiled. "Set your broth on simmer for a minute."

He propped himself on one elbow, gallantly slid the phone from beneath her shoulder, and presented it to her. "Hurry. I think my thermostat is broken."

Her smile faded. As she punched the Cove's number into the phone, she looked at him wistfully. "My sister deserves this kind of morning. She's still sitting in the middle of the woods with nothing but her pillows to hug. It's not fair."

"It won't do Sam any good for you to feel guilty about getting your bread buttered. In fact, you can help her more now that you're my purring little love beast. Give her and Jake positive reinforcement born from your new attitude."

"Purring little love beast," Charlotte repeated dryly. She held the phone to her ear and listened as it began to ring at the Cove. "*Kitten with a whip* is more like it."

"Hmmm. No whips. I might consider a soft pastry brush though."

"You're wicked. Wicked and creative. I like that in a cook. Damn. She's not answering. I'll give it a few more rings and then I'm . . . *Sammie*?" Charlotte sat up. "Did I wake you up? Oh? No, you sound a little strange. I, uh, came by yesterday but couldn't find you. Didn't see Jake either." A sardonic "as usual" stopped on Charlotte's lips. Ben nodded approvingly, as if he knew she'd resisted. She barely noticed. She was too stunned by her sister's reply. "Oh?" Charlotte stared at Ben, wide-eyed and distracted. "Uhmmm, okay. Bye."

Charlotte dropped the phone in her lap. Ben sat up quickly. "What's wrong? You look like you've been slapped with undercooked spaghetti."

"Let me see if I can recreate Sammie's side of the conversation—with sound effects. *I'm awake.* Gasp. *Fine.* Thunk. Phone receiver hitting the bedpost. *Jake's fine.* Voice about two octaves lower than normal. Breathless. *He's right here.* Sound of someone kissing something. *I'll call you back. In a while. Oh! Hmmm. Don't come over until I do. Ah! It may be a few days.*"

Charlotte shook her head. "That was as far as it went. I felt like I'd called dial-a-moan."

She and Ben traded a long, open-mouthed look. Finally he said, "I told you we'd inspire them. This is good. Must be something in the air. They'll put a few dozen dents in the mattress, then they'll start talking. He'll explain his mysterious newspaper clippings, and we'll all be happy."

"What if he doesn't? He didn't exactly lay his deepest thoughts on a platter before he went hunting for Malcolm Drury." Charlotte squirmed out of bed. "What if she gets blindsided by another round of his frontier justice?"

Ben grabbed her by one hand. "You make an excellent prosecutor but a lousy judge of character."

"I'm going to pay a visit to the great circled one." Her voice shook with nervous anger. "My cousin's ex-wife. Are you coming with me?"

Ben cursed wearily, and nodded.

The passenger window of his rusty blue Escort was scattered in pebble-size pieces across the patched bucket seat. He couldn't believe some bastard had the balls to rip off his crummy car in broad daylight on a busy city street while he was eating lunch in a deli not twenty feet away. That kind of shit happened in places like New York and Atlanta, not Raleigh.

"Hell, Bob, what'd they get? Your eight-track? Your collection of bottle caps?" A fellow reporter with standard-issue wise-ass newsroom sympathy peered over his shoulder as he unlocked the driver's-side door and jerked it open. What was missing? What the hell could anyone want out of his rolling junkyard?

He knew the instant his gaze fell on the empty floorboard below the passenger seat. "My briefcase!"

"Aw, come on, why? That thing had more duct tape on it than leather. Even a crackhead with no brain circuits left wouldn't go to the trouble to steal it."

Bob slumped in the driver's seat and banged the steering wheel in helpless fury. *But someone who wanted my notes on the Lomax story would.*

Chapter
Thirty

"What a dump," Charlotte said sardonically. She and Ben left his car and followed a brick walkway across a pristinely landscaped yard shadowed by dogwoods. "Just your average quarter-million-dollar cottage in one of Raleigh's finest neighborhoods. I hope she went through my cousin's assets with a bulldozer."

Ben glanced at her without a trace of appreciation for her acid humor. "I heard the divorce was amicable."

"You heard what the Lomax publicity machine wanted you to hear. She probably got tired of Tim punching her around."

"Interesting theory. Sam's mentioned that your cousin has an ugly temper, but I don't recall her saying he likes to beat up women."

Charlotte bit her tongue and bounded ahead of him

up brick steps to a terrace before an ornately carved door flanked by narrow windows of patterned glass. She rang the bell. "Act casual," she ordered. "We just dropped by to introduce ourselves to my ex–cousin-in-law."

"Sounds perfectly reasonable to *me*," Ben replied. "I know I'd be pleased if relatives of my ex dropped by unannounced. Maybe she keeps tea and finger sandwiches ready, just in case."

Charlotte glared at him. Eventually a delicate female face topped by feathery blond hair peered at them through a side window. Charlotte smiled as benignly as she could in response. The ornate door opened a few inches, tethered by a length of security chain. Wide blue eyes gazed at them worriedly. Interesting, Charlotte noted. Tim had married a woman who looked like a fragile version of his mother.

"Can I help you?" the poor thing asked in a breathless tone.

Charlotte found herself hunching down to peek back on the same level as those nervous eyes. "Gwen? Gwen Vanderveer?"

"That was my married name. What do you want?"

"I'm sorry to surprise you. I just wanted to meet you and say hello. I'm Tim's cousin. Charlotte. I was passing through town and I—"

"Tim's *cousin*? Alexandra's sending mysterious cousins to spy on me and harass me now?"

"No, no one sent me. Can't we talk a minute?" Charlotte gestured frantically toward Ben. "This is my, hmmm, friend. Harmless-looking, isn't he? Ben Dreyfus—"

"The lawyer?" Gwen Vanderveer's voice rang with horror. "You brought your lawyer to intimidate me?"

"He's not here as an attorney," Charlotte answered urgently. "I didn't realize he had such a reputation. He's only—"

"An innocent bystander," Ben interjected. "And totally confused."

"I'm through being bullied. You can't gang up on me. Leave me alone."

"But I'm not here to—" Charlotte began.

"*I've been pushed too far.* I'm not taking it anymore.

Get off my property. I'm calling the police." She slammed the door. The rattle of locks clicking into place was her good-bye. Stunned, Charlotte peered through a window and watched her flee around the bend of an elegant hallway.

The hot summer day surrounded them with the deceptively peaceful humming of slow bees above pots of colorful impatiens on the terrace. She looked at Ben with growing alarm. "Well, we know this much at least. Something's going on. Something seriously unnerving to the ex–Mrs. Vanderveer."

Ben took her by one hand. "Let's go before the police arrive. I have an aversion to visiting myself in jail."

"I think we have to tell Sammie about this." Charlotte let him pull her down the walkway. "Jake knows something's happening. She needs to know too."

"It wouldn't take Sherlock Holmes to deduce that divorced people are apt to loathe each other. They're probably still feuding over custody of a credenza and a pair of lamps."

"That doesn't explain why Jake circled her picture in the paper!"

He halted abruptly and faced her. "Do you want to disrupt Jake and Sam's first efforts at reconciliation with a lot of questions that don't add up to anything signif icant yet? Is that how you intend to *help* your sister?"

"No."

"Then be patient. We'll give them a few days. In the meantime, I'll put out some feelers and see what I can learn about the obviously *less*-than-amicable Vanderveer divorce."

Charlotte slumped. "You win."

He kissed her. "Hah. Don't flatter me." He searched her face with troubled intensity. "What made you suggest that Tim hits women?"

She froze. "That, my dear Watsonstein, was merely a logical deduction."

She sighed with relief when she heard the faint wail of a siren headed their way. Ben put an arm around her and hustled her to the car.

But she knew she'd sidetracked him for only a little longer.

Highview was shuttered like a fort under siege from invisible armies—the staff banished for the day, the front gate locked, the drapes drawn on the great arching windows, the incessantly ringing phones routed through a single line in an upstairs bedroom, where callers heard Barbara's efficient, polite voice on an answering machine.

The governor and Mrs. Lomax are not available for calls or visitors today.

Downstairs, Alexandra paced the elegant spaces of the vaulted living room with ferocious energy, thinking, planning, refusing to believe the foundation beneath her carefully built world was crumbling. Orrin huddled in an armchair, his stately face pale with anxiety, his shoulders hunched. He raked his hands through his silver hair every few seconds. Alexandra struggled to block his desperation from her mind; she had always been calmer and more tenacious than he, and she wouldn't let his fears pull her down. If she did, she'd begin to think of defeat, not solutions. The galling truth would seep through her defenses.

Everything they'd accomplished together, using the Vanderveer legacy as a stepping-stone, was threatened by the one part of that legacy she had never wanted but had been forced to carry along with her. William's son. *Her* son too, but only a perpetual reminder that she'd been required to breed like a prize mare in order to secure her hold on the Vanderveer name.

"This is what we've been reduced to," Orrin said suddenly, his voice hollow. He swept a hand toward a table littered with papers and notepads. "Sending one of my aides to steal the scribblings of a newspaper reporter."

Alexandra strode to the table and snatched a handful of the material. She shook the wadded papers at him. "Would you rather we have gone on guessing about his intentions? Hearing nervous reports from people who've been subjected to his prying questions? Not knowing whether he was simply playing with rumors or had significant details to back him up? Years of work, your political future, the party's consideration for much bigger things—all of it's at stake!" She threw the papers down. "I'll strangle this black son of a bitch with my own hands if he doesn't stop."

Orrin groaned. "I wish it were that simple. But someone is obviously feeding him information. Someone else knows." He dropped his head into his hands. "You realize the irony here, don't you? You and I have steered our way safely through the mine fields all these years. We've finessed our share of political deals that wouldn't stand up under public scrutiny. Yet none of them have come back to haunt us."

Alexandra knelt by him and clutched his shoulders. "I promise you, we'll be all right. He can ask all the questions he wants. The people he's talking to wouldn't be foolish enough to admit anything. They have their own interests to protect." She shook him lightly. "My darling, I've told you so many times that I'd take care of my son's stupid mistakes. I have. I know this situation inside and out. I've covered the weak points. I've insulated you from any consequences."

He laughed bitterly. "Don't you understand? If my stepson is accused of peddling his influence as a state senator to the highest bidder, the next step will be an investigation of the cover-up."

"But that will never happen. And you had nothing to do with it. I took care of everything."

"Alex, you're grasping at straws. You know how pathetic that defense would be." He spoke will dull sarcasm. "What should I do if my wife is implicated in hiding her son's criminal misuse of public office? Claim I had no idea of it? I'd rather not become a laughingstock as well as an accomplice."

She bent her head to his knees. "I swear it won't come to that. I was so careful, so methodical about damage control. Even if one of Tim's contacts were pressured into revealing something, it could be handled. No one knows enough to put the whole picture together."

"Even Gwen?"

"Gwen is a spineless creature muzzled by a large divorce settlement. She was no match for Tim or me. Tim has kept tabs on her. She's the least of my worries." She took Orrin's hands in a firm, reassuring grip. "Now, listen, my darling. I want you to relax. Leave this to me." She nodded toward the papers scattered on the table. "I'll find out who's behind this nonsense. It won't go any further."

She rose and turned at the doorway, cool, certain of the next steps to take. "I'm holding this family's public image together by sheer willpower. I haven't even decided how to maneuver Samantha and Charlotte yet. I'm not going to add an estranged son to the problems. Please, just let me deal with Tim."

Orrin sank back in his chair, looking defeated.

"Seen Jake much lately?" Joe asked. He sat on the porch steps, nursing a bottle of beer. Clara was ensconced in one of the rocking chairs, swaying slowly, her girth overflowing its narrow wooden boundaries, a glass of bourbon wrapped in her brown hands. Her hands and the glass rode her lap like a buoy on an ocean of flowered skirt. Sam, leaning against a porch post, was hypnotized by the patient motion. Every kind of rhythm made her think of Jake. Timing. The ebb and flow of wildly consummated reunions. She and he had been obsessed with the pulse of pleasure. It obscured the need for troubling conversations, but that couldn't go on forever.

Coming out of her trance, she found Joe and Clara watching her curiously. Joe repeated the question. Sam dropped to the edge of the porch and forced her restless hands to be still atop her jeans. "All the time. He moved back into the house four days ago."

She let that amazing announcement simmer for a few seconds. Clara stopped rocking. Both she and Joe studied Sam hopefully. Sam nodded. "Yep. I've got my husband back." She looked away, gazing blindly across the tree-shadowed yard, planning her words carefully. "At least in some ways."

Clara cocked her head and squinted at Sam. "What you thinkin', girl, askin' Joe and me to come visit today? You don't need a couple of wrinkled old chaperons around."

Sam smiled grimly. "Jake told me he'd be going into the mountains for a couple of hours this afternoon. Said he needs his routines. What he didn't say is that we've calmed down enough to start talking. He doesn't want to talk much. He knows what I want to ask him." Sam hesitated, then added pensively, "So I invited you two here to ask you about the subject he won't discuss. I believe y'all are the people most likely to know the truth about him."

"The truth?" Joe repeated. Something dark and worried glimmered in Clara's eyes. Sam homed in on it. "I went with him to track a lost child. I saw how he works. It's no ordinary skill. In fact, it's nothing short of miraculous. A gift."

Clara's eyes were burning holes in Sam. "Yes, it sure is," she said carefully.

"You've always known about it, haven't you? Both of you."

Joe looked from her to Clara, his mouth open. "I suspected," he said finally. "All the times I watched him go over a piece of ground like he was *seeing* the best spot to dig for gemstone. I've tried to ask him about that ever since he was a kid, but he was close-mouthed about it."

"And you?" Sam asked Clara. "How did you know?" Clara's silence made Sam scrutinize her worriedly. Without her false teeth in place, Clara could, when a dour mood struck, compress her lower face into a lipless hummock. *I'll need some pliers*, Sam thought with giddy despair. "Please tell me what you think," she urged.

"Granny Raincrow had the touch. The day Jake and Ellie was born, Granny told me they had it too."

"Ellie," Sam repeated, dazed. Her stunned thoughts went back to the night Ellie had coaxed Charlotte to tell the Raincrows about Tim's attack. Ellie's intuition about people who were hurt in some way.

"Don't be mad with me because I kept the secret from you. Jake's of his grandma's clan. Same as me. I got a duty to him. I wanted him to tell you about it himself. I couldn't do it for him."

"Do you know why he's never trusted me enough to tell me the truth? Why he still won't admit it to me?"

"Once, I told you that a clan of the little people live in the ravine back of this house, and you smiled real polite, like you thought I was a sweet old crazy woman."

Perplexed by the strange change of subject, Sam shook her head. "I'm sorry. But what—"

"Do you see very far? Can you look inside the shadows on the nights when the moon is full and see the spirits that might be looking back at you? Do you hear the almighty talking to you when you're lost?"

"I'm a . . . a practical person. I had to be that way, Clara, because my mother was just the opposite. So, no, I don't believe in ghosts or anything I can't, can't"—she held up her gloved hands—"anything I can't touch or create for myself with these ten fingers." Dropping her hands onto her stomach she added wearily, "I think of God as a high-school principal who's too busy to leave messages on the bulletin-board."

"Then you're goin' to walk a long road before you understand Jake."

"Please. Please help me to try."

Clara was majestically still. Then she said, "God talks, and Jake's got a rare gift for knowin' how to listen. He touches people and learns about 'em. He touches the things they touch, and those talk to him too. Even the mountains talk to him."

Joe whistled softly. "Man, that explains a lot."

Sam hugged herself and bent her head. "I've thought about all the times when we were kids. When he was there every time I needed him. I never understood how he *knew*."

"It's not that he don't trust you with it," Clara said. She was frowning harder every second, as if caught up in some dilemma she didn't quite know how to resolve. "It's that . . . well, he learns painful things about people, and it can bring on terrible trouble to talk about them."

"What do you mean? What sort of things?"

"I can't . . . I just can't talk for Jake. It wouldn't be right. You keep lovin' him, Sammie. You're right inside his heart and soul. You been there since the day he drew the first words out of you. It's a powerful bond—a man who can feel the good and the bad inside people—loving somebody the way Jake loves you."

Sam stiffened. "He's come home, Clara, but he hasn't said that he still loves me. I need to hear him say it."

"Words are just the icing on the cake," Joe interjected gamely.

"He never had any trouble saying it before."

Clara stared at Sam shrewdly. "You give him the old ruby back yet?"

Sam felt the blood draining out of her face. Her confusion, her questions, suddenly had a symbol. The seed of the bitter feud between her aunt and the Raincrows. Jake wanted it. What did he think it would tell him? What would it do to their lives again?

"Did you give it back to him?" Clara repeated sternly.

"No."

"Good. *Don't*. Don't never give it back to him."

Sam thought of the paths, those taken and those not, that had brought them, finally, together. The time he'd saved her from suffocating in an old trunk. How he'd tracked Charlotte and her when they'd run from Aunt Alex. And, with chilling comprehension, how he'd hunted Malcolm Drury down.

She thought of Jake locked in a cell, staking his trapped and battered hopes on her, scarring a vow into his skin. Believing she would be the one person who opened all the doors for him, and waiting for her, waiting endlessly. Believing that she would keep the ruby for him.

And the one question she was too afraid to ask began to haunt her.

If he could find anything he wanted, what kept him from knowing she'd buried the ruby beside his grand-mother's spring?

Tim glared at Alexandra and dismissed the reporter's notes with a disgusted flick of one hand. He radiated high-strung menace. "What do you want from me? An apology? I've played by the rules I learned watching the two of you. I'm sorry I'm not as good at it as you. But that's all I'm sorry for."

"You seem to forget," Alexandra said slowly, "that you're at the center of this mess. I'm concerned about *your* predicament, first and foremost."

"That's bullshit, Mother. You would have traded me like a stunted colt when I was a child if you could have. I don't doubt you'd still like to."

"Oh, please. Must your excuses always hinge on slights you imagined you suffered as a boy?"

"I didn't imagine that you despised me, Mother. I didn't imagine that Samantha was the child you wanted to raise, not me."

"How can you say that? You're my son. I have tried to protect you from yourself all your life. I've given you opportunities few children ever have."

"I'm a Vanderveer. That's the only thing that's ever meant much to other people. You didn't give that to me. All you did was destroy the one person who ever really made me feel loved. You and Orrin took that away."

"That is one of the most ridiculous accusations you've made to me in your life. And it has nothing to do with the subject at hand."

"Yes, it does. I don't care about proving my worth to you anymore. I just don't give a damn who knows what about me—or about you and Orrin."

"Until you snap out of that mood, at least stay out of my way and keep your mouth shut."

"I'm not the one you have to worry about." A caustic smile played on his mouth. "I've been to see Gwen. You know, I always treated her the way you treated me. I counted on some strange combination of love and fear to keep her under my thumb. But I underestimated her. Just as you've always underestimated me."

"Are you saying Gwen went to the newspaper with stories about us? I don't believe it. She'd have done it when she asked for a divorce, not now."

"The reporter came to *her* with information. She panicked. She confirmed everything he already knew, and even filled in the details." Tim took a step closer, leaning toward her. "It gave me a strange sense of satisfaction to hear what she'd done. Because I get to tell you *why* she was nervous enough to talk. She feared she was being spied on by another side of our family." His voice had dropped to a lethal whisper. He bent his head near Alexandra's. "One of your precious nieces had already come to see her. Charlotte showed up on her doorstep with Ben Dreyfus in tow."

Alexandra stared at him with sick fury. "What interest could Charlotte possibly have in meeting Gwen?"

"Gwen didn't talk to her long enough to find out. But you can put the puzzle together, can't you, Mother? Charlotte's just scouting for Sam. Oh, this is rich. Your pet is after you with all her pretty claws sharpened this time. But she's not the one who dug up dirt about us. It's Jake. I don't know how he did it, but I'm convinced he's the one. I doubt he's forgotten all the times you tried to take her away from him. Especially after he was sitting in jail." He hesitated, studying her face. "That scares you, doesn't it, Mother?" His voice was an accusing, satisfied hiss. "Jake's come home, and he's going to destroy us."

She slapped Tim. He drew back, his face flushing deeply, his eyes glittering. Alexandra trembled furiously. "Don't wallow in your self-destructive cowardice," she whispered between gritted teeth. "You really have no idea how ruthless I can be. Neither do Jake and Samantha. Any harm that's been done to me pales in comparison to the harm I inflict in return. Get out of here. I'll take care of this problem. As always."

Tim's expression had become a stony blank. "Not this time, I think." He turned and left the room. Alexandra waited until she heard the front door slam. Then she turned to Orrin. He sat with his head against the back of his chair. His face was ashen.

Alexandra composed herself by sheer willpower. She was quivering inside. "We can assume we've found the source of our trouble," she told him. "Now we simply have to determine a way to eliminate it. I promise you, we will. We'll be *fine*. We can pretend this episode never happened."

"Pretend," he said. He slurred the word. Then his eyes closed and he slumped sideways in the chair.

Chapter Thirty-One

He couldn't think when he was with Samantha. Couldn't think about anything but her. Her unanswered questions loomed over every brief, quiet moment when they were not dissolving into each other with blind need. So he'd visited his campsite for the first time in days, and gathered his totems to bring here.

The sun had dropped to the rim of the vast, rolling sea of mountains below, casting long shadows across the ledge of Sign Rock. Jake sat there with his collection of newspaper clippings spread before him. His own ancient guidemarks. Like the wind filling a high mountain cave, the familiar gnawing dread began to expand inside his chest. He had the terrible sense that something had gone wrong.

He trailed his fingertips over each sallow piece of paper, sorting through them, driven by something urgent and deep, an intuition that scalded him. Someone had intervened. Hands other than his own had touched what he was touching.

Samantha? No. He would have felt her presence easily. And if she'd examined his belongings, he'd have felt her silent concern—and her guilty invasion—every time he held her.

He closed his eyes. His hands lay flat on the photograph of Alexandra, Orrin, Tim, and Tim's wife. *Charlotte. Charlotte and Ben.*

He drew back in horror. He'd spent years chipping slivers of hard bedrock away from the hidden truth, infinitely methodical and patient, pushing Samantha away so she would not be caught under the hammer.

He had looked away from his work, looked only at Samantha, and shattered the stone. Now he pictured the truth bursting into sharp, glittering fragments as deadly and indiscriminate as shrapnel.

The wind caught his collection and scattered it into the high currents. He staggered to his feet. What door had he opened? What demons had he freed from Pandora's box? Jake turned back toward the Cove quickly, sick with fear.

"Going fishing has always relaxed me and helped me sort through my problems," Ben said darkly. He gave Charlotte a sideways glance as he cut his Jeep's engine. "I had hoped, with pathetic optimism, that the mood might rub off on you."

She pointed defensively to a patch of shiny fish scales clinging to the grimy, stained thighs of her jeans. "I cleaned. I gutted. Turning trout into nice little filets relaxes *me.*"

"Then why haven't you spoken to me all afternoon?"

"Because I didn't want to go fishing. I wanted to visit Sammie and see how she and Jake are doing. See if he really has come out of his surly cocoon. Find out whether he's explained anything to her. I want to know if he's told her his hobby is collecting scrapbook material on our relatives. And I want to ask Jake if he has any inkling why our mutual cousin's ex-wife is jumpier than a lobster in a pot of hot water."

She climbed out of the Jeep and slammed the door. Ben followed her to the door of her condo, muttering under his breath. Charlotte searched for her key in a pocket of her jeans, then lost patience and tried the knob hopefully. "Oh, great, I left the door unlocked again."

Ben shook his head. "As your lawyer and your main squeeze, it's my responsiblity to tell you that you qualify as an 'attractive nuisance.'"

"Don't worry. I have a built-in security system. Little invisible antennae that set off an alarm when anyone messes with me."

"That's the problem."

She shoved the door open, then batted her eyes at him. "But I gave *you* my secret entry code."

"Oh, you let me inside the premises, but you haven't given me the combination to the safe yet."

She stepped into the darkened living room and beckoned grandly for him to follow. "There's nothing in my safe, but I'll show you my—"

Tim moved out of the shadows and kicked the door shut between her and Ben.

It was nearly dark. Sam tried to concentrate on her loom, but kept wondering where Jake was. The low, mournful strains of a jazz disc played on the boom box by her feet, taking up some of the lonely silence. When she heard his footsteps on the porch she leapt up, then stopped herself. Something wounded and proud made her sink back to the bench of her loom. She tuned the portable player to a pop-rock radio station.

If he were going to wander the woods with his secrets for company, she would pretend to be content with her loom and Rod Stewart.

She jumped when she heard the front door slam. Bo's large, long-nailed paws clicked alongside the loud thuds of Jake's quick strides. Jake walked into her workroom with all the calm of a human tornado. Her heart pounding, she peered at him between the vertical strands of thread.

Have a nice walk? came to her lips, but by then he was pulling her off the bench. He said nothing, but held her in a tight, almost ferocious embrace. The breath bubbled out of her in a confused sigh, and she put her arms around him. Conversation was lost—as usual—in anticipation of another irresistible plunge into bed.

But he tilted her head back with his hands cupping her face, then studied every feature as if making certain nothing about her had changed. His scrutiny was so intense, so desperate, alarm shivered through her. She had barely begun to come to terms with his talent, or gift, or *curse*—she wasn't even certain what to call it. How well could he read her emotions, her thoughts?

"Clara and Joe were here while you were gone," she said hoarsely. He didn't look surprised. "I asked them questions. You've obviously kept Joe guessing about you, but not Clara. She told me I was right about you. What Hoke Doop said is true. You have a . . . gift."

He shut his eyes and cursed softly, bitterly. Sam rested her head against his shoulder. "I've always believed in you—your loyalty, your love. Having you in my life was the one miracle I never doubted." She slid her arms tighter around him and lifted her head. He opened his eyes. There were tears in them. Sam whispered, "Because of you, I can believe in this other miracle too."

He didn't say a word. No agreement, but no denial either this time. His unexplainable, unspoken suffering was wrapped around them like a silk web—deceptively fragile, as binding as steel. Sam burrowed her face into the crook of his neck. She felt the accelerated rhythm of his heart against her own chest. "It must color your whole life," she continued, hoping something she could say would wedge further inside the wall around him. "Who you are, how you deal with other people, everything and everyone you love. Or hate." Her fears merged into a tight knot in her throat. "It might explain why you tried to make me think you didn't want me anymore when you went to prison. And why you tried to keep me away after you came home. If you knew something about our lives you couldn't tell me. Something that might hurt me."

He dug his hands into her back. Could he sense her dread that she'd stumbled on the truth? Sam looked at him again. "We can't go on this way. You have to tell me everything. If you know what I'm feeling right now, then you know I'm afraid, but you also know I can deal with it."

But suddenly his head jerked up and he twisted toward the radio. Sam's startled attention went from him to it. "What—" she began, but he held up a hand.

". . . We'll update you on Governor Lomax's condition as details come in," the announcer was saying. "Recapping that story, Governor Orrin Lomax collapsed at his home in Pandora this afternoon and was taken to the hospital there. After doctors determined the governor had suffered a stroke, he was flown to the university medical center in Durham, where he has, at this time, been listed in critical condition. Mrs. Lomax was with the governor when he became ill, and went with him to Durham."

Sam gripped Jake's sleeve. The news was less shocking than the vivid emotions playing across his face. Satisfaction. Uncertainty. Every muscle in his body had tightened in defense. She called his name softly, urgently, as if trying to wake him from a nightmare.

The phone in the living room began to ring. She ignored it, her attention riveted to Jake. He pivoted toward the sound, head up, one hand closing like a hot clamp on her shoulder. His face was grim. "Get the phone," he ordered in a low, gravelly voice.

Sam shook her head. "Whoever it is, they'll call back. Please, talk to me. Tell me why you look as if you're about to explode."

"*Answer the phone,*" he repeated. A shudder went through him. "It's important. It's Charlotte."

"*Sammie*." Charlotte ran to her the instant Sam and Jake rounded the corner of the waiting area outside the doors to the emergency ward. The sight of Jake beside her sister, his expression fierce, clamped a torrent of words inside Charlotte's throat. Panic gave way to caution.

Sammie threw an arm around her shoulders and stared at the red scrape along Charlotte's jaw. "Tim did that to you?"

"He tried to grab my hair. I jerked away from him, and he caught the side of my face with his fingers."

"How's Ben?"

Tears slid down Charlotte's face. "He dislocated his shoulder when he rammed the condo's door open. And he got two cracked ribs when Tim threw him across my living room. *Sammie*, he was all broken up like that, but he kept trying to get up and fight. You remember how huge Tim is. It was David and Goliath, with me in the middle. All I could do was keep a stranglehold on Ben and hiss pathetic threats at Tim."

"What did Tim want?" Sammie asked. Her eyes glittered with fury.

Charlotte shook her head warily, watching Jake. When he reached out and took her chin with one huge, big-knuckled hand, she froze. How much should she say in front of him? It might be better to tell Sammie the details, then let her decide how to confront Jake.

A doctor pushed through the double doors of the treatment rooms and motioned to Charlotte. "We're going to keep your friend overnight. We've given him a shot for the pain. He's not very coherent, but he keeps asking for you."

Charlotte stepped away from Jake's bewildering grasp, then took one of Sammie's hands. "Come with me."

"Jake too," Sammie said quickly. "You have to tell us what Tim wanted. What he said."

"No. Please. Please, not right now. Just come with me, big sister. I'm feeling really *small* at the moment."

Sammie frowned and looked at Jake. He nodded. "Go on." She touched his arm. "I'll be right back."

"I know," he said.

Charlotte dragged Sammie into the examining area. The doctor pointed them toward a curtained cubicle. Charlotte ran to it and slipped inside. She forced a sob back when she saw Ben ensconced on a gurney, bare from the waist up, his right arm in a sling and a girdle of white tape binding his rib cage. She bent over him. He gazed up at her with groggy devotion but more than a hint of unhappiness. "Is it obvious," he mumbled, "that I'm a pit bull trapped in the body of a poodle?"

"You're no poodle," she declared tearfully. She stroked his hair and kissed his forehead, then carefully took the hand of his good arm in hers. She was dimly aware of Sammie standing close beside her. "We're *not* going to keep telling the doctor that you fell off a fishing dock. We're going to tell him the truth. My own cousin did this to you. State senator or not, he can't get away with this. I'm going to call the sheriff and report him."

Ben scowled sleepily. "I don't want to bring assault charges against him. I don't want to sue him for my medical bills. I want to *kill* him."

"*Don't say that.* You don't have to prove anything to me."

Charlotte bowed her head. Sammie took her by the shoulders. "Tell me what happened."

"He stood over us," Charlotte said raggedly. "He looked as if he'd beat us both to pieces if we got up from the floor. He wanted to give us a lecture, he said. He talked about me—what he did to me at Highview—the truth, just like it happened. He said he hated his mother and took it out on us, Sammie. He . . . pulled his hair back from the top of his ear—well, where the top of his ear used to be—and he said, 'See? See what you did to me? It's not as bad as what she did to me.' "

"His mother? Aunt Alex? Did he say what he meant by that?"

"Told us," Ben said, mushing the words with his drugged, elegant drawl, "told us he's glad Jake is punishing her."

"Jake . . . *what*?" Sammie's voice rose desperately.

"I don't understand it all," Charlotte interjected, looking at her sister's horrified face with sympathy. "Just that he thinks Jake is behind some kind of terrible investigation that's being done. He mumbled about his mother, and Orrin—how they deserved it. How *he* deserved it, because he'd never had the courage to fight back."

"Jake hasn't done anything to him, Aunt Alex, or Orrin," Sammie said, shaking Charlotte a little. "There's no reason for him to care about them."

"Oh, Sammie, you know how it's always been. You know it hasn't changed. Ben and I . . . a few days ago . . . we found some things in Jake's tent. Newspaper articles about Aunt Alex and the others. He's been involved in some sort of revenge against them, Sammie. And they've figured that much out." She shook her head wildly. "Tim said that, and then he just walked out. Just left us on the floor and calmly walked out, got in his car, and drove off."

"Hey, hey, look at me," Ben mumbled with moon-eyed determination. He tugged at Charlotte's hands and winced, but kept tugging until she clutched his arm to make him stop hurting himself. "It wasn't your fault," he said, apparently unconcerned with making sense or nonsense of anything other than his own train of thought. His voice was hoarse, loving. "You didn't do anything wrong. With Tim. He's insane. You understand? No more . . . embarrassment. Promise?"

Charlotte broke down, sobbing softly and squeezing his hand with infinite care. "I love you. I didn't want you to know."

"It's all right. When I can walk without my bones squeaking, I'll . . . kill him. Kill him for hurting you."

"*No!*"

She was so intent on soothing his lovely, violent attitude that it took her a moment to realize that Sammie had left them.

Jake was gone. *Gone.* Oh, God, he hadn't needed to hear the details. He'd gleaned the basics when he touched Charlotte. Sam realized that now.

And he'd encouraged Sam to go into the examining room so he could leave before she followed him. She stumbled into the parking lot and retched when she saw the empty space where their car had been. He'd been keeping so much more from her than she'd ever imagined. What it was, she still didn't know precisely. But it was deadly.

He had gone to take care of business without her—shut her out, just as he'd done ten years ago.

But this time she would find a way to save him from himself, and from the past, no matter what secrets it harbored.

Jake found Tim's car on an old logging trail deep in the lap of the Razorbacks. The cluster of high, thin ridges flanked the more rounded peaks north of Pandora. Jake had followed him there by memory as much as instinct. Tim had staked out one of the Razorbacks during high school; he had claimed the highest peak as his personal territory, the place he retreated to after football games, usually with a girl and case of beer in tow.

Jake climbed a narrow trail up the mountain. The pale half-moon barely crept down to the forest floor shielded by towering fir and spruce. He sidestepped boulders and rotting tree trunks with long, sure strides. The forest ended abruptly, and he stopped at the edge of the vast, ancient bald at the mountain's summit. Mysterious natural forces had stripped the forest away and created a meadow there. Its knee-high grasses and flowers were tinted silver under the moon.

Tim stood at the distant rim, looking outward, silhouetted against a canopy of black sky and stars.

Jake crossed the meadow soundlessly, walking in centuries of long-erased footprints. Hunters, shamans, explorers. Wanderers searching for the edge of forever. He halted a dozen yards from his cousin, and for a fleeting moment remembered the nervous towheaded boy who had been no threat to anyone. But then, they had both been helpless children once.

He called Tim's name.

Tim pivoted. "I thought you'd come after me," he said. "I knew I'd provoke you to make a move. How do you do it, cousin? What's your secret? You and Ellie—you were always odd. I looked up to you both. And I hated you for the power you had over my mother. You saw her for what she was. You were the only people I've ever known who frightened her. Ellie's gone, but my mother is still afraid of *you*. You're the one, aren't you? You used me to get to her."

Jake stood as Tim did—legs braced apart, quietly posed with the same moonwashed calmness. "I felt sorry for you," Jake told him slowly, "until the day you turned on Samantha."

Tim's bitter laugh echoed across the bald. "She and Charlotte got their ounce of flesh from me. You couldn't let it go? Hell, I didn't want anything more to do with them *or* you."

"It's not that simple."

"Oh? Congratulations, cousin. You've set the stage. My mother's hovering over Orrin and her lost ambitions right now. Hell, don't worry about me causing any more trouble. Worry about her—you've ruined her in the only way anybody could. She was a starmaker. Now she's just the mother of a criminal and the wife of an invalid. You did that to her. Cold-blooded. I still admire you, cousin."

Jake took several steps closer, then stopped again. "You don't know as much about her as I do," he said softly. "But you've always known what she did to your father."

The night wind moaned across the bald, enveloping Tim's long silence, settling on him, slumping his shoulders. Jake couldn't separate its mourning sound from the roar of his own pulse in his ears. "You've had to live with that," he went on. "Afraid to admit it, pretending it didn't happen, but never forgetting what you saw that night. Hating yourself because you couldn't stop remembering, because you still wanted her to love you, even if she'd killed—"

Tim threw his head back. A guttural shout of pain and fury rose from him. He stared at Jake. "My whole life has been about revenge. I'm the one who made it possible. Don't forget that."

He turned and stumbled the last few feet to the bald's edge. It cut the meadow off at a stony precipice. He whipped around and balanced there, arms outspread. Jake moved quickly toward him, reaching out. "Don't," Tim yelled. "By God, if you try, I'll pull you over with me. You want to live. You want to go home to Samantha."

Jake halted. Tim's face was a mask of white moonlight with eyes slashed in black shadow. "This isn't how it has to end for you."

"It's exactly how it has to end," Tim replied. He smiled—another slash of blackness in the mask. "There's an old Cagney gangster movie. He's lost everything. He's surrounded. Up on some roof . . . something like that. He knows he's going down. And all he can think about is what his mother wanted for him. *Top of the world, Ma*." Tim's voice dropped to a drone mingled with the tugging wind. "*Top of the world*."

He leaned back. The wind and the mountain took care of the rest.

Chapter
Thirty-Two

Clara lay, sleepless and alert, in a sagging recliner in her tiny, cluttered living room with the lights off and the door open. Beds were for young bodies undisturbed by aching joints and insistent bladders; beds were for people who hadn't begun to measure the years left to accomplish their tasks.

She was as secure in her place as the creatures who crept through the dark, secluded hollow around her house, peering through her unlatched screen door with their wild, curious eyes.

And when people called on her in the night for instruction and comfort, as they often did, she rocked herself out of the recliner and saw to their needs.

Tonight she was waiting for trouble.

Patsy Jones, a good girl who'd become a good woman, had gotten that degree in social work. She'd been at

486

the hospital, looking after one of her cases, when Ben Dreyfus came in with Sammie's sister. Ben Dreyfus had gotten busted up in an accident, Patsy said. Then Jake and Sammie showed up. Jake had walked off. Sammie was trying to find him.

When her dogs began to bark, Clara rocked forward and stared into the yard beyond her front porch. A car pulled in.

A few seconds later Sammie was knocking on the screen door's wooden frame.

"I'm right here," Clara said from the darkened room. She turned a lamp on beside her chair. Sammie bolted into the house and dropped to her heels beside Clara's recliner. Clara frowned at her ashen face and red-rimmed eyes, her rumpled shirt and jeans.

She held out a gnarled hand and Sammie gripped it gratefully. "Jake's disappeared," Sammie said. Her voice was hoarse and weary. "I've looked everywhere I can think of. Have you heard from him?"

"No." Clara leaned forward and listened intently as Sammie explained. Each word weighed heavier than the last. Clara had watched Sammie and Jake walk toward this crossroads their whole lives, had seen it looming on their horizon like a thunderhead. There was no turning away.

"Help me," Sammie begged. "You know what he's after. I can see that in your eyes. The ruby. My aunt. Tim. The fire at the Cove. The man Jake went to prison for killing. It all fits together somehow, doesn't it? *Please*, talk to me, Clara. If you keep it to yourself, he'll be all alone out there, the way he was ten years ago. If something happens to him"—Sammie clutched Clara's hand harder. Her eyes were wild and desperate—*"we've run out of second chances."*

Clara sighed. Her purpose in the journey had become clear to her. It was hard duty; she would gladly have shut her eyes and not recognized it. But she couldn't. She had promised Granny Raincrow she'd do her best.

The sun was rising at the tops of the mountains on the Cove's eastern edge in an apron of angry orange and red, promising another stormy summer day. Jake hoped for rain as he drove into the Cove. Clear the air. He wanted to wash the night's vivid stains from his mind, think, consider what to do next, what to tell Samantha about Tim, and what had happened on Razorback Bald.

He could no longer deny how he tracked people, or how he knew their ugly secrets. With that understanding bridging the past, he could tell Samantha how Alexandra had destroyed his uncle William. She would see how that had been enough to breed revenge in him— that, combined with Alexandra's cold-hearted greed and manipulation ever since, and Tim's violence.

It was enough. More than enough to explain himself to Samantha. She would never have to share the far more painful reasons behind his actions.

But she wasn't waiting for him at the Cove. Instead, he found Joe's Cadillac in the yard. Joe and Clara sat side by side on the porch steps. Bo lumbered out to greet him happily after a long night spent locked in the house.

Something sharp and terrible twisted in Jake's stomach as he walked toward the porch. He didn't have to touch Joe or Clara to sense their dark mood. *Where was Samantha?*

Clara hoisted herself from the step with Joe's help. She shuffled to Jake with one fist knotted over her broad middle and grim scrutiny in her eyes. "Did you push your cousin off Razorback?"

"No. But I went looking for him. And I was there when he jumped."

After a moment Clara nodded. "That's what I figured."

Joe stepped forward. "Everybody's heard about Tim. This has gotten to the point where it can't be stopped by you. The law is looking for you, boy. People haven't decided yet whether Tim jumped off that bald or got pushed. You seem a likely party to it. They want to take you in and ask you questions. Like where you were all night."

"I climbed down and found him, where he lay. I couldn't leave him there if he was alive. But he wasn't. I went to a pay phone over at Cawatie and called the sheriff." He started past them. He couldn't feel Samantha's whereabouts, and the emptiness froze his blood. Joe blocked his way.

"She's not here."

"She come to me in the middle of the night," Clara said. Jake pivoted toward her quickly. "She was searchin' for you, afraid you'd got yourself into awful trouble again." Clara peered up at him steadily. "I told her, Jake. It was time. I told her everything about her aunt."

Her announcement tore the breath out of him. He stared at her while a savage, gnawing fear hollowed him to the core. "*Why?*"

" 'Cause I've always meant what I said to you. You can't finish this alone. Much as you tried, it ain't possible. Hiding the truth ain't gonna stop no ravenmocker. Sammie's got to deal with the shame, now or sometime."

Clara took one of Jake's hands, stuck her clenched fist into it, and relaxed her fingers. The cool, smooth ruby dropped onto his palm. He stared at it in sick silence. "She told me where she hid it," Clara explained. "She'd buried it beside your granny's spring. You never even had an inkling, did you, boy? That's how I know I did right to tell her everything. 'Cause you're still deaf and blind." She closed his paralyzed fingers over the stone.

Samantha had returned it to him. Her apology. A lifetime of love glimmering like the star, but trapped, like it, inside the bloodred grief and shame he'd fought so hard to keep from her.

"She went after Alexandra?" His voice shook. "*You let her go?*"

"I told her it'd take both of you, but she wouldn't hear that."

"I've got to find her before she gets to Alexandra."

Joe clamped a hand on his arm. "The law's lookin' for you. If you go off half cocked, they'll pick you up before you get far."

"I have to take that chance."

Bo lifted his head suddenly and began to bark. Jake spun toward the narrow driveway. *A car on the Cove road*. The knowledge came swiftly, the silent, unmistakable song turning into a hideous shriek in his mind. It wasn't Samantha.

"Get in the woods," Joe yelled. "Go on. Wait out of sight. Me and Clara'll do the talkin'."

Jake heard himself utter a guttural sound of frustration. He didn't have time for hiding. He hadn't done anything to deserve blame. *Just like ten years ago, but you couldn't prove it. Can't prove anything now.* Clara tugged fiercely at him. "You won't be any good to Sammie if the sheriff latches onto you. *Git.*"

That sharp point cut his hesitation. He told Bo to stay, then walked swiftly into the forest. The ruby felt like a hot coal in his hand. Useless, burning his skin.

"Ain't seen him or Sammie," Clara told the deputy. "Joe drove me over so I could feed ol' Bo. I reckon Sammie and Jake are keepin' company with Sammie's sister. Her boyfriend got banged up in a accident. He's at the hospital."

The deputy scowled at Bo, who lay in the yard, looking toward the woods and whining. "What's wrong with him?"

"There's a yellow-jacket nest in a log over yonder," Joe said quickly. "They been after him."

"Well, I have orders to wait here until Jake shows up," the deputy said, frowning harder. "Sheriff wants to find out where Jake was when Senator Vanderveer took the short way down from Razorback."

Joe grunted with disgust. "Jake's got no reason to throw his cousin off a ledge. They went separate ways before either of 'em was grown. Probably haven't even crossed paths since Jake got out of prison."

"The governor keels over with a stroke and his state-senator stepson goes sky diving without a parachute. Maybe it's just a damn bad run of luck, but it's got every honcho in the state government running around like chickens with their heads cut off, looking for explanations."

"I say Tim Vanderveer did himself in," Joe said. "He always was a moody soul. Probably grieving over his step-father. I heard the doctors aren't giving the governor good odds."

The deputy threw up his hands. "Look, we're just rounding up anybody who might've seen the senator last night. Anybody who has a clue about his state of mind. *Somebody* found his body and reported it. We want to find out who that was."

"You got the call on tape, don't you? The sheriff knows Jake's voice. Did he think it sounded like Jake?"

"Aw, hell, the dispatcher was half asleep and havin' trouble with the system. It didn't record. For all we know, she could've been talking to Barney the purple dinosaur."

Clara fixed something akin to the evil eye on the deputy. "Jake'll come in and talk to you folks. He's got nothing to hide. We'll send him along when he gets here. You go on back to town. Jake don't deserve to be carted off in a patrol car."

"Probably not, but I've got my orders." He settled on the porch steps and stared at Bo suspiciously, then turned the same intense glare on Joe and Clara. "So I'll wait. Y'all have a seat and wait with me."

Watching from the cover of the woods, Jake broke into a cold sweat. He was alone, trapped, with only the unforgiving stone as a guide. It would not help him. He turned away from the house and began the long trek across the beautiful, merciless terrain, thinking, planning, praying.

His mind was filled with the soft, deadly whisper of a ravenmocker's wings.

"Mrs. Lomax? Is there anyone you want me to call?"

When Alexandra didn't answer, Barbara slid closer to her on the couch. Alexandra was vaguely aware of the low hum of voices outside the waiting room's closed door and the silent scream of loss and disbelief inside her own mind. Tim was dead. And less than an hour ago, she had held Orrin's limp hand and watched the doctors turn off machines that could no longer keep him alive.

Her secretary was crying for her; Alexandra was too numb to shed tears.

Barbara repeated the question. Alexandra shivered. "Who is left for you to call?" She stared blindly into space. "Who is left for me?"

Barbara gave a tearful cry. "There are reporters downstairs. Our people want your permission to issue a statement. Everyone from the governor's staff is waiting in the hall."

"They should tell the media that my husband died an hour ago and my son died last night. Nothing else is important."

"What do you want them to say about Tim?"

"My son loved his stepfather. He was in shock over his stepfather's illness. He had an accident."

Lies. All lies. Jake had destroyed her family. Jake and Samantha. Only Jake had a reason, but he had turned Samantha against her. Somehow he had pried open the doors to the past and taken revenge—ruining Alexandra's future through her loved ones just as she had ruined his.

It was not a fair trade.

She would make him pay his debt.

"I'm going home now," Alexandra announced. "I'm going back to Pandora. I need to take care of the arrangements. Have someone bring my car. I want to go to the airport. I'll fly the Cessna home."

"Mrs. Lomax, you can't do that. You're in shock. You don't know what you're doing."

Alexandra looked at her with measured, unblinking strength. "I have never been more aware of what I have to do."

The breeze across the airport runways smelled of oil and heat. Slate-gray summer clouds pressed the muggy air down on her, and the noise of the big jets in a distant sector of the airport was a low, unending drone in Sam's ears. She walked slowly through the wide arena of concrete and sky, an actress moving with intense concentration toward the stage.

Official-looking men and women were crowded around Alexandra's small airplane, and Sam could see them sweating in their business suits. The plane was a puddle jumper, one of those propeller-driven crafts that resembled an oversize toy. Sam glimpsed her aunt at the group's center, stately in her grief, an elegant murderer.

The woman who had manipulated everyone in her path. Who had sent a con man to plunder her own sister's savings and fragile independence. Who had spared no mercy for Sarah, Hugh, and Ellie. Who had let Jake go to prison for tracking down the truth.

Sam recognized Barbara in the group. At the same moment, her aunt's longtime secretary glanced Sam's way, gaped at her, then hurried over, hands outstretched. Barbara seemed relieved to see her. Sam halted rigidly as Barbara grasped her shoulders. "You couldn't have shown up at a better time," she told Sam. "I should have known you wouldn't let old misunderstandings keep you away. She's your *family*."

That word had the power to twist Sam's stomach. Yes, Alexandra was her family. A hopelessly entrenched poison, impossible to wash out. The reason Jake had kept secrets from her. The reason he couldn't bring himself to say he still loved her. "Blood's thicker than water," she answered.

"How did you find us?"

"Went to the hospital first. They told me she was here."

"She's determined to fly herself to Pandora. We've been trying to talk her out of it, but she won't listen. She keeps saying it will only take about an hour, and that she needs the time to think. She's in shock, Samantha. She won't talk about Orrin or Tim. She won't let go and cry."

Sam stared past Barbara. "I'll go with her. She'll talk

to me. I'm a very good listener." She walked on, the hair rising on the nape of her neck while a dark feeling of serenity grew inside her.

Her aunt's attention rested on her. Alexandra stiffened. Her head came up, and the look on her face gave away nothing—not surprise, or wariness, or pleasure. The crowd parted. Sam was dimly conscious of the stares. She steeled herself, put an arm around Alexandra's shoulders, and hugged her tightly. "I'm glad I caught up with you," she told her aunt. *I caught you*, Sam amended silently. *I caught you in your lies*. "I'll keep you company on the trip home."

Alexandra draped her arms around Sam. "See?" she said to the others. "My niece knows me better than all of you do. She doesn't expect me to fall apart." She looked at Sam—hollow-eyed but sharp. "We're very much alike. Strong. We'll get through this together."

Sam nodded.

Jake climbed a steep bank, pushed his way through a thicket of brambles, and halted, breathing heavily, along an empty road on the outskirts of town. The ribbon of pavement snaked along a man-made terrace carved out of the mountain's flanks decades earlier, shadowed by overhanging trees until it disappeared around a switchback curve ahead.

He would follow the quiet back road, hoping to catch a ride on one of the lumber trucks or tankers that sometimes used the road as a bypass around town. It might take hours to get a ride; even the toughest rig drivers would think twice about stopping for a dangerous-looking stranger in the middle of nowhere.

Jake began walking. He refused to think too much about his haphazard journey. Panic churned under his frustration, and he couldn't let it distract him.

The day was slipping inside gray clouds and mist; it was the kind of weather that would blanket the high places in dense white fog by night.

He had to get out of the mountains before then.

He sensed a car coming long before he heard it. Cars meant trouble—a deputy, the state patrol, a forest ranger—people who might be hunting for him. Locals who might tell someone they'd seen him. He cursed the lost chance and eased back into the concealing thickets.

A late-model pickup truck crept around the curve. Jake was instantly wary. It moved too slowly, even for the tricky road. Could be someone hoping to take potshots at the deer that grazed the road's grassy shoulder. Could be someone looking for him.

The truck rolled closer, inching along. The driver's window was open. A burly black arm in a short-sleeved shirt was crooked on the sill.

Hoke Doop, his dark, jowly face compressed in serious lines, scanned the thicket.

Jake bolted forward. Hoke jerked the truck to a stop. "I'll be damned," the detective called. "I heard the local boys were lookin' for you, and I figured you might need some help. I went prowling for you. My hunches are workin' like a Swiss clock today."

Jake swung the passenger door open and leapt inside.

They had not spoken a word to each other since climbing into the plane. For almost an hour now Sam had sat in the close confines without speaking. She wasn't sure what she was waiting for; she wasn't afraid. The plane bucked in the rough air. Clouds closed in around them, and streams of water whipped along the small window beside her face. She studied her fading reflection in that crying mirror, and relived her memories of Jake.

Summing up the happiness, the sorrow, the love. Tying up the loose threads; clearing her loom of the tapestry they had woven together. Wrapping herself securely in that intricate, marvelous cloth. That was why she had waited—to feel, to know, its reassuring warmth around her.

"We're coming into the mountains," Alexandra said in a soft, caustic tone. "Almost home. How long do you intend to keep up the sympathetic pretense?"

Her question jolted Sam. Time was up. She turned

toward her aunt, and for a moment she only studied her—the clean, delicate profile, the hard mouth and eyes, the unfailingly confident hands gripping the plane's controls. "Why wouldn't I feel sorry for you?" Sam asked.

"*Stop it.* I'm not a fool. You wanted to hurt me. You and Jake. What did you think—that you could hide behind a newspaper reporter and I'd never suspect? That you could tear down everything I've built and then live happily ever after, gloating over your victory?" Her voice rose. "The two of you *killed* Orrin. You *killed* Tim."

Sam leaned back and shut her eyes. "It's easier for you to believe that than admit the truth. But I'm sure you understand how one small push can start a chain of events."

"He's finished. Do you hear me? *Jake is finished.* I'm going to prove he was on that bald with Tim last night. I'm going to prove my son's death was no accident, no *suicide.*"

Sam opened her eyes. "You think you're invincible."

"Look at me. I'm still here. *And I will survive and prosper long after Jake is gone.*"

Sam laid a cool hand on her arm. "There's no way out this time. No more lies. No ... Malcolm Drury ... doing your dirty work for you."

Alexandra jerked. She turned a livid, searing gaze to Sam's condemning one. Her mouth worked. Sam straightened in the seat. They were so close together. Blood kin, opposite sides of the same hard coin. "Don't bother to say it isn't true. You sent him into my mother's life. You let him hurt her. Jake tracked him down that time and made him suffer for what he'd done. But you waited. You used Malcolm again—to destroy the Raincrows. And you let Jake go to prison for punishing Malcolm. Jake knew you were behind all of it, but he was trapped—not just by prison, but because he never wanted me to know what my own aunt had done to his family, and to him."

Sam paused, watching the words sink into Alexandra's expression. A kind of terrified fury glimmered in her eyes. Sam breathed evenly, measuring every second. "Please don't deny it. Because I'll never believe you." Her hand tightened on Alexandra's stiff, trembling arm. "And I'll never let you go."

Slowly, the horror that suffused Alexandra drained away. She appeared almost relaxed. Burned down to glowing, deadly coals. "How did he know?"

"There are some things I can't explain. Things you don't deserve to hear. But he does know, and so do I. And I won't let you hurt him anymore." She stared quietly into the mirror of unflinching blue eyes. "Understand? I'm here to finish what you started."

"Don't you see? Jake forced me to take steps to protect what was mine."

"None of it ever belonged to you. You stole it."

"I wanted to own everything that was precious in the world," Alexandra whispered. "That included you. More than anything else. My own perfect replica."

"No. I'm like you in only one way. I don't give up."

"If I said I won't land this plane until we reach a compromise?" There was an unspoken question underneath, a test.

Sam didn't hesitate. "I can't go home to Jake. You murdered his family. When he looks at me, he'll always see you." She placed both perfect, graceful hands on Alexandra's, riding the motion of the plane's control with them. "End it now."

Alexandra smiled at her. There was savage pride in it. Slowly, bonded by the only bleak victory they had ever shared, they drew their hands away.

"What's wrong? You sick, boy?" Hoke kept one eye on the interstate traffic and glanced anxiously at Jake, who had suddenly doubled over on the truck's seat. *Sick* wasn't a strong enough word for the way Jake looked. He had his forearms folded across his stomach as if something had been ripped out of him. He shook violently and gasped for air. "Stop," he ordered in a raw tone.

Hoke was too stunned to ask questions. He maneuvered his truck into the grassy median and rolled to a stop. Jake gripped the dash, white-knuckled, and pushed himself upright. Hoke had never seen so much pain and panic in a man's face. "Something's happened," he said. "Go . . . back. Toward the mountains."

The know-how had slammed into Jake like a sledgehammer. Hoke didn't doubt that something terrible *had* happened. He slapped the truck into gear, made a U turn that sprayed chunks of rain-soaked sod into the air, and headed back down the highway at full tilt. "Talk to me, boy," he commanded grimly. "Don't let your imagination get the best of you. Tune it out and give me something solid. 'Cause we're headin' in the wrong direction if Sammie's still in Durham, like you thought she was before."

Jake fell back on the seat and pressed his hands to his head. He made a guttural sound that chilled Hoke's skin. "She's not there anymore. She's not . . . all right anymore."

Hoke steered with one hand and grabbed his car phone with the other. "My brother's baby girl is a secretary at the hospital over in Durham." He punched a number. "Louise, honey? It's Uncle Hoke. Aw, got nothin' better to do on my day off than meddle in some gossip. You still got government honchos and reporters runnin' around there? You *do*? Heard anything interestin'?"

Hoke listened intensely, didn't like what his niece told him, said his thanks and good-bye abruptly, then dropped the phone back in its berth. "Miz Lomax left for the airport a couple of hours ago. Everybody's talkin' about it. Callin' her *steel magnolia,* and such. Because she was set on flying herself back to Pandora in her own plane."

He glanced at Jake, who was looking more torn out of the frame every second. Hoke took the phone again. "Got a fishin' buddy at the airport. Chief of security." Hoke punched another number, listened, then barked, "Teddy, you old sonuvabitch. This is Hoke. Got no time to hear you tell more lies about your prize bass. Checkin' up on something. Did the governor's widow come through there a while ago? Oh? Oh? Yeah, that must've been sweet. Bye."

Hoke put the phone down slowly, as if a ton of bricks had been dumped on him. He could feel Jake staring at him. "Real sweet thing, Teddy said." Hoke cleared his throat. "Miz Lomax was bound and determined to head home in her own plane, nasty weather be damned. Her niece showed up to keep her company. Went with her."

The last heartbeat before the end of the world couldn't have been any quieter. Then Jake said in a voice that made Hoke shiver, "Take me to somebody who has a helicopter."

"Where's Sammie?"

Charlotte stood in the yard, rain drizzling down her face, one hand on the open door of the second car she'd rented after Sammie had taken the other car in search of Jake the night before. She looked from Joe and Clara to the scowling deputy sheriff. All three were ensconced on the porch with Bo, who lay with his graying muzzle morosely planted on his front paws.

"We haven't seen her or Jake all day," Joe said.

"I've called a dozen times. Why didn't one of you answer the phone?"

Joe gave the deputy a sour glance. "Barney Fife wouldn't let us."

The deputy shifted awkwardly as Charlotte turned a furious stare on him. He said loudly, "I have my orders," against a background of dripping rain and the sporadic crackle of the dispatcher's voice conversing with other deputies on the tiny radio unit perched on his shoulder. "You find Jake for me, and I'll get out of your hair."

Charlotte exploded. "I don't know where my brother-in-law is, but I'm sure as hell not going to help you find him so your neo-Nazi interrogators can harass him. He and my sister are probably trying to learn what made our mutual cousin walk off the side of a mountain last night! Our cousin's dead, his stepfather's dead"—she waved toward Ben, who sat in the car's passenger side looking like a dazed, half-wrapped mummy—"my guy here is recuperating from a . . . an accident, so don't you think we have *enough* to deal with? I'm bringing my guy into this house and putting him to bed, and the next time the phone rings, *I'll* answer it. Now get your Dudley-Dooright ass out of my way."

"*Charlotte*," Ben interjected groggily. "I'm really not up for any *Bonnie and Clyde* theatrics at the moment."

The deputy rose hurriedly, looking wistful. "Ma'am, I have feelings too, you know. I went to high school with Tim, and Jake, and Jake's sister. Jake and Ellie kept Tim from bullying me and every other scrawny little 'Dudley Dooright' in town. My whole family loved Jake's daddy and counted on him to take care of 'em when they was sick. One of my folks' proudest possessions is a hand-painted portrait Jake's mama gave them on their first wedding anniversary." The deputy flailed his arms for emphasis. "Like most of the people around here, I'd just as soon leave Jake alone and wish him well."

Charlotte shook her head. "Then tell the sheriff that, and *go away*. Ben, say something. He can't commandeer this house and ambush Jake for no good reason, can he?"

Ben straightened gallantly but with obvious pain, his bad arm in a sling and his taped rib cage showing under the shirt draped around his shoulders. "I'll argue your case with every breath in my battered body. In the best tradition of my literary hero, Atticus Finch, I shall humble this unsuspecting officer of the law with my uncanny impression of Gregory Peck—"

"Hush," Charlotte said, suddenly ashamed of pressuring him for help when he was barely able to sit upright. She dropped down beside him and stroked his hair. "You've done more than your share of noble wrangling for me, Sammie, and Jake. *Shhh*. Relax and enjoy your medication."

"—and if all else fails, my love," Ben continued doggedly, "I will crawl out of this vehicle and bite your oppressor on the ankle."

Charlotte sighed. "I'll behave, for your sake. Sammie and Jake will show up eventually."

The deputy's shoulder radio emitted an electronic squawk, followed by the dispatcher yelling *Duane,* as if something had rattled the official procedure out of her vocabulary. The deputy jumped. He grasped the unit. "I'm right here."

"You still at the Raincrows'?"

"Yeah. All I've got so far is Jake's sister-in-law, and she's making my life miserable."

"Get out to the airstrip as fast as you can. Sheriff needs everybody over there. Mrs. Lomax was flying in from Durham, and she should've landed an hour ago. We think the plane went down in the fog."

Clara muttered something in Cherokee. Charlotte reeled with shock. In the space of twenty-four hours Orrin had died of a stroke, Tim had fallen or jumped from a secluded cliff, and now Aunt Alex was missing. It was as if some bizarre black hole were swallowing the family up one by one. *Where were Sammie and Jake?*

"I'm on my way," the deputy said.

"Duane!" the dispatcher called. "Wait!"

"Yeah?"

"Jake's sister-in-law is also Mrs. Lomax's *niece.*"

The deputy looked startled, as if he'd just remembered that fact. He squinted at Charlotte, who nodded grimly. "I don't think she's going to collapse if I leave," he said with drawling exasperation.

"Duane! You better bring her with you. Her sister was on the plane with Mrs. Lomax."

Charlotte's knees buckled. She sagged against the car door. Dimly she heard Clara speaking to Joe. One strange word stuck in Charlotte's terrified thoughts.

Ravenmocker.

Chapter
Thirty-Three

S am floated in a nightmarish dreamscape haunted
by confusion and terror, her life broken into small,
vivid pieces—rubies that glowed like eyes, hard
walls pinning her inside the antique trunk when she was
a child, looms that clattered like gnashing wooden mouths,
the lonely years when Jake was in prison, reluctant wak-
ings into empty mornings when she had to acknowledge,
before she opened her eyes, that he wasn't beside her.

She floated up through that crowded black land into
a cloud of agonizing pain. It jolted her eyes open and
made her gasp for air. A small part of her mind focused
on small details—the crushed sheath of the cockpit
clutching her legs and folding her forward, the sticky red
splotches on her outflung arm, the hard, bumpy surface
of the mangled control panel beneath her cheek. She stared
out the shattered side window at a steep slope of rock and

earth and broken trees shrouded in a ghostly gray mist.

Turning her head required all her willpower. Every inch of movement brought a fresh wave of pain. She concentrated on little details to subvert the torture. Wispy, fading light. The bizarre discovery that one of the plane's shattered wings lay across the nose. The startling canopy of trees beyond the broken windows. Trees were not that fully branched at ground level. She was gazing straight out into their crowns. That made no sense, and her bewilderment nearly segued into hopeless panic. *Think*, she chanted silently.

Creaking nails-on-chalkboard sounds caught her attention. The protests of metal shifting against metal. The unmistakable tremor that went through the plane's carcass. The lopsided tilt of her body, and the narrow band of the seat belt digging into her hip. She added up those details a dozen times, until they produced an answer.

The wreckage was balanced on rocks and broken trees, high on the side of a steep ridge.

She refused to concentrate on that frightening image. Sam shut her eyes, took a deep breath, and twisted her head to the other side in one wrenching motion. She rested her cheek on the weirdly upthrust panel of gauges and struggled not to black out. When the pain and darkness receded, she opened her eyes and slowly raised her head.

She met a startling barricade of pine branches. A limb of a massive tree had snagged the delicate plane, piercing the cockpit's windshield. Sam was dimly aware of lifting her left arm. Every muscle in it seemed to be tearing away from the others. She pawed the smaller branches. Her strength gave out and her arm sank limply atop them, pressing them down. Her fingertips grazed chilly skin and wet fabric.

Alexandra was trapped inside the hard claw of the tree. Her head was tilted back on the seat; her eyes were closed. She looked eerily composed, as if she'd fallen asleep. Except for the bloody splatters on her pale gray jacket.

Sam dragged her fingers across the material until she

found the edge of a lapel, then the softer fabric of the blouse beneath. She pressed her forefinger to the center of Alexandra's chest. The slow, thready heartbeat made Sam curl her hand away.

Alexandra's eyes flickered. She stared at Sam. With her head flung back and her eyes half shuttered, the gaze seemed imperious. Her mouth worked. A raspy whisper finally escaped.

He won't find you this time.

"This is goddamned crazy!" Jake heard the helicopter pilot's shouted words through a headset but didn't respond. His attention was riveted to the darkening blanket of fog around them. Trees, not far below, appeared and disappeared as if manipulated by a master magician. He had tried to quiet every thought and let intuition take over, but the bleakest fear he'd ever known kept racing through him. He *felt* they were headed in the right direction, but it might have been the fear disguised as a desperate wish. Hoke laid a hand on his shoulder. Jake ignored it.

"I said I'd take you as far as I could before the fog closed in," the pilot continued. "This is it. I didn't survive two combat tours in 'Nam to end up scattered all over a mountain at home."

"We got to turn back," Hoke said. He shook Jake lightly. "I'm drawing a blank, and I think you are too."

"No. I might not be close, but I'll get there."

"You got nothing to work with, boy. Not a scrap of your wife's clothes, no jewelry, nothing."

"Let me out. Find some kind of a clearing—there. Over there. That hilltop."

The pilot cursed loudly. "You mean that jumble of rotten logs? The pine borers would have to chew on that hilltop for another twenty years before I could set this chopper down."

"Just get close enough for me to jump."

"Oh, *man*, you'll break your damned legs."

"Do it." Jake twisted toward Hoke. "Go back and see what kind of help you can send. The north edges of the Etowahs. Tell 'em the plane went down somewhere between here and Mount Gibson."

"That's thirty miles of rough territory," Hoke answered. "A dozen peaks. A hundred little coves and hidden ridges and—"

"I'm not going back without her, Hoke. She's alive. That's the one thing I do know."

"I doubt I can get you much help before the fog lifts. That'll probably be late tomorrow morning."

"Do the best you can."

Hoke slumped. "Take this bird to that hilltop, Andy. The man'll jump out from up here if you don't."

"All right. They're his bones to break."

As the helicopter swung toward its destination, Hoke pressed Jake's shoulder a final time. "God bless you. You've come too far to lose everything now."

Jake tossed his headset aside, then slid his arms through the straps of a backpack the pilot had provided. A flashlight, matches, a blanket, a small coil of rope, a canteen filled with water, a hunting knife, and a pistol. The copter dropped slowly over the hill, the ethereal white mist surrounding it. Jake pushed his door open and studied the clutter of fallen trees.

"You got about a twenty-foot drop," the pilot yelled. "That's as good as it's going to get!"

Jake crouched on the rim of the door, found a patch of clear ground among the chaos, and jumped.

He hit the soft ground with a force that buckled his legs and sprawled him sideways. Dazed, he lay still for a few seconds, the wind from the copter's blades whipping him, then rose unsteadily. He looked up at the helicopter. Hoke scrutinized him from the still-open door.

Jake raised one hand, signaling good-bye. Hoke gave him a thumbs-up.

The helicopter rose and was swallowed by the fog. Jake stood a minute on the lonely, ruined hilltop, lost in the mist and gloom and the whisper of evening currents curling through vast forests.

He emptied his mind as best he could, let himself become a human compass, and hoped that the deep, faithful pull of Samantha's heart would show him the way.

Clara watched from a hard folding chair in a corner, keeping her own somber counsel, absorbing the chatter of official-looking people as busy as bees in a hive. They scurried around the hot, cramped space of the airfield office, carrying their opinions, like specks of pollen, from the wall maps to the telephones. She wished she could produce a sprig of bright-red bee balm to quiet them down. Especially Charlotte, who followed first one person and then another, asking questions that had no answers.

"What do you think?" Joe whispered to her. He was old and wise, like her, and he sat cross-legged on the floor by her chair, away from the traffic.

Clara bent her head toward his. "Jake'll find Sammie. No one else is meant to."

He sighed. Charlotte's voice cut through the room's noisy buzz. "There must be *something* you can do tonight!" She latched on to the shirt of a big man wearing a ranger's uniform.

The man shook his head. "We can't send any planes out in this fog. All we can do tonight is organize search teams and map out the most likely crash sites. By morning we'll have a couple hundred people and a dozen planes ready to go."

She jerked at his sweat-stained shirtfront. "You could send out professional trackers and their dogs tonight."

"They'd need to be airlifted into some of the rough spots we're talking about. And not even a professional tracker is going to risk stumbling over a waterfall or a cliff in the dark."

"My brother-in-law is a tracker—the best one in the state—and *he* wouldn't be sitting here thinking up excuses." Charlotte jabbed a finger toward the door. "He'd be out in the mountains with his dog, no matter what the weather was like."

"Well, there isn't anybody else like Jake Raincrow. And since we don't know where he is or if he even knows his wife was in that plane, what he'd do about it is a moot point. I'm sorry to put it that way. You've got a right to be scared and mad, but all you can do is wait for morning, like the rest of us."

"Charlotte." Ben slid off the edge of a desk, clear-eyed but hunched with pain, and put his good arm around her. She leaned against him with tearful defeat. The look on his face said he'd take on her pain too if he could. "I can't believe Jake hasn't heard that she and Alexandra are missing. You *know* he's looking for them."

"How can he? He didn't come home to get Bo, he didn't call anyone for information about the search or the plane's flight path—"

"Excuse me," a wiry young man said to them. "Could I intrude for a minute?" He had slipped through the crowd from his own quiet corner with only Clara noticing. She had been scrutinizing him for a while, wondering what he was forever scribbling in a notepad. "I'm Bob Freeman, from the *Raleigh*—"

"He's a newspaper reporter," Ben interjected, drawing Charlotte closer. She and Ben traded a startled look. Clara bent down to Joe and whispered quickly, "He's the one I told you about."

Joe jumped. "The one Jake sent the—"

"Yes sir."

"You think he's figured out where it came from?"

"I hope not."

Ben was studying the intruder shrewdly. "I recognize your name. I might be impressed. If nothing else, I'm impressed that you managed to get into this office while the rest of the media are camped outside behind barricades."

"Hometown advantage. I was born on a tenant farm near Pandora. The sheriff's relatives sat around a few moonshine stills with mine."

"My sister is all I can think about right now," Charlotte told him. She hesitated, then added, "And our aunt."

"I understand. You're a . . . close . . . family?"

"She isn't in very good shape to discuss the family," Ben said smoothly.

"It's all right. I need to talk," Charlotte replied. "It might help me make sense of what's happening." She squared her shoulders. "My aunt took my sister and me into her home after our mother died. It was the kind of experience you never forget. Our aunt couldn't be more involved in our lives if we were her own children."

"Had you talked to your cousin recently?"

"He dropped by for a visit yesterday. He was very depressed about his stepfather's stroke. I didn't have much time to listen, because I had to take my accident-prone friend here to the hospital. I feel lousy about running out on my cousin."

"Would you say he was a moody person?"

Charlotte nodded wearily. "But he had a side to him very few people saw. He really *cared* what happened to my sister and me. He'd show up when we least expected it, and if we were upset about something, he'd give his ear."

Ben coughed loudly, then winced. Charlotte turned her attention to him anxiously and helped him ease down on the desk again. "About your sister," the reporter began.

"My sister?" Charlotte fumbled with her shirttail and stared blindly into space. "My sister"—her voice trembled—"tell your readers that my sister always puts family first. That's why she got in that plane today. Maybe it was a foolish thing to do. But Sammie's never turned her back on our aunt."

"Just one more question."

There was a small commotion outside, and the office door burst open. Clara was entranced by the sight of another black man, this one grizzled and stout and rumpled, marching into the room. There were plenty of white and red people in the mountains, but not many black ones. Now there were two in the same room at the same time. It must be a sign.

"One more question, Charlotte," Bob Freeman repeated, glancing at the newcomer curiously. "Do you think it's strange that your brother-in-law disappeared at the same time the wrath of God, so to say, descended on his wife's family?"

Charlotte whirled toward him like a ferocious cat. "Every word I wasted on you is the truth. And so is this—Jake would never do *anything* to hurt the people Sammie loves."

"What's this about Jake?" the newcomer thundered. He plowed through the crowd, a towering, angry old bear of a man. "Y'all wondering where Jake's been? He's been with me since early last night, and any jerk-tailed man who thinks different is callin' Detective Hoke Doop of the Durham police a liar!"

Charlotte made a hoarse sound. "Where is he now?"

Detective Doop strode to a wall and thumped a section of a topographical map where the ridge lines tangled together like threads on a twisted skein. "There. Hunting for his wife and her kin. God help him."

Lost. The word had never had real meaning to Jake before. To become suddenly blind, deaf, paralyzed—he had always been able to imagine how those limitations would feel, but not this. He couldn't tell if he was moving instinctively toward Samantha or only wandering.

Muddy, wet, aching from the jump and the long, steep miles, he was doing little more than pushing one foot in front of the other. He scraped against tree trunks and stumbled over the jutting crowns of submerged boulders; he had put the flashlight away to save its batteries, and even his woodsman's skill at traveling had deserted him.

He was missing a piece of the puzzle; there was a blank space in his mind's eye.

The fog and darkness made an impenetrable screen at the end of his outstretched hands. He read the land solely by the slope under his feet—climbing, descending, flattening into narrow plateaus and fading into thin valleys, where he heard the gurgle of small creeks and felt them pouring over the toes of his boots.

He reached another crest, hesitated to take one reviving breath, then lifted a foot to make the next step. Suddenly pain shot through his leg, shooting, burning into the bone, spreading up that side to his arm. It brought him down like a sledgehammer, and he curled into a tight ball, gasping and half conscious.

This was what Samantha felt.

The realization made him groan. He had done this to her. His secrecy and revenge had sent her out, alone, to punish Alexandra.

Alone and unsuspecting.

No hard lesson had taught her to keep what she knew to herself. She didn't understand that ravenmockers killed the ones who recognized them.

The pain was ripping him apart. His hands convulsed against his thighs. The ruby made a hard kernel inside a leather pouch tied to a belt loop of his jeans. His fingers closed on it as recklessly as they had when he was a boy. He tore the pouch free and raised it in his shaking fist. *Take me,* he said aloud. *Take me and save Samantha. That's all I want.*

The pain vanished.

A new, calm strength flowed into him. He sat up, shook the ruby into his palm, and breathed the miracle of redemption.

The fog and darkness still surrounded him, but he wasn't lost anymore.

And he knew how to find Samantha.

The plane's wreckage shifted again. Sam moaned helplessly as the vibrations jarred bone and muscle. The netherland between sleep and shock was her only refuge. Her brief periods of consciousness were filled with silent battles. She argued against faith, hope, and survival.

Jake won't find you this time.

I have to believe he will.

Don't think like that! You did the right thing. It has to end this way.

She couldn't see anything, and sounds seemed magnified in the eerie void. She was forced to listen to the wind, the creaking of tree limbs, and the slow, raspy hiss of Alexandra's breath. When nightmarish panic won out, Sam imagined a hideous, hungry *thing* watching her patiently from its lair.

This plane was on the verge of tumbling down the mountain. Sam accepted that fate. She hoped the fall would kill her before she felt the nightmare creature's hot breath on her skin.

It was coming toward her. Sam tried to lift her head. The effort made her dizzy, but through the sickly ringing in her ears she heard twigs snapping under its feet.

Alexandra would eat her alive, then slip away in the mist. Sam had failed at the only act of love that could set Jake free.

Grief and defeat made her cry out.

"*Samantha.*" Jake's answer, a hoarse and exultant shout. Light crept over her face. She struggled to look up. His dear and familiar hand followed the light, frantically exploring.

A gust of wind rocked the plane. Sam moaned. "Get away, it's too late."

She hurt too much to notice whether he answered. Every bone seemed to be grating against its neighbor. The light went away. She knew when he took his hand from her face; the loss upset her.

She heard the metallic creak and scrape of metal, felt Jake's arm brush against her as he reached inside the broken, crumpled door. He lifted her left hand and pressed something into the palm, then gently pushed her fingers shut over it. The unknown gift was oddly comforting. "Hold on to that," he told her.

She did. Even when he jerked violently on the door frame, and pain washed over her in blind sheets.

The next thing she knew, his arms were under her, and he was easing her legs from the mangled cockpit. "I know it hurts," he said hoarsely. "You're almost out."

But there was a popping sound. Pine branches brushed her face; the limb that pierced the cockpit had cracked. The wreckage slid a little, then stopped. "You're almost out," Jake repeated. Her head bobbed against his chest. "I'm sorry, I have to pull hard now." He had both arms under her.

"No. My hand," Sam said. "*She's got my hand.*"

Alexandra's icy grip tightened like a claw. Jake uttered a soft, furious sound. Sam realized he couldn't let go of her to pry Alexandra's fingers away.

"You can't take her," Alexandra whispered weakly, as if all her strength were focused on holding Sam.

A tug-of-war. Her aunt would fight him, with Sam caught in the middle, just as she'd always done. Strangling fury rose in Sam's throat. "You're not going to get him. I won't let you drag Jake down with the two of us."

Jake's chest heaved against her cheek. "I'll come back for you, Alexandra," he said. "Let go of her. I'll come back in a minute and get you out too. I swear it."

She killed your family, Sam thought. She made a mewling sound of protest. *Don't you understand? She'll kill you too.*

Alexander's fingers dug into Sam's wrist. "Lying." The word gurgled. "You'll never . . . help me. No one has ever . . . helped me."

A convulsive shudder went through the plane. Jake said loudly, "Open your hand, Samantha." Sam was dimly aware of obeying. "Take it, Alexandra," Jake continued. "Even if you don't believe I'll come back for you, you *know* I'll come back for the stone."

Sam's feeble, shocked attempt to close her fingers over the ruby wasn't quick enough to stop her aunt from taking it. The instant Alexandra released her hand, Jake lifted Sam from the plane. The pain found new routes through her unfolded body, and all she could do was slump in his arms, gasping. He climbed a few feet up the precarious slope, then sank to his knees and laid her down gently.

He ran his hands over her. She heard his guttural sob and tried to move, tried to show him she could. He took her face between his hands. The damp, cool night hid him, but his touch was infinitely caring. "I love you," he told her. Sam tried to speak, but he placed a finger against her lips. "I love you," he repeated. "Alexandra doesn't have to die for me to love you again. I never stopped loving you."

He rose and walked back to the plane. Sam called desperately for him to stop. With her last ounce of strength she pushed herself up on one elbow and watched.

Jake anchored the flashlight in a jagged hole, then wedged his upper body into the cockpit. Alexandra stared back at him with fading blue eyes, her face stark and pale as the light. Pine boughs framed her softly; the only defiance was the fist she had curled against her throat. "You came for the stone," she said. Her voice was fading too.

"No. It won't bring my parents and my sister back. It's served the only purpose it was ever really meant for. I don't need it anymore."

"Then, why . . . why care whether I—"

"I don't want Samantha to suffer anymore for what you did. There's been enough revenge. I'll get you out of here—not because you deserve to live, but because it's the right thing to do for Samantha. And for me."

Jake began snapping the easy branches, clearing a way toward the bigger ones that enveloped her. He felt Alexandra watching him, but neither fear nor hate had any power over him now. "I am still . . . extraordinary," she said, her voice ragged. "You'll see why."

Jake bent a limb back. It was matted with blood. What he saw behind it made him gag.

The tip of the main limb had skewered Alexandra through the stomach. The mountain had pinned her to earth.

His gaze rose slowly to hers. Her thin smile taunted him and the rest of the world. "I . . . was raised to . . . endure . . ."

The wind kicked up. The roof of the cockpit began to buckle. Jake watched, helpless and repulsed, as the limb sank deeper into her. Uncle William. Mother, Father, Ellie. Whispering his own humanity to him. He had walked the path for them. There was no dishonor. He grasped the limb and pulled it free.

Sam screamed his name.

Alexandra threw her head back and writhed. "Go to her. I'm dying. I give her to you."

"Not yours to give," he said between gritted teeth as he struggled with the jammed latch of her seat belt. She cursed him, thrust her fist into his hands, and pressed the ruby into his palm, slick with her blood. Alexandra released it into his keeping. Her eyes bored into his with their last glimmer. "What good is anything precious," she whispered, "unless you're willing to die for it?"

Jake shoved himself backward as the plane tilted and began to slide. A jagged edge of metal caressed his cheek like a talon.

Suddenly he was sprawling beside Samantha, finally free.

The night consumed the falling body of a raven-mocker.

Chapter
Thirty-four

"Just where do you think you're going, Bob 'Clark Kent' Freeman?" Charlotte blocked the hospital corridor like a small defensive tackle.

The reporter didn't look too menacing, but her nerves were frayed. It had been the longest night of her life, followed by a sleepless morning that was now moving into a sunny, sleepless afternoon.

"Just a couple of questions," the man implored, looking past her to Ben, who lay on a gurney the nurses had allowed him to commandeer. Ben said darkly, "Don't eye me for help. I'm in charge of guarding the door to the room. I have no jurisdiction over the hallway."

Charlotte nodded. "Why should I talk to you again, Freeman? I don't even know how you're going to use what I said last night."

"I'll use it just the way you told it to me. Fair enough?"

"Maybe."

"How's your sister?"

"You can get that information from the hospital."

"Yeah, but it's about as useful as a laundry list. Broken leg, broken arm, cuts, bruises. I'd like to know how she felt when her husband rescued her."

"She wasn't surprised. He's still the best tracker in the state. She knew if anyone could find the crash site, it'd be him."

"I'd say he has a remarkable talent."

"I'd say he knows how to read maps. And he never gives up."

"Come on, give me some heart to go with the facts."

"Tell me what 'facts' you mean."

"Your aunt was dead when he got there. Your sister had managed to crawl out of the wreckage before it broke up."

"Well, that's the truth. Jake wrapped Sammie in a blanket and built a fire. The rescue teams found them a few hours later."

"Is Jake with her now?"

"Of course. He hasn't left her for a minute."

Joe walked out of the hospital room. "They're ready."

"Bye, *Bob*. Just tell the truth. That's all we need." Charlotte pivoted and strode away, then halted abruptly. She looked back at the reporter. "Wait a minute. All right. Come and see something for yourself. Tell people about it. You want 'heart,' I'll show you heart."

She and Joe wheeled Ben into the hospital room. Jake was seated beside Sammie's bed, on the side next to the arm that wasn't in a cast. He looked like hell. So did she. But he was holding her hand, and their eyes were locked in a poignantly intimate gaze. Clara sat in a chair in one corner. Hoke Doop stood by the window.

A minister stood at the foot of the bed. Charlotte waved for the reporter to take a place just inside the door. His eyes wide with curiosity, he did.

And then, with everyone who mattered sharing the blessing, Jake and Sammie got married all over again.

Memories and angels. The room was full.

A small brown mule was tied to the porch rail. A small, brown mule decked out in full harness attached to a two-wheeled cart.

It was an unexpected homecoming present, to say the least. Sam peered out of the car from her throne of pillows, then gingerly swiveled her head toward Jake. "Bo's changed while I've been in the hospital."

Jake smiled—one of the satisfied, easy smiles that were becoming part of their life again. Bo crawled out from a cool spot under the porch to disprove the rumor he'd grown hooves. He was waiting by the car's passenger door as Jake opened it. Sam stroked his grizzled head. "I am really home," she whispered.

Jake bent over her. She stroked his cheek with the backs of her fingers. "Really home."

He carried her to the porch and set her gently on the steps. "Why do we have a discount-size mule and kiddie wagon?" she asked.

He walked over to the fat, sleepy creature and scratched it behind one ear. "She's old. She and Bo ought to get along together pretty well. Do you remember the stories I told you about Grady?"

"The pony you and Ellie had? How could I forget? He sounded like the stuff of legends."

"He was. This is his daughter. He had a passion for donkeys. One wandered away from a farm at Cawatie and paid a visit to the Cove. She had a smile on her face by the time we hauled her home."

"So their love child has always lived with her mother's people at Cawatie?"

"Hmmm. Until now. I bought her." He looked at Sam tenderly. "I want our children to have what Ellie and I had." He hesitated, then added solemnly, "Except for the bite marks and stomped toes."

Sam studied him through a sheen of tears. "This is an old mule. We'd better start making babies soon." She looked away, struggling with shadowy regrets. "I can't even make love to you right now. Everything's either sprained, sore, or covered in a cast." She nodded at the arm and leg on her right side.

"We've got time. A lot of time." He came over and kissed her. "But it's not just your body. You're not letting go of that night on the mountain."

"It's hard to believe she's gone."

"I know." He went into the house and returned a few seconds later with an armload of sofa cushions. Without a word he arranged them in the cart then tucked Sam's pillows on top. She looked up at him in puzzled wonder as he lifted her onto the soft bed. "I'm taking you on a trip," he explained. "There's something we need to do."

They were headed to Sign Rock. Jake led the way with one hand on the mule's bridle. When the trail became too narrow and steep for the cart he hitched the mule to a tree then carried Sam the rest of the way up. His mission was still a mystery to her as he stepped onto the wide, windswept stone ledge with its ancient carvings. He put her down carefully and sat beside her for a while. Content with the silence and the serene vista in front of them, Sam held his hand.

"I told her the truth when I said I didn't want the stone," he said finally. "I found you. That's all I care about."

Sam closed her eyes and said a silent prayer of gratitude. When she looked at Jake again, he was studying her, a troubled and loving expression on his face. "It belongs here," he told her. "We don't need it."

"You want to just leave it for anyone to claim?"

"It ends up where it's supposed to be. It always has." He took the ruby from a pocket of his trousers and held it out. "Letting go is easy, if we do it together."

Sam touched the stone with a fingertip. A pledge to the future and a good-bye to the past. Jake rose and crossed the broad ledge. A narrow crevice cut through the rim of the ancient rock platform. He opened his hand. The ruby disappeared into the mountain's secret places.

He met Sam's adoring gaze. There was peace in him, and she shared it.

ABOUT THE AUTHOR

A multiple-award winner for her novels and contemporary romances. DEBORAH SMITH lives in the mountains of Georgia where she is working on her next novel.